TRAMP IN ARMOUR

TRAMP
IN ARMOUR

*

COLIN FORBES

THE
COMPANION BOOK CLUB
LONDON

This edition, published in 1970 by
The Hamlyn Publishing Group Ltd.,
is issued by arrangement with
William Collins, Sons & Co. Ltd.

AUTHOR'S NOTE

I wish to record my thanks to Mr. M. J. Willis
and to Mr. P. Simpkin of the Imperial War
Museum for their invaluable technical assistance.

*Made and printed in Great Britain
for the Companion Book Club
by Odhams (Watford) Ltd.*

SBN 60077127x
11.70 600871274

To JANE

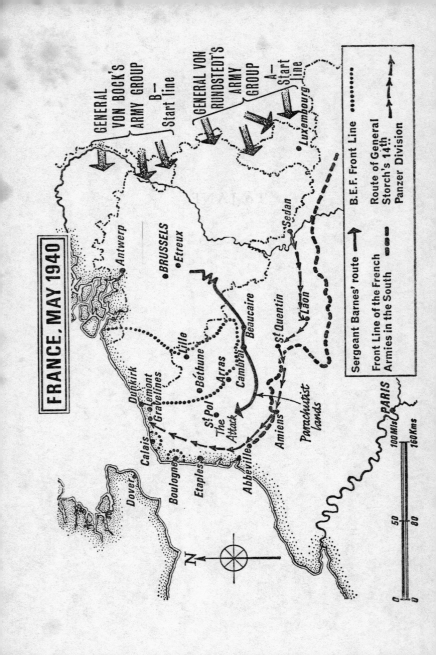

FRANCE, MAY 1940

GENERAL VON BOCK'S ARMY GROUP
B—Start line

GENERAL VON RUNDSTEDT'S ARMY GROUP
A—Start line

Antwerp
BRUSSELS
Etreux
Luxembourg
Sedan
Laon
Beaucaire
St Quentin
Lille
Béthune
Cambrai
Arras
Parachutist lands
St Pol
The Attack
Amiens
Dunkirk
Lemont
Gravelines
Calais
Boulogne
Etaples
Abbeville
Dover
PARIS

N

••••••	B.E.F. Front Line
→	Route of General Storch's 14th Panzer Division
⟶	Sergeant Barnes' route
▬▬▬	Front Line of the French Armies in the South

50   100 Mls
80   160 Kms

1. Thursday May 16

THE WAR had started.

'Advance right, driver. Advance right. Two-pounder, traverse left, traverse left. Steady . . .'

The tank commander, Sergeant Barnes, thought that should do the trick—when the tank emerged from the ramp on to the rail embankment, in full view of the German troops of General von Bock's Army Group B, the turret would rest at an angle of ninety degrees to the forward movement of the vehicle, the two-pounder and the Besa machine gun aimed straight at the enemy. The tank crawled upwards at a steady five miles per hour, still invisible to the German wave advancing across open fields to assault the embankment behind which the British Expeditionary Force waited for them, while overhead the sun shone down on Belgium out of a clear blue sky, the prelude to the long endless summer of 1940.

Barnes's squadron of tanks was positioned on the extreme right of the B.E.F. line, and the troop of three tanks which formed his own unit was stationed on the extreme right of the squadron. Somewhere beyond this troop the French First Army, the next major formation which faced the attacking German army group, reached out its left flank to link up with the B.E.F., but this vital link was not apparent, which was why Barnes had just received his urgent wireless instruction from Lieutenant Parker, his troop commander.

'Find out where the hell the French are, Barnes, and report back immediately, if not sooner.'

The natural route to the French, the road below the embankment, had been blocked by dive-bombers, and now what had

7

once been a road was a barrier of wrecked buildings, so Barnes decided there was only one way to go—up to the top of the embankment and along the trail track in full view of the enemy. The prospect of exposing his tank like a silhouette on a target range didn't greatly worry him: the armour on the upper side of the hull was seventy millimetres thick and none of the light weapons the German advance troops carried could do more than scratch the surface. As for the big stuff farther back, which was already lobbing shells into the B.E.F. rear areas, well, he'd be off this embankment before they could bring down the range of their artillery. Any moment now, he told himself, pressing his eye to the periscope.

Four men crewed the tank: Trooper Reynolds inside his own separate driving compartment in the nose of the tank, while in the central fighting compartment Barnes shared the confined space with his gunner, Trooper Davis, and his loader-operator, Corporal Penn. The fighting compartment in the centre of the tank was shaped rather like a conning tower, the upper portion protruding above the tank's hull; the floor, only a few feet above the ground, comprised a turntable suspended from the turret, so that when the power-traverse went into action the entire compartment rotated as a single unit, carrying round with it the guns and the three men inside, the traverse system controlled by the gunner at the commander's instructions.

They were very close to the top of the embankment now, but still the view through the periscope showed only the scrubby grass of the descending slope, while outside all hell was breaking loose, a hell of sound infinitely magnified inside the confines of the metal hull: the horrid crump of mortar bombs exploding, the scream of shells heading for the rear area, while the permanent accompaniment to this symphony of death was an endless crack of rifle shots, a steady rattle of machine-gun fire. It was only possible for the crew to hear Barnes's sharp instructions because he gave them over the intercom, a one-way system of communication through the microphone hanging from his neck which transmitted the words to earphones clamped over the crew's heads. Barnes screwed up his eyes, saw the wall of embankment disappear. They were over the top.

The view was much as he had expected, but there were many more of them—long lines of helmeted Germans in field grey advancing like the waves of a rising tide, running towards him across a vast field. Some carried rifles, some machine-pistols, and there were clusters with light machine guns. The tank had reached the embankment at the very moment when the first assault was being mounted.

'Driver, straight down the railway—behind those loading sheds. Two-pounder. Six hundred.' Davis set the range on his telescope. 'Traverse left.' With a hiss of air, turret and crew began to swing round, the tank still moving forward. 'Traverse left.' The turret screamed round faster, the guns and the fighting crew now at an angle of forty-five degrees to the tank hull. 'Steady,' Barnes warned, his gaze through the periscope fixed on the anti-tank gun in the distance as a fusillade of bullets rattled on the armour-plate. 'Anti-tank gun,' he snapped, pin-pointing the target.

'Fire!'

Davis squeezed the trigger. The tank shuddered under the recoil, the turret was swamped with a stench of cordite. Barnes didn't hear the explosion but he saw it—a burst of white smoke on the gun position, a brief eruption of the ground. Then they were moving behind the loading bays which the ramp served, out of sight of the enemy for swiftly passing seconds, emerging again as Barnes gave fresh orders.

'Besa . . .'

The destroyed anti-tank gun was the only immediate menace to Bert, as they called their tank. Now for the German troops. The tank had scarcely moved beyond the sheltering wall of the loading bays when the Besa opened fire, the turret traversing in an arc from left to right, pouring out a murderous stream of bullets which cut down the first wave of Germans like a scythe. The turret began to swing in a second arc, the Besa elevated slightly to bring down the second wave, and all the time the tank moved forward down the rail track while Penn, who had already re-loaded the two-pounder, attended to his wireless. Parker, the troop commander, was speaking to Barnes now.

'What's the picture, Barnes?'

'German assault waves just coming in—they'll be over the top in your sector any second now. They stretch as far as I can see, sir. Over.'

He pressed the lever on his mike which controlled wireless communication and waited. Parker sounded exasperated.

'But the French, Barnes—can you see the bloody French?'

'Nothing so far, sir. I'll report back shortly. Off.'

All the way up the ramp and along the embankment so far the turret lid had been closed down, so Barnes had relied on the periscope to let him know what was happening outside, a method of sighting which he found restricted and unsatisfactory. Now that he could no longer hear the clatter of bullets ricocheting harmlessly off the armour-plate, he risked it, pushing up the turret lid and lifting his head above the rim. For once, he was wearing his tin hat. A quick glance told him that no Germans were close to the section of the embankment they were advancing along. Instead, the troops in that area were running back across the field away from him: they had seen what had happened to their mates. To encourage their flight he gave orders to fire the two-pounder twice and then called for a burst from the Besa. If he was really going to see what was going on he would have to lift his head well out of the turret. He clambered up and stood erect, half his body above the rim, gazing all round quickly as he gave Reynolds instructions automatically.

'Driver, full speed ahead down this railway. All the speed Bert will give.'

The tank began to pick up speed, one caterpillar track outside the railway, the other travelling midway between the two iron lines, while inside the driving compartment Reynolds had his eyes glued to the slit window in front, a window protected by four-inch armoured glass. Normally, he sat on his jacked-up seat with his head protruding clear of the hatch in the front hull, but now this seat was depressed so that he sat inside the hull and a steel hood was closed over the hatch above his head.

He vaguely wondered what Barnes was going to do next, a line of thought which was occupying Barnes himself at the same moment.

To the left the fields of Belgium stretched away to disappear inside a curtain of black smoke, the result of R.A.F. bombing and B.E.F. heavy artillery fire. In front of the curtain small figures moved like the inhabitants of a disturbed anthill, but always the apparently chaotic movement was forward, except in the sector ahead of the tank. They were now perched **a g**ood twenty feet above the surrounding countryside and to Barnes's dismay he realized that the embankment was gradually rising all the time the farther south they progressed, the sides growing steeper, making their descent from the railway more difficult every yard they moved forward. His eyes scanned the ground on the Allied side of the embankment and saw nothing which comforted him. As he had anticipated when he had decided to mount the embankment and make a dash along the railway, it gave him an excellent view of the battle area. The outskirts of the Belgian town of Etreux had been badly battered by the Stuka raids, but even at this early stage of the campaign he was becoming used to these scenes of devastation. What he had not expected was that the desert of rubble would be *unoccupied*, and as his eyes searched and searched again for signs of life a chill began to crawl up his spine. The wireless crackled: someone was coming on the air again.

'Hullo, hullo! Troop calling. Parker here. Anything to report, Barnes?'

'Barnes here, sir. No sign of our friends yet. Repeat, no sign of our friends. I am a quarter of a mile out and no sign of them yet. Repeat, at least a quarter of a mile. Over.'

'Are you quite sure, Barnes? I've got to report to Brigade at once. I must be quite sure. Over.'

'Quite sure, sir. I'm twenty-five feet up here and the place has been flattened, so vision is good. I'm a quarter of a mile out at least and there's no sign of them ahead. Do I proceed farther or return? Over.'

'Proceed a farther quarter of a mile if you can, then report again. Over.'

'Barnes O.K. Off.'

At least it was a convenient distance. The tank was still moving ahead along the railway line, the embankment straight as a ruler, and about a quarter of a mile farther along the line disappeared into a steep hillside. Barnes could see the arched opening of a tunnel clearly now. So the distance was all right, but the timing probably wasn't. He glanced at his watch and calculated that within the next two or three minutes the Germans would have wirelessed back for artillery support to lay down a barrage along the top of the embankment. Soon the first ranging shots would be falling, a spotter would be reporting their fall, and unless Barnes was very much mistaken they would hardly have completed their quarter-mile run before the shells began to bracket the tank. The fact that the embankment was so damned straight would make the German gunners' work that much easier. He wondered how the others liked being stuck up silhouetted against the skyline and glanced down inside the turret. Davis had the shoulder-grip tucked into position and he couldn't see the gunner's expression, but Penn happened to look up and on his thin, intelligent face Barnes thought he detected signs of worry, but then it would always be Penn who worried first because Penn had the imagination to think of all the things which might happen. Too much intelligence could be a distinct disadvantage when you were locked up inside a tank. He spoke briefly into the mike, urging Reynolds to keep up the speed.

Below him the ruins of Etreux glided past while he continually watched for the first sight of a gun position, for French troops. There had been a muck-up, the certainty of this was growing on him. First, there had been the hectic rush forward on May 10 when news of the German invasion of Holland and Belgium had come in, a rush from behind prepared defences on the Franco-Belgian frontier out into the open to meet the German onslaught in head-on collision. And now it was Thursday May 16, only six days later. To Barnes it felt more like six weeks later, but at least they were stuck into them. For a brief moment he glanced back to where the line of German dead lay, victims of the Besa's murderous sweeping arcs. He felt not a trace of pity, but he also felt no exultation, only perhaps a certain satisfaction that one of the few British tanks with the B.E.F. was already proving its worth.

The railway tunnel was very close now, barely two hundred yards away, the black arch coming closer every second as the tank ground forward. And still no sign of the French, no sign at all. He'd have to report back soon now. Even in this sector there was a lot of noise—the heavy boom of the big artillery, the whine of shells—and this was why Barnes failed to detect the arrival of the enemy. Also, in his concentration on Etreux, he had neglected to search the sky for the past minute. It happened with terrifying suddenness—the appearance of a plane above his head screaming down in a power dive. He looked up as he dived inside the tank, saw the Messerschmitt hurtling earthwards, its guns blazing straight at Bert, and rammed down the lid, almost crushing his fingers in his haste. But he was just too late—one bullet whistled in under the closing lid, missing Barnes by millimetres, and terror entered the tank.

With the driver's hood closed and with the turret lid down, the occupants of a Mk. II Matilda tank in 1940 could feel themselves reasonably secure against everything except a direct hit. On the other hand, if by some mischance a bullet from a rifle or a machine-gun were able to enter the armoured confines of the tank, then what had once been a haven of comparative safety immediately became a death-trap. Entering the mobile fortress under the impetus of its own tremendous velocity the bullet has to spend its velocity somewhere, and it does this by richocheting back and forth off the armour-plate hull of the *interior* of the tank, flying about unpredictably in all directions until its force is spent—normally by its entry into human flesh. As soon as the bullet entered, the three men knew what they were in for, and knew that there wasn't a thing they could do about it—except to wait and pray. The biting sound of bullet tearing from one metal surface to another only lasted for a brief period in time, but nerves stretched to breaking-point by the wear and tear of battle reacted to screaming pitch as the danger flashed into three battered minds, drawing from them in seconds reserves of physical and mental strength they would normally have expended over hours. Then there was a momentary silence while Reynolds drove at top speed towards the tunnel. Penn was the first to speak.

'I think it went into the wireless set.'

Barnes checked his communications and banged the microphone while he looked at Penn, who was examining the set. Then suspicion flooded into his mind and he scrambled up the turret, pushing the lid back and staring up into the clear morning sky. The clever bastards! They'd sent the Messerschmitt down not hoping to hit anybody but to get him *to close the turret*. In this way his vision would be restricted and he wouldn't see what was coming next, but he could see it now coming from the east—an arrow-shaped formation of ugly, thick-legged birds—Stuka dive-bombers coming for Bert. He spoke into the mike, his voice dry and harsh, using his driver's name.

'Reynolds, we're going to be dive-bombed unless you get us into that tunnel first.'

He stayed in the turret to check the course the Stukas were taking, remembering that these were the planes which had battered Poland. He might well die in this war, he knew that, but not yet, not yet! He wanted to see Germany smashed first. With narrowed eyes he watched the tunnel draw closer as the Stukas came over at a bare thousand feet. Yes, he'd been right—they were coming for Bert. They'd changed direction now and he waited for the first one to peel off, waited for the hair-raising shriek of those screaming bombs which would put fear into the dead.

'Lights on,' he ordered automatically as Bert thundered towards the tunnel.

The first Stuka was peeling off now, falling sideways, ejecting black eggs from its belly. Barnes slammed down the lid, dropped to the turntable floor and rotated the periscope so that he saw the tunnel moving towards them.

'Wait for it,' he warned the others, but mainly to warn Reynolds who was driving.

They heard it coming, a high-pitched whistle growing to a piercing shriek which easily dominated the engine sound, penetrating the armoured walls as though they were papier-mâché. It's a direct hit this time, thought Penn. He looked at Davis, but the gunners' eyes stared fixedly at the turntable floor, his jaw muscles clenched, his forehead moist with sudden sweat. Penn looked at Barnes, but the sergeant had his eyes glued to the periscope as he watched the tunnel coming closer. God, thought Penn, he's got no nerves at all. The thing was screaming like a banshee now. Would it never land? Up in the nose of the tank Reynolds could hear it coming, too, but he was wrestling with two separate fears. Reynolds had no imagination but as he saw the mouth of the tunnel looming towards him through the slit window he remembered a story he had once read in a newspaper. It had happened in Spain during the Civil War—a scout car racing towards a tunnel to escape bombing had met an express train coming out of the tunnel at high speed . . . But nobody would be running trains in the battle area. The tunnel mouth yawned towards him and the bomb exploded.

The shock wave dealt the armour plating such a blow that it rattled the plates, seeming for a moment about to blow the tank off the embankment. Fitments clattered down on to the turntable floor and the detonation reverberating inside the metal room was so loud that they were all deafened. Then they heard the next one coming. First the whistle, then the scream. This time Barnes felt fairly sure they were going to get it: the scream was much louder, its aiming point seemed to be dead centre down the turret. It had to happen to someone during the war—a bomb dead centre through the lid, exploding inside that confined space . . . The bomb hit, detonated. It rocked the tank like a toy, smashing at the plates with a hammerblow, the acrid smell of high explosive seeping inside the fighting compartment. That one had been close! He glanced at Davis, who still stared at the floor as though his life depended on it. Penn had gone as white as a sheet, his small neat moustache quivering before he clenched his lips together and then unclenched them to speak.

'Knock, knock. Who's there?'

Nobody laughed, nobody smiled. They just looked at each other strangely as they heard the next one coming. In the driver's seat Reynolds kept the tank going full out, conjuring up reserves of speed from Bert that even he hadn't known existed. The tunnel mouth now filled the breadth of his slit window. He had forgotten all about trains coming out of hillsides. His hands holding the steering levers were as wet as though he had dipped them in water. Sweat streamed off his broad forehead and dripped into his eyes, but he kept them open, seeing the beams of his headlights inside the tunnel now. Then the third one started to come down. The tunnel rushed closer and closer as the bomb fell lower and lower, louder than its predecessors. Please, Bert, *please*! Reynolds whispered to himself. The walls of the tunnel rushed forward and they went inside as the bomb detonated. The force of the explosion seemed to take hold of Bert's rear and shove him inside the hill, followed by an appalling clattering sound, a low rumble behind them, then the ground under the tracks shook and they felt the vibration inside the tank. Barnes swore, swivelled the periscope through one hundred and eighty degrees, and stared back to where should have been an arched frame of daylight, seeing nothing but pitch blackness. The last bomb had caught the top of the entrance, blowing the hillside down over the track and sealing off the outside world.

'Halt,' Barnes rapped out into the mike, 'but keep the engines revved up.'

The last thing he wanted inside this tunnel was an engine failure. He looked at the others and they stared back, stunned now by the nerve-racking silence. Except for the engine sound it was uncannily quiet. No shells whining past, no projectiles screaming down from above.

Cautiously, he climbed into the turret and pushed back the lid on its telescopic arms. It was like emerging into an underground cavern, a subterranean cave weirdly lit by Bert's headlights. Barnes felt a tightening of his stomach muscles as he swivelled his torch beam into the dark corners, moving it slowly over the enormous rock pile. Through the intercom he told Reynolds to switch off the headlights and at the same moment he doused his own torch. Not a glimmer of light anywhere: the entrance was well and truly blocked. He climbed down off the tank and used his torch to guide him to the rock wall. Still no sign of daylight. The only way out was forward to the far end of the tunnel. When he climbed back into the tank he found Penn was still examining the wireless set. He put on his headset and ordered Reynolds to switch on the headlights. The corporal looked up and pulled a wry face.

'It's hopeless. Two valves went when the bullet charged in. Mind you, I'd sooner have it nestling in there instead of in my pelvis, but I haven't any spares so we'll have to wait till we get back to squadron H.Q.'

Barnes tested the intercom again. At least that was still working, but being cut off from Parker was serious. Thank God he had sent out one warning about that gap in the French lines.

Taking the map case out of the rack he climbed down on to the hull and Penn followed, watching over his shoulder as he spread out a large-scale map of Belgium and Northern France over the engine covers at the rear of the tank. His torch focused on the area round Etreux.

'This tunnel's a damned long one, Penn. We'll just have to jog through it and then make our way back as best we can, Jerry permitting. At least we'll have a pretty good report on the area when we do eventually land back.'

'It's going to be a long way round, isn't it?' queried Penn. 'As soon as we get out of the tunnel that canal bars the route back for miles. We'll have to go over that bridge, then follow this road . . .'

His finger traced a wide semi-circular course which would take them back into the rear outskirts of Etreux. Barnes agreed that this was the only way and he cursed inwardly at the breakdown in wireless communication. Parker would be wondering what on earth had happened to them and meanwhile he'd have to fight the German onrush with two tanks instead of three. It couldn't be helped, but they'd better get cracking. Climbing back inside the tank he explained the position to Reynolds and Davis, giving Reynolds a word of caution over the intercom.

'This tunnel won't be straight, you can bet your life on that, so keep your speed down to five miles an hour or less and watch for bends. I'm going up into the turret to help guide you. What's the matter, Davis?'

The burley gunner with the squarish face and red hair had a hunted look and an air of tension radiated from him. He opened his mouth and closed it again without speaking.

'Come on, spit it out, man,' snapped Barnes.

'You'll think it's stupid, sergeant, but I've always had a horror of tunnels. I was a miner once, as I told you. I was in a colliery disaster in 1934—we were locked in for five days and we thought we'd been buried alive . . .'

'Well, Davis, this happens to be a railway tunnel and we'll be through it in ten minutes, so get your mind on your guns. You never know,' he smiled grimly, 'we might meet a Panzer division coming up from the other end.'

He had reached the turret and given the order to advance when the hollowness of his joke struck him. If the Germans had just happened to break through at the other end it might seem a very good idea to send tanks along the tunnel in the hope of taking Etreux on the flank. He decided that he'd better keep a close lookout ahead and his mind began to calculate the possible effect of two-pounder shells exploding inside the railway tunnel. The powerful headlights penetrated some distance into the tunnel and soon Barnes was warning Reynolds of a curve in the line. Now that they were away from the battle area the driver had rolled back the hood from the hatch and jacked up his seat so that his head protruded above the hull like a man in a Turkish bath cabinet. The journey along the tunnel was eery and strange, the grind of the tracks and the throb of the engines echoing hollowly, probably very much like riding through a mine shaft, Barnes thought, and he glanced down into the compartment below. Penn was still fiddling with the wireless set as though hoping to perform an act of faith, but Davis sat rigid as a stone behind his guns, his body thrust hard into the shoulder-grip, his hand on the

18

two-pounder's trigger. Undoubtedly, Trooper Davis's idea of a private hell was meeting a Panzer column deep underground.

The engine noise sounded far too loud with its reverberations hemmed inside the tunnel and the grind and clatter of the steel tracks conjured up the advance of the biggest tank in the world. Barnes looked at his watch again and then gazed ahead. They should be seeing daylight soon now if the map was anything to go by, and leaving the tunnel was going to call for some pretty careful reconnaissance. Barnes had absolutely no idea what the position might be on this sector of the front: what he had seen from the embankment gave him little cause for optimism as to what might face them once they reached the far end. One part of his mind concentrated on the probing beams while another considered the various possibilities they could encounter—calling on the one hand for a swift dash out into the open or, on the other, for a more cautious passage. As far as he could tell from the map, the railway emerged into open country with no sign of an embankment; there should be fields on both sides with the canal barring the way to the west, the way they wanted to go. They'd just have to see. The headlights were now beginning to sweep round a gradual bend. Somewhere round this bend they should see daylight, probably a first glimmer, than a distant archway. When that happens, Barnes told himself, I'll halt the tank and go on foot for a recce. Just so long as we don't have any trouble with Davis. He glanced down again and saw that Davis was sitting in exactly the same position, gripping the two-pounder as though his very life depended on it, a posture of such implacable rigidity that Barnes was none too happy about his gunner's likely reactions.

'We'll soon be there, Davis,' he said down the intercom. 'Penn, get back to your seat just in case. Be ready to halt, Reynolds, as soon as I give the word.'

The tank ground on, the left-hand track rumbling over wooden sleepers while the right-hand track scattered pebbles, so that the tank was tilted very slightly to the right, the three sounds complementing each other—the throb of the engines, the grumble of the tracks, and the slither of pebbles. Abruptly,

Barnes gave the order to halt, saying nothing more while he wondered how to break it to them. The headlights penetrated the darkness and then half way along the full extent of their beams they splashed out over solid surface, a wall surface with boulders protruding from a scree of soil and rubble which resembled a landslide. This end of the tunnel was blocked, too. They were sealed off inside the bowels of the earth.

On May 10 the B.E.F. had moved from France into Belgium and Barnes' unit had moved with it. On May 10, four hours earlier at 3 a.m., General von Bock's Army Group B had advanced across the frontiers of Holland and Belgium with the express purpose of tempting the B.E.F. and three French armies to leave their fortified lines. Before the end of the day the movement of these vast forces was quite apparent to London and Paris, but a third movement of even more massive forces had so far gone unnoticed.

At the point where Belgium, France and Luxembourg meet lies one of the least known areas of Western Europe—the massif of the Ardennes range, a remote zone of high hills enclosing steep wooded gorges along which snake second-class roads. This was the sector of the huge front from Belgium to Switzerland which the French High Command had long ago declared 'impassable,' and it was opposite this sector that they had placed their weakest forces.

During the early hours of May 10 General von Rundstedt's Army Group A began its secret forward movement through the 'impassable' Ardennes, an army group more powerful than any the world had ever seen. It comprised a force of forty-four divisions, including the main mass of the Panzer divisions which contained over two thousand armoured vehicles. All night long the army group penetrated into the twisting defiles, drawing ever closer to the French border. The tanks drove in close formation, each vehicle guided by the hooded rear light of the tank ahead, an exercise they had practised over and over again. Seen from the air through the eye of an infra-red camera the German host would indeed have resembled a snake, or rather a series of snakes—armoured snakes threading their way through the darkness towards the Meuse near Sedan.

The leading Panzer division was commanded by a thirty-two-year-old general who had won his spurs—and his promotion—in Poland. His unit had led the Wehrmacht into burning Warsaw and now he looked forward to leading it into burning Paris. Without aristocratic connections, on sheer ruthless ability, the general had risen in a few brief years to command the very tip of the spearhead aimed at the heart of sleeping France. His was, in fact, the first tank, and now he stood in the turret erect as a fir tree, night field glasses dangling over his chest, the Knight's Cross suspended from his neck, his eyes fixed on the motor-cycle patrol ahead.

Under his high peaked cap his hawk-like face was calm and without a trace of emotion. His gloved hand rested lightly on the turret rim, without tension, to correct his balance as the huge vehicle made its way along the insidious road. He might well have been on manoeuvres, looking forward to the congratulations of the umpires later and a drink with his fellow officers in the mess. Except for the fact that the general neither smoked nor drank, and except for the further fact that he was leading the advance guard of the coming onslaught, confident that he was about to play a decisive part in the total annihilation of the British and the French.

The tip of the German spearhead reached the Meuse on May 12, crossed it on May 13, and by Thursday May 16 the general was in Laon, deep in the heart of France. He led the advance still erect in his tank, still wearing the peaked cloth cap in spite of the earlier entreaties of Colonel Hans Meyer, his G.S.O.1, to exchange it for a steel helmet.

'It won't be necessary, Meyer. You will see,' the general had said, 'we shall cut through them like a scythe.'

Meyer withdrew the helmet as he sourly recalled a conversation he had had with the general a month earlier during the final war manoeuvres near Wiesbaden. To Meyer it now seemed that the conversation had taken place at least a year ago since already the Panzers were pouring over the pontoons across the river Meuse.

'There will be two or three major battles,' the general had said, 'and these will take place soon after we have crossed the Meuse. We can expect the fiercest resistance for two or three weeks and then a total collapse of the enemy.'

'I wonder,' Meyer had replied dubiously.

The general was a little too confident for Meyer's liking, particularly when he remembered that his commanding officer was a nobody whereas Hans Meyer was descended from one of the oldest families in East Prussia. One must move with the times, of course, and Meyer was only forty-three years old. As he watched the endless Panzer column advancing into the fields of France Meyer reminded himself that he expected high promotion in this war and that this largely depended on the general's goodwill. So he must compromise, keeping his doubts about the general to himself.

Once beyond the Meuse the Panzers met with only sporadic resistance—the frantic firing of a few shells from artillery pieces, a rattle of machine guns, an irregular thump of mortar bombs falling somewhere. The general drove his division forward non-stop along the main road, thundering across France in a cloud of dust while the early summer sun beat down on the iron column. Away from the road, women working in the fields stopped to watch that dust cloud which rose like a smokescreen against the hot blue sky. It was a beautiful morning, the sky cloudless, the sun building up the intense warmth which suggested leisured ease rather than total warfare. Some of the women thought that the dust cloud marked the progress of a French column, although it was travelling in the wrong direction. Others stood and wondered, a feeling of depression and fear clutching their hearts, but still not able to accept the fact that the German army had broken through.

For this is exactly what it had done—it had broken clean through the French lines where the Ninth and Second armies met—the least defensible point along any continuous front. And so far, since the dive-bombers had smashed all resistance on the west bank of the Meuse, there had been no fierce battles, none at all. Because the general was young, in the prime of life and endowed with enormous funds of energy and optimism, his sixth sense was beginning to tell him something. It was a matter of keeping going, of not stopping for anything. This mood was not shared by Colonel Hans Meyer.

There was an ugly scene when the general's tank halted briefly in the centre of a French village. Behind him four more heavy tanks rumbled into the square and halted, their huge guns revolving slowly round the upper windows of the old square, menacing even the thought of resistance. Meyer climbed down from his tank and approached the general, who remained in his turret, still standing erect, his face expressionless as he handed down his map.

'Meyer, the patrol has taken that road,' he pointed with his gloved hand, 'but is it the right one? They have assured me that it is—what do you think?'

Meyer examined the map quickly, looked round at the exits from the square, consulted his own map, and handed the other back to the general.

'I'm sure they are right, sir.'

'We'd better check with the locals. You speak French. That man over there—ask him.'

The general took off his glove, unbuttoned his holster flap, extracted his pistol, and pointed it at a middle-aged man with a grey moustache. It was an astonishing scene: the sun shining down so that it was almost hot, the inhabitants standing in the old square rigid with fear, like waxwork figures out of a tableau.

Only five minutes earlier they had been going about their daily routines with a touch of anxiety but with no real fear. Then it had happened—the scared boy running into the square shouting something about a huge dust cloud. He had hardly finished telling his story when the motor-cyclists had flashed across the square, tyres screaming at the corners, vanishing as they raced off to the west. People had come out of their houses at the commotion, completely bewildered. A woman had seen German soldiers in the sidecars, helmeted figures carrying machine-pistols. Arguments had broken out. She must be mad, must be seeing things. And while they argued and wondered the general had arrived with five tanks.

23

The village was paralyzed as he unsheathed his pistol and aimed it.

The man with the moustache stepped forwards and sideways, presenting his body to the pistol muzzle, shielding a woman instinctively. His wife. A hush of horror fell on the sunlit square. Even Meyer was disturbed. He spoke quickly.

'That won't be necessary.'

'Ask him, Meyer.'

The gun remained levelled at the man's chest. Meyer stepped forward, his face stiff with anger. He even placed his own body between the man and the pointed muzzle as he addressed him in excellent French.

'Which is the direct route to St. Quentin? You see what we have with us, so think carefully before you reply. The direct route to St. Quentin.'

The Frenchman moistened his lips and glanced sideways as an army truck drove into the square. Before it had pulled up men were jumping out of the back, German soldiers armed with rifles and machine-pistols. Their sergeant held a map in his hand, a detailed map of the district. He glanced round quickly, pointed, and a detachment ran into a building. Outside in the square, the moustached Frenchman had taken his decision: he had his wife to consider, and the other villagers. He pointed in the direction the motor-cyclists had taken, his hand wobbling.

'That is the way to St. Quentin—the only direct way. I swear to God.'

Meyer nodded and turned round, his body still shielding the Frenchman while the general put away his pistol.

'He says the route is down that street. He's telling the truth, I'm sure of it.'

'Good, good. As long as we're sure.' The general turned round in his turret and called out to the sergeant who stood by the truck with several of his men.

'Tell them we come as liberators. Tell them also that at the slightest sign of resistance they will all be shot.' He broke off impatiently. 'You know what to say, I should hope. We are pressing on.'

He issued the order to his driver and the tank rumbled away from the square, leaving Meyer to scramble up inside his own vehicle while the villagers stood perfectly still, not yet able to grasp the nightmare which had arrived in brilliant sunshine.

I'm right, the general told himself as the tank advanced into open country beyond the village, I do believe I'm right. He allowed a little of the exultation to well up inside him. *There isn't going to be any real resistance.* Those people in the village were symbolic: the shock of the armoured hammer had smashed French morale, had brought on a state of psychological paralysis. We must keep moving, on and on. And on and on raced the German spearhead, a spearhead tipped by the 14th Panzer Division, commanded by General Heinrich Storch.

The tank crew had been entombed inside the tunnel for over twenty-four hours and the strain was telling. In spite of the fact that they had spent over two-thirds of their time in back-breaking toil, removing large boulders with their bare hands, carting away hundredweights of debris with the shovels they carried on the tank, their state of near-physical exhaustion still couldn't prevent them from thinking, and the longer they remained trapped inside the hill the more they began to wonder whether they would ever leave the tunnel alive. Barnes paused to lean on his shovel, wiping sweat from his dripping forehead as he looked at his watch in the headlights. Seven o'clock in the evening of Friday May 17.

They had driven into the tunnel at eleven o'clock on the morning of the previous day and there was still no sign that they had more than scraped the surface of the landslide. At the rock face, its impenetrable solidity only too apparent in the pitiless headlight beams, Davis and Reynolds wrestled to haul out a massive boulder from the left-hand side of the wall. The two men were working together as a team while Barnes and Penn wielded the shovels—a sensible division of labour since the two troopers were easily the strongest men in the crew. Barnes stood back and watched them working while he began his fifteen-minute break. He had organized the work routine so they had fifteen minutes off in every hour, and he had further arranged that the breaks should be taken in pairs, so that each man had someone to talk to, but at the same time he was encouraged by still seeing the work in progress. Four men resting at the same time, all voicing their fears, could have a disastrous effect on morale.

'Time for a break, Penn,' he called out.

'In a tick—I'll just finish shifting this lot.'

Thirty-four years old, Barnes was not only the oldest member of the crew, he was also the smallest, Barely five foot seven inches tall, he was small-boned and slim, but his frame was wiry and on a long-term endurance basis he could probably outlast the other three on sheer will-power alone. His face was lean, clean-shaven, and above prominent cheekbones his brown eyes were still alert and watchful as he studied Reynolds and Davis. In size there wasn't a great deal to choose between them; they were both large, heavily-built men, but there was an enormous difference in temperament. Whereas Davis, the ex-miner, was subject to moods of melancholy, Reynolds could be relied upon to carry out any task he was set until he dropped, showing neither enthusiasm nor depression at any stage.

As for thirty-year-old Corporal Penn, he was easily the most intelligent and best-educated of the four men. At the outbreak of war he could have obtained a commission but he had turned it down for reasons which were never quite clear. Slim and tall, he was the most light-hearted of the crew, and at the same time the most sensitive. Dropping his shovel, he wobbled over to Barnes in an exaggerated manner.

'There should be extra pay for this, there really should. Working underground doesn't come within my agreed sphere of duties, you know. I'll have to look it up in King's Regs. Mind if we take a stroll along the promenade?'

Along the promenade was Penn's version for walking through the tunnel, so Barnes got up off the hull where he had been sitting and walked with Penn, his torch beam showing the way. As soon as they were out of earshot of the other two men Penn began talking.

'I don't like the look of Davis. I don't think he can stand much more of this.'

'He'll have to—it's the same for all of us and we may be through to the other side any moment now.'

'Do you really think so? That wall could be twenty feet thick. I imagine the Germans blew in the entrance.'

'It looks like it—or they might have been bombing the railway and dropped one which started a landslide. It doesn't make much difference now—we've just got to get far enough through to be able to use the two-pounder.'

'The two-pounder?' Penn stopped in the middle of the rail track. 'You're joking, of course?'

'Look, Penn, by the time we see daylight we're going to be pretty tired. And in any case we've been away from troop for well over twenty-four hours. God knows what's been happening on the outside but our job is to get back as fast as we can —and the way to do that is to shoot our way out when we can. We'll wait until we have a hole big enough for me to crawl through and do a recce. Then Davis can take his mind off things by shelling the rest out of the way.'

'Just so long as Davis lasts out the course—and always assuming we ever reach your little hole.'

'Now you're beginning to talk like Davis. It doesn't seem to have struck any of you that being cooped up inside here is a damned sight safer than being bombed by Stukas.'

Penn glanced at Barnes in amazement. He had really meant what he had said, Penn felt sure of it. The idea that they might be trapped inside this tunnel until they were out of water, out of food, out of lighting when the batteries ran down—none of this seemed to have crossed Barnes' mind. In his usual way he just assumed that they would make it, that it was only a matter of time before they broke through that terrible wall. Well, if faith moved mountains, Barnes was likely to move that wall, and their tank commander had a habit of backing up his faith with planning and forethought: they were still enjoying meals of bully beef and biscuits because of Barnes's insistence that they should always carry provisions for one week. He turned and followed Barnes back to the rock face, sensing

27

trouble as soon as they arrived. Davis had apparently been waiting for their return and now the burly gunner was glaring at his sergeant, his voice an insubordinate growl.

'We'll never get through this bloody wall.'

'No, we won't—not if you just stand there,' Barnes agreed mildly. 'So get on with it.'

'We're wasting our time . . .'

'No, Davis—we aren't. At the moment you are the one who is wasting time, so get on with it.'

Barnes' voice was still very mild. He stood close to his large gunner with a relaxed air, his eyes never leaving Davis's.

'We're going to die down here—*die*, did you hear me? And one day they'll open up this bleedin' tunnel and find four corpses—four skeletons.' His voice was close to hysteria now, his mouth and hands working as though on the edge of a complete breakdown. 'I'm a miner—I know what this means. I've . . .'

'Davis!' Barnes's tone was sharper now. 'You haven't by any chance thought yourself into thinking that this *is* a mine shaft, have you?'

'No, but . . .'

'So, instead of being hundreds of feet below the surface we're actually at ground level—right? The fact is, Davis, that your being a miner is just about as relevant as the fact that Penn was once a draughtsman. Now, do you expect Reynolds to shift that boulder all by himself, or are you going to give him a hand?'

'It may take a fortnight to shift that lot,' Davis persisted stubbornly. 'There could be hundreds of . . .'

'Davis, I'm beginning to lose patience with you. It's just possible that it will take all four of us to break through, so we can't afford any spare wheels round here, and that's what you are at the moment. For the third time, I'm ordering you to get on with it.'

'Why not have a go at the other end—the wall may be thinner there.'

Barnes's face tightened. He prodded a stiff finger hard into Davis's chest, punctuating his words with prods.

28

'You have been given an order three times and three times you have refused to carry it out. As soon as we get back you're on a charge. In the meantime you will do your bit with the rest of us, and since you've wasted five minutes gassing, your next break period will be ten minutes instead of fifteen. Give Reynolds a hand with that boulder at once.'

He turned away and went back to sit on the tank hull, checking his watch to see whether his fifteen minutes was nearly up, putting his hands flat on either side of his body as he watched Davis start work again. Beside him Penn grinned and whispered. 'He thinks he can be Bolshie now we're on our own.' But Barnes made no reply and his face was grim. It had been a close run thing. They only needed one rotten apple in the barrel for the infection to spread, and the most contagious infection of all is fear. Outwardly, Barnes remained perfectly confident, his every word and gesture indicating clearly that it was only a matter of some hard slogging before they reached the outside world, but inwardly he didn't like the look of it. They were marooned in the centre of a battlefield and the war could rage backwards and forwards over the front for weeks as it had done a quarter of a century earlier. While that went on there would be a certain shortage of people to go round digging out buried tunnels, even supposing that the idea seemed important to them. There was no real problem of air —the tunnel was long enough for them to breathe inside it for weeks—but their water and food supplies would only last for several days, to say nothing of Bert's batteries. And when the batteries went they would be plunged into darkness, which would make working on the wall face almost impossible. For the first few hours of their entombment Barnes had mainly fretted about being cut off from his troop, but as the hours passed and they entered on a new day he found his mind beginning to think like Davis's, and the analogy of the mine disaster was only too apt, which was why he had shut up Davis at the earliest possible moment. He glanced at his watch again, nodded to Penn, and went forward to pick up his shovel.

Twenty-four hours later, in the evening of Saturday May 18, they had removed an incredibly large mass of rubble and rock, but still the wall face was intact. They worked now by the light of the oil lamp which Barnes always carried inside the tank, and the reason for this was not only to save Bert's headlights: Barnes foresaw that later, when morale was sagging, switching on the headlights again might just keep them going a while longer, but he kept the real reason for this decision to himself. In the middle of the afternoon there had almost been a fatal accident when part of the wall suddenly came away and slid forward of its own momentum. Only Reynolds's speed and strength had saved Davis when he had grabbed the gunner's arm and hauled him sideways out of the path of the tumbling boulders. It was a measure of their anxiety that even when Davis had just experienced this shock he was the first to recover, running away from Reynolds to gaze up at the centre of the wall in desperate hope, his voice hoarse and strained.

'Maybe we're through now.'

'Keep back. I'll see,' snapped Barnes.

Gingerly, he had climbed up the rubble slope, expecting at any moment a fresh fall, but when he had reached the rock face and pushed it was like leaning against the side of a fortress. So they had started again, Barnes and Penn working furiously with their shovels to remove the fresh rubble so that the other two could reach the rock face with their crowbar. It was just after seven o'clock in the evening when Penn made his remark during their rest period. Barnes sat alongside him on the tank hull, watching Reynolds prising out a fresh boulder while Davis sought to give extra leverage by pulling with his bare hands.

'It's funny, but ever since we've been in here we haven't heard any sound of the battle.'

'We've probably driven them back a bit—besides, there wasn't so much going on this side of Etreux.'

He left it at that, wondering why the obvious and macabre conclusion had not been drawn by the others long ago. The fact that they could not hear even faint sounds of the huge bombardment taking place in the outside world demonstrated more clearly than anything the immense thickness of the wall which barred their escape. The thought had occurred to Barnes twenty-four hours earlier and had so worried him that he had waited until the others were asleep before walking back down the tunnel. When he reached the far end he had listened carefully at the blocked entrance but no sound had penetrated from the outside world. They were well and truly sealed in at both ends. Taking a sip of water from his mug, he frowned. Then, very carefully, he put the mug down on the hull and walked over to where Reynolds and Davis were working. He faced the wall and then turned sideways as though listening. It was a dramatic moment and Penn instantly guessed that something had happened because he got down off the tank and walked forward. Something in Barnes's attitude had attracted the attention of Reynolds and Davis and they stopped working.

'What is it?' asked Penn.

Barnes shook his head and faced the wall again, his hands on his hips, his eyes searching the surface carefully. When he spoke his voice was quiet.

'I think we're nearly through.'

'Why?' Penn asked quickly.

'I can feel a faint current of air—come and stand here.'

'My God! You're right! You're right!'

They began to work feverishly at the point where Barnes had traced the air current's entrance, a point about four feet above the level of the tunnel floor. A quarter of an hour later they experienced another heart-lifting moment when Barnes told them to stop working for a minute while he put out the lamp. For a short time there was no sound in the darkness of the tunnel while four pairs of eyes strained to see any sign of daylight in the wall. It was Barnes who spotted it first—a narrow, paper-thin slit along the upper surface of one large boulder.

'We're through,' shouted Davis. 'We're really through. Dear Mother of God, we're through!'

'Take it easy now,' warned Barnes, 'this could be tricky. There's still a solid mass of rock up there.'

He relit the oil lamp and when he turned round Davis was already inserting the crowbar into a corner near the end of the slit they had seen, his hands gripping the iron with a ferocious intensity as he drove the end deeper into the wall and began to twist and turn for leverage. Barnes opened his mouth and closed it again without speaking. The poor devil must have gone through even greater agonies than the rest of them with his memories of the mine trap he had escaped from. Barnes had realized this when he had treated Davis roughly, but any display of sympathy at that time could have destroyed the morale of all of them. And Barnes never forgot the dictum of Napoleon—morale is to the material as three is to one. So now he let Davis break loose as he dug and rammed the bar into the remaining barrier, punishing his hands with the force of his efforts and never even noticing the punishment. Penn spoke as he shovelled debris to expose the base of the remaining rocks.

'I'll tell you now, I never thought we'd make it.'

'We'll face tougher things than this before this war's over.'

Within ten minutes Davis had prised the boulder loose and Reynolds was helping him to haul it back out of the wall, a boulder as large as the oil stove they carried inside Bert for emergency cooking arrangements. It came away suddenly. One moment Davis was leaning his full weight against the crowbar, sweat streaming down the sides of his face, and then the rock was shifting inwards, swaying gently before it toppled back into the tunnel, so unexpectedly that the two men had to jump sideways to avoid it. Picking up the oil lamp, Barnes held it behind his back and they all stared at the oblong of daylight. It was a memorable moment. Four men, each of whom had secretly felt that they would never make it, knew now that they would live. There was a pause when no one spoke, no one moved. Then Davis went berserk.

Seizing the crowbar which had fallen with the boulder, he rammed it behind the rock above the opening and began heaving and twisting with all his strength. Barnes shouted a warning, but Davis either didn't or wouldn't hear him. He felt the rock moving easily and dropped the crowbar. Reaching up to his full height he pushed, both hands flat against the rock, which fell outwards, enlarging the window considerably, enlarging it enough for Davis to climb up into it, crouching inside the alcove on his knees as he pushed with his hands at the loosened rock above. Barnes was still shouting when disaster struck.

The upper rock was held in position over the opening by ledges on either side of the aperture, but it moved loosely on the ledges so that when Davis again pushed his full strength against it the rock wobbled and then fell outwards under the fierce pressure of Davis's hands. As it fell away it unhinged the centre of gravity of the wall above. Davis was still crouched in the aperture when there was a low rumbling sound. The whole upper wall began to quiver and disintegrate. Barnes was running forward to grab Davis when Penn grasped his arm firmly and hauled him back against the side of the tunnel. A second later an avalanche of rock and rubble poured down over the floor where Barnes had been standing, spilling tons of debris along the centre of the rail track, filling the tunnel with a roaring sound which deafened them. Then they were bending over and choking and spluttering as the dust invaded their lungs and blinded their eyes.

It was only when the dust began to settle that Barnes saw what had happened. On the far side of the tunnel, his back against the wall, Reynolds was safe. Beside Barnes, Penn was wiping his eyes to try and clear his vision. But it was the entrance to the tunnel which was the most awe-inspiring sight. The new landslide had completely cleared the upper part of the tunnel, leaving a great gap above the rubble slope which now stretched deep inside the tunnel, a gap through which they could see the blessed evening sky, a gap through which Bert could be driven once he had mounted the slope.

It took them several minutes to locate Davis, and they found the gunner only a few feet away from where Barnes had been standing after Penn had jerked him back out of the path of the falling wall. At least, they found Davis's head. The rest of his body was buried under the fall and it needed only a second's examination for them to realize that he was dead.

2. Saturday May 18

SOMETHING VERY STRANGE had happened to the world in this part of Belgium. The war had gone away.

Before they drove the tank out of the tunnel, up the rubble slope, and down the other side, Barnes had made a personal reconnaissance in the brilliant warmth of early evening. The first thing that struck him was the incredible silence, a silence which was intensified by the only sound, the peaceful twittering of an unseen bird. Beyond the tunnel the railway stretched away across open country, the track empty, the green fields deserted, not a sign of life anywhere, Etreux, or what was left of it, must have petered out farther along the hillside, because over to his right there were no buildings, no people. Only the still waters of the broad canal which barred their easy way back to Etreux.

He found the silence, the absence of gunfire, so disturbing that he climbed a little way up the hillside above the wrecked tunnel entrance, but still he heard nothing, saw nothing. The war had gone far away—to where? And which way? He sat down for a moment on the grass, his nerves strangely on edge as though the peaceful landscape were full of sinister meaning. He sat there blinking against the strong sunlight, drinking in the fresh air, then he got up quickly, went back to the tank, and gave the order to advance.

There had been no question of burying Davis, for Davis was already buried under a ton of rock, so they wrote his name, rank and number on a piece of paper and left this under a rock close to the head. Then they drove away, too exhausted to feel much emotion other than shock at the suddenness of the gunner's death. The thought uppermost in Barnes's mind now was that his crew was reduced from four to three. They were all capable of firing the guns in an emergency and he told Penn that when the need arose he would act as gunner. As they moved along the rail track Barnes stood in the turret, map in hand, and his mind weighed up the situation grimly. At least they had almost full fuel tanks, which meant that they could travel one hundred and fifty miles along the roads, a distance which would be reduced by fifty per cent once they began moving across country, but this was the only credit point he could muster. One crew member short, the wireless out of action, no knowledge of where Parker might be: they almost resembled a warship sailing into uncharted seas with no means of communicating with its base. Half his mind pondered the dubious likelihood of rejoining his troop while the other half toyed with the glimmer of an idea which was to grow. *Whatever happened, they must find a really worthwhile objective.*

A mile from the tunnel the track reached a level crossing and it was at this point where they turned off the railway line and began to move along a second-class road which ran between low hedges bordering fields of poor grassland. Six miles farther on they should turn right along a road which would take them into the rear area behind Etreux. But where were the armies?

Standing upright in the turret Barnes strained his ears for sounds of gunfire, strained his eyes for sight of smoke or planes. The fields stretched away, empty; the sky, a vault of pale blue, stretched away uninhabited. The uncanny feeling grew, a feeling of men moving into unexplored territory. The tank tracks ground forward at top speed, the engines throbbed with power, as though determined to enjoy to the full this race across open country after the confinement inside the tunnel, and then Barnes saw the first traces of battle—the faint marks of tank tracks in the fields, the occasional crater where a shell or bomb had exploded, and as they proceeded along the deserted road the traces became more frequent, less reassuring. At one point Barnes ordered Reynolds to halt while he got down to examine

35

wrecked vehicles by the roadside. They were burnt-out tanks, five of them, and they were French Renault tanks which looked as though they had fought the entire German army on their own. A little farther along the road he stopped again and Penn climbed out with him to look at a mess of French equipment. In the ditch rifles lay there as though they had been thrown down in panic flight from something awful and overpowering. When Barnes picked one up he found the weapon was still loaded. A few yards farther along there were abandoned army packs, abandoned helmets, all French. Search as he might, Barnes could find no German equipment. Two of the helmets were occupied, the bodies lying on their backs facing the sky. Then more rifles, all of them loaded.

'I don't like the look of it,' said Barnes. 'The loaded rifles, I mean. It looks as though they just ran for their lives. Tanks against men, probably.'

'They've retreated, then,' remarked Penn quietly.

'Looks like it. A helluva lot must have happened while we were bottled up in that tunnel. According to the map there's a village about five miles farther on—we should get news there. I may halt Bert outside and go in on foot. I don't like the look of this at all.'

'It could be Jerry who has retreated,' said Penn thoughtfully. 'Parker may be on the Rhine now.'

'Wars don't move at that speed, Penn, not in either direction. As to Jerry retreating, I still don't like the look of those loaded rifles in the ditch—they smell of French retreat. We'd better get on.'

As they moved along the road Barnes saw more and more evidence that the scythe of war had passed that way, more and more burnt-out Renault tanks, smashed guns, still figures lying sprawled in the fields, helmets. And always they were French helmets. He was still waiting to see even one sign of German casualties in either men or machines, and he had not found it when he saw in the distance the first indication of life in this eerily empty landscape—a horizontal line of smoke. The line crossed the sky just above the ground and it hung perfectly still as though drawn in with charcoal. But at one end, the end which was approaching the road half a mile farther on, the line was growing and he realized it was smoke from a train's engine, a train which was still invisible below the level of an embankment. He scanned the sky and stiffened, his hand tightening on the turret rim. High up in the blue vastness a formation of planes was flying on a course which seemed to parallel the direction of the train. He raised his glasses and focused them. It was impossible to be sure but they looked like a squadron of British Blenheim bombers and his heart lifted at the sight of them.

As the tank trundled forward he watched the planes coming closer and then, focusing his glasses along the road, he saw the level crossing which the train would pass over within the next minute. He swivelled his glasses back to the aerial formation and caught his breath. They were moving into line now— *coming in for a bombing run.* He gave the order to halt and warned his crew over the intercom.

'I think there'll be some bombs dropping in the vicinity shortly. Don't laugh—but they'll be coming from our chaps.'

No one laughed as they waited in the stationary tank, the engines still ticking over. Should they reverse, wondered Barnes, and then he rejected the idea. They might just as easily reverse into a bomb. He prepared to slam down the lid but for the moment he waited, curious to see whether the Blenheims hit their target.

'What are they after?' Penn called up.

'A train, I think. It's just about to cross the road farther along, so get ready for it.'

His glasses brought up the road ahead now and he saw the smoke line emerge from behind the embankment. The train began to move across the road into the fields beyond. Two engines, drawing a line of goods coaches. He sucked in his breath as he saw tiny figures clustered round a long barrel on a flat truck. A Bofors? He could hear the gun now as it began pumping shells into the sky. When he looked up the first bombs were falling, small black dots against the warm blue, too far away to menace Bert, thank God, but they were going to be close, mighty close, to that train. The stick of dots vanished behind the smoke and he waited for the detonations. As he stood there, his eyes glued to the smoke line, a colossal explosion murdered the evening, far more enormous than it should have been. The first shock wave swept along the road as a coach went hump-backed. The wave buffeted against the tank hull and Barnes started to scramble inside, the words screaming through his brain. Ammunition train! The second, more devastating shock wave hit the tank when he was half way down, his hand inside the turret, the lid still open. The tremendous force of the wave unbalanced his footing and his head smashed back against the steel rim. At that very moment the undetected Messerschmitt swooped in a power-dive, all guns blazing, but Barnes was already unconscious.

Saturday evening, 7 p.m. The 14th Panzer Division was racing deeper into France, now well beyond Laon, coming close to the Somme. General Heinrich Storch not only had the nose of a hawk, he also had the eye of that predatory bird, and this eye was now fixed on a hump some distance away across the fields. Whipping up his glasses, he focused on the object, letting out his breath in a hiss. He spoke briefly into the microphone hanging from his neck as a shell screamed across the field towards the tank column. A 75-mm. gun, Storch told himself, the best artillery piece in the whole French army, probably the only gun capable of taking on a German heavy tank. He looked back as the shell exploded over the road and in the field beyond. A ranging shot. The column was already obeying his command.

Storch's tank increased speed, rumbling along the road like an angry dinosaur while the gunner followed Storch's orders, traversing the turret which carried the barrel of his heavy gun towards the French artillery position. Behind him four tanks were moving at different speeds, so that in less than a minute they were well spaced out, making the French gun-aimer's task infinitely more difficult. He could now aim at only one target, while at the same time four tanks were firing back without fear of retaliation. The Panzer column stopped, five long barrels aimed across the field towards the camouflaged hump. A second shell screamed towards them, fell just short of the centre tank, and exploded in the grass, scattering a rain of soil over the hull. The Panzers replied.

One hand gripping the turret rim, the other holding his field glasses. Storch felt the recoil of his own heavy cannon. This shell also fell short of its target, sending up a cloud of smoke in front of the 75-mm. position. Storch spoke briefly, confident that the next shot would be on target, but his gunner never had the opportunity to fire because a shell from the tank behind landed squarely on top of the French position. It exploded, smoke blotting out the target, then there was a second explosion as the 75-mm. ammunition went up, hurling the mangled bodies of the gun crew across the field. Two more tanks fired, and as though encouraged by the marksmanship of their neighbour, both shells landed inside the billowing smoke, scattering the relics of the smashed gun. Storch issued the order to cease fire, his field glasses on the target, his voice quiet.

'Congratulations, Meyer. Your duck-shooting experience is bearing fruit.'

Inside his own tank turret Meyer tightened his lips. It was typical that Storch could not pat him on the back without in the same breath digging him in the ribs. The duck-shooting remark was a slighting reference to his aristocratic background, he had no doubt about that. While they waited, Meyer polished his monocle and screwed it back into position. He wore it on every possible occasion simply because he knew that it annoyed Storch, who regarded the eye-glass as a badge of caste. Then he heard the general's high-pitched voice through the crackle of his earphones. They were on the move again.

Storch's sense of exultation was growing. In his mind's eye he was already racing ahead to the distant objective of Amiens, only twenty-five miles from the sea. His Panzer division was in the lead of the extraordinary advance and he was determined that it should maintain that position. Speaking into the microphone, he ordered the driver to increase speed, even though there was a danger that they might overtake the motor-cycle patrols, but the spotter plane had just radioed back to say the road ahead was clear.

Following up in the second tank, Meyer wiped his face clean of the dust kicked up by Storch's vehicle, his mood very different from that of his commanding officer. Soon they were passing through yet another French village without stopping, witnessing once again the same astonishing scene: another church, another village square, the inhabitants standing petrified against the walls, too scared or too astounded to rush indoors as the Panzer column thundered past. This can't go on much longer, Meyer told himself grimly. They had already far out-distanced the infantry and he was going to have a word with Storch about that at the next stopping point. All Meyer's professional instincts revolted against this wild headlong rush into the blue.

They left the village and emerged once again into the open French landscape, a sea of fields stretching away for ever, the sunlight shining down on dry pasturelands. And whereas Storch saw every evidence of a French collapse in the deserted view ahead, Meyer saw a panorama full of hidden dangers. He was well aware that the Manstein Plan envisaged a tremendous encircling sweep which would cut off the northern group of Allied armies from the French forces in the south, a sweep which would be completed when they reached the sea, but it seemed to Meyer that this plan was based on the extraordinary assumption that the Allies would sit back and let this happen. From his Great War experience Meyer knew this to be the assumption of a madman. At any moment the enemy counter-attack would erupt, rolling like a tidal wave against the armoured columns stretched out far ahead of the main German army. He only hoped to God that the counter-attack would not materialize *behind* them. Another instruction came as they approached a crossroads. Storch was waiting in his stationary tank as Meyer arrived. Climbing down out of his own vehicle he walked over and stood looking up at his general, who spoke first.

'The spotter plane reports something on the road ahead— it's investigating.'

'I know.' Meyer took a deep breath, wishing that Storch would come down out of his turret. 'I've been expecting this—

there'll be a heavy counter-attack at any moment. May I suggest that we wait here until the infantry catches us up? It might even be wiser to withdraw a few miles—to consolidate.'

'Why?'

Storch's voice was silky. He leaned over the turret to examine Meyer, who was at a further disadvantage because the general's peaked cap shaded his face and he couldn't see his expression.

'Because we have no supporting troops to hold the ground we have taken.' He took another deep breath. 'In fact, what we have taken may mean very little without troops occupying the ground we are rushing over like the Berlin Express.'

As soon as he had spoken he felt that he had gone too far, but having spoken he was determined not to back down and he prepared to defend himself. In any case, if things did go wrong this might well be a useful conversation to repeat at a military court of enquiry. The general did not reply immediately. Instead, he turned his head sideways, cocking his ear as though listening to something almost beyond the range of human hearing. Storch did have exceptional hearing powers and he attributed these to his total abstinence. Looking up, squinting against the sun's glare, Meyer had a view of Storch's profile now—an arrogant curve of nose, the thin wide mouth, the sharply pointed jaw-line.

'It sounds like bombing,' the general commented. 'Our Stukas must be taking out the next town. So, you think we ought to stop here do you, Meyer?'

'Or withdraw to a less-exposed . . .'

'May I remind you, Colonel Meyer,' Storch paused, still listening, 'that this Panzer division is under my command, and I, in turn, am responsible to the Corps Commander, General Guderian,* who takes his instructions from General von Rundstedt?'

---

* General Guderian, who had carefully studied General de Gaulle's work, 'The Army of the Future,' was chiefly responsible for the development of the Panzer divisions. Guderian later took the armoured host to the southern approaches of Moscow.

Meyer was appalled. What on earth was coming? Surely Storch was not contemplating sending him back to base? He stood stiffly as the awful realization of his tactical error dawned on him. For Storch could easily interpret what had just been said as faint-heartedness in the face of the enemy. Meyer said nothing as Storch continued in the same silky tone.

'And may I also remind you of General Guderian's orders that the Panzers are to be let off the leash—to push forward as far and as fast as they can while their petrol lasts out?'

For the first time the general looked down at his G.S.O.1, as he pulled down his earphones in position, listened, and then lifted them again. His voice was harsher now.

'It may interest you to know that the spotter plane has located and identified the obstacles in our path—two French farm carts. I don't imagine, Colonel Meyer, that we should allow ourselves to be troubled by such opponents.' He stood up in his turret, erect as a ramrod. 'Meyer, please return to your tank—the advance will continue in the general direction of Amiens.'

Barnes sensed that something was wrong, that this was no normal waking, so he resisted the temptation to open his eyes immediately. He listened. His mind felt muddled and he was vaguely aware that he had been dreaming, dreaming something unpleasant, something to do with the war, but it had receded from his realms of consciousness. He always woke up quickly and how he pushed the dream, the nightmare, away, struggling to grasp where he was.

Where the hell was he? It was very quiet inside the building and he was lying stretched out on his back staring up at a beamed and raftered ceiling far above his head, alarm gripping him as memory surged back. The Blenheims, the long smoke line, the ammunition train, the terrible explosion, a feeling of something tearing into his right shoulder, then oblivion. Still lying on the blanket, his fingers reached up and explored the shoulder, contacting a thick dressing, sticky plaster. Yes, they'd got him, all right. But where was he now—and where were Penn and Reynolds?

He tried to sit up on the blanket and flopped back as a wave of dizziness rolled over him. His head was aching horribly and he felt weak and washed-out, hardly able to concentrate. Under the dressing his shoulder throbbed and at the pit of his stomach was a sensation of sickness. Tentatively, still lying down, he tested his legs by crooking them at the knee; first the right knee, then the left. They seemed to be in one piece. Now for the arms. He worked them round over the blanket, clenching and unclenching his fingers. As far as he could tell his main handicap was an appalling weakness which had reduced his normally wiry frame to the consistency of a jelly. Turning his head to one side, he saw his boots standing a few feet away, placed neatly together, the toecaps gleaming like black glass. He knew they were his own boots because he recognized a tiny scratch on one toecap, and the sight of these boots heartened him because they had recently been cleaned with great care, which meant that Reynolds must have cleaned them. To take the weight off his shoulder, he moved his body over sideways, lifting his head to examine his quarters. He was inside some kind of out-building, probably part of a farm. Yes, in the far corner he could see an old plough and beside it some of their army kit—a dixie supported on an improvised tripod, suspended over the ashes of a fire, and two enamel mugs. Then he saw something standing against the wall which gave him a bad turn. A German machine-pistol with the magazine protruding below the barrel, its strap coiled in a neat loop.

He tried to stand up to reach the loaded weapon but his legs gave way, so he crawled from under the blanket over his body and wobbled his way across the wooden floor on his knees, naked from the waist upwards. He collapsed as he reached the weapon. Gritting his teeth, he forced himself up on to his knees again, grabbed the pistol by its long barrel and then crawled back to his blankets. Sitting up, he began to examine the machine-pistol, extracting the magazine before he fiddled with the firing mechanism. As he found out how the gun worked it came back to him. Someone had attended to his wound, a man with red cheeks and a bushy white moustache. The same man had given him an injection, he could remember

43

the prick of the needle in his right arm, and later the stranger had come back to re-dress his wound. He could remember that very clearly because he had resented being woken up. But how long had they been inside this place? Six hours? Twelve hours? He looked at his watch and the face was cracked, the hands stopped at 7.45. That would be about the time when the ammunition train blew up. Through a window high up in the wall he could see that it was broad daylight, another glorious day with the sky blue and hot. It must be Sunday morning or afternoon, Sunday May 19. Then he heard someone coming. Re-inserting the magazine, he pulled a blanket up over him and sat still, the gun concealed under the blanket, his left hand under the barrel, his right hand round the trigger guard.

Two men walked in through the huge door at the far end of the building. Penn and a stranger, a lad no older than eighteen, who wore a blue denim jacket and trousers, his shirt open at the front. He looked the picture of health, tall, well-built, his manner radiating an air of vitality. His fair hair was combed neatly back over his head and his blue eyes looked down at Barnes with curiosity. Penn looked surprised as they stopped near his bedside.

'You're awake, sergeant.'

'What did you expect to find—a corpse? Who's this?'

'This is Pierre. He speaks English, Pierre, meet Sergeant Barnes.'

'I am happy to meet you, sergeant.'

The lad bent down and to Barnes' embarrassment he solemnly shook hands. Then he stood up and waited without saying a word.

'Where's Reynolds?' demanded Barnes.

'He's on guard outside.'

'Guarding Bert, you mean?'

'Yes, Bert's in the next shed. Don't worry—he's well out of sight.'

'And what does that mean—why should I worry?'

'How are you feeling?' Penn inquired. 'You've had . . .'

'Well enough to wonder what the devil is going on. How long have we been in this place, Penn?'

44

'You've had concussion. When the Jerry fighter dived at us you caught a bullet in the shoulder and banged your head a fourpenny one on the turret.'

'I can remember that,' Barnes snapped irritably. 'Do get to the point and answer my question. How long have we been here?'

'Four days.'

The answer hit Barnes like a thunderclap. For once in his life he was speechless as the implications of Penn's statement raced through his brain. Where was the troop? Come to that, where was the B.E.F.? Sitting up was making the throbbing of his shoulder wound worse: he would have loved to lie down again but that was out of the question. He blinked away the muzziness of his vision as Penn spoke again.

'You'd better listen to what Pierre has to say—he knows more about it than I do.'

Barnes looked up at the lad, his voice polite but firm.

'Pierre, would you mind going outside and staying with Trooper Reynolds for a few minutes?'

He saw Pierre's face drop and Penn frowned. When the lad had gone out and shut the door Penn protested.

'I wish you hadn't done that—we may need him. You don't know the position here.'

'And I won't until you tell me.' Barnes dropped the blanket and laid the machine-pistol on its side.

'What did you want that for?' asked Penn.

'I'd no idea what was happening when I woke up—a couple of Jerries might have walked through that door. Now, what's the position?'

Penn paused and then burst out with it. 'We're a helluva long way behind the German lines. Maybe twenty miles or more.'

'We can't be . . .'

'The Germans have broken through along the whole front. They've torn a tremendous gap in the lines and it's a bloody great mess—just how great it's hard to tell because there are so many rumours . . .'

'It could be a rumour that they've broken through, then.'

45

'No chance of that—I heard this morning that the Panzers have reached Arras. The Luftwaffe has the whole show to itself —our lot and the French air force were shot out of the sky in the first few days. The Germans have hundreds of tanks and thousands of planes. You've got to face it—we're miles and miles behind the German lines.'

'Today is Thursday, then?'

'Yes, Thursday, May the twenty-third.'

'And where exactly are we?'

'Just outside a place called Fontaine. We're fairly close to the French frontier.'

'What?'

For the second time in five minutes Barnes was staggered, but this time he simply stared at his corporal grimly as he climbed to his feet. He felt his legs giving way at once, but sheer willpower stiffened the flagging muscles. Leaning a hand against the nearby wall, feeling the sweat trickling down his back with the effort of staying upright, he smiled wintrily.

'Penn, if I haven't gone potty I seem to recall that when the ammo train went up we were a good forty miles from the French frontier.'

Penn's moustache quivered and then his sense of humour got the upper hand and he spoke lightly.

'Sergeant Barnes, you have been away from this wonderful world of ours for four days—in other words you've been out cold, so it was up to me to see you home safe and sound, if you can call this home, although personally I've known better ones. Supposing you just let me tell you what's happened and then you'll feel a lot happier. You won't,' he added with a grin, 'but you know I always phrase things in the most tactful way.'

'The floor is yours.'

'When the train blew up we were attacked by a Messer-schmitt and you collected one in the shoulder. You managed to smash your head good and hard at the same time. On the way down you did get the lid shut, and that's why I'm talking to you now—I heard half a beltful of bullets rattling on the turret before Jerry pushed off. When I checked the state of

46

your health you were dead to the world and bleeding like a stuck pig, but I managed to get a dressing on.' He took a deep exaggerated breath to illustrate the drama of it all. 'For the next few hours, till well after dark, we were dodging Jerries. It was a sheer fluke that we got away with it—mostly by driving across open country. Eventually, hours later, we ended up here and here we've been ever since.'

'You drove through the night?'

'Yes, there was a moon, which helped, considering we daren't use the headlights. When we got here I hadn't the slightest idea where we were. And before you blow my head off about that, you can't read a map at night when you're travelling across country, keeping an eye open for Jerry, and popping down to see whether your tank commander is still in the land of the living. At least,' he ended with a grin, 'I can't.'

'You did damn' well, Penn. Thanks. What made you stay in this place?'

'I found a Belgian doctor who was willing to look after you without letting anyone know we were here. These buildings are outside Fontaine and the village still don't know about us. The doctor's a nice old boy called Lepin and the last time he called he said it was just a matter of changing your dressing and waiting till you came round. I doubt if he'll be back again— he could be shot by the Germans for treating you. The main thing is we haven't been spotted yet . . .'

'Pierre has spotted us.'

'I'll come to him in a minute. How are you doing?'

While they had been talking Barnes was testing himself, walking slowly round the floor and keeping close to the wall as he forced his reluctant legs forward. The wound was thumping him good and proper now but the dizziness was receding.

'Fine,' he said quickly. 'Go on.'

'Lepin was a godsend. You probably don't remember it— and that's your good luck—but while you were drugged he took out the bullet. He said you'd need at least ten days' rest—that's a week starting from yesterday.'

'Arras—where did you get that news about Arras?'

'It came through on the radio bulletin. I go into Fontaine

47

once a day to listen in. Lepin's house backs on to a field and he leaves the wireless set in a shed for me.'

'The French radio may not be reliable.'

'I'm talking about the B.B.C.'

A chill ran down Barnes's spine. Arras was half way to the sea. He still found it difficult to grasp the extent of the catastrophe and he still held on to the hope that the reports were wildly exaggerated.

'We must have some idea of how far behind the German lines we are,' he said sharply.

'I've no idea at all.'

Barnes paused to hold himself up against the wall. 'Look, Penn, there must be a front line somewhere. Don't the radio bulletins give any indication at all?'

'Sergeant, you still haven't grasped it. The French to the south of Etreux took an awful bashing. The whole weight of the German armour was thrown against them from what I can make out, and there isn't a front line down here any more. Everything's all over the place. Jerry has torn a bloody great gap in the line and it's getting bigger every day. And the B.E.F. is a long way west of Brussels now.'

'There are no Germans in Fontaine?'

'Not up to this morning. A column of tanks went through two days ago but that's the way they seem to be operating— they didn't leave a single soldier behind.'

Barnes found that interesting. He thought about it while he picked up his clothes and started dressing with difficulty. At least he was still wearing his battledress trousers so he wouldn't have to struggle with them. Then he resumed his cross examination.

'The tank's next door, you said. In what condition?'

'Engines are in full working order. The Besa's O.K. So is the two pounder. The wireless is still U.S. but the intercom's O.K. We can talk to each other but we're cut off from the outside world. Reynolds and I have spent most of our time on maintenance while you were playing Rip Van Winkle.'

'One thing bothers me, Penn. This lad, Pierre. How does he come into the picture?

48

'He's helped us enormously. He saw us coming into this place when we first arrived and he's been around ever since. He knew we were here so I thought the best thing was to make friends with him—and the fact that he speaks English as well as his native French is a godsend . . .'

'He's Belgian?'

'Yes, his parents come from the north and he's lost touch with them. He was visiting an uncle in Fontaine when the war started.'

Barnes asked a lot more questions while he finished dressing and among other things he learnt that it was now two o'clock in the afternoon. At the end of the conversation he returned to the subject of Pierre.

'You said he was visiting an uncle here when the war started —you mean way back in September last year?'

'No, I meant when the Germans attacked Belgium a fortnight ago. I still say Pierre could be useful. We both know a little French but if we're going to get out of this we'll need someone who can talk to the locals, and he's as keen as mustard to come with us. How the hell will we know where we are if . . .'

'Bring him in to me.'

Barnes picked up the machine-pistol, extracted the magazine again and began testing the mechanism.

'Pierre brought that . . .' began Penn.

'I said send him in.'

Barnes went on fiddling with the gun after Penn had brought in Pierre and he kept him waiting while he went on examining the weapon. He was looking down at the gun when he fired his question at Pierre.

'Where did you get hold of this?'

'I found it on the road outside Fontaine. I saw a car stop and the driver threw it into the ditch. Then he drove away very fast. It is in good order, Sergeant Barnes.' He pronounced it 'Burns.' 'I tested it myself. After first taking out the magazine,' he added proudly.

'I see. Where did a lad of your age learn about things like this?'

49

'My father works at the Belgian small arms factory at Herstal. He can fire all the pistols and machine guns.' Again the hint of pride. 'Including your own Bren gun. They call it by that name because it was first made in the city of Brno in Czechoslovakia.'

'You have an uncle living in Fontaine?'

Barnes looked directly into the lad's blue eyes and his gaze was returned steadily. Pierre's eyebrows were so fair that he almost appeared to have none, which gave him a curiously older appearance.

'Not any more,' he replied. 'My uncle fled from the Germans three days since.'

'I see. Why didn't you go with him?'

'Because I am not scared. I am going to fight the Germans.' He went on talking quickly. 'I shall be eighteen years of age by July so I am quite old enough and my knowledge of weapons means that training is not necessary. Corporal Penn said that I could come with you.'

'Steady on, laddie,' Penn interjected. 'I said you'd have to ask Sergeant Barnes and that isn't the same thing at all.'

Barnes opened his mouth to say that he couldn't come under any circumstances and then he changed his mind. There was no point in antagonizing the lad before they left Fontaine. Instead, he asked a question.

'Where did you learn to speak such good English?'

'Thank you, sergeant.' Pierre glowed with pride. 'My father sent me to spend six months with the British firm of Vickers in Birmingham so that I could learn about British weapons. They tell me that I have a Midland accent.'

'You'd better go and talk to Trooper Reynolds, Pierre, while I have a look at the tank with Corporal Penn.'

Barnes started to explain to Penn how the machine-pistol worked, handing the weapon to him to demonstrate a point while Pierre was leaving the building.

'The temptation with this gun is to hold on to the magazine, but you've got to grasp it higher up just under the barrel . . . that doctor, Lepin, did you talk to him much while he was here looking after me?'

'Hardly at all—he's a very quiet type and I left Pierre to interpret for me.'

'You've been into Fontaine yourself?'

'No, I kept well clear of it except when I visited Lepin's garden shed to hear the news. I thought the Germans might occupy the place at any moment and I wanted to lie low till you were better.'

'Who owns these buildings—they belong to some farmer, I imagine?'

'Yes they do, but he's cleared out with the refugees so we should be all right here for a while until the roads are quieter. The main one through Fontaine is still crammed with refugee traffic and the place itself is lousy with them. We may have to sit it out here for several days.'

'Get the map for me, Penn. Staying in one spot behind the German lines for four days isn't a healthy idea at all and I'd say our luck is due to run out at any moment. We must get moving.'

'You've only just got up . . .'

'And I intend to stay up. Warn Reynolds to make any last-minute checks he thinks necessary so that we're ready to move at a moment's notice. And I could do with something to eat if there's anything left.'

The atmosphere was changing already with every word Barnes said, and Penn could sense it. A feeling of urgency had begun to animate Barnes and that feeling communicated itself to Penn, but he made one last effort.

'I still think you ought to rest up at least . . .'

'I'm going into Fontaine with Pierre to see for myself. When I get back we must be ready to move. Make no mistake about it, Penn, we'll be out of this place well before nightfall.'

The feeling that they ought to be on the move, away from this place, tugged insistently at Barnes as he marched steadily along the road to Fontaine with Pierre. The afternoon sun shone down brilliantly over the fields of France, beating down on their faces and warming their hands, a physical sensation of pure heat. Barnes had two reasons for his reconnaissance: he

51

wanted to smell the atmosphere for himself and he wanted to test his own staying power. The blazing sunshine added to the discomfort of his wound, so that now as well as the throb-throb he could also feel a pricking sensation round the edges of his dressing, a sensation which made him want to tear off the bandage. His head was aching and he walked rigidly, forcing himself to take long strides, each footfall thudding up into the sensitive shoulder like the impact of a small road-bumper. But he was still on his feet, so he was all right. In his holster he carried the Webley .455 revolver and the flap was un-buttoned.

'There's the village, Sergeant Barnes.'

'What on earth is that lot on the road?'

'They are the refugees. They go through Fontaine all day and all night. It is difficult to cross the main square.'

A grey slate church spire rose up from a huddle of stone-walled buildings and from that distance they could see on both sides of the village a road which ran at right-angles to the road they were walking along. The main road was packed with an incredible congestion of traffic, a slow-moving column which travelled at such a snail's pace that it hardly seemed to move at all. Barnes turned off the road and began to cut across the fields diagonally along a course which would take them to the eastern outskirts of the village.

'Are we not entering Fontaine?' inquired Pierre.

'I want to have a look at that column. Later, I want to go in to buy some food.'

'You will not get any—the village store is empty and the storekeeper has left two days before. He was very frightened and said it was time to go.'

'Frightened of the Germans?'

'No, of the villagers. He said that soon they would take what they wanted without paying him a franc. One man did call him a robber—I saw it myself. Other people in the store were threatening him.'

The incident had an ugly ring and Barnes began to feel alarmed. The sooner they got out of this area the better, but he must check the state of the roads first. We're in a jam, all right, he told himself. If all the main roads are like this we'll have to move across country, and that will slow us down and double our fuel consumption. They were approaching the refugee line broadside on, a line which stretched as far as the eye could see. A dozen yards from the roadside they stopped in the field and watched the spectacle. The road was crammed from verge to verge with a swollen river of fleeing humanity—several cars, a large number of horse-drawn carts piled high with bed linen, mattresses and a jumble of household goods. On one cart he saw a brass-posted bed which threatened to lurch over the edge at any moment. But above all the road was congested with people on foot and Barnes had never seen more pathetic faces, the faces of men and women at the end of their tether, their expressions weary and despairing, their eyes fixed dully on the vehicle ahead as they trudged along under the merciless heat of the sun.

'We'll never get through that lot,' he said eventually.

'There is a road which turns off over there,' Pierre pointed across the fields to a low hedge. 'You could take your tank along that road. No refugees have come from that direction since the Germans attacked.'

'Do you know where it goes?'

'Of course. It leads to Arras. I have never been there but my uncle has told me. I have been along it for many miles and it is wide enough for a tank.'

What Pierre was saying agreed with the map Barnes had studied and he found his thoughts turning more and more towards the town of Arras. Penn had told him that a news bulletin that morning had reported an Allied counter-attack developing in the area of Arras, a counter-attack of British tanks, and the town was the one fixed point where the Allies seemed to be engaging the Germans. He looked to the right as he heard a car coming closer, its horn blaring persistently. It was an open touring Renault, a green four-seater, and super-ficially it had the appearance of a military staff car. For one split second Barnes thought he might have re-established con-tact with the Allied forces, and then he saw that the only occupant was a woman. The horn blared again and again as she stopped and then edged forward a few more yards. Barnes felt that she must be crazy, but as he watched her he was filled with a sense of unease, an odd foreboding. To add to her idiotic behaviour she had not even offered a lift to any of the exhausted wretches who trudged in front of her on foot.

'How provocative can you get?' growled Barnes.

'Pardon?'

The German attack came without warning, without mercy, came out of clear blue sky from in front of the sun so that it was almost impossible to detect their approach, but Barnes heard them coming.

'Down!'

He shouted the word again and again to the bewildered crowd and then dropped flat on the grass beside Pierre as the first Messerschmitt swooped along the column, its engine screaming, its machine-gun blazing non-stop. The crowd was dazed, stunned with terror, unable even to attempt to run for safety in the shock of the sudden onslaught. In front of him Barnes saw an old man turn and stare at the plane as it came straight along the road with a scream and a stutter. He must have taken a dozen bullets in the chest before he crashed back against a cart. As the first machine screamed past Barnes tugged out his revolver and waited for the next one, steadying the gun barrel across his arm. The second Messerschmitt pulled out of its dive and sped over the procession almost immediately. Barnes saw the outline of the pilot's helmet, the black cross on the fuselage, the swastika on the tail. He fired three times in rapid succession, knowing that it was hopeless. Unless a .455 bullet burst through the petrol tank he might just as well be armed with a bow and arrow, but he had to try something. The third machine was coming now, its nadir so low that it almost skimmed the heads of the panic-stricken refugees. Barnes fired, swearing foully as he switched his eyes to the west where another one was coming, and at that moment a horse went berserk, dragging its cart off the road as people scrambled desperately to escape this new menace.

There were six machines altogether, and when they had flown away from the carnage the afternoon was suddenly horribly quiet. Only the heart-broken cries of sobbing women disturbed the stillness as Barnes clambered to his feet and ran over to the stationary Renault. When he reached the car and looked inside he clenched his teeth: the woman in the Renault had taken the full blast of the machine gun and now she was hardly identifiable even as a blood-soaked corpse. The engine was still running so he leaned over and switched off the ignition. He would give these refugees what help he could and then head for Arras non-stop.

The tank rumbled southwards at top speed and the road ahead was clear as far as the eye could see, another panorama of Belgian pastureland spreading away with hardly a tree anywhere, which meant no cover from air attack.

Standing in the turret, Barnes concentrated on keeping all-round observation: the deserted road ahead, the road behind, the fields on either side where people worked a long way off and never seemed to notice the passage of a British tank, and above all the sky overhead where the most instant danger could strike without warning. Below him Penn occupied Davis's old position behind the guns, while in the nose of the tank Reynolds sweltered as he handled his driving levers, his head thrust up through the open hatch, relieved that once again they were on the move and that Barnes was in command. To Reynolds, all was well with the world so long as Barnes was in command. Behind the turret sat Pierre. He was perched outside the tank on the engine covers and already had grown accustomed to the gentle wobble of the hull as the huge tracks ground farther south with every revolution. There had almost been a row between Barnes and Penn over taking the Belgian lad. At first, Barnes had refused point-blank.

'We need him for information,' Penn had protested. 'He knows the country and we don't. Supposing we're inside a town close to the battle area—accurate information will be vital. Our lives may depend on it and the only one who can get it quickly from the locals is Pierre. He's taken some chances with us already—he was with us in the building all the time the Panzer column was moving through Fontaine. We didn't know it at the time but if he'd been caught with us they'd have shot him. And he brought food for us.'

It was probably the gesture of bringing food which had finally persuaded Barnes to let Pierre travel with them until he could drop him off in an area more peaceful than Fontaine. They were on the point of departing when Pierre had come running back from the village with sticks of French bread under each arm and a satchelful of tinned meat hanging from his shoulder. He even had a packet of coffee in his pocket. No one had inquired too closely as to how he had obtained these provisions: after all, there was a war on.

And now, as the tank left Fontaine far behind them, Barnes was weighing up many things. It was pleasant to have the sun shining down on them, but it was from the sun that the Luftwaffe made its sneak attacks, so frequently he shaded his eyes to scan the sky, straining his ears for the first warning sound of approaching engines. The landscape ahead was beginning to undulate and he kept a careful observation along the ridges to detect any signs of gun positions which might lie in ambush. So far they had only met Belgian horse-carts on this lonely road which seemed to go on for ever, horse-carts which plodded past while their drivers stared at the tank as though hardly able to believe their eyes. As he kept up his vigilant watch Barnes was also trying to locate on the map the road they were travelling along and he was puzzled. There was a road from Fontaine which led south-west in the general direction of distant Arras, but this road had gradually turned until they were heading due south. Without mentioning his discovery, he kept an eye open for landmarks.

They were going to run into trouble soon now, Barnes could feel it in his bones. They were travelling with their guns loaded and the power-traverse on, and Barnes had given Pierre strict instructions that in case of trouble he must immediately leave the tank and take cover. The farther they moved along this peaceful road, the only witnesses to their progress cows grazing in the fields, the tauter Barnes's nerves became. It was only a matter of time before they met something big and when that happened he'd have to take a lightning decision. He only hoped that he was up to that. He had reached the stage where he accepted the throbbing and pricking of his shoulder as a permanent burden, as much a part of himself as breathing, but he did wish that the dreadful pounding headache would go away. Under the circumstances it was remarkable that he reacted at all when the emergency arose, and the fact that he reacted instantly was little short of a miracle.

At the time they were travelling at reduced speed on his instructions because they were approaching a hump-backed bridge. The character of the countryside had changed again and now there were low hills close to the road. Even from the elevated vantage point of the turret he found it impossible to see the stretch of road immediately beyond the bridge, so as they drove forward his gaze was fixed on the crest which was still a hundred yards away. Instinctively, he didn't like the look of the bridge. He began to give precautionary orders, just in case.

'Two-pounder. One hundred. The bridge ahead.'

Below him, Penn's head was pressed hard against a padded bracket, his eye peering steadily through the telescope at the small circle of countryside which centred on the bridge crest. The two-pounder's leather-bound grip was fixed tightly round his shoulder, under his armpit, so that only the slightest movement of that shoulder automatically raised or depressed the muzzle of the gun. His left hand gripped the power-traverse lever while the other hand gripped the trigger handle. Now the cross-wires inside the glass circle were aligned dead centre on the bridge crest. The range was set, he was ready, and all this had taken only a few seconds.

Barnes had hardly completed giving the orders, Penn had just completed obeying them, when it happened. Straight over the crest of the hump-back, travelling at high speed, recklessly high speed, hurtled a large covered truck. Barnes registered its identity in a flash—even to the soldier peering round from the back, leaning well out, a pudding-shaped helmet set squarely on his head. A German detachment of motorized infantry.

'German truck! Fire!'

The barrel dropped slightly, because now the truck was over

the hump, still tearing towards them. Knowing what to expect, Barnes gripped the turret rim. The tank shuddered under the stomach-jerking spasm of the recoil, the shell screamed forward, its target rushing to meet it. The two missiles met in frightful collision, the shell smashing into the truck just above engine level, exploding with a roar, ripping apart metal, canvas, flesh. Inside the turret the air reeked of cordite fumes as Barnes, who was now behind the gun, reloaded, flipping in a fresh round with a certain force to make the breech-block close. Then he scrambled back to the top of the turret, the tank still trundling towards its target. In the nose of the vehicle Reynolds stared at the truck with grim satisfaction. God, that had been a close one!

The truck was pulverized, but the force of explosion plays strange tricks and this explosion had hurled from the open back several German soldiers still clasping their machine-pistols, throwing them out on to the grass verge where they lay stunned for a second. But when Barnes looked out from his turret they were recovering, jumping up off the grass, the reflex of fear speeding their movements as they darted into the field, spreading out the target. In a matter of seconds, if they were well-trained, they would be circling round the tank. Barnes gave instant orders.

'Driver, right, off the road, right. Besa. Besa. Right. Well right. Fire!'

Penn's trigger hand jumped to the Besa. Reynolds swerved off the road, through a low wire fence, over the grass, heading straight for the running men. The Besa began to stutter, a hail of bullets catching the man on the right-most flank, catching him in mid-stride, in mid-air as he began to flop, his body hiccuping convulsively, the machine-pistol falling from his grip.

'Besa. Traverse left, left . . .'

Coolly, without panic, Penn's mind and hand paralleled Barnes' intentions and the turret began to swing, taking the flail of bullets with it. Get the one on the far right first, then sweep left against the forward movement of the running men, catching all five men as they desperately tried to spread, depressing the Besa to sweep it at ground level over those who had dropped to the grass. In half a minute it was all over and Barnes gave the order to take the tank back on to the road.

The smashed truck sagged grotesquely to one side, still on its wheels but keeled over at a crippled angle, flames licking over the bonnet, the torn canvas at the back catching alight. Then the petrol tank went up, a dull thump. Flames soared up and the canvas flared, burning rapidly, exposing the metal framework. Halting the tank, Barnes waited until the conflagration had died down, his eyes scanning the summer sky constantly for aircraft, but it was empty of any sign of war. Only on the ground death disfigured the gloriously sunny day. As soon as the flames began to peter out Barnes gave the order to move the tank forward. The shelled truck now blocked the way, the wreckage standing in the middle of the road. Carefully he guided the tank along the grass verge, turning it so that the front hull faced the truck broadside on.

'Driver, move forward slowly and tip it over the edge.'

The tank crawled forward, its tracks bumping the side of the truck. Foot by foot, it thrust the truck backwards towards the slope at the end of the bridge, a slope which Barnes now saw led down to the canal. From the turret he could see over the hump of the bridge and the road beyond was clear for miles. He could also see on the floor of the cab and inside the truck itself a huddle of clothes which bore little resemblance to uniformed soldiers. The truck was almost on the brink now, pushed backwards by the tank which was manoeuvring the vehicle like a bulldozer shifting waste material. As the truck began to topple a helmeted figure scrambled out from under the bodies, dropping to the roadway and swinging his machine-pistol round in one movement. God knew how he had managed to survive the holocaust but now he survived only seconds. As the machine-pistol came round Barnes fired his revolver at the same moment as the Besa began to stutter. The German fell back over the edge a few seconds before the truck toppled, crashing down the slope on top of him with a jarring grind of crumpling metal as the vehicle landed on the edge of the

canal, settling like a crushed concertina. There was an unpleasant smell of burnt rubber as Barnes gave the orders to
reverse, drive forward over the bridge, and halt on the far side.
Then he clambered down into the road and went back over the
bridge.

He saw Pierre in the distance, climbing up out of the ditch
where he had jumped as soon as the truck appeared. Now he
walked slowly along the road as Barnes scrambled down the
slope to investigate the carnage. It was like a miniature battlefield. In its fall down the slope the truck had thrown out its
grisly load, scattering bodies along the canal bank. One man
lay half in the canal, face downwards. The smashed and
twisted bodies were all dead, all except one. Grimly, Barnes
walked over to the moaning man, the moans reminding him
of an animal in mortal pain. Both his legs had been blown off
and he lay on his stomach, the lower part of his body a blood-
stained stump. He had lost his helmet and appeared to be
biting the ground. It was quite clear that in a short time, half
an hour at the most, he would be dead, but during that half an
hour he was a creature who would be racked by unendurable
agonies. Christ, thought Barnes, why didn't you have the sense
to die too? He clenched his teeth bitterly. You poor bastard.
He mouthed the words silently for fear that the man might
hear him, might even manage to turn his head. Leaning down,
unaware that his teeth were locked rigid, he held the muzzle
of the revolver within an inch of the man's head and before
he could think about it he pulled the trigger. The German gave
a quick convulsive movement and lay still. Barnes let out his
breath. As he straightened up he sensed that he was not alone
and he turned round. Over the parapet of the bridge two faces
stared down. Penn and Pierre.

'Pierre,' shouted Barnes, 'come down here a minute.'

The lad came down slowly, watching his feet as he slithered
down the slope, not looking at what lay beneath him. Up on
the bridge Penn still looked down, his face like stone. When
Pierre reached the bottom he stopped and looked at Barnes,
his hair freshly combed, his expression blank.

'Take a good look, Pierre,' invited Barnes. 'This is the war you were so eager to get mixed up in. When you reach your age group you'll get called up—and it's my bet the war will last long enough for that. But don't ever think that it's going to be fun.'

Pierre's eyes wandered over the bodies, his face still devoid of all emotion. He stood very erect.

'Take a good look,' went on Barnes, watching him closely. 'These are the bastards who machine-gun women from tanks and planes.'

'Can I go now?' Pierre asked coldly. He omitted to add the word 'sergeant.'

'Yes, go straight back to the tank and wait there with Trooper Reynolds. Penn, come down here a minute.'

He waited. Pierre had disappeared over the bridge when Penn reached the tow-path, his eyes blazing, his voice sharp-edged.

'Did you have to do that to him?'

'I had my reasons. Now find two machine-pistols in working order and as many spare magazines as you can. That'll give us one each and they may come in handy.'

They worked in silence. Barnes counted the bodies and as far as he could make out the truck had carried a complement of twenty men including those lying in the field on the other side of the road. He would have liked to search the clothes of the officer who had undoubtedly sat in the cab beside the driver, but in this jumbled horror such a search would have taken hours. Instead, he went back to the man without legs, felt under the body, and extracted his army pay-book. Gustav Freisler, the 75th Field Regiment. At least that's what he thought the long German word identifying the unit meant. He put the pay-book in his pocket. It would positively identify the unit when he reached the Allied lines and also he wanted the report of this poor devil's death sent back to Germany via the Red Cross as soon as possible.

When they returned to the tank, Barnes spent a short time explaining to Penn and Reynolds how the German machine-pistols worked and he made them practise using them without magazines. While this was going on Pierre sat on the engine

61

covers and gazed up at the sky without taking the slightest notice of Barnes. Penn practised with his pistol diligently and said hardly a word, climbing up into the tank when the exercise was over with an expressionless face. Only Reynolds seemed unaware of the coolness in the atmosphere and he spoke with conviction as he turned to get down inside his hatch.

'Good old Penn. He can really use that two-pounder.'

'Good job he can—there were twenty of them inside that truck.'

Good old Penn, Reynolds was right there. If he hadn't clobbered that truck with his first shot the dead German officer might well be examining their pay-books now. But it was what lay ahead of them that was occupying Barnes's thoughts now, and as he screwed up his eyes to check the late afternoon sky he felt sure that they couldn't hope to get through the coming night without very serious trouble.

There was an element of danger in his decision, but Barnes took a calculated risk when he decided to spend the night by the river bridge. Since leaving the shelled truck by the canal they had experienced an evening of tension which had played havoc with their already strained nerves, and since both Penn and Reynolds had taken it in turn to mount guard during the four nights when Barnes lay unconscious at Fontaine, all of them were in a state close to physical exhaustion. Probably the factor which more than any other drained their resources was the knowledge that they were moving behind the enemy lines, that at any moment they might encounter an overwhelming German force which would easily annihilate them in a matter of minutes. Most of all, Barnes feared that they would meet a Panzer column head-on.

The rising tension made itself felt in different ways. Two hours had been wasted by the roadside when the engines broke down and they struggled to find and repair the defect. During this time Pierre, who had to leave the tank when they pulled open the engine covers at the rear, sat on the grass verge without speaking. Barnes suspected that even Penn was beginning to wish that he hadn't been so keen to bring the Belgian with them, but he couldn't be sure because the corporal himself was unusually silent. Reynolds worked stolidly on the engines, noticing nothing wrong, but then Reynolds was never over-sensitive where atmospheres were concerned. They found the cause of the trouble eventually, repaired it, had a drink of water, and then moved on, leaving the road to circle round a town. So far they had avoided three towns by moving across open country in wide sweeps, returning to the road well beyond each town. This tactic, too, had caused an argument with Penn.

'Why don't we risk it?' he had pressed. 'We have Pierre and one of us can sneak in with him to get some news.'

'We may have to do that later, but not yet,' Barnes had replied firmly. 'I want to have some better idea of where we are first.'

'Doesn't the map tell you that?'

The engine had just been repaired and before starting out again Barnes and Penn had wandered off into a nearby field as Reynolds made his final checks.

'No, it doesn't, Penn. We'll go round this place like we went round the last one.'

From where they stood they could see the town in the distance. A tall church spire, several factory chimneys, a long line of buildings. A flight of Stuka dive-bombers crossed the sky very high up, heading for the north-west. Since leaving Fontaine they had stopped four times while enemy planes flew out of view. Irritably, Penn persisted.

'But if you just trace the road down from Fontaine . . .'

'Penn, the road we're travelling on doesn't correspond with the road we thought we were taking. It doesn't correspond with it at all. We're travelling south-west now, I know, but for a long time we were heading due south.'

'The compass may be playing up. It does sometimes with all that metal . . .'

'I'm going by the sun—that isn't affected by the metal, is it?'

'You mean we may have got back on to a different road when we made one of our detours?'

'I mean there's something damned peculiar about the whole business. So,' Barnes spoke emphatically, 'we're not going near any town today. We'll go round this place, wherever it is. We'd better get moving.'

It was very close to dusk when Barnes saw the bridge, a large stone affair with a broad span which could easily take two lanes of traffic. They were in the middle of open country miles away from anywhere and within half an hour they wouldn't be able to move without putting on the headlights, a course of action he was anxious to avoid at all costs.

As they came closer he noticed a copse of trees to the right of the bridge. He stopped the tank and went forward with Penn to investigate.

'This might be a good place,' Penn suggested. 'Bridges are lucky for us. We could park Bert in these trees.'

But the copse was a hopeless cover. It was simply a handful of thin-trunked saplings staggered at intervals through the grass. No matter how they parked the tank, Bert would still be visible from the road, and it was the road which worried Barnes. Penn thought differently.

'This is an ideal spot, particularly at night.'

'Not correct, Penn. Any vehicle coming over that bridge from the south will swivel its headlights straight over this spot. We've been lucky so far—I think the German invasion has cleared all normal traffic off this road but that doesn't mean Jerry won't be sending more troops this way. We've got to find somewhere we can park Bert completely out of sight. Under that bridge might do the trick.'

'*Under* the bridge . . . ?'

But he was talking to himself. Barnes strode off back to the road and scrambled down the bank by the side of the bridge, pushing his way through thick brambles to the river at the bottom. Yes, there was ample room under the high stone arch, but how deep was the river? Bert could comfortably wade through three feet of water provided the fording flap was closed over the rear air outlets. He found that under the bridge the water was less than a foot deep and blessed the fact that it hadn't rained for over a fortnight. Even better, the bed of the

64

river was surfaced with smooth rocks and between the rocks was a fine gravel.

An old footpath ran along the north side of the river, a footpath half-submerged under weeds and tall grass, and this would give them a place to sleep close to the tank. Looking up under the arch he judged that there was sufficient clearance to take Bert's overall height of eight feet. Now for the question of concealment. He walked along the footpath under the bridge, pacing out the distance. Twenty-six feet. Bert's overall length was eighteen feet so he would rest well inside the archway. The only problem lay in getting the tank down to the river bed—the banks were at least twelve feet high and steeply inclined, their slopes covered with a jungle of brambles and undergrowth. He went back to the tank and issued instructions, leaving Pierre by the roadside while he guided the vehicle some distance across a sun-baked field and well away from the bridge before they attempted the descent to the river bed: he was determined to leave no traces of their presence by smashing down undergrowth close to the bridge.

He checked the river depth again, returned to the tank, and ordered Reynolds to switch on the headlights, disliking the precaution but knowing that it was essential because it was almost dark now below the level of the banks. Then the tracks began to descend, smashing down undergrowth, dropping with a bump as the tank's centre of gravity pivoted on the brink and then plunged downwards, slithering and grinding over the brambles, hitting the water with a splash, the tank turning as Reynolds briefly halted the right track so that the revolutions of the left one swung the hull round through an angle of ninety degrees to face downstream. When Barnes shone his torch beam he saw that the river level was no more than a foot up the side of the tracks. As usual, Reynolds was handling the driving brilliantly even in this unusual environment. The tank advanced towards the bridge, a clearance from the banks on either side of several feet, moving forward over the firm river bed until they halted under the archway. Inside the hull Penn sat listening to the peaceful lapping of water round the tracks.

'Now,' said Barnes briskly, 'time for supper. Penn, you take up temporary guard duty on the bridge while Reynolds brews up—I'll come up and relieve you as soon as it's ready. I wonder what the devil has happened to Pierre?'

He climbed down to the footpath and started to climb the bank when he heard Pierre coming along the footpath from upstream; the lad was carrying something in his hands. When he switched on his torch he saw that Pierre was holding a large fish.

'I caught it in a pool higher up—we can have it for our supper. There are many more—easily enough for one each.'

Penn paused, half way up the bank on his way to the bridge.

'What a marvellous idea—my mouth's watering already. Pity we haven't some chips to go with them.'

'Give it to me!' Reynolds thrust an eager hand forward and Barnes remembered that the driver had been a fishmonger before he had signed on. 'I'll start cleaning it as soon as I get the brew-up going.'

'You really want raw fish for supper?' Barnes asked quietly.

'Raw?' Penn protested. 'We can cook the damned thing in no time.'

'There'll be no cooking here tonight. It's a warm evening, the air's absolutely still, and a cooking smell could linger round this bridge for hours. I'm not risking it. We'll have to make do with tea and bully beef. We've got the French bread Pierre brought, too,' he added.

'For Christ's sake!' exploded Penn.

'You're supposed to be up on that bridge keeping a lookout,' replied Barnes with deceptive calm.

'Sorry,' Penn spoke stiffly, turned away, and clambered up to the top of the slope.

Reynolds said nothing and went back to preparing a brew-up on his little stove. Barnes waited for the Belgian lad's reaction with interest. Putting his hand back behind his head, Pierre hurled the fish as far as he could downstream and sat down on the footpath, not looking at Barnes. Under the archway, Reynolds worked in silence, unpacking his spirit stove, inserting

66

white metaldehyde tablets, applying a lighted match, and then replacing the metal cap over the flame. When he went off upstream to fill his kettle he was gone for several minutes and Barnes guessed that he had taken water from Pierre's pool so he could look at the fish.

The stove was not standard issue, but many of the items they carried, such as their sheath knives, had never appeared on any official list of equipment: Barnes had long ago decided that his tank must be able to operate as a self-contained unit without the normal supply facilities when necessary, although never in his wildest theorizing could he have visualized a situation like this where they would find themselves behind the enemy lines, cut off from all contact with their own army, let alone their own troop. I took the right decision, he told himself as he thought of Penn's irritability and watched Reynolds's abnormally slow movements in preparing the supper. Those two haven't enjoyed more than four hours' sleep a night since we landed at Fontaine and today was no picnic. Until we get some rest none of us is capable of taking part in action against the enemy, so the only thing to do is to keep our heads down until we've recovered. I hope to God we get a peaceful night. He went up to the bridge to relieve Penn.

Too tired to talk, they ate in silence by the light of the flickering spirit stove—Pierre, Penn and Reynolds sitting side by side along the pathway under the arch while the water gurgled past the tank's tracks. It was quite dark now and in the pale blue flame the tank looked enormous and strange, as though it stood in some war museum. Penn clapped a hand on the back of his neck and swore: it was after ten o'clock but the air was warm and muggy and the mosquitoes were active. He could hear one buzzing close to his ear and the blighter wouldn't go away. He hurried his meal because until he had finished, Barnes, who was standing guard on the bridge, would have to go hungry. Now that he had got used to the idea, Penn rather liked the feeling of security of being tucked away under the bridge: it was like camping out in a cave, something he'd always enjoyed as a boy. He must remember to change Barnes's dressing and he'd insist on taking first guard

67

duty on the bridge. It would make up for some of his grumbling during the day.

Half an hour later he had changed the dressing and had gone up to the bridge to mount guard. Barnes was sitting on the footpath as he put on his jacket again, thankful that the emergency dressing had been applied and feeling sufficiently better to appreciate his own state of incredible fatigue, but at least he felt more comfortable. As he dressed himself he looked sideways at Pierre. He had been conscious of the lad's fixed stare for several minutes.

'We may find somewhere to drop you off tomorrow,' he told him.

'That is for you to decide.'

'Yes, it is, isn't it? You'd better get some sleep now. We may have a long day ahead of us.'

'Can I take my share of guarding the bridge, sergeant?'

'We'll see. Shut up chattering now and get down.'

Five minutes later Pierre was stretched out full length along the path, his feet to Barnes's head, his back against the wall of the bridge, an army blanket loosely draped over his body. Reynolds had finished washing up in the stream and was settling down at the foot of the bank on the other side of Bert. Normally, he was a restless sleeper and he had wrapped himself in his blanket for fear of throwing it into the water during the night, but he had hardly put his head down before he was snoring loudly, deep in a sleep of sheer physical exhaustion.

Barnes, on the other hand, felt exhausted but not sleepy. It was eleven o'clock and in two hours' time he would take over guard duty from Penn and later hand over to Reynolds for the last turn. His mind raced round like an engine out of control: the great thing now was to find some really worthwhile objective, to give the Germans a tremendous blow on the nose. Without realizing it, he eventually fell into uneasy sleep, in spite of a tiny portion of his mind which desperately begged him to stay awake.

3. Friday May 24

'SERGEANT! Wake up! *Wake up!*'

Barnes opened his eyes instantly, blinking once, his hand automatically closing over the revolver he had hidden under the blanket.

'What is it, Penn?'

'Come up to the bridge—we've got company.'

Barnes had slept in his boots and now he sat up with the minimum of movement, glancing back at Pierre as he switched on the torch, shading it with his hand. Switching it off again immediately, he clambered to his feet and nearly fell into the river. Pierre lay in exactly the same position as when he had fallen asleep, one large hand resting limply outside the blanket. From the far side of the tank came a deep-throated snore. Reynolds was still putting his time to good use. Following Penn, Barnes climbed up the bank, digging in his toes and using his hand to follow the line of the wall. The illuminated hands of his watch, the watch he had borrowed from Penn, registered 1.30 a.m. Another two-and-a-half hours to dawn. And Penn had let him oversleep by thirty minutes.

Coming up on the bridge he stopped as a chill ran through him. The moon was up and through the palely illuminated night to the south a column of lights was advancing towards them. In the heavy stillness of the early morning he could faintly hear the purr of many engines. He made a quick estimate of the number of vehicles, stopped counting when he had reached twenty, which was only a fraction of the total number of tiny lights.

'Penn, go down and wake Reynolds—quietly. Tell him to get his damned boots on.'

'What about Pierre?'

'Don't wake him on any account.'

Barnes stood and waited, shivering a little from the cold. The nearest lights seemed closer now, the sound of the engines distinctly louder. This was no procession of refugees heading for the bridge: he could tell that from the orderly advance of the headlights, just sufficiently well spaced out to allow the whole endless column to move forward at a rate of about twenty miles an hour. Cocking his head to one side he listened carefully, but there was no sound of aircraft in the cloudless sky. Standing there on the bridge he could hear the gentle lapping of the river as it swirled round Bert in the cavern below, but the water sound was now being muffled by the steady revolutions of the motors of the approaching armada, which he was quite certain now was an army column of enormous striking power. British, French, or German? Their very lives might hang on the answer to that question. A few minutes later he was listening even more intently as Penn stood by his side. No, he had not been mistaken. Above the engine rhythms he could detect a familiar sound—the steady rumble of tank tracks. They were standing in the path of an armoured column.

Scrambling down the side of the bank, finding his way by feel, he went in under the bridge and switched on his torch briefly. Reynolds was up and standing on the same side of the river as Pierre who had just laced up his shoes. The lad's hair was freshly combed and he was staring up at Reynolds who held a revolver in his hand.

'They'll be coming over the bridge in a few minutes,' Barnes snapped. 'It may be a Panzer column. Whatever happens you both stay here until I come back. Get it, Reynolds?'

He looked meaningfully at the driver and then scrambled back up the bank to where Penn still waited at the northern end of the bridge, just in time to see the corporal leave the road in a hurry as he plunged down the far side of the bridge. Instantly, Barnes moved sideways along the bank and hid himself behind a thick clump of wild shrubs. The next moment he heard the buoyant burst of a motor-cycle. Lights flashed, crossed the bridge, swerved round the corner and headed north, immediately followed by a second cycle. The lights of the second patrol briefly lit up the first and in the side-car he caught a glimpse of a seated soldier who wore a pudding-shaped helmet, a machine-pistol cradled across his chest. It was Jerry all right. Christ!

Instead of following the first patrol towards Fontaine, the second motor-cycle reduced speed, swerved on to the grass, its headlights sweeping over the shrub where Barnes lay, then stopped, its engine still running. The soldier in the side-car stepped out and the cycle drove off, leaving the sentry who walked back to the bridge. Barnes lay very still as the German peered over the parapet on his side. A powerful torch beam flashed on and swept over the bank where they might have taken Bert down by the direct route to the river bed. Then it went out and he heard the sentry's feet march back to the end of the parapet. The torch flashed on again, pointing down the bank. It began to move forward and behind it feet slithered, recovered, and then started to feel their way down over the brambles. Barnes gritted his teeth. This was a thorough bastard. *He was going to check under the bridge.*

Without a sound, Barnes brought his right hand up to his hip, grasped the hilt of his knife and withdrew it from the sheath. The sound of the oncoming engines was much louder. He would have no time at all to work this trick. He lay still, listening to the sentry moving down the bank, praying that Penn wouldn't open fire. The German was only a few feet from Barnes as he passed him and his feet were making a row as they trod through the undergrowth. Lifting himself carefully to his feet, Barnes moved across to the wall under cover of the sentry's shuffling feet, leaning out his hand to contact the stonework. Then he began to follow the German down, left hand on the wall, right hand gripping the knife. He had to finish him with the first thrust. He could see the silhouette of the sentry clearly against the torch glow: any second now the torch would swivel left and shine on the stationary tank. What the German's reaction would be when he found that under the bridge was really something for the book. Stealthily, he went down the bank. There was one horrible moment when he nearly slipped, digging in his right heel desperately, his knife hand waving all over the place, but he regained his balance without the sentry hearing him. The German was about four feet ahead of him now, and beyond the bridge the purr of the motors grew steadily louder. He had to get a little closer. He stepped down farther and at that moment the German swung his torch sideways and the beam glared full on the menacing hull of the hidden tank, its two-pounder pointing downstream. Barnes sprang forward, knife held high, his body lunging forward and downward in one leap. The knife reached the sentry's back and stabbed clean through the greatcoat, penetrating the body deeply under the impetus of Barnes's violent thrust. They fell forward together on to the bank, the sentry groaning once as Barnes landed on top of him. The torch splashed in the river.

As he fell, Barnes smashed his forehead on the German's steel helmet, which stunned him for a second, but his brain forced him to his feet, still holding the knife hilt which he was pulling at savagely. It wouldn't come out. Penn appeared from under the arch.

'I was just going to shoot him.'

'That's what I was afraid of. Here, hold this.' He handed him his own torch which he had switched on. Then he was tugging the German over on his back, unhitching his steel helmet, which was a struggle because the head flopped back inside it. He got it loose and thrust the helmet at Penn. 'Get this on . . . someone's got to act as sentry—they'll expect to see him. I'm too short so you've just volunteered. Grab his machine-pistol, man.' He was unbuttoning the greatcoat, trying to push the body over on its stomach and only succeeding when Penn helped him. The throb of the advancing engines resounding in his ears. 'Reynolds, you stay there with Pierre.' They had the sentry over on his stomach now, both of them hauling a sleeve over limp arms.

'The knife,' said Penn, 'we can't . . .'

'Yes, we can. You stand with your back to the bridge wall so they can't see it.' The sleeves were free now. Taking a firm hold of the coat, Barnes ripped it clean up over the haft of the protruding knife and helped Penn inside the coat. 'Now, follow me, but keep out of sight till I tell you—we may be too late . . .'

Scrambling back up the bank like a terrier, ripping his hands and face on the brambles, he reached the top and peered over the parapet. The leading vehicle was alarmingly close but its headlight beams hadn't yet reached the bridge. He could hear that deep-throated mechanical rumble clearly. They had tanks, all right.

'Just in time, Penn. Here, your top button's undone. Get over that side, *your back to the wall*. Hold the machine-pistol across your chest. All you have to do is to stand there so they see you. Away you go!'

Penn dashed across the bridge and took up his position. With a last look at the headlights, Barnes felt his way rapidly back down the bank, hand scraping over the wall. At the bottom he trod straight into the river and retrieved the sentry's lighted torch. Switching it off, he flung it under the bridge and got back on to the bank. Now for the really difficult part. Feeling around in the dark, his hands touched the sentry's legs, grabbed his ankles. He took a deep breath and began to move backwards under the arch, hauling the German with him. He wondered if he was going to make it: the body weighed several stones more than Barnes and it was like trying to shift a buffalo, but inch by inch he pulled it back until it was well under the arch. Then he bent down and toppled it over the edge so that it fell into the water between the river bank and Bert's right-hand track. As he stood up he found that his legs were trembling with the effort and sweat was streaming down his back and over his forehead. In standing up he bumped into someone. Pierre. His voice sounded strangled.

'I think I'm going to be ill—Reynolds attacked me.'

'Reynolds,' growled Reynolds, 'shoved a revolver into his belly—he was trying to play hero. Wanted to come up and help.'

'Don't be ill over us,' snapped Barnes. 'You asked for it.'

'I think I will be all right.'

73

'Sit down, Pierre, and stay down.' Barnes reached out a hand in the dark and pushed it against Pierre's chest until he felt him sitting down on the footpath. 'And if we have one cheep out of you Reynolds will empty his gun into you . . .'

He stopped speaking, holding the wall for support. A vehicle rolled over his head. Twin beams swept over the river bank and briefly passed over the small copse in the field. Then they were gone as the vehicle proceeded north. In no time at all more wheels moved over them, more beams swivelled, then vanished. To make sure that Pierre understood the situation Barnes touched his head lightly with the muzzle of his revolver, bending down to whisper:

'Just keep it quiet, laddie, and you've nothing to worry about.'

Nothing to worry about, that's a good one, thought Barnes. Four more vehicles rolled over and then he heard a different sound coming, the smooth grinding clatter of heavy caterpillar tracks. The arch seemed to shiver as it rumbled over, little more than twelve feet above them, a German tank moving at medium speed. Before the rumble had disappeared they could hear the next monster approaching the bridge, reducing speed slightly, the tracks clanking like the tread of a small leviathan. As he leant against the stone wall Barnes felt scared stiff and he wondered how poor Penn was feeling.

Penn was petrified, gripped by such a paroxysm of fear that he had almost lost all sense of feeling any emotion. He had just taken up his position when the first vehicle arrived, headlights briefly glaring in his face, then sweeping over the bridge, round the corner, and up the road towards Fontaine. An armoured car. Penn had stationed himself at a point where the bridge wall curved away from the road, so that he presented a profile to the oncoming vehicles—a profile of a pudding-shaped helmet, a greatcoat, and a machine-pistol. He held the weapon at an angle, its muzzle pointed across the road to be sure that they would see it. Another armoured car swept past and Penn began counting: Barnes would want to record the make-up of the column afterwards, always assuming that there was going to be an afterwards. As he stood there Penn was horribly aware that it only needed one vehicle with an officer to stop and he would be done for. Four more armoured cars drove past and then Penn experienced an ever sharper terror as he heard the approach of a familiar rumble. The tanks were coming—they would have commanders erect in their turrets, men who would have time to look him over as the huge vehicles turned the corner. He froze rigidly, his hands locked so tightly over the machine-pistol that the muzzle began to quiver. Hastily, he loosened his grip and prayed as the first tank mounted the bridge, his eyes staring ahead at the opposite wall. When the vehicle drew level with his position his eyes were fixed at a point on the lower turret and he was conscious of the figure above. The tank moved past, went round the corner, picked up speed. He let out the breath he had been unaware he was holding and wondered how much more of this he could stand. The second one was coming over now . . .

In times of danger Penn had learnt to practise a little mental exercise which he called to himself 'putting the mind into cold storage.' It involved suppressing all feeling, all normal reactions, and was in fact a temporary suspension of the brain's activity by concentrating on one thing only: now he concentrated on his counting. He had counted the passage of twenty heavy tanks when he realized something—not one of the commanders had spared him a glance. As they came over the bridge they were far too concerned with getting their tank round the corner to bother about a sentry whose presence they accepted as part of the night landscape. Penn even reached the stage where he welcomed the arrival of a tank because he had discovered that the trucks of motorized infantry were far more dangerous. The first one to arrive gave him a frightful shock. As the headlights passed beyond him he was able to see it clearly—a replica of the one he had blown up with the two-pounder. The truck drove forward slowly and from under the rim of his helmet Penn saw the officer sitting beside the driver in his cab. The officer looked sideways at Penn, then the cab was past. Without warning the open back presented itself to

Penn, a back crammed with helmeted-German infantry nursing their weapons. A sea of blank faces stared out at him as the truck back-fired at the corner and almost stopped. For God's sake keep moving, keep moving! The truck went round the corner and vanished. His hands were so wet now that he had difficulty in holding the weapon straight. Count, keep on counting. Nothing else matters but counting. He wiped his hands quickly on his greatcoat. Another truck now. The same frowning glance from a peak-capped officer, then the sea of staring faces at the back of the truck. He could do without any more of those. Send me some more tanks, please. He almost giggled at the thought and his own reaction bothered him. Was the fearful strain driving him round the bend? Watch it, another damned truck. As the vehicle disappeared he heard Barnes's voice from behind the parapet at his back.

'Keep it up, Penn. You're a bloody marvel.'

Hearing Barnes's voice made him feel better: it counteracted the dreadful feeling of being mercilessly exposed to the enemy. And it can't be all that much fun down there, he thought. It's probably even worse not being able to see what's going on. He began counting again. Half an hour later, as though his nerves had not already been shredded, battered to a jelly, and then shredded again, fate decided to turn the screw tighter, to take him to breaking-point and then beyond to a region of terrified desperation he could never have dreamt existed, and the trial came without warning.

The truck approached the bridge like its predecessors, the headlights catching him briefly in the face. It rode up over the slope and passed him, first the cab with the officer and then the open back with its huddle of staring faces. As it started to turn the corner it back-fired explosively again and again. The vehicle slowed down, its engine coughing and spluttering unpleasantly although it still took the truck forward. Penn could hear the driver fighting to keep the engine going and for a few seconds it throbbed perfectly. Then the awful coughing started again and the truck turned off the road, its headlights beamed directly on the copse. Driving forward a few yards farther into the field it stopped.

In a daze of horror Penn watched men jump down from the back and begin to walk about in the field. An officer and a soldier, undoubtedly the driver, had the bonnet up and they were peering inside at the engine. The sentry Barnes killed, Penn thought grimly, must have some chums in this division and they could be outside that truck. How long would it be before a soldier came over to him? Even in the face of this new nightmare Penn realized what was happening as the next tank came over the bridge. Every vehicle must have the same instructions—in the event of a possible breakdown they had to get off the road at all cost. Whatever happened they mustn't impede the movement of the Panzers. And this lot could quite easily still be here by daylight.

'Penn!' Barnes hissed the name from behind the parapet. 'I know what's happened. Just keep still. They may get that truck moving in a minute . . .'

He broke off as another tank crossed the bridge, pressing himself flat against the wall so that it was impossible for the commander in the turret to spot him.

'Penn, I'm right behind you with one of their own machine-pistols if the balloon goes up. Don't move—just . . .'

The rest of his words were lost as another tank clattered by, but knowing that Barnes was waiting behind the wall gave Penn's morale a desperately needed boost. He gripped the machine-pistol tighter. If this was it, well this was it and there was nothing he could do except to keep up the masquerade to the bitter end. Several of the men from the truck were moving closer to the road and the officer and the driver were still bent double over the engine. If they didn't get it started pretty soon some of the waiting troops were going to cross the road to come and have a chat with him. He saw one soldier start to cross, then headlights flared and a truck swept over the bridge too quickly, pulling up at the corner with a squeal of brakes, gunning the engine as it navigated the corner. The soldier had stepped back on to the grass and stood there hesitantly. Something had to give soon.

Barnes had left the wall behind Penn and now he was scrambling up the southern bank, the bank nearest to the oncoming column. His hands were torn to pieces, covered in congealed blood from earlier struggles with the brambles, the congealed blood in its turn covered with a film of fresh blood so that both palms were sticky with gore and damp with sweat. He reached the top and fell flat as another vehicle arrived, waiting until it had passed before he parted the branches of a shrub, sucking in breath quickly at what he saw. They were almost too late. He scrambled down the bank again, picked up his machine-pistol from the path, plunged into the river, and climbed the other side. He waited until the next tank had crossed and then spoke rapidly.

'Penn, only four more vehicles to come—the last two are probably motor-cycles.'

'I think that truck in the field is leaving . . .'

'I know, I heard them starting the engine. Now listen. You let two more vehicles pass and then you get down here like a bat out of hell when I tell you.'

'But the truck in the field . . .'

'Shut up!'

It was going to be a damned close thing, Barnes knew that. He was peering round the end of the bridge where he could watch the truck. Soldiers were climbing into the back and the officer and the driver were inside the front cab. The last patrol at the rear of the column would be stopping on the bridge to collect Penn and they would have to deal with that patrol, but everything depended on the truckload of soldiers in the field driving away in time so that they had the bridge to themselves, and Barnes realized that the timing was going to be split-second. All the troops were aboard now, the tail-board had been pulled up. The truck started to turn in a half-circle. Another vehicle went over the bridge, an armoured car. One more to come. The truck was driving forward towards the road, bumping across the uneven field at a painfully slow pace. Would it slip on to the road before the next vehicle drove past, the last one before the patrols arrived? He gripped his machine-pistol firmly, his mind on edge for the lightning decision he would have to take within the next sixty seconds. The truck reached the edge of the road and paused to make sure that the way was clear. Barnes watched it grimly—that truck was the real enemy, the enemy which could mean the difference between life and death for his unit. It seemed reluctant to depart, almost as though the driver sensed that there was some unfinished business to attend to here. A thought flashed into his head and he hoped to heaven they were not about to die by mischance—the mischance that the officer in the cab would decide to collect the sentry himself. Then the truck turned on to the road and drove off as an armoured car came over the bridge, skidded round the corner, and followed the truck along the road to Fontaine. Barnes jumped up.

'Penn! Now!'

He grabbed Penn's arm as he came round the end of the bridge and hustled him along the bank.

'Down behind these bushes. Whatever happens, don't open fire unless you've got to. The first patrol will probably drive on, leaving the last one to pick you up. If the first one does stop we'll have to wipe them out and then deal with the second one.'

'They're bound to search for . . .'

'Not necessarily—they may think you were picked up by one of the last trucks when they can't find you. I'll be over on the other side.'

Barnes ran back flat-footed to avoid tripping. He crossed the road in a sprint, ran farther along the bank and dropped down behind some bushes twenty yards back from the road. From this position he commanded the northern side of the bridge and the road beyond. With Penn facing him they would have the patrols in a crossfire, although he hoped that it wouldn't come to that because the tail-end of the Panzer column wasn't far enough away yet. Let them be tired, he prayed, too tired to start poking around under the bridge. Then he saw lights and the first motor-cycle and sidecar arrived.

It came over the bridge at speed, braking with a snarl of exhaust, screaming round the corner explosively, then it was gone. It happened so quickly that it almost took Barnes' breath away. Now they were only faced with the last patrol, the one which was bound to stop to pick up the sentry. He pressed himself closer to the earth, the machine-pistol stretched out in front of him, also flat on the ground to avoid any danger of light reflecting off it. He could hear the machine coming now, coming flat out as though anxious to collect the sentry and catch up the column. An impatient type. That might just help —someone who didn't like to spend too much time hanging around lonely bridges in the middle of the night. Through the bushes he could see the light now, blurred by the tiny branches and leaves of the bushes, a light which rushed towards the bridge.

His leg muscles tensed, his hands grasped the pistol. The roar of the motor-cycle was almost on top of them, the light showing on the parapet. Then it arrived, crossed the bridge, swerved, skidded madly on the corner, recovered its balance, and raced off up the road after the column.

Barnes laughed silently, weakly, the spasm shaking his aching body. Of course! He'd got the system wrong! He must need a refresher course. The real sentry would have kept a close eye on the progress of the column and then waved down one of the last trucks to pick him up: motor-cycles had no wireless communication, no way of being told that there was a sentry ahead to be collected, and that last patrol which had gone over the bridge already carried a soldier in the sidecar. All that tension, all that nerve-wracking anxiety—all for nothing. He went across the road and told Penn.

'Jolly good,' was all Penn could find to say. 'Anyway, now we can relax,' he added.

'I'm afraid not—there's one fatal question we need the answer to before morning.'

It was half an hour before dawn and beneath the bridge the world was pitch black. Barnes switched on his torch and shook Pierre awake. The lad stirred, blinked in the glow of the beam, sat up, and ran his hands through his hair.

'More trouble, sergeant?'

'No, but you seem anxious to do your bit. We are all just about exhausted and I'd like you to relieve Reynolds from guard duty if you would. It means three hours on the bridge because we won't be moving off before seven.'

'Certainly!' Pierre began to lace up his shoes. 'I am most willing to take my turn with all guard duties. I said so.'

'We'll see how you make out. All you have to do is to stand on the bridge and listen. Don't assume that if a vehicle is coming it will have its lights on—and remember, it may not be coming from the south like the others. In fact, I'm more worried about them sending someone back from the north if they find out they're one sentry missing.'

'I will watch very carefully.'

'At the first sight or sound of anything coming you run down here and wake me—is that clear?'

'Perfectly.' He reached out for the machine-pistol, but Barnes's hand closed over the weapon. 'I'll need something, won't I?' Pierre protested.

'Yes—your eyes and your ears. I'm not risking you letting loose at something in the dark which turns out to be a shrub instead of a crouching man. Up you go.'

Barnes waited until Pierre was climbing up to the bridge and then he ran back under the archway, crossed the river without making a sound, clambered up the opposite bank, and settled himself behind the shrub which had concealed him when he had watched the progress of the Panzer column. He was now hidden on all sides because the lower part of his body was submerged under a clump of brambles. From where he lay he could hear Pierre and Reynolds talking on the bridge, followed by the sound of the driver slithering down the bank as he returned to the archway. After that the only noise came from the bridge itself where Pierre had begun to patrol backwards and forwards, his footfalls a soft tread in the night. Gradually, Barnes found that he was able to see the patrolling figure as a vague silhouette beyond the parapet, a silhouette completely unaware that he was being checked. By the time the false dawn began to glow in the east Barnes had come to the conclusion that Pierre would make an excellent sentry: at frequent intervals the lad paused at either end of the bridge to listen for a whole minute before he resumed his march back and forth, and once or twice he glanced over the parapet wall and looked along the river as though he feared they might be subjected to a surprise attack either upstream or downstream. Dammit, thought Barnes, he might have been trained for the job.

The real dawn was beginning to show, pale shafts of cold light low down on the horizon, when Barnes found himself in difficulties. He had lain quite still ever since he had taken up his position, putting up with an ache in his right leg which steadily grew worse, when suddenly he was subjected to an attack of cramp. Forcing himself not to move, he felt the cramp take hold, compressing and kneading the leg muscles of his calf mercilessly, to such a fierce degree that he had to dig his fingers into the ground to bear it. He was determined not to move since Pierre had now stopped at his end of the bridge, his face turned towards where Barnes lay as he watched the dawn grow stronger, and any sound would alert Pierre and warn him that he was under observation. Sweat began to trickle over Barnes's face as he struggled with all his will-power to keep the leg flat until the pain receded, which gradually it did, and when the cramp had gone Pierre resumed his patrol, almost as though he had waited so as to cause Barnes the maximum agony.

Through the shrub Barnes could now see the field beyond which rose gently to a ridge. From his personal reconnaissance of the area shortly after they had first arrived he knew that beyond the ridge the ground fell away sharply to a lower level. It was, in fact, the one blind approach spot in the vicinity of the bridge, the one place where an enemy patrol could come close to the bridge without being observed at a distance. It was also the spot to which his eyes were now glued, and as he watched the line of the ridge grew clearer until it was sharply outlined against the dawn sky which was streaked with splashes of grey and gold, the genesis of another glorious day. Pierre had stopped again, this time on the far side of the bridge, and the absolute silence of early morning seemed uncanny, unreal, a silence that Barnes imagined he could almost *hear*. It was also chilly and several times he shivered as the cold penetrated his battledress and began to freeze his body, the low temperature accentuated by the presence of early morning dew which had settled on his uniform and coated his hands with a film of moisture. Beyond the ridge a spiral of white mist was rising from the ground, the curtain of vapour blurring the dawn light so that he could almost convince himself that there was movement behind the mist. A few minutes later he detected human movement beyond the ridge.

Gradually, the vague figure moved higher up the ridge and then stood stock still. Barnes tensed, fingers closing over the revolver in his right hand, his eyes staring at the silent figure half hidden in the mist so that it was impossible to identify the clothes it wore. The figure was two-dimensional, without depth, faintly outlined against the light behind it until the mist swirled away and he saw that it was the upper half of a soldier wearing a greatcoat and a pudding-shaped helmet. He could hear Pierre crossing the bridge again and then the footfalls ceased abruptly; when he glanced sideways Pierre had disappeared, crouched down behind the parapet wall. This will test his reflexes, Barnes told himself grimly.

The helmeted soldier remained motionless, staring in the general direction of the bridge as though he sensed danger. Now the silence was heavy and ominous, like the moment before the storm breaks. Barnes waited. Pierre waited. The German soldier waited. The soldier stood so still that he might have been a statue, and now Barnes's attention was concentrated on two points—the ridge in front of him and the parapet wall to his side. Then without warning the soldier marched up to the crest of the ridge and came down the other side, a slow deliberate approach as though he had not seen anything yet but he still didn't like the look of the bridge. He could easily be the advance guard of a patrol sent to find out what had happened to the sentry, a patrol which had been clever enough to cross the river higher up so that they could approach the area unexpectedly from the south side in the hope of taking the enemy by surprise.

He came forward holding a machine-pistol across his body, a body which stooped forward, the face blurred by remnants

83

of dissolving mist. Barnes heard a rustle from behind the parapet where Pierre crouched, and when the rustle stopped the only sound in the heavy stillness was the faint tread of the oncoming soldier's boots, a tread so light that Barnes knew he was trying to walk cat-footed as he crept forward. Half way between the ridge and the bridge he stopped, head to one side, listening. Then he began to advance again and Barnes raised himself slightly. This was it. Any second now. He heard a scrabbling sound from the bridge and Pierre stood up, his hands in the air. He was calling out as he walked forward into the open, walking more rapidly when the soldier didn't open fire, calling out urgently. Barnes stood up, his battledress rumpled, hands by his sides, and also emerged into the open as Pierre reached a point midway between the bridge and the soldier who now swivelled his machine-pistol to train it on Barnes. Turning, Pierre saw Barnes and called out again, one hand pointing, jabbing in Barnes's direction. He began to run towards the soldier, shouting at the top of his voice, insistently, continuously. A short distance from the helmeted figure he stopped abruptly, his voice dying away as Barnes walked briskly across the field towards the two men. Pierre had been shouting non-stop in German until he saw the face under the helmet, the face of Penn wearing the German sentry's greatcoat and helmet.

'You were right about this rat, then.' Penn levelled his machine-pistol at Pierre's stomach.

'Strange behaviour for a Belgian patriot,' said Barnes. 'Very strange behaviour. He sees a German soldier come over the top and instead of calling me he runs up to him.'

Penn held the butt of the pistol under his arm, one hand still round the trigger guard while he used the other to undo the top button of his German greatcoat.

'This thing chokes me. As you were saying—I thought he'd never react. So we've trapped ourselves a dirty little spy.'

'He didn't react at once because he thought a whole infantry platoon would be coming over the ridge behind you. My appearance on the scene jolted him into action. You made several mistakes, Pierre.'

'What mistakes? I do not make mistakes.' Pierre drew himself up, a sneer on his young face, making no attempt to deny the charges. He even ran his fingers through his hair to straighten it.

'That, for one thing—you've an obsession with your personal appearance. After we'd shot up that truck yesterday you arrived on the scene with your hair neatly combed—and you'd just been sprawling in a ditch. No normal lad of seventeen would react like that. But a trained soldier who was fantastically conceited about his good looks might do that automatically —providing he was very tough and a bit of a bastard into the bargain. It was your lot we shot up, remember.'

Pierre's eyes blazed and he stood very erect. 'It was not possible to take any action at the time.'

'No, you were biding your time till you could hand over a Matilda tank intact for inspection by your own people. And another thing—your reaction to that cemetery round the wrecked truck wasn't right either, not for your supposed age.'

'The German soldier is not trained to hide under bridges from the enemy.'

Penn took a step forward but Barnes restrained him with a look, his voice still mild when he spoke again.

'Let him spit away—he's going to be shot in a minute unless he gives us some information.'

For the first time Barnes thought he detected a flicker of fear in the staring blue eyes, eyes which looked quickly over Penn's shoulder and then back at Barnes. He tried to speak indignantly but his voice couldn't quite manage it.

'That would be murder, Barnes.'

'You'll address me as sergeant, and I would remind you that since you are not wearing uniform this puts you into the category of a spy who can be shot out of hand. What is your unit, Pierre?'

'I don't have to answer your questions.'

'No, that's right, you don't. You can be shot instead.'

'I might be prepared to answer certain questions.'

'That's better. How old are you?'

'Twenty.'

85

'And still with fluff on his cheeks.' Barnes looked at Penn. 'Maybe they wean them late in Germany.'

Pierre clenched his hands and stood rigidly, his feet close together, a pink spot on either cheek.

'What's your real name, Pierre?'

'Gerhard Seft. Sergeant Gerhard Seft.'

'And your unit?'

Silence. Seft's mouth was a tight line and he looked quickly over Penn's shoulder again.

'You haven't seen any real war, then?' Barnes goaded him.

Seft's voice changed. He stiffened his shoulders and almost barked his reply as he glared at Barnes.

'I served with the Wehrmacht in the Polish campaign. I was at Warsaw. We cut the Poles to pieces, smashed them—and I was there!'

'Well, you really know the position of a soldier caught in civilian clothes, then.'

The German's eyes flickered and he changed the subject quickly. 'How did Corporal Penn get away from the bridge without me seeing him?'

'He slipped off up the river bed while Reynolds was handing over the guard to you.' Barnes waited for a reaction but the German said nothing, gazing back blankly as though waiting for something. 'Seft, why did they push you out on a limb—send you in civilian clothes behind enemy lines? I want to know. Why?'

'Because I speak perfect English and French. My mother was French.'

Had he put that last bit in to arouse sympathy, to remind his captors that he, too, was human? Barnes suspected as much and his hostility towards Seft grew. His voice was harsher now.

'Where does this road lead to?'

'Towards Arras—I told you.'

'You told me a lot of bloody lies, my lad. And while we're on the subject where have we come from?'

'From Fontaine, of course.'

Seft's manner was growing more confident again, a trace of

the arrogance returning as he realized that he wasn't going to be shot out of hand.

'From Fontaine?' queried Barnes. 'Try that one again, too.'

'But he's right there,' protested Penn in surprise.

'Is he? Did anyone in the village except Seft tell you that it was Fontaine? I thought not. The road we were supposed to have taken from Fontaine runs south-west on the map, but this road ran due south for miles before it turned south-west. And we should have passed through at least a dozen villages—instead we came across four towns and not a single village anywhere. Seft's game was to lead us deeper into German-held territory until he got the chance to hand over Bert intact —and that would have been a feather in his cap. The German High Command would love to have one undamaged tank so they know exactly what they're up against. He must have been doing his nut when Reynolds held a revolver on him while a whole Panzer division rolled by overhead. And that, Seft, was a further mistake. You were just a little too anxious to come out from cover when your lot arrived. Now, what is the name of the village you called Fontaine?'

He stood looking up at the German, his eyes half-closed. This was his first encounter with a fanatical young Nazi and he found the attitude of sneering arrogance an interesting reaction under the circumstances. It neither startled nor impressed Barnes, he simply thought that it amounted to sheer bloody stupidity. Seft spoke loudly, his voice clipped.

'I am not permitted to reveal information which may be of assistance to the enemy. You are my enemy. Heil Hitler!'

Penn hit him across the side of the face, hit him hard with the back of his hand and the blow left a red weal across the German's pink flesh. He took a step back as Penn snapped at him.

'You've been told once, Seft, and you won't be told again. When you address Sergeant Barnes you address him as Sergeant. Next time you forget, you'll be minus a few teeth.'

Seft looked carefully at Penn as though memorizing his face. Then he deliberately rotated his cheeks and with an expression of supreme contempt spat on the ground. Again, Barnes's look restrained Penn.

'Don't waste your strength on the lad. He's hardly out of his diapers.'

Whether he understood the word or not the insult galvanized Seft. He stood very erect, his chin thrust forward, his voice rasping like a drill sergeant's as he stepped forward.

'The German army will be here very shortly. You are standing in German-occupied territory and you are now my prisoners-of-war. Sergeant Barnes, surrender your pistol.'

Taking two more steps forward, his face flushed with uncontrollable fury, he reached out to grab at Barnes's hand. The effrontery, the blind insanity of the manoeuvre, momentarily stunned Penn but Barnes reacted as though he had been expecting just such an attempt. Stepping backwards, he brought up the revolver from his side and swung it in a vicious arc. The barrel smashed against Seft's left temple and the blow was so powerful that the revolver almost leapt out of his hand. He took another step sideways as the German fell forward and slumped to the ground, his arms stretched out beyond his head, his fair hair all over the place. Barnes bent forward, felt the neck artery, and then looked up at Penn.

'The fool's dead. Just as well—we can't afford to be lumbered with prisoners at this stage.'

'He must have been stark raving bonkers.'

'He's a fanatic who thought he could get away with anything, but not completely bonkers. Take a look over your shoulder. I think Seft must have spotted them earlier than I did.'

A long way off to the south, where the road was now clearly visible in the early morning sunlight, Penn saw a thin trail of toy-like vehicles moving up the road towards them. The rear of the column was hidden behind a rise in the ground but more and more vehicles were appearing as the column advanced steadily forward. Barnes spoke grimly.

'I'll check with my glasses but that's another Panzer column on the way, bet your life on it. So that route's barred. And if we head back to so-called Fontaine we'll run into the other lot.'

'What the hell are we going to do? We'll never get away with it a second time.'

'Get out of here with Bert as fast as we can by the only route still open to us.'

4. Friday May 24

AT 4.30 A.M. they were fleeing for their lives. Moving at five miles an hour the tank emerged from under the bridge and drove along the river bed between the high bramble-covered banks like a monster metal barge sailing downstream. Standing up in the turret, Barnes was enormously relieved to find that he couldn't see over the tops of the banks which were two or three feet above his head, so that meant the enemy couldn't see them either. As they left the bridge behind he looked back to make sure that the tracks weren't leaving traces of their passage, but apart from a muddying of the water there were no traces to give them away. Ahead, the river ran almost straight for about a hundred yards and then it disappeared round a bend. They had to reach that bend and get round it before the advance elements of the Panzer column reached the bridge. He rated the chances of success a good deal less than fifty-fifty, but it was their only hope of survival.

About half way from the bridge to the bend a line of trees covered the banks on both sides, their branches spanning the river to form a tunnel of foliage which roofed in the water below, and it was so dark inside the tunnel that he couldn't see the river clearly. If it suddenly went deeper, they'd be finished anyway. Behind him the fording flap was closed down over the rear air outlets so now Bert was amphibious—amphibious, that was, in up to three foot six of water. He looked down at the grisly load roped on the back of the tank and hoped that they hadn't left their departure too late.

Their departure from the bridge had been held up by the necessity of disposing of the two bodies—the sentry's and

Seft's—and since he was determined to leave nothing near the bridge which might arouse suspicion and provoke a search, he decided that the only safe thing to do was to bring the bodies with them. The bodies were now lying on the engine covers at the rear of the hull, attached to the turret by separate ropes.

The greatest danger was the motor-cycle patrols which he had seen through his glasses moving ahead of the column. They would follow the same procedure as the previous column, he felt sure of that. A patrol would arrive, halt to drop a sentry, and then drive on. The sentry would move on to the centre of the bridge and look straight down the river. Barnes looked down the river: yes, it was a good hundred yards to that bend. And there were other things to worry about. Driving a tank along the bed of a river, even a comparatively straight river, is not the easiest of manoeuvres, and he was constantly talking into the mike to guide Reynolds's progress between the banks. They might just make it, *so long as the river bed remained firm.* From his elevated position he strained his eyes desperately to see the ground ahead under the water, searching for any sign of a large area of mud or softness or, worse still, a threat of rapids. And then there was always the chance that the engine might stall, leaving them in full view of the approaching Germans. He put that thought out of his head quickly as Penn climbed up to join him.

'Think we'll make it?' Penn asked him quietly.

'If we get round that bend in time.'

'Can't we get up a bit more speed—we're crawling.'

'Deliberately. This isn't the Great North Road, you know, and I'm bothered about the river bed—it's getting deeper.'

The water level was rising up the tracks quickly and he guessed the depth at over two feet. Three foot six was the maximum Bert could take. At the same time the river banks were closing in so that Reynolds barely had half a foot clearance on either side. The tracks ground forward, sloshing through the water, rattling over unseen rocks, grinding up mud discoloration, sinking deeper and deeper below the surface. Penn pulled a face as Barnes glanced back at the bridge.

'Must be three feet at least now.'

'All of that,' Barnes said tightly.

They were half way between the bridge and the tunnel of trees when a new anxiety assailed them—the sound of a plane. From the light-toned beat of the engine Barnes guessed that it was a small plane and it was flying very low. The Panzer column was using a spotter plane to check the ground ahead, which meant that the pilot would be searching every inch of countryside below him. If that plane flew over the river they were bound to be seen. Barnes could visualize it all clearly— the plane circling overhead while it wirelessed back to command HQ, the arrival of heavy tanks on both banks—in front, behind, above them. Then the remorseless shelling at point-blank range until Bert was reduced to a shattered hulk. It looked as though he'd taken them straight into a death-trap. He spoke into the mike.

'Driver, increase speed by five miles an hour. Follow my instructions exactly. You're too close to the left bank . . .'

The tunnel of trees still seemed a terribly long way off, and that tunnel could hide them from the plane if only they reached it in time. The sound of the plane's engine was very close and it was flying lower. It had probably spotted the bridge and was coming in to reconnoitre the whole river area intensively. At that moment the tank almost collided with the right bank and Barnes corrected Reynolds sharply, which wasn't fair because although the driver's head was poked up through the hatch and he had a clear view ahead, his vision was limited at the sides and he couldn't see the edges of the banks. The plane was losing even more height, Barnes could tell from the engine sound.

'This is going to be dicey,' Penn remarked.

'Keep an eye on the bridge, will you? I want to concentrate on the sky from now on.'

He wanted to concentrate on several things—checking the sky, observing the bridge, watching the clearance on either side of the tank, and keeping a sharp eye on the river course ahead, but it was impossible. As usual, Reynolds was doing a marvellous job—any other driver would have stalled the engines, driven hard into the bank, committed any number of

understandable errors, but Reynolds ploughed stolidly on . . .
Barnes lurched sharply as the whole tank *dropped*, a really
noticeable drop. Penn's face went white and he quickly glanced
down and then resumed observation of the still-deserted bridge.
They must have dropped at least another foot and now they
were semi-submerged under the river. The hull would soon be
awash. Barnes grunted, checked the clearance on both sides,
and scanned the sky. They'd have to gamble now, gamble on
the desperate hope that the river stayed the same depth. That
plane was almost on top of them—his hand tightened on the
rim as he waited for it to flash into view. The tank rocked over
an obstacle and his moist hand slipped. He was recovering his
balance, still looking up, when a roof of foliage blotted out the
sky, a tangle of branches thickly covered with many layers of
leaves. Above the green network the spotter plane sped across
the river and continued on its course to the north.

'So far, so good, as the man said to the girl,' joked Penn.
'There's still the bridge.'

'Not a sausage yet, not even a German one.'

Barnes looked back. The stone arch was much smaller now
and it looked amazingly peaceful from inside the tunnel of
trees, the sunlight showing up its white stone with great clarity.
It seemed incredible that at any second the engines of war
would be streaming across it on their way to a battle zone.
Barnes turned round to face the front, feeling the coolness of
the foliage-wrapped tunnel on his face, and his heart leapt into
his mouth. Their road was blocked.

The light was dimmer inside the tunnel, which was why he
hadn't spotted the obstacle—in the very centre of the river,
barely ten yards ahead, a giant boulder projected from the
water. The rock was black and pointed at the summit, its near-
side sheer and massive, forming an island round which the
river divided into two separate channels. Bert was capable of
mounting a vertical obstacle two feet high, but the height of
the boulder was at least four feet. In the time it took the tank
to move forward a couple of yards Barnes considered the
alternatives: climbing it was out of the question; ramming it
could be suicide—they'd stall the engine or damage the hull;

bypassing the obstacle by driving Bert out of the river and along the bank slope would be near-suicide. But the third alternative was the only possible one so he immediately began issuing warnings and instructions to poor Reynolds who was now being asked to overcome the insuperable. The operation called for no less than taking the tank from the river bed up on to the steep slope and then endeavouring to pass above the boulder with the vehicle tilted at a precipitous angle high above the river. Penn listened with a drawn face until Barnes had completed his preliminary instructions and when he spoke his voice was strained.

'Can we manage that? You could topple us over sideways.'

'It's the only way—we'll have to manage it. Keep a sharp lookout on that bridge.'

'Well,' said Penn lightly, 'it's a good job we've got plenty of time.'

'Do watch that damned bridge, Penn.'

Penn hadn't taken his eyes off the bridge except for the brief downward glance when the tank had dropped precipitately, but at that moment Barnes was in no mood for his corporal's pleasantries. They were very close to the boulder and the closer they came the more immovable it appeared. Yes, the only way was up the bank and along its side. Reynolds commenced the manoeuvre under Barnes's watchful eye, braking the left track so that the right one turned the tank towards the bank. As they left the water and mounted the left-hand slope a spasm of alarm ran through Barnes: the bank was much steeper than it had appeared. Instead of the undergrowth sinking several feet under the tank's weight it flattened down no more than a foot, enormously increasing the hazard because when Bert tried to move along the slope parallel to the river it would be like a cyclist riding up the wall of death. We could topple sideways, Penn had suggested. Well, Barnes knew what the likely result of that would be for the men in the turret: they would end up on the river bed with twenty-six tons of deadweight tank on top of them. The tracks moved forward, the tank inched up the slope, and then began to turn which could prove quite fatal. Reynolds had braked the right-hand track and now the revolutions of the other track slowly swung the massive weight round on its axis, then he stopped briefly. The tank was parallel to the river below, the turret tilted out over the water, tilted so steeply that Barnes and Penn had difficulty in keeping their balance and their bodies were perched at an acute angle. Now for it.

They were all only too aware that even the slightest error of judgement would take the tank over sideways, and that even if they survived, which was unlikely, Bert would land on the bed of the river flat on his back like a helpless beetle, his tracks churning the air. And to Barnes it was quite clear that it all hinged on a few degrees of tilt; even a few extra pounds of weight on the right-hand side could be sufficient to start the fatal sideways topple. He gave the order. The tank began its forward movement. Foot by foot the tracks advanced, clutching at the earth below the undergrowth, and no one spoke, no one moved, every nerve end geared to the painfully slow revolutions of the steel tracks. They were beginning to creep past the huge boulder below when the crisis came. Barnes saw the left-hand track start to lift gently, increasing the tilt by several degrees. His hand gripped the turret rim as he took his decision. The bodies of Seft and the sentry were sliding over the engine covers to the right—he saw that when he glanced over his shoulder—and those bodies were adding well over twenty stone to their dead weight. Literally, dead weight, he thought grimly.

'Penn, cut those ropes—quickly!'

Reacting instantly, Penn pulled out his sheath knife and nervously leaned down over the back of the turret, being particularly careful not to lean sideways. The ropes were taut with the weight of the slithering bodies and he sawed rapidly, his nerves so keyed up that he observed each strand giving way until the rope, thinned to a few strands, suddenly snapped of its own accord. Seft's body rolled off the sloping hull and fell with a great splash into the channel of water alongside the boulder. Penn was so preoccupied in trying to watch the bridge while he cut through the second rope that he never even saw the first body land, but Barnes had a quick glimpse of the corpse sinking below the surface before he switched his gaze back to the front tracks. They were pressing down the undergrowth slowly, like an animal feeling its way across treacherous ground, and he knew that even the merest extra lift could unhinge Bert's precarious balance.

On his jacked-up seat in the nose of the tank, Trooper Reynolds was drawing on all his experience of the engines as he desperately tried to judge just how slowly he could keep moving without a fatal stalling of the motors, because if that happened he was sure that even the vibrations of re-starting the engines might well tip them into the river, and this was an experience that no training had prepared him for. Only his intimate knowledge of the tank's structure and idiosyncracies could pull the trick if anything could. For several minutes Barnes had not spoken a word, knowing that words were useless and that he must leave it entirely to Reynolds to perform this diabolical operation. They were three-quarters of the way past the boulder when Barnes saw the upper track move against a clump of brambles, but instead of pressing them down the track began to climb as it mounted some unseen obstacle beneath the undergrowth. Here we go, Barnes told himself. He prepared to shout to Penn to jump, knowing that he had to stay on board himself because Reynolds wouldn't have a dog's chance of scrambling up out of the hatchway in time. The track was still climbing, but Bert still clung limpet-like to the side of the bank, poised at an impossible angle. Then Barnes felt the *wobble* as the tank began to heel over. At that moment Penn sawed through the final strands of rope and the sentry's body broke free, toppling off the hull into the river. The wobble stopped, the upper track savagely trampled down undergrowth and dropped at least six inches to lower ground. They had recovered their balance. Penn's voice was breathless.

'Thought we were going, then. Two passengers couldn't stand the strain—they got off.'

'I think you were just in time, but we're not out of the wood yet. Any sign of the Panzers?'

'Bridge still like a picture postcard. Can't last like this much longer.'

'No, it can't. Keep watching.'

They weren't out of the wood yet because now Reynolds was faced with a fresh manoeuvre which promised to be at least as tricky as the one he had just completed. The upper track was still moving forward over the smooth slope so Barnes decided that they'd better get on with it before that track started to climb again. And they had passed the boulder now. He gave instructions and then waited, watching intently without saying another word to Reynolds. Again, it was strictly the driver's baby.

To move back down to river level Reynolds had to brake the right-hand track, keeping the upper track churning so that it revolved the tank on its own axis to face down the bank at an oblique angle. Here again there was ample opportunity for a fatal mistake: it was not only a topple that Reynolds feared, he was frightened that the revolutions of the upper track might cause a side-slip. He paused to wipe his clammy hands on his trousers and then firmly gripped the steering levers, knowing that Barnes was relying on him to pull it off. The upper track speeded up and they began to turn. Reynolds handled the manoeuvre largely by feel, handled it magnificently, although in his own estimation he lost a few marks when Bert slithered the last yard or two and flopped into the water with a thunderous splash, but he redeemed himself in his own eyes by missing the far bank as he completed the second turn. The tank now faced downstream again. Barnes spoke quickly.

'Well done. Now, drive like hell . . .'

Reynolds accelerated, the tracks churned up the water into a cauldron as the tank surged forward, pushing the river out of its way, heading non-stop for the bend which was now so close. South Pole or bust, he told himself, and increased speed more still. He could see part of the way round the bend now, could see that it turned gradually so there was no need to slow down. Instead, he speeded up! In the turret two pairs of eyes stared back at the distant bridge which was still deserted, the stone intensely white in the sunlight. Barnes turned to see how close they were to the bend, shouted a warning to Penn, and two heads ducked down inside the turret. They heard the crack of the overhanging branch as it broke against the metal. When Barnes lifted his head Penn was already standing upright as he observed the bridge, his knuckles white with tension as he gripped the turret. They felt the tank veering under them as it entered the bend, saw the bank on their right gradually screening the bridge from view until it vanished altogether. Ahead, Barnes saw another long stretch of river still hidden under the tunnel of trees. They had made it.

Less than half an hour later, as though their shattered nerves had not already been tested almost beyond endurance, a new crisis burst upon them. German tanks were approaching from *downstream*.

They had halted Bert a hundred yards or so beyond the bend, had climbed the southern bank to catch their first sight of the advancing column they had so narrowly escaped, arriving at the top in time to see the first motor-cycle patrol reach the bridge. Because of the bend in the river they could see clearly across open fields to the bridge and Penn gulped as he peered through the trees: the cycle had stopped in the very centre of the bridge while a soldier dismounted from the sidecar, and even at that distance Penn felt quite sure that the sentry was staring clear down the stretch of river they had just negotiated.

'God!' Penn gasped. 'That was closer than the shave I didn't get this morning.'

'Which reminds me,' Barnes replied, 'we'll have to clean up as soon as we get the chance.'

He focused his glasses and the bridge came up to him—the sentry walking to the northern side, gazing down over the parapet, making his way down through the brambles to check under the bridge before the column arrived. Yes, it had been damned close. He swivelled the glasses and the twin circles ran along the column—stubby armoured cars, squat self-propelled guns, heavy tanks with their deadly barrels pointed up the road. The lot, in fact. He began counting, recording the count cryptically in his notebook, a form of shorthand which only he could decipher, adding it to the notes he had already made under the bridge when he had recorded the composition of the previous column while he waited to wake up Pierre for his test watch.

Behind them Reynolds had stayed with the tank which was now resting in mid-stream like a strange steel island, the sunlight forming a patchwork of shadow across the hull where it penetrated the overhead foliage, foliage which was still dense enough to mask them from any spying plane which might fly over. The river was shallower at this point so the water flowed past no more than three feet up the sides of the vehicle, but it was also much wider and there was now a good three foot of clearance on either side. For Reynolds, who was seizing the opportunity for a little maintenance, it was more like scrambling about on the deck of a boat. Since he was over twelve feet down below the level of the banks he didn't hear the menacing rumble of the Panzers, a sound like the distant chunter of a concrete-mixer.

Under the trees Barnes made a further note while Penn stood with his arms folded as he asked his question.

'What happened to the bodies when they went in? I was too busy trying to observe the bridge at the time, you may remember.'

'They both sank—they've probably floated miles downstream by now.'

He finished his note and frowned. The throb of powerful engines and the clattery grind of tank tracks drifted across the field as a muddled purr, but his acute hearing had detected a different sound. No, the same sound, but from a different direction. As he turned his head Penn noticed the movement.

'What's up?'

'Quiet.' He looked across the fields to his right. About half a mile away the ground sloped up gently to a low ridge so that the area beyond was hidden from view. Was there another road beyond that ridge? The sound of approaching engines was more distinct now, distinct enough for Penn to hear them.

'Not another lot?' He groaned in mock despair, but his feelings of despair were real enough, and he hadn't yet recovered from his ordeal on the bridge during the night, to say nothing of that mind-breaking experience when Barnes had taken the tank up the bank and past the boulder. It was not yet 6 a.m. and Penn's morale was at its lowest in the early hours, on top of which he was unshaven, unwashed and unfed. There had been no time even to have a drink of water since they had left the bridge and now he was hungry and thirsty and his stomach was full of wind.

'I'd better take a look,' said Barnes eventually. 'You stay here and keep on counting—start with that tank just coming up to the bridge now.'

'If it's Panzers coming up the river, they're bound to spot us.'

'Just wait here.'

Barnes was away for fifteen minutes, although to Penn it was more like an hour, and since he had loaned his watch to Barnes there was no way of checking the passage of time. Glumly, he went on with his counting, half his mind on making notes while the other half listened to the distant throb of engines downstream. We're caught in a pincer movement, he was thinking, trapped between two columns of the bastards. It was bound to happen, our luck's run out . . . He turned as he heard a trampling of undergrowth and Barnes came up the bank behind him.

'It's Panzers, all right. About a hundred yards farther on there's another bend with a bridge just round the corner. It carries a road behind that ridge and there's another column going over the bridge—probably to protect the flank of this lot.'

'We're the meat in the sandwich.'

'Something like that. It's a good job we stopped here instead of pushing on downstream—we'd have run into them, or they'd have seen us after we'd passed the bridge. The river goes through open country just beyond there. And they've posted a sentry, of course. The chap was looking this way when I had a dekko through some trees.'

'So we just sit tight?' Penn made a note in the book Barnes had left him. 'I could do with a drop to drink before you start counting again.'

'I'll get your bottle from the tank.'

Barnes turned to make his way down the bank and froze. Something had just floated downstream past the tank, a misshapen object which was now picking up speed in the current. Reynolds hadn't seen it because he had an engine cover up and was kneeling on the hull with his back to the near-side channel, but Penn had spotted it and he swore foully.

'That's the sentry's body—that German on the next bridge will see it.'

'You stay here!'

Barnes stumbled and slithered his way down the slope and then started to run along the overgrown bank side as though all the devils in hell were after him. He ran flat-footed, hammering his feet down and then lifting them straight up again to try and avoid tripping over the brambles which snared his path, and as he ran black despair threatened to smother his mind. Of all the bloody bad luck. It had all seemed so simple up to this moment: all they had to do was to keep their heads down and remain out of sight until the Panzers on both roads had disappeared to the north. And now this. It was like a drowning man within an ace of the shore suddenly feeling himself swept up by an ebb-tide. And the tide of the river was carrying their safety away from them in the form of the dead sentry's body. What the hell could have happened? It must have got caught on something and then later the current had freed it again. Barnes could have wept; instead, he kept on running, watching the ground but continually glancing up to see the progress of the corpse which was so clearly that of a German soldier.

The body was face down in the water but the shoulders and back and legs were well above the surface, exposing the jacket and trousers of a German infantryman, and it wouldn't take some bright officer too long to wonder why this had appeared now on a stretch of river between two bridges being crossed by the Wehrmacht. He increased speed, took several paces forward, and fell flat on his face. Scrambling up again he hardly noticed the tear and rip of the thorns as they re-opened recent wounds, but he had fallen sideways on his right shoulder with a heavy thump and he did notice the sharp throb of his wound which immediately started up again. Swearing briefly, he ran on desperately. He had to reach that corpse before it swept round the bend and flowed on in full view of the sentry on the bridge, a sentry who had been looking this way. He fell flat again, his foot trapped by ropes of bramble, dragged himself to his feet, began running and then stopped. The floating body was approaching the bend, still drifting in the centre of the river. It was now or never. He threw off his battle-dress tunic, tore off his boots, and dived in.

The chill of the water took his breath away but he ignored the shock and began swimming rapidly downstream, his arms flashing through the water, his body shooting forward under a momentum which was increased by the flow of the current. While stationed in India as a professional soldier before the war Barnes had been champion swimmer in the division but he broke all records now, swimming as though his life were at stake, which it probably was—and the lives of two others. Under his shirt the wound was throbbing steadily, sucking away his energy when he needed it all for just the next few minutes. He swam with his teeth clenched, knowing that he was beginning to overhaul the corpse. Foot by foot the gap closed, and foot by foot the bend came closer. He was only a few yards behind the floating body when his leg hit a rock under the surface, the blow sending an agonizing pain from his kneecap to his thigh. It stopped him for a second, then he was swimming on, his eyes fixed on the bend which was almost on top of him, the corpse still several yards ahead. The hump of German uniform picked up a little speed, bobbing slightly as it swept round the bend in full view of the bridge. He hadn't made it.

He had a quick glimpse—the curved bridge, the low parapet, the sentry on the far side, his back turned. Barnes took a deep breath and dived under, swimming now almost along the bed of the river, thrusting forward with powerful strokes until he saw a grey mass above him, barely one foot above him. He reached up with one arm, grabbed the body round the middle, hauled downwards with all his strength, feeling he was trying to drag down a ton-weight. It came down suddenly, rolling over sluggishly, and now his arms tried to swim two men. The bridge was very close to the bend but the distance seemed endless as he swam forward while the body tried to take on a life of its own, threatening at any moment to slip from his grasp. As he fought to retain control he was keeping a close eye upwards for the first sign of a change in the light which would warn him he was going under the bridge, and at the same time he was fighting his bursting lungs, his teeth a tight trap to hold back the carbon dioxide, to force his lungs to hold out just a few seconds longer as he felt the blood pumping like a steam-hammer. No sign of a light change yet. He began to expel air, saw a shadow on the water surface, heaved upwards, broke surface under the bridge, blew out, took in oxygen as he threshed to the bank and grabbed at it with one hand.

A tank was crossing the bridge, he could hear the steel rumble, so no one would hear him threshing about. He clung on to the bank with his left hand while the right pinioned the sentry. Now for the rough part—getting out. The tank had gone, so he waited. When the next one approached he started to climb out and then he had the devil's own job hauling out the sodden body which seemed suddenly to have increased its weight tenfold, at one point almost dragging Barnes himself back into the water as he lay face down in brambles while he struggled to heave the leaden burden up over the edge, both his arms wrapped round the waist and his hands locked together to make quite sure that it wouldn't slip back and float into view at the last moment. It was a grisly task and it became even more grisly when he succeeded in hoisting the corpse on to the bank because it rolled and he rolled with it, lying for a moment flat on his back with the sentry almost on top of him, sodden, dripping with water, its face close to his, the hair plastered flatly over the white skull.

He waited until another tank arrived and then he worked furiously to push the body deep inside a jungle of brambles, treating it like a sack of cement as he finally jerked the legs and bent them to thrust them after the rest of the corpse. The bridge he now lay under was much smaller than the one higher up, wide enough only to take single-line traffic, and the foot-path had disappeared altogether long ago when the brambles flourished and took over the whole bank up to the stone wall. There, he'd done it. No one would find the sentry unless they searched for him and by now Barnes was becoming familiar with German bridge procedure: they checked underneath it before the column arrived but they certainly wouldn't come poking around down here a second time. Not unless he attracted attention.

Barnes was temporarily exhausted, the wound playing him up badly now, his kneecap aching steadily, his hands and face scratched to blazes with the ripping of the brambles. He lay quite still for several minutes, his revolver in his hand, although whether the weapon would work after its soaking was any-body's guess. He listened to the column rumbling past over-head and gradually he revived, his mind revolting at the thought that he was back to square one again. When he cautiously peered through the far side of the arch he saw the long shadow of the sentry above him spread over the upper bank, the top half of his body, the pudding-shaped helmet absurdly stretched out. The bastard was on the right side of the bridge—downstream—and Barnes had had a bellyful of being cooped up under bridges. He decided to risk it. And Penn would be doing his nut if he didn't get back soon. The real danger was that his swimming form might be spotted under the water before he reached the bend, but the river here was about four feet deep so he'd just have to swim with his face on the bed. Because a tank commander erect in his turret has an elevated view Barnes waited until one of the vehicles had moved across the bridge and then he took a deep breath, slipped back into the river noiselessly and began swimming upstream along the river bed.

This time he was going to swim the distance in two stages, pausing half way along the stretch under the lee of the bank where long grasses trailed into the water. In fact, swimming as he was now against the current, he was going to have to take two bites at the cherry, a favourite Penn phrase for seeing the same girl twice. His face close to the flat-rocked bed, he was having to swim all-out to make headway against the current which was stronger than he had expected; he began to veer in close to the bank, expelling air slowly, his eyes gazing ahead for under-water boulders as soft mushy weeds brushed against his face unpleasantly. When he reached the bank and surfaced behind the trailing grasses he found that he had covered half the distance. He stood crouched against the bank, his nose just above the water, watching the approach of yet another German tank, and it was rather like observing it through a green bead curtain, his first close-up look at the weapon which was sweeping across the plains of France in an annihilating wave.

As he waited hunched under the bank his mind raced over the problems ahead: taking Bert downstream when the coast was clear was something they might just manage in this depth, and beyond the bridge he could leave the river where the banks came lower, a fact he had observed from under the bridge. The tank was crossing now, the commander leaning out of the turret to check clearance. Once we get away from this lot, Barnes thought, we'll head west-south-west: in spite of Seft's deception he was confident that he had a rough idea of where they were because he had found two places on the map which could correspond to the fictitious Fontaine. And west-south-west should lead in the general direction of Arras. The tank had crossed now. He slipped under the water.

He was immediately aware that his movements were slower, that his strokes lacked thrust, so he redoubled his efforts, determined that this time he must get round that bend or else he was going to be spotted. He had pushed his luck to the limit and far beyond, so whatever happens, keep going, he told himself, for God's sake keep going. In his anxiety to succeed he took a short cut, veering to the left to take himself straight for the turn in the river, seeing a forest of trailing weeds ahead and projecting himself through the diabolical mess. He was almost through when he felt a tug above his right kneecap, the one he had injured, and when he endeavoured to swim forward he remained anchored to the spot where the weeds had twined themselves round him. Pausing for a split second, he lunged out savagely, felt the weed stranglehold tighten, and he didn't move forward an inch. He was running out of air: the only thing to do was to surface. He made to swim up and the grip tightened like the tentacles of an octopus. You can't drown in four feet of water, Barnes. But you can, you know—if your upper leg is locked down tight close to the bed. A tremble ran through his brain and transferred itself to his body as he felt panic rising. Grimly, he fought down the emotion and concentrated on freeing his damned leg. Think it out, quickly! Forward is no use—try sideways, out into mid-stream. His lungs were protesting again, building up a horrible balloon-like pressure, the water gyrating oddly, a singing in his ears growing. He thrust out sideways, felt the weed tighten. God, he really was done for this time. Keep moving, Barnes! He made one last effort, felt the weed tearing away as though reluctant to give up its victim, then he was free, stroking his way upstream, still under water until he came to the surface choking and spluttering as he gulped in water, his head turning automatically to check his position. He was round the bend.

And if it goes on like this much longer he thought as he headed for the bank, we'll all be round the bend. But his instinct told him that it would probably get worse.

Eight-and-a-half hours later, at three o'clock in the afternoon and thirty miles away from the bridges, the tank was like a hunted animal, still alive but only because of the sharp eye and keen instinct for danger of its controller who had saved it on four separate occasions from detection by the hunters. At the same time the animal was still viciously armed with over seventy two-pounder shells and ten boxes of Besa ammunition secreted within its innards.

By 8.30 a.m. the Panzers had gone from the river area and by 9 a.m. the tank crew had shaved—at Barnes's insistence—and they had eaten bully beef and the last of the French bread Seft had brought, which reduced their rations to a meagre quantity of remaining bully beef and nothing else: the two tins of meat Seft had supplied were found to be blown, whether by accident or on purpose didn't matter any more, but it did mean that they were desperately short of food. They were also running low on water but this was due to an accident and an oversight which were the result of chance and fatigue. Before leaving the river they had attended to the radiator and filled a dixie with water for their own use: the accident had taken place an hour later when they mounted a steep bank into a wood to escape being spotted by a flight of Stuka bombers. The dixie had fallen over and spilt its precious contents on the turntable floor. The oversight was the fact that only Barnes had remembered to fill his water-bottle—he blamed himself for not checking to make sure that the others had filled their own. In a word, there was now one water-bottle to quench the growing thirst of three men. Although only briefly mentioned, the thirst was the reason for a bitter argument between Barnes and Penn soon after one o'clock.

'I think we ought to risk going in,' Penn had said emphatically, pointing towards the town on the skyline.

'We'll go round it, instead—across country,' Barnes had replied quietly.

Across the sun-baked fields, the town—another church spire and a line of buildings—had looked like a mirage as it trembled gently in the dazzling heat haze, an impression heightened by the absence of workers in the fields, although normally the farmers would have been busy at this time of the year. This absence of people troubled Barnes and strengthened his decision.

'It is possible to get a bit too cautious,' said Penn hotly.

'It's also possible to walk into something we won't get out of. There's no one about and I don't like the smell of it.'

'There's been no one about for miles—what makes this place so ruddy different?'

'The fact that there's a town over there. If it's under German occupation the locals may be lying low indoors—these are cultivated fields so there should be someone working them.' Barnes put a foot on the hull to climb back into the tank. 'Any more questions before we start?'

'We've seen no sign of Jerry on the ground since we left the river—what makes you think he's anywhere near here?'

'Penn, I've no idea where Jerry is. From what I've seen and from what you told me about those radio bulletins my guess is that the Germans have torn a huge gap in the Allied lines which may be up to twenty miles wide*—at the moment we're somewhere inside that gap but until I know more about it we'll avoid all towns and villages as long as we can. We're moving off now.'

Two hours later they were moving along a deserted country road under the furnace blaze of the afternoon sun, and during those two long hours they had stopped three times to avoid detection by aircraft, halting twice in the lee of hedges and sheltering once inside an abandoned dairy farm where they had been surrounded by empty milk churns. As they had waited for the Stuka bombers to disappear a small herd of cows had gathered behind a fence, their udders horribly swollen, their strange cries a pathetic sound which had affected them more than the distant roar of the Stuka engines. But there was no one to milk the beasts so they had gone away, thankful when Bert's engine drowned the echoes of animal pain. It was not only people who were suffering in this war, Barnes had thought.

As they drove steadily along a hedge-lined road between a sea of empty fields which stretched away on all sides Barnes knew that he was feeling the strain, the strain of standing upright in the turret for long periods while the sun beat down fiercely on him, so fiercely that his shirt and trousers were almost as generously soaked with sweat as they had been with water when he had emerged from the river. His task of endless observation was arduous enough to test the strength of the fittest person since it involved keeping up a constant watch— on the road ahead and behind, on the landscape on both sides of the road, and above all on the sky, since they had good reason to know now that a moment's unguarded relaxation might be punished by the sudden swoop of a Messerschmitt. But Barnes was not feeling at his strongest and a further drain

* Barnes had badly under-estimated the position: at this moment the gap torn in the Allied lines by the Wehrmacht was between fifty and sixty miles wide.

on his strength was the non-stop pounding of his shoulder wound which he was finding it impossible to ignore, while at the same time he had to take his weight on the left leg because the right kneecap was badly bruised where it had struck the underwater rock. Mentally, Barnes was still functioning, but physically he was in a state.

Shading his eye against the sun's glare he stared along the road to where a small building stood by the verge, or rather to where the relics of a building stood. It must have received a direct hit from shell or bomb. But what caught his attention was a pole which spanned the road outside the wreckage, a red and white striped pole. He spoke into the mike.

'The frontier's dead ahead. We are just about to cross the border into France.'

He could see now that the Customs post beside the pole had camouflaged the existence of a gun position, a gun position which had been completely wiped out. The 75-mm. barrel lay by itself and several French helmets were scattered across the ground, but there were still no German helmets to indicate that the enemy had also died. Bert rumbled forward, smashing aside the pole like matchwood. They were on French soil. When Penn asked permission to come up into the turret for a minute Barnes readily agreed. It must be like an inferno down inside the tank this afternoon.

'Back on home ground,' remarked Penn lightly.

'We're still a long way from home,' Barnes replied grimly.

'Any chance of a drop of mild-and-bitter?' He meant water.

'Not yet. We're down to half a bottle.'

'I do think we should have gone into that town,' Penn said hoarsely.

'And run into a Jerry ambush most likely. Tanks aren't for towns—not tanks on their own roaming about behind the enemy lines. It only needs a couple of anti-tank guns at either end of the street with us in the middle and we're finished. You should know that by now.'

'Well, we can't go on like this much longer. Reynolds must be near the end of his tether stuck out there in front driving on and on hour after hour.'

'Reynolds has not complained,' Barnes answered drily.

'But Reynolds is a good boy.'

'If this is going to be the quality of your conversation you'd better get back behind your gun.'

Penn clambered down into the fighting compartment without a word and Barnes immediately regretted his reply, but having said it he had to leave it. God, the strain must be telling for him to say a damned silly thing like that, but the tension was the product of strain. He reckoned it up. In twenty-four hours he had enjoyed barely two hours of uneasy sleep and Reynolds had made do with the same ration, but Penn hadn't slept at all, and prior to that both of them had made do with four hours' sleep a night for four nights while Barnes lay unconscious. Yes, they badly needed a safe bivouac for the night. And eight hours' sleep. He scanned the sky again.

Inside the hull the temperature was ferocious, the air almost non-existent. Penn sat in his vest and trousers, hugging the shoulder grip, his hand close to the trigger guard. Their experience with the lorryload of German infantry which had roared over the bridge in their faces had impressed on all of them the need for a constant state of alertness, although at this moment it was purely a reflex action with Penn to take up the position. His brain was becoming numbed, numbed with the heat, with the diesel fuel odour, with the endless throb of the engines, with the hypnotic grind of the tracks. He had reached the stage where he was frightened he might faint and this was why he had gone up into the turret. The dizziness increased and he kept shaking his head to clear it. The thirst he was suffering from was so intense that his tongue clove to the top of his mouth and he could almost see foaming tankards of beer, wishing to God that his imagination wasn't so strong. The tank ground on.

In the nose of the tank Reynolds wore a stolid expression. He was hot and sticky and he was thirsty, too, but they would get a drink when Barnes gave permission. In the meantime he could wait. He was neither worried nor resigned—he was just doing his job, driving Bert in accordance with instructions. He had experienced a little trouble with the monotony of the road rolling towards him on and on like a slow-motion conveyor belt which never stopped, but he countered this by glancing sideways across the fields frequently. So they were inside France now, were they? It didn't seem to make much difference to Reynolds—one field was like another and if they hadn't put up that pole you'd never have noticed any change. Fuel was going down, of course, but Barnes would do something about that. The tank ground on.

Water, fuel, ammunition, food. These were the basic commodities, in that descending order of priority, vital to their existence as a fighting unit, and they always loomed in the front of Barnes's mind. They loomed large now while he was coping with his aching wound, his bruised kneecap, the heat and the thirst, maintaining all-round observation at the same time. He knew exactly what the position was—they had sixty gallons of diesel left, but the tanks at the rear of the hull had a capacity of ninety gallons; they had half a bottle of water; a meagre quantity of bully beef, sufficient for another meal, and some tea. They were stuffed to the gills with ammunition, of course. A pity they couldn't eat that. He began to think that perhaps they had better investigate the next place they came to and he shaded his eyes to make sure that he wasn't seeing things. No, there it was—a line of buildings on the horizon straight ahead of them. He spoke into the mike.

'We're approaching a town. I'll be taking us in to have a look at the place.'

From that moment the whole atmosphere changed for the better. Glancing down inside the turret Barnes saw Penn looking up at him. The corporal grinned and winked. Even Reynolds reacted, sitting up a little higher on his seat, straightening his shoulders, gripping the steering levers a little more tightly. It was like the approach to the promised land for them. Water, fuel, ammunition, food. If they were very lucky they might load up with everything they needed. And information, an item which Barnes was tempted to add high on his priority list. If they could only know exactly where they were what a weight off his shoulders that would be! He called to Penn to come up out of that hothouse again and the corporal almost sprinted up into the turret, his voice positively light-hearted.

'Maybe we'll be off the old bully beef tonight. I wonder what's on the menu at the Restaurant de la Gare.'

'We're behind the German lines,' Barnes reminded him.

'Even so, providing their lordships aren't in residence we may get a slap-up supper. Now, let me see, I wonder what I fancy.'

'A bottle of water to start with.'

'Boeuf a la Bourguignonne with haricots verts would be acceptable. Yes, that's it. Washed down with several bottles of vin ordinaire, of course. We can't really afford vintage wines on army pay, can we?'

'Don't count your chickens.'

'Chickens? Well, poulet rôti might do at a pinch. It's rather plebeian, of course.'

They chattered on for several minutes and Penn's lively banter, plus the sight of the approaching town, revived Barnes, but soon he sent Penn down into the tank again as a precaution. It would be just their luck to meet another lorryload of German infantry leaving the town. He repeated his routine, scanning the hot blue empty sky, searching the surrounding country-side for signs of danger, and all the time the tank rumbled forward, taking them ever closer to the unknown town, which he now had difficulty in seeing because the road was turning and the sun shone straight into his eyes.

As the town came closer he found himself shading his eyes more frequently, straining to catch the detail of the silhouette which looked oddly still in the blazing sunlight. Once again he checked his all-round observation and then quickly looked ahead, his hand forming a peak over his eyes, his sense of unease growing. This town had been badly bombed. What he had taken for buildings from a distance on closer inspection revealed themselves as stone façades of irregular shape, and now he was sure that at least half the town was in ruins. But in a place of this size there must be someone left, someone who could tell him the name. And they must find more diesel. A tank running low on fuel was a sitting duck, its second weapon

—movement—immobilized. He'd better break the news to them. He spoke quietly.

'This place looks a bit of a wreck—I think Jerry has been here before us and he dropped a few carefully placed bombs.'

They were less than a quarter of a mile from the town now, a small town of possibly about thirty thousand inhabitants he estimated. He held his hand up again, screwing up his eyes, his mouth tight. It reminded him of pictures he had seen of Ypres taken during the First World War, although the one thing he did know was that they were many miles away from that ill-fated Belgian town. Grimly, he watched the advancing silhouette.

The outskirts had been gutted, no other word for it. The walls which were still standing were windowless, the upper frames like sightless eyes enclosing clear sky beyond. Half way down the walls the scree slopes began, slopes of rubble and debris. These were relics of buildings and there was no sign of life anywhere—no women working in the fields nearby, no men clearing the mess out of the streets. Just nothing, nothing at all. And over the devastation there hung a curious atmosphere, a horrible silence which seemed even more unnatural in the bright sunny afternoon. Water, fuel, ammunition, food . . .

They crawled through the outskirts at minimum speed, hearing the tank tracks grinding their way over pieces of masonry, feeling the hull drop slightly as the stone was crushed to powder. Barnes ordered Reynolds to drive down the very centre of the rubble-littered highway as he anxiously watched the spectral walls of the bombed buildings they were passing, wondering whether they should turn back at once. It was by no means certain that the vibrations of the tank movement might not bring down one of those hanging walls. Some of them seemed to stay upright by a miracle of balance. Cautiously they edged their way round a corner and drove deeper into the town.

The devastation was getting worse, no doubt about that. Whereas before many buildings had at least one wall standing they were now entering an area of almost total annihilation.

113

Any relationship between what Barnes saw and a town could only be visualized by stretching the imagination to its limits. He calculated that an area close to a quarter square mile was a sea of rubble. The rubble was arranged in cone-shapes which rose up between huge craters, a scene more like a moon landscape than a town in northern France, and the going was getting worse.

'Driver, halt. Keep the engines running.'

He gave Penn permission to come up and climbed down to the street, resting one hand on the hull and then snatching it off as the heat seared his flesh. Changing his mind, he told Reynolds to switch off so that he could listen carefully to hear whether he could detect any sign of life; he still found it hard to believe that a town of this size had been abandoned.

'There's always someone who stays behind,' he told Penn, 'someone who tries to make the best of it.'

'The Panzers may have been through as well,' objected Penn.

'But they're not here now, are they? If they have been this way they'll just have passed through without occupying the place—that's the sort of thing that's happening from what you told me about the news bulletins.'

'But no one would stay here—just look at the place.'

'I know, but it may not be so bad on the far side. We'll take a look.'

'I'd be quite happy to clear out altogether, thank you.'

Penn was voicing the feeling of all three men. There was something horribly oppressive about the deserted town, as though it had been sacked by barbarians who had taken all the inhabitants away into slavery. On the far side of the rubble sea a wall swayed gently, leaned and toppled out of sight. They heard a dull thud and saw a huge cloud of dust floating upwards. Barnes was still listening when suddenly he was galvanized into action, ordering Penn down inside the tank, warning Reynolds to close his hood, leaping up into the turret himself and ramming on his headset as he issued instructions.

The tank headed into the heart of the rubble sea, threading

114

its way between the cones, clipping down the slope of a crater, crossing the floor and mounting the other side. They were near the centre of the area before the first planes appeared, a squadron of Stuka bombers flying low. Barnes issued the order to halt in the middle of a wide crater, went down inside the tank, slammed the lid closed and waited. The first stick of bombs fell some distance away, growing fainter as they fell further off. Penn's voice was bewildered.

'Surely they couldn't have spotted us?'

'No, I think they were coming here anyway. I wanted us well clear of those walls.'

'But they've already smashed the place to bits . . .'

He stopped and they listened, staring at each other. The scream was starting again, the scream of a Stuka falling into a high-speed dive before it released its deadly load. Another stick was coming, but this one was different. The first explosion was a long way off, the next one closer, the third closer still, a frightful nerve-shattering crump. Penn began conducting an unspoken conversation with himself. It will be the next one that gets us, the next one . . . The bomb exploded in their ears and the shock wave was like a hammerblow. The hull of the tank shook, wobbled, settled again. Then a fifth crump further off. A sixth, fainter still.

'They must be stark raving bonkers.' Penn sounded indignant, a highly strung form of indignation. 'They did the job last time—are they running out of space to store their perishing bombs?'

'There's an encouraging side to this,' said Barnes, going on quickly as he saw Penn's expression. 'They must have come back to make the place absolutely impassable—which looks as though they're frightened Allied reinforcements will be moving up here soon.'

'Glad to hear it. I feel so much better, sergeant, now you've told me that.'

The scream of another plane starting its dive commenced, a plane which sounded to be directly overhead, the scream rising to a crescendo as it came down as though the machine were out of control, a scream which sent cold water down

Barnes's spine. Then the explosions came, heart-shaking crumps landing all round them, pinpointing Bert's position. Between explosions he heard another distant sound, a heavy thump. One of the remaining walls had gone. At least he had taken them clear of those insidious hanging walls. Barnes was well aware that the majority of casualties during an air raid on a built-up area are caused by the inhabitants being buried under collapsing masonry. He glanced at Penn to see how the corporal was standing up to the bombardment and Penn looked back, deliberately quivering the ends of his moustache in mock terror.

Mock terror? Penn's nerves were shuddering like plucked violin strings. Another bomb exploded almost on top of them and the tank rattled like a toy under the impact, fitments coming loose and falling on to the turntable. Bombing is a grim experience wherever the recipients may be hiding, but it is particularly grim for those inside a tank. Penn had an awful sensation of being exposed: the brick wall of a building may give as little protection as the 40-mm. steel which protects the lower sides of a tank, but inside a building there *feels* to be more protection, and locked inside the Matilda the assault on the eardrums was tremendous. As Penn sat tensely the sound of the explosions seemed to slice clean through the metal skin, but once inside the hull the cannonade reverberated from wall to wall as though a ten-ton hammer were beating on the plates, setting up vibrations which shook him to the guts. While the raid proceeded he struggled to put his mind into cold storage, as he had on the bridge when the Panzers were moving past, but now the method didn't work. He had decided to count up to a hundred explosions, telling himself that long before he reached that figure the raid would be over, but already he had lost count and he gave it up, living now from one explosion to the next.

In the nose of the tank, locked away from the other two men, Reynolds sat huddled forward, his hands still gripping the steering levers, his brain dazed with fear. It wasn't so much the thought of a direct hit which frightened him, because if that happened there would be nothing to worry about. Instead,

Reynolds was desperately trying to forget a technical factor in the construction of Bert—the four six-volt batteries which were housed in the nose of the tank. And above all else Reynolds had a gibbering horror of being blinded. He was well aware that even a near-miss could deal the hull such a shattering blow that those batteries might burst—spilling sulphuric acid all over his face and hands. He sat there silently, waiting for the next one, cursing the man who had designed the Matilda for exposing him to this terrible hazard. Miss us or kill us, he prayed, gripping his hands even tighter as they slipped wetly on the levers. Here it comes, right in front of me. Oh God, no! The explosion battered the nose and he heard debris spatter the armoured glass beyond the slit window, then he realized he was all right this time. He still sat with his head down, facing his lap, his eyes tightly closed.

'So far, so good,' said Barnes, repeating Penn's joke.

'Yes.'

Penn spat out the word, wondering how much longer it was going to last, his imagination working at a feverish pitch as he saw so clearly what was coming—the bomb which was a direct hit. The hull would rip open, letting inside the monstrous gases which are the product of high-explosion, tearing their flesh apart, disintegrating the three men and scattering their pulped relics across the rubble. No one would ever know what had happened to them: they would simply disappear. 'Reported missing in action . . .' My God, he thought, my poor people. I was just going to write to them the day we moved across the frontier. That was how many days ago? He couldn't work it out and he didn't even try to any longer as the next stick came down, straddling the tank so that for a few agonizing seconds three men were convinced that they were on the verge of death.

The raid lasted fifteen minutes and during that time they were bombed almost non-stop. After a short pause they endured a series of near-misses which terrorized poor Reynolds very close to breaking point: it was probably only the unseen presence of Barnes just beyond the plate behind him that saved the driver from opening the hatch and climbing out to escape those dreaded batteries. He had reached the stage where he was quite prepared to take his chance out in the open. Then the second pause came, a pause which went on and on while they waited for the bombardment to start again. It was Barnes who recovered first, climbing up into the turret and cautiously raising the lid, starting to cough as soon as he had poked his head up into the dust-laden air, feeling the heat of the sun on the back of his neck. The turret rim was hot to the touch.

Many of the hanging walls were no longer there and over the whole area was suspended a pall of dust, a pall so dense that the sun was a blurred disc. He looked down and saw that the hull was coated with a film of dust as though Bert had been camouflaged to operate across a grey desert, and when he stepped down on the hull his foot slipped and he almost banged his knee again. He told both of them to get out of the tank and join him where they could breathe in the dust for themselves, but at least they were out in the open, outside the claustro-phobic confines of what had so nearly become a metal coffin.

The tank stood inside an old square in the western, less-ruined sector of the town while its crew waited for the unknown intruder to make his appearance, the first sound of life they had met since entering the devastated town. The square was enclosed by hanging walls and the weird tomb-like atmosphere seemed to grow as they waited, Reynolds still in his driver's seat, Penn standing in the turret grasping a machine-pistol, while Barnes stood next to a corner of the square with his back to a wall. Instinctively, he did not lean against it and he held the revolver across his chest so that the muzzle was aimed at the corner.

Little more than ten minutes after they had stopped inside the square for Reynolds to check the tank, Barnes's acute hear-ing had detected the sounds, odd rustling sounds as though the approaching feet were scuffling furtively through rubble. The footsteps were very close now, moving more quickly. Barnes elevated his gun and at the same moment Penn aimed his machine-pistol. A man came round the corner and stopped abruptly.

Over his shoulder he carried a limp sack and for an instant his bony face expressed extreme fear, but he recovered quickly, removing a cap from his head and smiling unctuously. Small and lean, he was dressed strangely, his suit old and shabby, but round his neck he wore an expensive silk tie and Barnes caught a glimpse of a gold wrist-watch before he wriggled his sleeve. His feet were encased in a pair of brand new crocodile shoes. Barnes spoke quietly.

'Sorry we frightened you, but can you tell us the name of this place?'

'British soldiers, yes?'

He was still smiling in a forced way and he had begun to step away from Barnes, shooting a quick glance at the tank as though he expected it to advance on him at any moment. Barnes tried again.

'We're British soldiers. There's nothing to worry about—we won't hurt you. But I would like to know the name of this place.'

He began jabbering away in French, speaking at a tremendous rate, so quickly that neither Barnes nor Penn could understand what he was saying, and as he went on talking he retreated step by step. He was close to the next corner when he lifted a hand and gestured furiously in the direction the tank had come from, waving his cap and then replacing it on his head. Barnes was walking slowly towards the tank when the man with the sack scuttled round the corner out of sight. Penn looked puzzled and sounded irritable when Barnes reached the tank.

'Why didn't you grab him? He could have told us . . .'

'Quick, Penn—give me that machine-pistol.'

'What . . .'

'Hurry it up, man.'

'Here . . . what's the big idea?'

'Both of you wait. If you hear me using this thing get a move on—but come with Bert.'

He ran to the corner, peering round just in time to see the man leave the road as he scrambled over a heap of rubble in the distance. He followed him, running lightly on the balls of his feet and holding the machine-pistol across his chest. The man had vanished behind the wall of a building and when he reached the point where he had scrambled over the rubble he was vanishing again behind the stunted relic of a house, still without a backward glance. Barnes slowed down as he approached the house, and now he held the machine-pistol under his arm ready for instant use as he peered round the end wall, quite unprepared for what he saw.

Beyond the house was a road comparatively free of debris and standing in the road was a single-decker bus, its sides covered with dust. Four people stood outside the bus and they appeared to be arguing. The bus was empty of passengers but its interior was crammed with a motley collection of goods, and beyond the open door he saw a seat piled high with miscellaneous articles. Bottles of wine, their necks protruding from a wicker basket, some red material which might be curtains or a bedspread, an upended silver tray, the upper half of a small chair with a brocaded back, and an old hunting rifle with a silver-plated stock. The quartet which stood arguing were almost as strange a collection as the contents of their bus.

The bony-faced man stood on one side, putting in a word every now and again, while the other three men formed a circle, facing each other as they talked. The leader of the group appeared to be a short squat man with a swarthy complexion and a large black moustache. He wore a crumpled business suit, a dark slouch hat pushed well back over his head, and round his neck was tied a coloured handkerchief. Barnes was reminded of a Corsican he had once met in a bar at Port Said when his troopship stopped there on the way home from India. The other two men were very thin and tall and they seemed to defer to the swarthy individual when the argument became too heated; they were dressed in blue denim jackets and trousers and wore black berets pulled tightly over their heads. Barnes walked out from behind the wall, his machine-pistol aimed at the group, his voice harsh.

'What the devil's going on here?'

Three bodies spun round to face him, then froze. The

Corsican was the first to recover and he came forward a few paces, smiling as he said something in French.

'Talk in English,' snapped Barnes.

The Corsican made a show of not understanding. Jabbing forward his pistol, Barnes rasped out the words.

'Get your hands up or I'll cut you to pieces.'

The Corsican shot up his hands, saying something quickly over his shoulder, and three more pairs of hands jumped above shoulder level.

'I'm glad you speak English,' Barnes commented. 'Who are you? Come on—be quick about it.'

'Joseph Lebrun, sir. Fur salesman from Le Cateau.'

'What's the name of this place?'

'Beaucaire, sir. You are the British Army?'

'The advance guard. That road which comes into the town from the west—where does it lead to?'

'To Cambrai. Arras is beyond.'

God, Barnes was thinking, we're miles further south than I'd thought. He stepped back several paces because Lebrun was showing a tendency to edge closer. He kept his voice crisp and hard.

'Stay where you are. Lebrun, how close are the Germans?'

'They have gone.' Lebrun looked astonished. 'They passed through here several days ago soon after the first bombing . . .'

'Soldiers in trucks, you mean?'

'No nothing like that. It was a long column of huge tanks, enormous guns.'

'But no soldiers in trucks?' Barnes repeated.

'No, nothing like that.' He stared at the machine-pistol, frowning. 'That is a German gun?'

He's quick, this one, Barnes warned himself, and probably treacherous. He kept the pistol aimed at Lebrun's stomach as he pressed home his cross-examination.

'How long ago was this? You said several days ago—exactly how many days?'

'Six or seven days since. We did not see them ourselves—we were told. We do not live here.'

He stopped quickly and his face went blank as though he

had said the wrong thing. Barnes went on talking quickly, determined to extract the maximum information from this gangster while he was still off-balance.

'Lebrun, where are the Germans now?'

'In Abbeville.'

Barnes felt as though he had been rabbit-punched. If this were true the B.E.F. and the French armies in the north would be severed from the main French armies to the south, a catastrophe without precedent during the whole of the First World War. Then he recovered. The so-and-so was lying, of course.

'Abbeville's on the coast, Lebrun. Now try again and this time be a bit more careful.'

'I tell you.' He became excited, waving his hands above his head. 'I tell you, they are in Abbeville—we met refugees who were from the town. The German tanks are everywhere. They have thousands of tanks and they are all over France.'

'But not near here?'

The squat man's eyes became cunning and he stared hard at Barnes before replying.

'Only the big tank outside Beaucaire—on the road towards Cambrai.'

'A German tank, you mean? How far along the road outside Beaucaire?'

'Seven or eight kilometres—we passed it on our way back here. It is there by accident, I am sure. It has broken down in a field and four soldiers are trying to make the repairs. They are working stripped to the waist like peasants. This was two hours ago.'

'On which side of the road as you drive towards Cambrai?'

'To the right, about half a kilometre from the road.'

Barnes nodded and gave them instructions, forming them into a line spread out across the full width of the road with plenty of space between each man. Then he marched them back towards the square, halting at a side turning which led down to the road from the square. At the corner he made them lie down in the dust, flat on their stomachs with their arms stretched out full length, firing one burst from his machine-

122

pistol into the air. The prone bodies jumped and he knew that for a brief second they had believed they were about to die. In the distance he heard the throb of Bert's engines and he fired a second short burst, bringing the tank round the corner. Only Lebrun plucked up the courage to look over his shoulder as the tank pulled up.

'Who are these birds?' inquired Penn from the turret.

'Looters.' Barnes spat out the word. 'While their own chaps are trying to hold off Jerry this lot goes round scavenging. There's a bus-load of the stuff up the road.'

'How did you catch on?'

'Bony-Face was wearing some of it. He's wearing a filthy old suit but the tie and the shoes don't go with it—to say nothing of the gold watch.'

He ordered Penn to stay in the turret while Reynolds searched the four men. From Lebrun and one of the thin men the driver extracted two pistols, German 9-mm. Luger pistols, and when Barnes asked where they had obtained these Lebrun explained that they had taken them off two dead German soldiers they had found lying beside a crashed motor-cycle and side-car. Barnes made no comment on the fact that only German officers were armed with Luger pistols and he left Penn to guard the four men while he walked back to the bus with Reynolds.

The seats of the bus were littered with a variety of loot which included a glass case containing old gold coins and Barnes was burrowing deeper into the strange cargo when he heard Reynolds give a whoop. The driver had thrown out of the door the hunting rifle, the silk curtains, the little chair and the silver tray when he called out. Barnes looked up.

'Found some champagne?'

'Yes, for Bert!'

He was holding a heavy rectangular can and had taken off the cap while he examined the contents. Replacing the cap, he carried it off the bus and put it down on the roadside as though it were a fragile glass vase. Then they began searching the bus ruthlessly, finding more cans of the precious diesel fuel which they carried to the roadside. Within five minutes Reynolds had arranged twenty cans in a neat row and still Barnes found it hard to believe their good luck. Bert ran on diesel fuel and possibly the only vehicle in Northern France which used this was a bus. Reynolds stood guard over the cans as though he were afraid they might walk away, his voice almost purring.

'They must have pinched the bus from a depot, so they pinched plenty of spare fuel to go with it.'

'You can load up Bert now, but get a move on.'

While Reynolds was carrying the cans back to the tank Barnes made a further search of the bus and when his fingers pressed through a coverlet he felt bottles underneath. At least not only Bert would have plenty to drink. Ripping away the coverlet he found a dozen bottles of mineral water: clearly, Mr Lebrun liked to dilute his wine. And underneath the last two mineral waters he found the jackpot—a half-bottle of Five Star Bisquit cognac.

He carried his own treasures back to the tank and the four men were still lying sprawled in the blazing sun while Penn mounted guard over them from the turret. Reynolds was humming to himself as he fussed about the tank, lifting back the engine cover, removing the cap and inserting the large tin funnel which he used to fill up with diesel. As he poured in the precious liquid he was taking as much pleasure over the operation as if he were enjoying a five-course dinner himself. They had almost completed the loading operation when Lebrun couldn't stand it any longer. Lifting his head cautiously, his face streaming with greasy sweat, he spoke over his shoulder, his tone of voice petulant.

'Please, sir . . .'

'What is it, Lebrun?'

'Please leave us two or three of the containers for the bus.'

'Too late—we've poured it all in the tank.'

Lebrun glared savagely and Barnes was startled by the look of bitter hatred in the squat man's eyes. He had his mouth open and between the thick lips several mis-shapen gold teeth showed. Barnes told him to get his head down, took a heavy wrench from the tool kit and went back to wreck the bus's engine. He smashed the motor systematically, putting it completely out of action. Lebrun wouldn't be using this bus again to plunder his own people and now there was no risk of the looters driving out of Beaucaire ahead of them to warn that German tank of Bert's existence. When he returned to the tank Lebrun was settling his face back on the ground as Penn swore at him.

'He's a sensitive soul,' Penn explained. 'The noise you were making was getting on his nerves.'

'I wish you'd told me that—I'd have wrapped a cloth round the wrench.' Barnes's voice hardened. 'Lebrun, get on your feet. The others can get up, too.'

Lebrun said something quickly in French and rose slowly to his feet, facing Barnes alongside his companions, an expression of the utmost venom on his face. He's an ugly customer, this one, thought Barnes, but he can't do much without his Lugers. He spoke abruptly.

'You can all push off now—that way, to the east. If we see any of you again we'll shoot.'

'The Germans come from the east . . .' began Lebrun.

'That's right. I doubt if they'll like you any better than we do. Get moving.'

They followed the four men down the road in the tank and then halted after they had turned on to the highway which led westward. Amid the sunlit ruins they ate a quick meal and quenched their thirst with mineral water while Barnes pointed out their position on the map and outlined what the Corsican had told him. The news almost spoilt Penn's appetite.

'The Germans in Abbeville!' The corporal looked stunned. 'You don't believe that, do you?'

'With these Panzers roaming all over the place I'm not sure what to believe. I just hope he's wrong, that's all.'

'We're heading for Cambrai first then?'

'It's in the right direction, if there is such a thing.'

They talked about the problem—a single tank roaming behind the enemy lines, unaware of its position, because they couldn't be absolutely sure that this was Beaucaire, the Germans unaware of its presence—and then Barnes said it was time to move, but at the last moment he jumped down to the ground again. 'What's up?' inquired Penn, leaning out of the turret.

'I'm going back to the bus—I forgot to look in the tool box at the back and there may be something useful in it.'

He left Penn standing in the turret, hurried back up the road, and turned the corner out of sight of the tank, the machine-pistol under his arm. As he reached the bus he glanced down at the pile of loot which Reynolds had thrown out and wondered why it looked different. Dismissing the thought as imagination, he boarded the bus and made his way to the back. All the windows were closed and it was appallingly hot and airless and there was a smell of wine. His foot kicked an empty bottle which rolled under a seat and he stiffened: the bottle hadn't been there when he left the bus. Inside the tool box he found a large wrench which he put in his pocket, still trying to work out how that bottle had appeared. He was leaving the bus when his glance fell again on the pile of loot strewn across the ground and a warning signal flashed in his brain. *The rifle had gone.*

A sense of foreboding gripped him as he ran back towards the corner. Why take an old hunting rifle? Lebrun must have doubled back round the ruins while they were eating, must have found a bottle of wine, drank it and made off with the weapon. He was midway to the corner when he heard the sound of a single report, one sharp crack, then an awful silence. He reached the corner and at first sight nothing appeared to be wrong: the tank was where he had left it and Penn was still in the turret, but as he ran closer Reynolds scrambled clear of the hatch and stood on the hull close to Penn who was no longer standing erect. When he reached them he saw that the driver was holding Penn up, his right hand sticky with blood. Penn spoke hoarsely, his face ashen.

'Blighter got me in the shoulder . . . Lebrun . . . watch it—he's behind that building . . .'

'Take it easy . . .'

Reynolds spoke quickly. 'It's all right, I can see to him.'

Barnes ran across the rubble towards the stunted house from where he had first seen Lebrun and his gang, ran crouched low, his eyes everywhere, the machine-pistol held forward in front of his stomach, his mind calculating and murderous. The house came closer and he watched both corners, watched a window which faced his approach, the only three points from which Lebrun could take him by surprise. As he ran he cursed himself for overlooking that rifle, but who would dream of checking an ancient weapon like that? Some idiot must have kept the damned thing loaded in his house and Lebrun had pinched it because of the silver-plated stock. He reached the house, crept round the outer walls, looked inside through a half-wrecked doorway, and saw the entire ground floor at one glance because the internal walls had collapsed, leaving only a stone staircase which led upwards past the still intact ceiling. On an impulse he stepped inside and carefully mounted the staircase which trembled under his footsteps. He emerged on to a flat roof, the floor of the upper storey which had vanished, and it gave him an all-round view over the rubble-strewn desolation behind the house, a region of large bomb craters. Inside one huge hole something flashed in the sunlight.

Lebrun knew instantly that Barnes had spotted him and now he began to scramble to his feet, kicking up dust from the crater floor, shouting hysterically at the top of his voice as he lifted the rifle and waved it harmlessly. The silver on the stock flashed again and again in the sun. Was he saying that the rifle wasn't loaded, was he begging for mercy? Barnes neither knew nor cared. Without pity, without any real emotion, he lowered the muzzle of the machine-pistol, braced his legs and fired, sweeping the fusillade of bullets over the crater floor where they coughed up spurts of dust. Lebrun was on his feet and suddenly he jerked, then he fell over backwards and lay still. The bombed zone was terribly silent.

Barnes pulled a face. His tank crew was now down to two men.

5. Friday May 24

PENN was in a bad way. Barnes only had to look at his face to tell that; a face which was normally pink and fresh was now the colour of grey mud and his eyes lacked life. He sat up on his seat inside the tank, a folded blanket behind his back, and Reynolds had just finished cleaning the wound which was in the right shoulder, a similar wound to Barnes's, but in Penn's case the bullet had entered from the back instead of from above. Reynolds was just about to apply a field dressing but he waited while Barnes examined it. The driver constantly had to swab up fresh blood and Barnes wasted no time.

'What's the verdict?' Penn asked weakly.

'I've seen worse, much worse, and they survived.'

'I'm afraid I'm not much use at the moment . . .'

'You will be, soon enough. Put the dressing on.'

As Reynolds applied the dressing Penn stiffened his back against the blanket and took the bottle of cognac which Barnes had opened for him.

'Just a few sips now—don't get greedy.'

'Rationing me?' Penn managed the pale imitation of a smile.

'You can have a stiffer tot in a minute. Do you think you can stay in that seat when Bert's on the move?'

'Course I can—anything to get away from this bloody hole. This place gives me the creeps. Did you get Lebrun? I heard . . .' He stopped and winced as Reynolds tightened the dressing.

'Yes, he's dead. He took half a magazine in the guts.'

'I should have seen him . . . my fault . . .'

'No, it isn't. There was no reason for you to think that he might be armed, or even come back at all for that matter.'

'Anything in the tool box?'

'A big monkey wrench—it will replace the one we lost at Etreux. We'll get you out of this beauty spot . . .'

'Join the army and see the world. Thanks, Reynolds, that's better. What was I saying? Oh, yes. The people you meet in this man's army. When this is all over I'll publish my memoirs. You didn't know I was keeping a diary, did you, sergeant?'

'No,' lied Barnes.

'Strictly against regulations. You'll have to put me on a charge. Three days' C.B.—confined to Bert. Looks as though I'll be confined to him anyway.'

He laughed feebly and then stopped abruptly, his face cramping in a spasm of pain. Barnes handed him the cognac bottle again and told him to take several mouthfuls, watching him closely. The vital thing was for Penn to stay conscious until they got clear of Beaucaire. At least a little colour was flowing back into his face as the alcohol penetrated his bloodstream. Reynolds gathered up a number of blood-soaked swabs and climbed out of the turret. Barnes didn't like the look of those swabs—Penn must have lost a lot of blood and among the swabs there had been two sodden field dressings, which meant that Reynolds had twice failed to stem the flow.

'We'll be moving off now, Penn. I'll try and avoid the rough patches but it won't be like driving along Brighton prom.'

'Let's get on with it. We're heading for Cambrai?'

'In that general direction, yes.'

'Don't forget the Jerry tank Lebrun warned us about—the swine could have been telling the truth about that. Sorry I can't handle the gun,' he repeated.

'Don't worry about it. I'll act as my own gunner till we get you fixed up.'

'Bet you could do with a bit of a sit-down yourself.'

'More fresh air up there, my lad. We'll get under way now.'

Yes, I could do with a bit of a sit-down, Barnes thought as he gave the order to advance from the turret. It was five o'clock in the afternoon and the sun scorched down as the tank headed westward, the tracks grinding up fresh clouds of dust from the powdered rubble, dust which obscured his vision so that he was constantly waving his hand in an attempt to see clear ahead. To ease the strain on Penn he had told Reynolds to move at low speed, but it was not entirely a feeling for his corporal's comfort which prompted his instruction. He wanted Penn to be as strong as possible when the time came—the time to take out the bullet.

Heaven knew when they would find a doctor and Barnes was not prepared to leave the leaden obstruction festering in Penn's shoulder. He wished that he knew whether a missile fired from an old hunting rifle was more or less dangerous than a .303 bullet lodged in the same place. He simply had no idea, but there was one small mercy—the bullet appeared to be close to the surface, wedged in down the side of the bone. Extracting the bullet successfully was not likely to be an easy matter, but at least he had had to perform a similar operation once before in India when they had come under fire from hostile tribesmen in a remote spot. He hoped that he could remember how he had managed it then. One basic thing it did involve and that was laying Penn face down on his stomach, and there were less cruel surfaces than dust and rubble for such an operation. He shaded his eyes and gazed ahead, eager for his first sight of open country and fresh green.

They reached the end of the town without warning. One minute they were driving through a street of badly bombed houses and then they turned a corner and France spread away in front of them, a vast landscape of green fields as far as the eye could see, a haze of shimmering heat close to the horizon. Barnes heaved an audible sigh of relief.

Half an hour later there was still no sign of the German tank which Lebrun had mentioned but they were approaching a spot which seemed ideal for Barnes's purpose. They had just come over a small rise and close to the road stood a large empty farm building: he could see that it was empty because the large double doors had been left wide open. There was no sign of a farmhouse nearby and he could scan the road in both directions for over a mile. Nothing in sight anywhere. The building provided perfect cover for Bert in case enemy aircraft flew over while he was at work, and bombing was the last activity he wished to attract while he was treating Penn. He gave Reynolds the order to turn off the road and they moved along a short track which led inside the building. As the engines were switched off he went down inside the tank and saw that Penn was looking better in spite of the ride.

'Penn,' he said, 'you'd better treat yourself to another tot of cognac. I'm taking out that bullet.'

The floor of the farm building showed traces of animals, which would increase the danger of infection enormously, so reluctantly Barnes decided that they would have to do it out-side. At least the light was better there. They spread blankets over clean grass and laid a groundsheet over the blankets. Then Penn lay stomach down on the groundsheet while Reynolds boiled water. He was stripped to the waist now. Barnes had removed his jacket and rolled up his shirt-sleeves. When the water was ready he took one last look along the road in both directions, scanned the sky, and started.

'Reynolds is going to sit on your shoulders,' he explained. 'We've got to be sure you're kept perfectly still.'

'I can dig my fingers into the ground.'

'You'll be doing that, anyway, my lad. And Reynolds will be holding down your elbows.'

'Good old Reynolds. With his weight he'll probably flatten me to a pancake.'

'And don't be in such a hurry to kiss mother earth, Penn. Here, drink this.'

He poured a generous quantity of cognac into a mug and made Penn drink it quickly. If only he could get him drunk that would help, but he knew from previous experience that Penn's ability to absorb alcohol was phenomenal.

'There'll be the same for you afterwards,' he told him.

'Almost worth it—to get rations like this.'

'Ready?'

'Get it over with.'

Reynolds sat his whole weight on Penn's shoulders, twisting himself sideways so that he could press his huge hands over Penn's elbows. The field dressing came off with a quick rip and Barnes used antiseptic cottonwool to sponge off a mess of

131

ooze. Then he reached for the knife in the boiling water: he was using Reynolds's sheath knife, a knife the driver kept honed sharp as a razor, the point like a needle. Barnes took a deep breath, he wanted to get this over with quickly.

It took him five long minutes, and whether this time was longer for Barnes or Penn no one would ever know. Only Penn experienced the searing, agonizing, hellish pain which went on and on, stabbing and gouging into the ultra-sensitive wound like a red-hot poker, then turning and grinding and driving deeper and deeper until he thought that he must have reached the ultimate of all pain, only to feel through the burning hot scalpel another wave of torture twisting and disembowelling flesh which had become a million times more sensitive to even the lightest of touches, let alone to this fiendish probe which was thrusting and tearing right through his body until his brain pleaded and screamed for relief, for death, for anything but a continuation of this incredible agony . . .

Barnes drew the knife firmly between bullet and bone, and the scrape of knife on bone brought on the ultimate agony for Penn. He really felt that his entire shoulder was being amputated with a blunt butcher's knife. Moaning horribly, as he had been doing for several minutes, he buried his fingers deep in the ground, biting his teeth together like a steel vice. In some superhuman way he was still managing to keep his tongue at the back of his mouth, knowing in a strangely disembodied corner of his brain that he was in grave danger of biting clean through his tongue. And at that moment Barnes remembered and his hand almost slipped. He'd forgotten. He should have rammed a handkerchief into Penn's mouth. *He'd bite his tongue in half.* He couldn't stop now. He pressed the knife in deeper between bone and bullet, not realizing that it may have been this omission which kept Penn sane and conscious—the knowledge that he must protect his tongue, keeping it well back, well back. And in his stupefied state Penn had no idea that Barnes was in trouble: the bullet wouldn't shift. He had cut all round, he had loosened it from the bone, he had prised underneath, but the bullet simply wouldn't shift. Then he heard the planes coming.

Glancing up he saw the flight of Messerschmitts. They were flying in formation about a thousand feet above the ground, their course roughly parallel with the road. Without hesitation Barnes put his head down and went on with his task, refusing to allow the oncoming roar of the engines to divert him. Penn had his fingers dug deep in the groundsheet now, turning his head from side to side as he moaned quietly like an animal in its death throes. Reynolds was leaning his whole weight on the elbows, and he hadn't looked up once when he heard the planes coming. If it was all right with Barnes it was all right with him. They were almost overhead now, and then they sped past, unaware of the drama below. Barnes took a deep breath, said *Sorry, laddie* under his breath, and scooped much deeper, turning the knife with great deliberation, then he hoisted. The bullet flicked up from his knife and landed on the groundsheet. Done it!

As he disinfected, sponged, and dressed the wound he tried to tell Penn that it was all over, that it was all right now, but Penn was too far gone to understand. Barnes applied the dressing quickly but carefully, feeling an enormous wave of relief, and then a wave of fatigue swept over him and he nodded to Reynolds to get up as he gripped Penn's left arm.

'It's done, Penn. The bullet's out and I've put a fresh dressing on. It's all right, Penn.'

Penn turned his head, his eyes dazed, his face wet and drawn, looking at Barnes without seeing him.

'It's all right now, Penn. You can have your cognac.'

Penn opened his mouth to say something and fainted.

'Damn him,' said Barnes. 'Why couldn't he have done that five minutes ago?'

It was close to dusk and the tank was rumbling steadily forward when they first saw the farm, an isolated spot in the middle of nowhere. Would the inhabitants be friendly, Barnes wondered, and he prayed that they would be because the tank crew was near the end of its tether.

It had been eight o'clock in the evening before he had felt that Penn was fit enough to travel, as far as any man could be said to be fit to travel inside a tank two hours after a bullet had been removed from his shoulder. While Penn rested, Barnes and Reynolds had worked non-stop under the heat of the sun attending to the tank's maintenance. Their work completed, they had turned to the nightmare task of lowering and settling Penn inside the tank and as they wedged him in with several blankets he had protested.

'You don't have to make all this fuss. For your information I'm already feeling a lot better with that bullet outside me.'

'Shut up and try to get some rest,' Barnes had told him. 'You ought to be blind drunk now with the cognac you've consumed.'

'When I was in London, sergeant, the deb girls used to have some trouble getting me drunk.'

'I thought it was supposed to be the other way round.'

'Then clearly you weren't in demand like I was.'

Even this short exchange of banter seemed to exhaust Penn and he relapsed into silence as Barnes checked the firing mechanism and then climbed back into the turret. Giving the order to advance, he forced himself to stand erect as the tank left the building, proceeded down the track and turned on to the road to the west—the road to Cambrai, with Arras beyond.

An hour later Barnes was still in the turret and the tank was still rolling forward. To make sure Reynolds kept alert he spoke to him frequently over the intercom because by now even the driver was showing signs of strain and Barnes was hoping to God that they wouldn't meet the enemy before nightfall. The unit was in no shape to fight a cat at the moment. They were approaching the top of a hill and he couldn't yet see over the other side. Standing up on his toes, he waited for the moment when he could see what lay ahead. When they moved over the top he saw the farm.

It was standing by the roadside half a mile ahead. Focusing his glasses he saw a farmhouse, several outbuildings, a haystack close to the verge, and a man working in the fields. As they came closer he saw a woman leave the man to walk back to the farmhouse while nearby another man was driving across the fields on an orange tractor. From the farmhouse chimney a coil of smoke rose, climbing vertically into the evening sky as the sun neared the horizon, a blood-red disc which promised yet another glorious tomorrow. Would they be friendly? Was it possible that they could tell him of a place where the tank and its crew could spend the night out of sight? And, above all else, would they sell them some food? He doubted it. They were under partial German occupation and probably already they were learning to watch their step. 'German occupation.' The phrase ran through his mind and he thought of what Lebrun had said. 'The Germans are in Abbeville . . .' Lebrun must have lied about that: if it were true it could mean that the war was lost. Perhaps at least this farmer would be able to tell him about Abbeville. As they drew close to the farm the man left the field and stood waiting by the roadside, and as he watched him Barnes heard a familiar sound a long way off, no more than a distant mutter but he immediately identified the sound of heavy artillery firing. The guns of Arras? They were approaching the battle area. It was the evening of Friday May 24.

Four days earlier, at 7 p.m. on Monday May 20, the Panzers entered Abbeville. Before dusk General Storch had set up his new headquarters inside a school building on the northern outskirts of the town.

He always made a point of establishing new field headquarters as close as possible to the point where his next advance would begin, and the new direction for the Panzer onrush would be north, north towards the Channel ports. But as he completed inspecting his temporary new home Storch was in a state of almost uncontrollable fury, a fury which as usual he vented on Meyer.

'They must be mad,' he thundered, 'completely insane. Out of their minds, Meyer!'

'The High Command, general?'

Meyer straightened some papers on the desk, making a neat pile by squaring them up with the palms of his hands. He was standing up because Storch had just risen from his chair, sending it over backwards with the abruptness of his movement, but in spite of the fact that he was the victim of Storch's tirade Meyer was in an excellent humour.

'The people who drafted this order, Meyer.' Storch waved the wireless message savagely. 'All Panzer divisions are to halt temporarily on their present positions pending further instructions. Why stop when you are winning? Always go on to the end, Meyer, always go on as long as your tanks have a litre of petrol left. That is the way to win wars.'

'I suppose General Guderian has his reasons.'

Their normal roles were almost reversed, because now it was Meyer who spoke silkily, careful to keep his voice sympathetic, but underneath he was experiencing a sense of triumph. At last the High Command was seeing the folly of this reckless onrush into the unknown. But here Meyer had overplayed his hand because Storch had a sensitive ear for voice tones and now he regarded his G.S.O.1 thoughtfully, his manner suddenly calm.

'You mean General Guderian is worried about the Panzers?'

It was a subtle manoeuvre and Meyer instantly felt that he was losing ground. Everyone was aware that Guderian, the Corps Commander, was almost as great a firebrand as Storch himself, and Meyer had little doubt that Guderian was at this moment raging and fuming about the order he had been compelled to pass on to the divisional commanders. So if Storch took it into his head to dismiss Meyer from his post Guderian would completely agree with the decision—once it came out that Meyer had said Guderian wished to halt the Panzers.

'I was referring to Army Headquarters,* of course,' he said hastily.

But now Storch was re-reading the message and the cynical expression under the peaked cap bothered Meyer. Surely he couldn't twist this order to his advantage? Storch threw the

* Meyer was actually referring to the Army Group commander, General von Rundstedt, who personally sent this halt order. The conflict between the two schools of thought—those for advancing non-stop and those who preached caution—raged ferociously through the entire campaign.

message down on his desk and asked Meyer to read it again, then went on speaking.

'They probably don't realize that we are still as fresh as when we came over the bridges at Sedan. It's understandable, is it not, Meyer, when you think of the remoteness of Army Headquarters? I think a little reassurance would help. Send this message. Road to Boulogne open. Division ready to advance.'

'Ready to advance?' Meyer stared in amazement at Storch. 'Fifty per cent of our vehicles are in desperate need of maintenance and the men have had very little sleep for over ten days.'

'You mean half our tanks have broken down?'

Meyer swallowed. Storch knew perfectly well that he hadn't meant that. 'No, sir, but there may soon be breakdowns . . .'

'The tanks require urgent maintenance?' Storch's own voice was silky now, almost a purr. 'That's what you mean, isn't it, Meyer?'

'Yes, sir.'

'I agree. You are right, of course. It therefore becomes a matter of top priority to work on the tanks through the night.'

'We have arranged for a night shift . . .'

'*All* the fitters, Meyer. They must all work non-stop through the night if they are capable of standing on their feet. Any fitter on the sick list who is capable of walking must immediately be put to work.'

'But the men themselves . . .'

'I expect you to supervise the operation personally. Through the night,' he added maliciously.

Meyer screwed in his monocle, his face blank. Storch was well aware that he had been up most of last night and Meyer was a man who needed eight hours' sleep. He's punishing me, Meyer thought, punishing me because I dared to look pleased at the order to halt the Panzers. He waited, seeing that Storch hadn't finished with him yet. The general picked up the order again.

'I think we have misunderstood what lies behind this message, Meyer. It ends with the words "pending further instructions." I think I can predict that those will be for us to resume our advance, so it becomes vitally important to be ready, Meyer. Do you not agree?'

'Yes, sir.'

'We are now close to the jugular vein of the British Expeditionary Force—the Channel ports. Once we start moving north we shall capture Boulogne, Calais and Dunkirk within two days, maybe even only one day. Then the British are finished.'

'Two days?' Meyer was stunned.

'At the most. Now, you must hurry.' Storch walked to the door and then turned before leaving the room. 'And don't forget that message, Meyer. Road to Boulogne open. Division ready to advance.'

The farmer's name was Mandel, and without hesitation he invited them into the farmhouse, but first he asked them to hide the tank in a distant outhouse which lay about half a kilometre from the Cambrai road. Before parking Bert, Barnes and Reynolds helped Penn to walk from the tank into the farmhouse where they lowered him into an arm-chair in the kitchen. Barnes was almost too exhausted to worry about other people but he did warn Mandel that it could be very dangerous for him if the Germans arrived and found them helping the British.

'You do not worry about that,' Mandel assured him. 'Once the tank is hidden in that distant outhouse the Germans will never find it. As for yourselves, Etienne, my nephew, will keep watch. We can see the road for a long way in both directions, so if anything happens there will be time for you to hide in a ditch well away from here.'

This was another stroke of good luck—the fact that Mandel spoke good English. Barnes asked him where he had learned the language.

'In your country, of course! For several years I worked as an onion-seller. I come from Brest, you see, where I was employed by the Syndicate. I used to take my bicycle on the boat over to Southampton, collect my onions from the depot and then cycle all round Hampshire and Surrey. You soon learn English that way!'

'We'd better park the tank.'

'Etienne will show you. You go up the track and . . . I will leave it to Etienne.'

As far as Barnes could see there was no sign of a telephone, so it wouldn't be possible for Mandel to phone the Germans to tell them that they were here. Not that he thought there was any likelihood of that happening for when he looked at Mandel he felt pretty sure that he could trust him. The farmer was in his fifties, a short, heavily-built man with a strong red face and a large grey moustache which matched his great bush of hair. Even his wife, Marianne, showed no signs of alarm at the arrival of these dangerous visitors. A woman of about the same age as her husband, she wore her hair tied back in a bun and her features were shrewd and decisive. She said she would prepare a meal for them and went away before Barnes could protest. They made a formidable pair.

Leaving Penn with the Mandels, he followed Etienne to where Reynolds had returned to the tank. The track was stony, barely visible under the grass, and Etienne had to guide them along it to the distant outhouse. He could hardly speak a word of English but frequently he banged his fist on the side of the turret and said 'Good, good!' He was probably just under military age, Barnes decided, very close to his seventeenth birthday, the age Seft had claimed. But Etienne was very different from the German fifth columnist. This lad was thin and wiry, his freckled face fresh and alert, and there was a look of wicked humour in his eye. He'll be a devil with the girls, thought Barnes as they reached the isolated building. Etienne jumped down off the hull to open the huge doors.

While Reynolds was driving the tank inside Barnes walked all round the building which stood in the middle of nowhere. Green fields stretched away to the skyline and the only approach was by the track they had driven along. He was on the horns of a dilemma because his small unit was now reduced to two effectives—himself and Reynolds. Leaving Bert here meant either leaving the driver to guard it or not guarding the vehicle at all. Reluctantly, he took a decision which would have horrified his troop commander—he decided to leave Bert on his own for the night. They had to keep some sort of watch through the hours of darkness—for the sake of the Mandels as well as their own—and he knew that in their present state of exhaustion keeping awake and alert all night was impossible. He would have to split the guard duty between himself and Reynolds, so both of them would take turns in watching the road, because it was along the road where any danger would come from. As they walked back with Etienne through the gathering dusk he still wasn't happy about putting the Mandels at risk by staying with them, but the fact was they couldn't move another kilometre without rest. On one point he was quite determined: they wouldn't sleep in the house.

Well after dark they sat down to the hot cooked meal which Marianne had prepared. Roast chicken, potatoes and some green vegetables they didn't recognize. They ate together at a scrubbed wood table in the huge kitchen at the back of the house, the stone walls hung with burnished copper pans, and the family ate with them. Barnes was famished and joined Reynolds in attacking the meal with vigour, but Penn held his knife and fork and then put them down. Marianne said something and Mandel, sitting at the head of the table, smiled sadly.

'Your friend can't eat—it will be his wound.'

'I'm terribly sorry . . .' began Penn.

Marianne spoke rapidly in French, taking up his glass of wine and making insistent gestures that he should at least drink. Then she took away his plate and when she came back Penn was drinking. Nodding to herself with satisfaction, she said something to Mandel, who nodded in his turn.

'I can manage a gallon of this,' said Penn.

Mandel spoke to his wife in French and laughed at her reply.

'She says that as long as he drinks a gallon he will be all right. And, Sergeant Barnes, do stop listening so carefully while you are eating—Etienne is outside watching the road and will warn us if there is anything coming.'

'It's just that it's well after dark. Would he see them?'

'Of course! These Germans drive through the night with their lamps blazing away as though they owned France. Les salles Boches!' He made a gesture of cutting a throat with his knife and Marianne frowned, which caused Mandel to laugh again as he reassured Barnes. 'Do not worry. She is a good woman. Because I want to help you that is enough for her—she wants to help you also. Certainly we are more happy to see your tank than we were to see the others.'

'The others?'

'Yes, a tremendous column of Germans which went on and on past our front door—huge tanks, big guns, armoured cars. I think it was a whole division.'

'When was this?'

'Six days ago—last Saturday. There have been others since, but they are mainly supply columns. The first one was the big one. Of course, you know that the Germans are in Abbeville?'

'We had heard a rumour,' said Barnes slowly.

'It is true, I fear. We may have a visitor from Abbeville later tonight—my other nephew, Jacques. He comes from Lemont near Dunkirk, where he lives with his father, but at the moment he is living with his married sister in Abbeville. He may have interesting news for you.'

'How will he get here—you're behind the German lines.'

'I know, but this is not like the last war. The Germans are in Abbeville but only with tanks and guns—so if you can get the petrol, and if you are crazy like Jacques, you can drive about as you wish so long as you avoid their road-blocks. He has already made the journey once and he said he might come to see us again tonight. It has become a game with him, but do not ask me how he gets the petrol—he will not even tell me. I am sure that he has stolen it from a German store.'

'He'll get shot.'

'Do not look so surprised—it may not be as difficult as you think. The Germans seem very short of troops to guard even important places like petrol and ammunition stores. The foot-sloggers—is not that the right word—the foot-sloggers have not caught up with the tanks yet. I was a foot-slogger myself once.'

Mandel nodded towards the fireplace where a frame hung above the mantelpiece. Inside the frame hung Mandel's Croix de Guerre, the medal polished, the ribbon faded. Barnes was frowning as he spoke.

'I find that hard to believe, Mandel—that they don't guard their ammunition dumps.'

'I did not say exactly that—I said that they have not enough troops to guard them properly, as with the petrol. You can ask Jacques yourself when he arrives, he learnt to speak English when he lived with a British family. You see, his father has ideas that one day the boy will be a great international advocate.'

'What happens when the Germans pass here, Mandel?'

'They make us stand by the roadside so that we can see how powerful they are.'

'Very good of them. Where are the nearest Allied troops now? Do you have any idea?'

'In Arras, I believe. You are going to Arras?'

'Possibly.'

'It would be suicide.' Mandel waved his knife. 'The German army is between here and Arras and the closer you get to the front line the more of them there are, naturally. You would do far better to go west beyond Cambrai and then turn north towards the Channel ports. That way you might just meet the Allies before you met the Boche.'

They went on talking and eating but still half Barnes's mind strained to hear any unusual sound outside the farmhouse. After spending days in the open with the tank he felt nervous indoors and he couldn't get out of his mind the thought of Bert lying unprotected in that outhouse. He was picking up his last piece of chicken when he saw Penn staring at his fork. Without a word, Marianne went to the oven at the far end of the kitchen and came back with a plate which she put in front of Penn. Mandel grinned.

'She kept his meal warm because she thought that would happen. When he sees other people eating his appetite returns.'

He raised his glass to Penn. '*Bon appetit!*'

While Penn wolfed down his chicken the others tackled their second course, an almost unlimited supply of cheese. Again Mandel returned to the question of which way Barnes should take in the morning and while he spoke Barnes listened without committing himself. Half an hour later they were all drinking strong bitter coffee when Etienne came into the room and spoke quickly, a hint of urgency in his voice. Mandel stood up.

'A car is coming along the road from the west at high speed. It may be Jacques, but I think you should hide.'

Mandel led the way out of the farmhouse and across a field with his torch, stopping as they reached a large haystack close to the road.

'Wait behind here until I call you. It is rather too early for Jacques but one never can tell—he drives like the devil. If it is him, I will come out and shout.'

'Should he know we are here?' queried Barnes.

'The last time he was here he spent the night with my brother who lives at Fontenoy, a village close to Beaucaire. But he did not sleep much—he was up half the night with some friends. They tied a piece of telephone wire across the road just high enough to catch a motor-cycle rider. The Germans always send such patrols ahead and they caught a fish. At seventeen-and-a-half he has killed his first German, the young devil.'

'Pretty risky, isn't it? You might get reprisals.'

'Like the last one, this war will last four years and we shall get many reprisals, and Jacques will join the army soon and will kill many more Germans. But it is spirit like his which will save France. Now, I must go. And don't mention any of this in front of Marianne—she doesn't know and sometimes she understands a little English!'

They could hear the car's engine as Mandel hurried away, the engine of a car being driven at recklessly high speed, and now the headlights were coming closer. Penn's voice whispered in the dark.

'These people seem all right.'

'Yes, you want to forget about Lebrun and his gang. It's

people like the Mandels we're fighting for. Keep well in—I hope to God this is Jacques.'

Jacques was more mature than Etienne, more heavily-built, and he had the face of a monkey, a monkey with jet-black hair. His eyes were intelligent and quick-moving and Barnes took to him at once as he shook hands all round with a firm grasp.

'Uncle has told me about you, Sergeant Barnes. The Germans are in Abbeville with their Panzers. I have just come from that town.'

'How did you manage to get here past the Germans?' Barnes asked quietly.

'By knowing the side roads very well, by keeping my eyes well open, by asking friends on the way what the situation was.'

By keeping his eyes well open. They were large eyes and they had the same look of the devil in them which Barnes had detected in Etienne, but they were bolder, more challenging, and now they seemed humorously to challenge Barnes to call him a liar.

'So you came most of the way by side roads?'

'No, sergeant.' Was there a hint of mockery in this young man's expression? Barnes thought so as the lad went on. 'I came most of the distance along the same main roads the Panzers have used, but I turned on to side roads to avoid road-blocks.'

'There are a lot of road-blocks?'

'There are three—all outside Abbeville. But you should not go through Cambrai. They have set up some kind of head-quarters in the town hall and there is a curfew at sunset. But no one takes any notice of it because they have so few troops to see that their orders are carried out.' He grinned. 'Even so, your tank will not be welcome in Cambrai.'

Damn! thought Barnes. I wish Mandel hadn't mentioned Bert to him. I'm sure he trusts too many people. He hesitated. It didn't seem quite the thing to cross-examine Mandel's nephew in front of them all. Marianne was washing up and

Reynolds was helping her while Penn sagged in the armchair. Mandel finished lighting his pipe and laughed.

'Go on, Sergeant Barnes, ask him questions. He expects it!'

'So apart from Cambrai and the three road-blocks the road to Abbeville is open?'

'It was for me this evening. I took side roads to miss the road-blocks and Cambrai but otherwise I came straight here. It was easy.'

'Are there many Germans in Abbeville?'

'The town is full of their tanks and guns.' He frowned, his black eyebrows close together, moving swiftly like a comedian's. 'That is not quite correct. Most of the tanks and guns were on the north side two days ago and I haven't been to that district since. There is a curfew, too.'

'When does the curfew start?'

'Half an hour before sunset and it goes on until half an hour after dawn. They have said they will shoot anyone they find outside during the curfew but that has not happened yet. I could take you towards Abbeville,' he added hopefully, 'and then you could turn north to Boulogne. The Allies are in Boulogne.'

'I should damned well hope so. What about German aircraft —are there a lot about during the daytime?'

'Yes, there are, but they fly very high. If there were many of you I think they might see you, but not just one tank if you are careful. There are many miles where you do not see any Germans except for the occasional supply column. And they will not be expecting you in this area,' he pointed out shrewdly.

'Thanks, Jacques. There may be some more questions I'll think of to ask you—you'll be staying here for the night, I suppose?'

'No,' interjected Mandel quickly, 'he will be staying with my brother at Fontenoy, but there is plenty of time to ask him as many questions as you wish.'

It wasn't a matter of more questions to be asked, but now he knew that Jacques wasn't going to spend the night at the farm, Barnes's mind was filled with foreboding, driving away in a flash the soothing effect of the food and the wine, forcing his tired brain to weigh and calculate just when he had hoped that for a few brief hours at least he would be able to relax, to recuperate from the terrible strain of the events of the past two days. The lad was probably loyal: Mandel seemed confident enough and the Frenchman was no fool. But was it only a question of loyalty? Supposing he went out again tonight with his friends on one of those wild escapades, that he was captured and interrogated, possibly even by the S.S.? Since there was nothing he could do about it he smiled amiably.

'That's all right. I've asked all the questions I can think of for the moment.'

Mandel offered them two bedrooms but Barnes firmly refused, saying they would sleep outside by the haystack in case the Germans arrived unexpectedly, and he suspected that Mandel was secretly relieved at his refusal. Before they left the house the farmer said that they must listen to the news bulletin and Barnes was interested to see that he automatically tuned in to London as though he regarded that source as being the most reliable at the moment. They listened in silence as the calm detached voice of Stuart Hibberd began speaking.

'. . . fighting in Boulogne.'

It was after eleven o'clock when they opened their bed-rolls which they had carried back from the tank after parking it, and they laid them out behind the haystack. As they arranged the blankets the moon was coming up and Barnes welcomed this pale illumination since it would make their watch on the road easier; he was by no means convinced that the Germans would announce their arrival with warning headlights. Firmly, he gave Penn his instructions.

'You get to bed and stay there—you'll have little enough sleep as it is.'

'When do I go on duty?'

'You don't—I'm sharing it with Reynolds.'

'And may I ask at what hour reveille will be blowing?'

'At dawn—four o'clock on the dot.'

'That's five hours away, which means you'd get two-and-a-

146

half hours' sleep each. It's not good enough. I'm afraid you're in for a touch of insubordination—I'm doing my whack.'

'And you're due for a whack on the head if you don't shut up. Get down and stay down—that's an order, Penn. If I need you, I'll wake you.'

He only had to wait a few minutes before Penn was fast asleep, dead to the world, lying on his left side to take the weight off his wound. He gave Reynolds his orders.

'You go down as well. I'll do two-and-a-half hours and then wake you at one-thirty. After I've gone down you're to wake me at four—we must be away very early tomorrow. While you're on guard it's just a matter of keeping a sharp eye along the road in both directions. Down you go.'

A few minutes later and with some trepidation he watched Jacques drive away towards Beaucaire in his four-seater green Renault, still unable to rid himself of the feeling that this was the fly in the ointment. Physically, he was having an awful time keeping on his feet and he walked up and down the moon-lit road to take his mind off his gently throbbing wound, realizing now that it would have probably been wiser to change the dressing, but his brain went on racing round. They'd have to head north for the Boulogne-Calais area, not so far from where Jacques came from. It would mean the devil of a right-hand sweep, west and then north, and he doubted whether they'd ever make it, but at least on the way they might meet some really worthwhile objective. The search for some massive objective against which they could deal the Germans a hammer-blow was now looming larger in Barnes's mind than finding a way back to the Allied lines. The position was becoming terribly serious, the news bulletin proved that. It was a warm muggy night and this didn't help to keep him on the alert. He'd be glad when morning came, and then they could get on with it. As he paced up and down Barnes had a strong feeling that this was the last haven of peace they would find, that from tomorrow they would be in the thick of it all the way.

Shortly after midnight the lights in the farmhouse went out and he heard a window open and then close. It was probably Mandel listening to him pacing up and down. In the distance he could still hear the mutter of those guns, but just before it was time to wake Reynolds the guns stopped, and this disturbed Barnes greatly as though it were an omen of disaster. He woke up Reynolds and settled down to sleep under the stars, which seemed far bigger than usual. An hour later he was still awake, his mind twitching with anxiety, then without knowing it he fell asleep. The emergency he had feared came just after dawn.

THE TANK EMERGED from the outhouse into the eery light of the false dawn. It seemed to kick up the devil of a row as it moved slowly down the stony track, following the beams of the headlights which made the pale grey gloom even weirder. Across the fields coils of mist floated above the ground and a curtain of vapour fogged the beams.

They had risen at four like ghosts in a half-world, bleary eyed, thick-tongued, thirsty, hardly able to carry their bedrolls along the stony track, but they had the world to themselves, a world which was dark and chilly. They had brewed-up, drunk their tea and, at Barnes' insistence, had a shave. After the tea and the shave they had begun to revive sufficiently to eat some of the remaining bully beef and a packet of biscuits which Reynolds had quietly kept for an emergency. There was general agreement that the morning qualified. The horizon was a faint line against a bleak glow when they drove out of the building and along the track. Barnes already realized that Penn had not benefited from his night's rest to anything like the extent he had hoped and the corporal's peevishness had confirmed this.

'What about the Mandels?' he had asked. 'Are you running off and leaving them without a word of thanks?'

'Of course not. We'll park Bert by the road and then I'll pop back to see them.'

As they moved down the track he saw that lights had appeared in the upper windows of the farmhouse. Mandel must have heard them coming. It seemed ungrateful not to warn him the night before of their plans for a very early start but

Jacques had been there until they had left the farmhouse. Rubbing his arm to get the chill out of his bones Barnes looked both ways along the road and saw nothing. It would be an enormous relief when they had left the Mandels in peace. Within ten minutes they would be on their way towards Abbeville. He had chosen that route because it was the only one they had heard to be clear of traffic. They were very close to the farmhouse when he stiffened, swore, and gave the order.

'Halt! Lights off!'

From the direction of Beaucaire tiny headlights glowed in the distance, just one pair. They'd have to let the vehicle go past without seeing them. He issued more orders and the tank moved across the field until it was completely hidden by the dim bulk of the haystack, when he ordered a halt. Standing in the turret behind the stack he saw that the top was at least six feet above his head and when he leant far out from the rim his fingers touched the edges of projecting hay. Jumping down, he checked the front and rear: there was at least four feet of stack which concealed the tank from the road at either end. It was just a question of letting this early bird drive past before he went to see Mandel. He might even be able to buy some food off the farmer.

Going down on one knee behind the rear track he waited, feeling the early morning dew soak through his trousers, gripping the revolver in his right hand. His brain was becoming very alert now as he watched the headlights growing larger, a sense of alarm beginning to sting his nerves: this could be trouble, but at least there was only one car. Pull yourself together, Barnes—one car could contain four Germans armed with machine-pistols. Climbing up on to the hull he told Penn to hand him up a machine-pistol, then he resumed his position behind the track. The car was very close now, moving at a tremendous speed, probably well over sixty. Tension built up inside him like the crackle of electricity. Thank God he had got them up early. With a scream of brakes the car turned off the road, headlights sweeping over the rear of the tank, then it stopped.

Had they seen the tank? The headlights had continued in their ninety-degree turn without a quiver, but a strong-willed driver might manage that. The slam of the car door. Footsteps. A solitary figure reached the front door and hammered on it like a German drill-sergeant demanding entry. Barnes lifted the gun as the front door opened, shedding a pool of light into the yard and then closing again. Could it be Jacques? The parked car looked like a Renault although in this weird light it was difficult to tell. He wasn't at all sure that there weren't other people inside the darkened car. He'd better check this.

He ran, racing forward until he reached the side of the house out of sight of the car, creeping along the wall to a window which showed light behind curtains. He couldn't see through the material but faintly he heard voices, one of them excited. This voice was doing most of the talking. Cautiously he crept towards the front of the house and as he reached the corner he heard the front door open. Footsteps came into the yard. He froze.

'Sergeant Barnes, it's only Jacques. He's brought some news, some alarming news. Barnes!'

'Here, Mandel.'

He stepped out into the courtyard, lowering his machine-pistol, and when Mandel saw it he must have recognized the gun since he looked at it in surprise but without comment. Beside him stood Jacques, his chin unshaven and his collar open, while Etienne waited in the floodlit doorway. Mandel hurried forward, his shirt only half-tucked inside his trousers, speaking quickly.

'There is great trouble. From his bedroom in Fontenoy, Jacques can see across the fields to Beaucaire—or rather to the road here from Beaucaire—and he heard something early this morning. Then he saw a lot of lights so he walked across the fields and hid behind a hedge close to these lights. A large German column has reached Beaucaire, has come round it to the south, you understand, and camped on this side of the town . . .'

'Camped?'

'No, that is the wrong word. Apparently it has halted for a

151

short time. When they move again they must come this way—past here.'

'What makes him say it has only halted for a short time?'

Jacques stepped forward, his manner so different from the night before that he seemed a different person. He spoke urgently.

'May I explain? It is part of a Panzer division—the usual big tanks and guns. It has to come this way and may move at any time. They are using this route as their highway to the west—but can you keep ahead of them?'

'We'll have to. We'd better start at once. Mandel, can I buy some food off you or are you short yourselves?'

'Etienne.' Mandel turned and took a parcel from his nephew and handed it to Barnes. 'Take this—my wife packed it before we went to bed last night. No, any suggestion of payment will be taken as an insult. Now you must go!'

Thanking him, Barnes tucked the parcel under his arm and ran back to the tank. The three Mandels followed him and waited while he climed into the turret, put on his headset and gave Reynolds the order to start the engines. While he waited he looked down and saw grey stubble on Mandel's chin. Looking back in the growing light he could see no sign of traffic on the road from Beaucaire. The engines coughed, sputtered, and died. Barnes said nothing and waited. Reynolds tried again. The engines repeated their surly reaction. Mandel put his hands on his hips and waited. They all waited while Reynolds fought desperately to start the motors. Five minutes later the dawn light was spreading gradually over the fields and now there was a glint of gold in the east. Soon it would be broad daylight. Reynolds tried again and again but not once did the engines give any sign of activating. Patiently, Mandel stood waiting without showing any traces of alarm but the two lads were now staring fixedly along the road to the east.

'No good?' Barnes called down from the turret to Reynolds.

The driver's head inside the hatch turned to look up. 'I think it's the starter system.'

'Do your best—that Panzer column may be here soon.'

'I'll still have to look at the starter wiring.'

'How long do you think it will take?'

Immediately he regretted the question. How on earth could Reynolds be expected to predict that? It was the sign of only anxiety Barnes had allowed himself to show.

'Could be two minutes, could be two hours. I noticed it was coughing nastily when we came down that track.'

'Have another go before you start checking.' Barnes leaned over the turret to speak to Jacques. 'What exactly made you think the column would be on the move soon?'

'The men in the tanks hadn't left them—they were eating a meal and they had stayed in the towers to eat.'

Barnes looked down at Mandel. 'That sounds as though it's just a short stop and then they'll be coming this way.'

'I think so, too.'

'We'll have a few more shots at starting.'

Reynolds was persisting non-stop now and while he struggled to coax life out of Bert it became daylight. Again no one spoke. Barnes stared backwards at the distant hill crest which was now clearly to be seen, the crest over which the Panzers would appear. Jacques and Etienne stood stock still, hands in their pockets to keep warm. Only Mandel was moving during the agonizing wait when nerves were stretched and a fresh chill, the chill of fear, seeped into the waiting men. Walking round the haystack, Mandel disappeared from view and then reappeared at the other side in front of the tank. His face was thoughtful, his thick brow scowling, and he looked at the tank closely and then spoke quickly to Etienne. The lad ran away across the field to an outhouse just behind the farm.

'Sergeant, it's no good,' said Reynolds firmly. 'I've got to have a look at the engines. It may take quite a while.'

'Just do the best you can as quickly as possible.'

He had just finished speaking when he heard the purr of a motor. Turning round, he saw Etienne emerging from the building as he drove a large orange-coloured machine towards them. In front of the machine a huge power-grab shovel was hoisted at an angle, wobbling as it moved closer. Mandel came forward and stood directly under the turret.

'The tank will not move. Is that not so?'

'Not yet, anyway.'

'And the German tank column will soon be on the move and will pass here?'

'That seems pretty evident,' Barnes replied irritably.

'So the only solution is to hide the tank. Is that not so?'

'You can't shift it with that power-grab machine. This tank weighs twenty-six and a half tons and you won't budge it an inch with that thing. You're pretty well-equipped out here, aren't you?' he added.

'I borrow it from a wealthy neighbour to clear my ditches. Now, I agree that this machine won't move your tank, Sergeant Barnes. So we must proceed logically—we must leave the tank where it is and yet still hide it. That is the only possible solution.'

'I don't follow you.'

'We shall have to turn it into something else—a haystack.'

'How the devil are you going to manage that?'

'This haystack is constructed of square bales of hay which have been placed on top of each other—this method makes it easier for us to take away only a small portion of the stack when we require it. The bales were lifted up by the power-grab, as you call it. All we have to do is to take the haystack to pieces and then rebuild it round the tank which will, of course, sit in the hollow inside it. But we must start at once—all of us helping.'

'Even if it would work there may not be time.'

'It will be much quicker than you think. Etienne!'

He poured forth a stream of French as Barnes told Reynolds to help Penn out of the tank. Between them they got him sat down on the grass and by now Etienne was working the grab to Mandel's instructions. To start with he tackled the corner of the stack nearest the road, driving the machine forward, inserting the huge metal hand and emerging with a bale of hay which he dumped on the ground. Immediately he began repeating the process as Mandel developed his idea.

'We leave the wall of hay next to the tank because we can use that where it is. To surround the tank will take a lot of

154

hay but there will be plenty left over by the hollow inside. We shall use that hay to build the roof over the tank.'

While he was talking Etienne was moving more bales, dropping them at random as he attacked the haystack ferociously along the side nearest the road. Barnes looked again towards the east. In the light of day the deserted highway bore a sinister aspect and he could just picture the scene. One moment it would be still like this, a peaceful scene devoid of traffic: then the first tank would crawl over the crest and head towards them, followed by a whole armada of Panzers. And if they found the tank here all the Mandels might well be shot. He made up his mind.

'We'll try it. Penn, your job is to watch that hill crest. At the first sign of movement bellow like the bull of Bashan. Reynolds, stop tinkering with that engine, there's work to do.'

Between them, Barnes and Mandel organized a work system: while Etienne dismantled the stack on one side, Reynolds and Jacques began lifting bales of hay and moving them to form a wall parallel to the rear of the tank. At the same time Barnes and Mandel formed a second team, carrying their own bales to build a wall across the front of the tank. Even here, Mandel was showing foresight.

'If the Panzers arrive too soon,' he explained, 'we may at least have two walls up. If we were very lucky they might not see the open back.'

'Let's hope we don't have to be that lucky.'

Half an hour later it all seemed to be taking too long to Barnes. The Germans would arrive and catch them in the middle of it. He urged everyone to move faster. It was still chilly but they were all working feverishly, their jackets lying on the ground as they heaved the huge bales up, balancing the load between them, staggering across to the walls to lay their new 'bricks', and then going straight back for another load. The two side walls were still only half-built when Marianne appeared with a tray of coffee. Laying it on the ground she watched them working for a minute and then went indoors without a word. Mandel grinned across a bale at Barnes.

'You have misunderstood her—she knows that when men

are working women must keep out of the way. She is the same when she brings us wine in the fields.'

'She must be worried, though.'

'We are all worried. So let us finish building our new hay-stack and then we can stop worrying.'

He's wrong there, Barnes thought. If we do get the job done in time the big worry will then start—will the Germans find the tank? He glanced towards where Penn stood leaning against a fence as he stared towards the ominous hill crest. They're going to catch us in the middle of this, Barnes felt sure of it.

'Mandel, whether we get the tank hidden or not in time I think you should clear out until the Germans have gone—take your family into the fields.'

'We could hide, certainly—and if they come too early we shall. But if we have finished, then we must stay. It would look strange if the place was deserted at this hour of the day.'

'No, it won't. People are fleeing all over France.'

'Yes, my friend, but they take things with them. Anyone who goes inside our house will see that we have taken nothing and will know we are hiding. They might well burn down the house. And do not forget Jacques' car—that will show someone is about.'

'Hide that in the outhouse where we hid Bert.'

They had laid the fresh bale on top of the wall in front of the tank, a wall which was now about the same height as the rear wall Reynolds and Jacques were building, and so far both walls only concealed half the hull. It was all taking far too long.

'Your idea about the car is good,' said Mandel. 'If they ask to see Jacques' papers they will see that he comes from Lemont and may wonder why he is here—so take him with you when you hide and I will get him to move the car at once.'

An hour later they were making tremendous progress, encouraged by the sight of the tank sinking lower and lower behind the walls of hay. The work had been considerably speeded up by Etienne who had now completed dismantling three-quarters of the haystack and was using his power-grab to transport the loose bales right up to the walls, so that all the others had to do was to manoeuvre the 'bricks' into position. Soon the end walls were finished and within another half hour the rear wall was over five feet high: even at the back only the turret still protruded, looking rather like the conning tower of an invisible submarine submerged in a sea of hay. They were all working in a frenzy now, standing on the rear wall, on the hull of the tank as they wrestled the bales into position, never stopping for a moment. The unspoken thought that they might just fail for the sake of a few bales gave added impetus to their efforts and now Mandel and Reynolds worked stripped to the waist, their bodies running with sweat in the warm sunshine. It was going to be another lovely day—for the Germans.

There had been no traffic along the main road since they had started, not even a farm cart, and this puzzled Barnes until he mentioned it to Mandel who laughed grimly.

'No one comes this way at the moment because they know that the Panzers use the highway, so what happens? My neighbours go miles out of their way along side roads when they could use this road easily, but they will not risk the Panzers.'

'What happens when the Panzers meet something?'

'If they meet a vehicle or catch it up they tip it into the ditch. Nothing must stop the progress of the Panzers. That is why people are keeping away from here. You see, Sergeant Barnes, soon we shall be finished.'

With the four walls completed they turned to the final task —the roofing-in of the new structure. Putting the icing on the cake, as Mandel called it. From this stage Barnes and Reynolds stood on top of the walls while Etienne handed up bales with the power-grab. It proved to be a more difficult stage than they had anticipated, because first they had to fill in the area round the turret, dropping bales down on to the hull and tracks and fitting these in round the gun. The gun was a nuisance because they had to wedge in bales round the long barrel and it slowed them down, but they persisted and then suddenly they had done the job. The drawback was that they ended up with an irregular roof which looked strange; once again Mandel came up with the solution, telling Etienne to use the power-grab in a certain way. Standing back on the road Barnes watched as the machine moved forward, the grab hoisted to its highest elevation. When it stopped Etienne brought the shovel down full force again and again, hammering the roof of hay flat. When he had completed the job even Barnes had to agree that from the road the haystack looked perfectly normal and he could hardly believe that Bert nestled inside the new structure. Then his eyes dropped to the ground in front of the stack and his mouth tightened. The earth was littered with hay relics and flattened dead grass which described a neat rectangle clearly locating the original site of the stack.

'Mandel—the Germans will see that. It's a dead giveaway.'

'All has been prepared. Do not worry. You will see!'

Reynolds and Etienne were now walking slowly back from the farm and between them they carried an enormous tarpaulin which they proceeded to spread over the marked area under Mandel's guidance. When it was in place the farmer began pulling hay from underneath the sheet and throwing it at random over the top.

'Now it means nothing. Perfect camouflage! This cover could have slipped off the haystack or been pulled off to let the sun dry the stack out. So now we can go inside and wait for them.'

'I still think you ought to hide in the fields with us.'

'No, we shall stay here to welcome them. More camouflage! So long as we line up on the roadside acknowledging their achievements they are quite happy. You will come in for some wine?'

'No, I'll wait here and relieve Penn. Why is Etienne dumping those spare bales in your yard?'

'To create a diversion. If something exciting is happening when they arrive it will take their minds off other things—including that haystack. Leave this to me and do not worry if you see signs of fire when the Boche comes. Marianne will bring a glass of wine to you and inside we shall drink a toast. To the tank!'

Barnes went into the middle of the road and waited alone as he watched the deserted hill crest. Supposing that after all

158

their trouble the Panzers didn't come? But they were halted on this side of Beaucaire and he remembered that apart from one or two country lanes there had been no major road leading off this one. Could they possibly get away with it? He looked at the stack again, amazed by its appearance of normality. Just so long as they didn't start pushing bayonets into it, although it would need a pretty long bayonet to reach Bert through those walls. And this, he thought, is a method of camouflage you won't find in the text-books.

Frequently he looked behind him along the road towards Cambrai and then he looked up into the brilliantly blue morning sky. Not a cloud anywhere, but more important still, not a plane either. Again, it was hard to believe there was a war on. A few minutes later, at 7.15 a.m., he was running at top speed towards the house when he met Marianne on her way out with a glass of wine, a glass he knew that he would never drink. He had just seen the first German tank coming over the hill crest.

They lay full length in a ditch some distance from the house but at a point where Barnes could still see it. The ditch was dry and disused and thick with tall weeds. A German would have to be on top of them before there was the remotest chance of their being spotted, and the ditch was a long way from anywhere. A long way from the road and a long way from the outhouse where the Renault was now hidden. Penn, Jacques and Reynolds were sprawled out along the ditch behind him and the machine-pistol rested in front of his chest. Barnes had deliberately placed Jacques between the two men because he was fairly sure that they would have to lie there for two or three hours and he had no knowledge of the lad's endurance. When he had taken Reynolds aside his instructions had been quite precise.

'If he gets panicky and there's no other way out—knock him on the head with your revolver butt.'

Through a clump of weeds Barnes could see the farmhouse and a section of the road. The view looked incredibly peaceful, a pastoral scene with not a soul in sight. His eye fell on the haystack, an innocent piece of furniture one might expect to find anywhere out in the country. For the second time in twelve hours Bert was all on his own. He stiffened. From the road beyond the house he heard the high-pitched engine sound of a motor-cycle: a patrol must have overtaken the leading tank and roared on ahead. A cycle with a sidecar came into view, turned, and drove out of sight into the farmyard. Penn kept his voice down as he spoke, although it wasn't necessary.

'Have they arrived?'

'Just a motor-bike and sidecar. They've gone into the yard.'

'Let's hope Mandel can handle them.'

'He'll handle them all right just so long as they don't start investigating that haystack.'

'Something's smoking—look, just beyond the roof.' Penn rested his chin on the edge of the ditch. 'They can't have set the place on fire already.'

'Got it! The artful old devil set fire to those spare bales Etienne dumped in the yard. That's his diversion to keep them occupied.'

For the first time Barnes wondered what rank Mandel had attained during the First World War.

'Any sign of the two Jerries?' inquired Penn.

'No, they must still be at the house . . . keep your head down! Tell the others.'

Along the road from behind the house the first German heavy tank appeared, its commander erect in the turret. The machine seemed to glide along the highway and across the field they could hear the low grumble of its revolving tracks. He estimated the vehicle's speed at fifteen miles an hour and the gun barrel was elevated at an angle of about ten degrees. Another tank moved into view, then another and another. They were certainly in a hurry to get somewhere and he was surprised that they were not spaced farther apart. The column's commander was either foolhardy or else he had very good reason to know that they risked no danger of air attack. Grimly he watched the enemy tanks and then thought of the Mandels again.

What on earth was happening at the farm? There had been no sign of the Mandels and the motor-cycle patrol was still on the premises. Gradually, the smoke from the fire died down until only a thin wisp rose above the rooftop. By the side of the machine-pistol lay Barnes's field glasses but he was reluctant to use them except in an emergency—the sun could so easily reflect off the lenses and if one of those commanders in the turrets spotted it the fat would be in the fire. He settled himself down to a long wait. Providing all went well at the farm there wasn't a great deal of risk to fear: it was largely a matter of patience, of waiting for the enemy to go away. This comfortable thought had just passed through his mind when he heard the plane.

Instantly he was reminded of the machine which had spied out the ground for the Panzers crossing the country south of Fontaine. He would always remember that place as Fontaine. His body tensed, his nerves twanged as he realized the implications, and he could have kicked himself for his complacency. The element of comparative safety had now been turned into one of maximum danger. He could tell that the plane was flying very low, and from the way its engine sound faded and then grew louder he guessed that it was travelling in a circle. It was the one hazard which he should have foreseen, the one which had completely escaped him. Turning on his side he spoke rapidly over his shoulder.

'It's a spotter plane, probably flying very low. From now on no one moves a whisker. Pass it on.'

'I'm the only one with a whisker to move,' said Penn.

From observation on land they were completely concealed but aerial observation was quite a different matter. There were four of them stretched out close together and the machine sounded to be only a few hundred feet up. They should still escape detection so long as they remained motionless, but in that still empty countryside only a small movement at the wrong moment could easily locate them. Pressing his body into the ditch. Barnes slowly turned his head to one side until he could see a narrow oblong of pure blue sky. The plane was very close now, almost on top of them from the sound, then it flashed into view. It was barely two hundred feet up, so low that he could see the outline of the pilot's helmet, a helmet which was tilted downwards. Then it vanished. Barnes wet his lips and then stiffened again. The plane was turning to come back again. Surely they couldn't have been spotted so quickly? Unless someone had moved. Jacques flashed into his mind and he stifled a groan. If he had moved Reynolds could hardly have warned the lad in time, the damage would have been done. Yes, it was definitely turning back, coming closer. What on earth could have attracted the pilot's attention? Suddenly he went ice-cold as the reason for the pilot's return flashed through his brain. *He was coming back to examine the haystack.*

With an awful clarity Barnes saw their fatal mistake. He had personally checked the appearance of the stack from the road which had seemed the obvious danger point. But he had forgotten the air! In his mind he relived the final stages of the camouflage operation. The roof of the stack had looked bumpy so Etienne had used the power-grab shovel to flatten the top. Supposing some of the bales had sunk into the hollow, perhaps falling down into a space between the tank and the hay walls? It could easily have happened and this meant that from the air Bert was now exposed to view. Penn's finger tapped him on the shoulder.

'Anything wrong? I saw your hand grip the pistol.'

'No,' said Barnes firmly, 'but keep absolutely still. That plane's coming back.'

Even though he couldn't see it yet he could hear it quite clearly now. The machine was describing another circle, but this time it was a smaller circle, a circle whose centre could well be the farmhouse—or the haystack. Very slowly, inch by inch, he raised his head above ditch level, taking care not to disturb the weeds. The Mandels, all three of them, were out standing by the roadside as a self-propelled gun rolled past. There was no sign of the motor-cycle patrol which must have driven off while his head was buried in the ditch. He studied the Mandels, trying to tell something from the way they stood. Then between the weeds the plane darted into view, flying straight towards him across the road. He kept perfectly still, resisting the temptation to duck. As it went over the Mandels looked up and then dutifully turned their gaze back to the road as another heavy tank rolled past. The commander's head was turned towards them. Had he made some remark? The spotter plane swooped even lower and roared over their heads. What had caught his attention?

He tried to put himself in the position of the pilot. What would he do? At his first sight of the tank inside its huge box of hay he would hardly believe his eyes, so he would circle in again for a closer look, which could well be the operation he had just completed. Then he would circle again and come in for a third and final look before he wirelessed the commander of the column. At least that's the way I'd handle it, Barnes told himself grimly. Had the plane gone away? He strained his ears for the sound of its engine. His wound was throbbing badly this morning and lying in that fixed position he could feel his right knee stiffening, the knee which had struck the underwater rock. No, the bloody plane hadn't gone away—it was coming back now for the third time round. It flew directly over the haystack and headed straight for him, waggling its wings from side to side. Why the waggle? Was it a signal? He felt stiff, clammy and sweat-soaked. They were trapped and all they could do was to wait inside the trap, hoping that these alarming manoeuvres of the plane had some other explanation. It passed directly over them and turned back to follow its familiar course. Still counting, he watched the endless column of vehicles move past to the west.

It was only ten minutes later when he was still waiting for a plane that never reappeared that he grasped the fact that Bert had not been spotted. For over an hour he refused to accept the idea completely, expecting that at any moment the haystack would be surrounded, but still the column rolled past and still the Mandels patiently witnessed its progress. Just how many Panzers did the Germans possess? He made a rough-and-ready estimate of what they had seen since leaving Etreux and then doubled it, arriving at the conclusion that the German High Command must be deploying three or four full-equipped Panzer divisions in northern France.* The B.E.F.

* Barnes underestimated. General von Rundstedt's Army Group A deployed seven Panzer divisions—over two thousand armoured vehicles.

complement was one tank brigade and one tank regiment. A tap on his back told him that Penn wanted to speak.

'I thought you might like to know, sergeant, that I've got ants crawling all over me and cramp in my leg. It's nothing to worry about, mind you, but I knew you'd want to know.'

'Good of you to keep me informed, Penn.'

'I'll be issuing regular bulletins from now on.'

The ants were crawling over Barnes, too, crawling inside his uniform. He had first felt the tickle of their tiny bodies when the plane was flying over, at the very moment when they had to lie as still as death. Since then he had been constantly aware of this minute enemy. Lying full length in the ditch there was no way of ejecting them and by now the tickling sensation had invaded the lower part of his body, crawling over his stomach and his groin until he thought that he would go mad if this went on much longer. Penn tapped him on the shoulder again.

'I haven't heard anything recently . . . what's that?'

'The end of the column's gone, I think. A staff car's just stopped . . .'

'It's probably the general—they always ride at the rear of the column!'

'The officer's just gone into the house with the Mandels. It shouldn't be long now—the driver's stayed with the car.'

Fortunately Barnes was too far away to hear the conversation which had preceded the Mandels' return to their home, otherwise his mind might have been racked with anxiety.

Outwardly Mandel showed no traces of alarm as the staff car slowed down and then stopped. His expression was sleepy, the hands by his sides limp, but he sensed that just at the moment when he had thought all would be well fate had dealt him a bad hand. The major who sat by his driver's side was immaculately dressed, his uniform newly pressed, the peaked cap resting squarely on his head. He stared down the road after the tail of the Panzer column when he first spoke, presenting them a profile which might have been carved out of stone. His French was highly guttural.

'I trust that you are now convinced of the invincibility of the German army after what you have seen?'

'We could hardly fail to be,' Mandel replied quietly.

'Good, good.' The major stood up, got out of his car, closed the door and stared down at Mandel from his great height. 'You still have plenty to eat?'

'We have sufficient for the moment, but as to later . . .' He spread his hands and dropped them.

'And to drink?'

'For the moment, just enough.'

'Good, good. Aren't you going to ask me inside? I may even furnish you with a certificate saying you are reliable citizens. That could come in useful when the next column arrives. There have been cases of French civilians firing on German troops and some commanders are a trifle hasty in their judgement.'

Without a word Mandel turned and led the way into the farmyard, his face still expressionless. When he reached the front door he stopped to let his wife and Etienne enter first and then waited for the German officer. The major had stopped in the middle of the yard to take a cigarette from a gold case. While he lit it he looked towards the remnants of burnt hay.

'I see that you have had a fire here very recently.'

'It started just before your column arrived—two of your men very kindly helped us to put it out.'

'That does not surprise me—in spite of what the lying British propagandists say the German soldier is always chivalrous. Now you will be able to tell your friends the truth in future.'

Mandel made no reply and the officer stood for a minute looking round him while he smoked. Gazing at the haystack he pointed with the cigarette.

'It is a good thing something like that didn't catch fire—that would be a tragedy for you, I'm sure.'

'We take care not to smoke near it,' said Mandel, feeling it wiser to make some reply.

'Ah well, we must not keep your good lady waiting. And I'm sure she dislikes smoking inside her house.'

He threw down his smoking cigarette among some pieces of

165

straw which began to burn almost at once. Seeing that there was no danger of the fire spreading Mandel walked after the German and found him standing in the kitchen looking at the framed decoration above the mantelpiece.

'The Croix de Guerre! I am in the presence of an old soldier then. I imagine you earned this fighting in the last war?'

'Probably at the same time as you obtained the Iron Cross on your tunic,' Mandel replied politely.

The officer glanced at him quickly, fingering the cross. Marianne stood by the table, her arms folded over her chest as she stared out of the window across the fields. Mandel wished that she had gone upstairs but he was aware that she was staying in the hope of keeping down the temperature. By her side Etienne gazed into the fireplace. The major spoke abruptly, his voice harsh.

'You said you had plenty to drink. Since my men so kindly helped you to put out the fire I think they should be suitably rewarded. Would you not agree? Two or three bottles of cognac would be acceptable, I'm sure.'

So that's it, Mandel thought, he's after loot. And they make a man like this an officer. Since he's a heavy cognac drinker his temper is probably uncertain. I'll have to watch this carefully.

'I have no cognac, major, but possibly a bottle of wine or two? Would your men prefer red or white, do you think?'

'They would prefer cognac.' His voice was a whiplash now. He stood very erect, his nostrils flared, his eyes glowing. 'Since you say you are running short we will give them three bottles only, which is a meagre enough reward. Had the fire spread this house might have been burnt down. And understand this, my men are here to fight a war—not to help profiteering French farmers save their capital!'

'I'm sorry—you can search the place. We have wine but no cognac. Not a single bottle.'

The German eyed him grimly. 'You hid it when the first column came through here. I have little doubt of that.'

Casually, he unbuttoned the flap of his leather hip holster and withdrew the pistol, holding it sideways in one hand, the muzzle pointing towards Marianne. Mandel moved quickly in front of her, while behind him his wife slipped a hand towards her throat. He saw Etienne's eyes on the heavy poker in the fireplace and almost imperceptibly he frowned, giving a little shake of his head. Knowing that at any moment there might be a tragedy he took the initiative quickly.

'Major, the cupboard in that corner is full of wine—may I show you and then you can make your choice?'

Slowly he moved towards the cupboard and the pistol turned away from Marianne to point at the wall. Without further hesitation Mandel threw open both doors and started lifting out bottles on to the table. The German waited until a dozen stood in a row and then he put away his gun.

'That will have to do if you persist in being obstinate. You and the boy—bring all the bottles on the table out to my car.'

They hurried out across the yard, three bottles under each arm, while the officer followed slowly. The driver snapped something at them, indicating that they should store the bottles on the back seat. When they had emptied their arms he leaned over and pulled a greatcoat across the bottles to conceal them. The major had left the yard now and strolled along the road to stand close to the haystack. He looked at it with interest while he extracted a fresh cigarette and lit it in a leisurely fashion. Mandel sent Etienne away to the farmhouse and waited tensely, feeling quite sure that their ordeal was not ended yet. From the direction of Beaucaire a motorcycle patrol drove up, slowing down and then speeding away as the officer waved them on. The driver had started the engine of the staff car but the major seemed in no hurry to depart: in fact, the haystack appeared to fascinate him and he began to walk round it as he took short puffs at his cigarette.

Nothing shows, Mandel told himself, nothing shows at all. He cannot possibly suspect anything so why is he taking such a great interest in it? With a tremendous effort he compelled himself to assume an attitude of complete indifference, even going so far as to clasp his hands over his stomach while he looked up at the sky as though checking the weather situation. The major had walked right round the haystack now and he made a small gesture with his free hand. Driving forward, the car pulled up close to the officer who now stood with his back to the road facing the haystack. Again he spoke without looking at Mandel.

'I do fear that the cognac you so stubbornly concealed is going to prove a most expensive proposition.'

Raising his right hand he aimed with great care, tossing the burning cigarette high in the air so that when it fell it landed out of sight on top of the stack. Then he stood and waited, one hand close to his holster flap, studying Mandel's face closely. Appalled, the Frenchman showed only the reaction expected. Hanging his shoulders, he gazed at the stack in glum despair, then very slowly he turned away and walked back to the farmhouse, forcing himself not to hurry, hoping that by removing himself from the scene of the conflagration the German would lose interest and go away.

The officer stood watching the top of the stack which was now crackling and spluttering, suddenly flaring up until the entire roof was a crown of flames. Satisfied, he got back into his seat and the car drove off at a high speed.

Only by exerting his will-power far beyond its normal limits was Barnes able to keep himself pressed down inside the ditch. He had seen the German officer studying the stack, he had even seen that he was smoking because now he risked using his field glasses. But as if some telepathic intuition had been transmitted between them he had understood Mandel's action when he slowly trailed back to the house. Seen from this greater distance the burning stack presented an even more alarming spectacle as grey-black smoke billowed in a huge cloud above the road, and from where he lay Barnes could see red tongues of flame licking their way along the full length of the roof of hay. He felt Penn stirring as Mandel walked away.

'We'd better get moving—we've got to try and put that lot out. We can shoot those two while we're about it.'

'Keep yourself down,' Barnes rasped. 'We're not moving till that staff car is well on its way.'

'You've got the machine-pistol,' Penn protested. 'And we've got our revolvers.'

'And they've got their car, you idiot. As soon as they see us coming they'll drive off and then be back with half that column.'

It wasn't only the unit he was thinking of. More important still he had no intention of putting the Mandels into further danger, no matter what the cost. And the cost could be very high.

'You're just going to let Bert burn?' Penn protested again.

'The car's off now. No one gets up till I give the word.'

Lifting himself cautiously only a few feet, his body still well-concealed behind the weeds, he watched the car racing away. When it reached the next hill crest and vanished he started running, running as he had never run before, keeping easily ahead of the others in spite of his smallness. The stack was roofed with flames, flames which drove the smoke several feet above the top of the stack. He was drawing close to the conflagration when he heard the power-grab coming across the field, moving forward so fast that the elevated arm was swaying wildly. They were all arriving at once—Etienne with the power-grab, Barnes, Mandel hauling and heaving desperately at a huge coil of hosepipe.

'Give Reynolds the grab,' Barnes shouted. 'I'll take that hose. Leave this to us—the tank is full of diesel and it may blow at any minute. Get back inside the house.'

'No!' Mandel shouted back. 'Etienne knows how to use the grab. Help me with this hose. It will take all of us to save it. The tank, I mean—the stack is gone.'

Marianne came running forward with several pitch-forks and Mandel told her to drop them and go straight back to the house. It was developing into a horrible muddle until Barnes took charge. Pitch-forks for Reynolds and Jacques. Etienne was left to work the grab. Barnes began to unloop the hose while Mandel fixed the other end to an outlet pipe from a small pump-house. While he worked Barnes was shouting instructions for Mandel to pass on to Etienne.

'Get Etienne to scoop the burning bales off the top—he's to drop them well clear of the stack so the men with forks can carry them to the road. But the grab must be used to clear off the burning hay. I'll hose down the lower walls—we'll never save the top.'

They worked like demons. As Barnes directed the powerful jet of water on the lower walls he tried to keep an eye on the spread of the fire, scared stiff that at any moment the fuel tanks would go up, wondering whether there had been a blow-back of fire from the top down into the hollow interior, a disaster which might not be seen until the whole stack suddenly burst into flames. And there was high-explosive inside that inferno—seventy rounds of two-pounder shells and ten boxes of Besa ammunition. He was close to the front wall now, spraying his jet in a steady arc, while nearby the grab was scooping up burning masses of hay above his head and throwing them clear. As the scorching bales hit the ground they crackled and spat angrily like live things. The heat was almost unbearable and Barnes was shielding his face with one hand while he held the bucking hose in the other, hardly able to see was was happening as acrid smoke filled his lungs and blinded his eyes. Behind him the men with pitch-forks were skewering the burning bales and carrying them over to the road where they dumped them and then ran back for more. Each bale was so heavy and unmanageable that it took two men to spear one bale and then lift it between them, and unknown to Barnes his corporal had seized a fork and formed a team with Mandel, holding the fork low down because he found it impossible to lift his right arm.

The turret of the tank was visible now, again protruding strangely like the conning tower of a submarine, but this time like a submarine trapped in a sea of burning oil. It gave Barnes a pang to see it standing there and for a moment he moved back out of the smoke to assess the position. It looked quite hopeless. They had removed the greater part of the upper walls and the roof but the haystack still seethed with smoke and from inside it he could hear that horrid flame crackle working further down. He saw Penn helping Mandel to carry away another bale and he opened his mouth to stop him, then closed it again without saying anything as he directed the water jet on to the hull of the tank. The temperature inside there must be ferocious and never for a second could he forget that Bert was bloated—bloated with fuel, with shells, with ammunition —a state of affairs which only a few hours ago he had congratulated himself on but which might now bring about the death of the tank and several of its would-be rescuers. They were working at such a frenzied pitch that they hardly realized the injuries they were suffering from the scorching heat, but Barnes had already noticed that Reynolds's right forearm was an ugly mass of blisters. As he began hosing down the outer walls again Barnes himself narrowly escaped the most appalling injuries. He was directing the jet low down when he heard a shout from Etienne above him. Instinctively he jumped sideways. A mass of burning hay which had been balancing precariously in the power-grab shovel smothered the spot where he had stood a moment before. He swivelled the jet and drenched the hay, but it took several minutes to put the fire out and afterwards he couldn't understand why it hadn't set light to the main wall low down.

Some time later he again stepped well back from the stack to see how much progress they were making, almost bumping into Reynolds who was carrying a blazing mass of hay towards the road when suddenly it disintegrated, almost collapsing in the driver's face. He just had time to jump clear but a shower of red-hot sparks sprayed over his already badly-blistered arm. Wiping his hand over his sweating forehead, Reynolds headed back to the stack while Jacques, who had been leaning on his own fork, joined him.

'We've nearly done it,' said Mandel.

'Have we?'

Barnes was astonished. Once he had emerged from the clouds of smoke the stack looked far quieter than he could ever have dared to hope. Bert was now exposed to halfway down his hull at the front, and although the turret was only occasionally visible behind the pall of smoke the vicious redness of the flames had died away. He paused to wipe his eyes with his handkerchief and then ran forward, switching on the hose: a line of flame had appeared along the top of the front wall and was growing with alarming speed. They'd never get the thing out. And close to the tank the temperature was still incredible, so fiercely concentrated that it seemed to come towards him in an invisible glow from the metal plates. It would happen so suddenly that they would probably have no warning—fuel first, one blasting outward thump, then the series of sharp explosions as the ammunition started to burn, but they would probably never hear that second sound being as close to the tank as they were. It's like being on top of a ruddy great bomb he thought. Through the smoke he could see figures moving without knowing who they were. Then, some time later, he thought they at last had the inferno finally under control. It should only be a matter of dousing with water until even the smoke faded away. At that moment he heard a frenzied shout from Reynolds.

'A burning bale's just dropped down Bert's side—it's flaring up close to the fuel tank.'

Barnes tried to run forward through the smoke and was jerked backwards. The hose was trapped round the wheel of the power-grab. He lost precious seconds releasing it and then jumped up on to the front wall. The flaring bale had fallen down over the far side but someone had got there first. Reynolds. He lifted his pitch-fork behind him to the fullest extent and then rammed it down like a bayonet, plunging the fork deep into the huge bale which was trapped between the hull and the rear wall of hay. Twisting it to tighten the fork's grip, he began to lift. From behind him Barnes could see the veins standing out on his left arm under the frightful strain. Two men had been handling these intact bales and now Reynolds was trying to hoist one by himself, to hoist it upwards from a position below him. Incredibly, the bale began to come loose, edging upwards as flames danced round the buried fork. Reynolds went on lifting, his legs splayed wide on the hull, his broad back arching. The bale came up suddenly with a rush, but Reynolds was ready for that and he regained his balance by leaning back against the turret. He must have seen Barnes waiting with the hose because as he turned he shouted, 'Get out of my way!'

Without the least idea of what the driver was going to do Barnes leapt back to the ground. Reynolds began to swing the bale in a slow arc through a hundred and eighty degrees, holding the massive weight at arm's length as the fire spread towards him along the fork. Stepping down off the wall he nearly lost his balance, but again he recovered as flames burst out all over the bale. Then he calmly walked across the grass to the road, still holding the flaming mass at arm's length. He had almost reached the road when it ignited into a small inferno, burning back and enveloping Reynolds. Barnes saw him hurl the bale forward, pitch-fork and all. It landed in the road and burst as Reynolds turned round to face the stack, both arms badly burned now, his hair singed, his face a brick-red colour. Ten minutes later Barnes was moving the hose over hay which barely smoked and the fire was out, but he still played the hose over the remaining walls and across the hull. He had sent the others back to the house and now only Mandel wandered round the relic of the stack, holding a pitch-fork and finding nothing to do with it. Leaning over the wall Barnes touched the hull and quickly snatched his hand away.

'You think it's safe now?' asked Mandel. 'The petrol, I mean.'

'If it was going up it should have gone up by now. Can you get Etienne to use his grab to shift the hay in front of the tank? When it cools down I'll have another go at the engine, but that won't be for a while yet. You'll be damned glad to see the back of us, Mandel.'

'This is our war effort. Who knows—your tank may strike a decisive blow at the enemy.'

A decisive blow? It seemed a little unlikely to Barnes at that moment and even less likely when later he followed them into the house to assess the damage to his crew. The kitchen had all the appearances of a casualty clearing station. Jacques who was now outside watching the road, and Etienne, had escaped with only minor burns, but Penn and Reynolds had borne the brunt of the injuries. Reynolds seemed to be in the worst state: he was sitting in a chair with his arms stretched out across the table and both arms had been bandaged by Marianne from wrist to just below the shoulder. As Barnes came in the driver stood up swaying slightly, and Mandel began to help him on with his shirt while Marianne attended to Penn who was flopped in the armchair. She had just finished applying a bandage which covered the whole of his left forearm and he winced as she tied the knot. But when he saw Barnes he managed a grin.

'Now it really looks as though your crew has been in the wars.'

'How are you feeling, Penn?'

'Like a fortnight by the sea. Would Abbeville be a good idea do you think?'

'What about you, Reynolds?'

Barnes turned to his driver with a special anxiety because without Reynolds the status of the unit was definitely non-combatant. Barnes could drive the tank but he couldn't from the driving compartment at the same time keep close all-round observation and operate the guns when necessary. Clinically he watched the process of Reynolds finding his way back inside the shirt Mandel was holding, noticing that Reynolds was able to bend his elbows and seemed to have full use of his hands. It was his face which worried Barnes most at the moment. Normally, Reynolds looked the picture of physical well-being, his complexion ruddy like that of a man who spent most of his life outdoors, but now the driver's face was chalk-white, drained of all colour.

It's hitting him, thought Barnes. He's in a state of shock. It just depends on how he comes out of it. Reynolds still hadn't replied to the question and he remained silent while he fumbled with the shirt buttons. Then he reached for his battle-dress jacket but Mandel lifted it off the table, holding it open for his arms. Carefully, Reynolds slipped inside it, doing up the cuffs and then the buttons down the front. When he had finished he sat down heavily on the chair and picked up a glass of wine, draining the contents in one long swallow. Putting the glass down he looked up at Barnes, his voice a growl.

'Give me half an hour and I'll drive you to the coast.'

174

He's indestructible, Barnes told himself. He's been driving almost non-stop most of yesterday; he had two-and-a-half hours' sleep last night, less the night before; both his arms have been badly burned, and even now his voice sounds vigorous. He decided he still had a driver and went over to Penn, another face as white as death but here there was an awful weariness, and whereas Reynolds sat stiffly upright at the table Penn sank back limply as thought he might never move again. He grinned up at Barnes.

'I'm not as bad as I look. Fortunately.'

'Of course you're not. I didn't see your arm—what's it like?'

'A bit of a mess—but you should see Reynolds! I suppose you know the back of your own hand could do with a little attention?'

He had just made the remark when Marianne took charge of Barnes, guiding him over to the sink where she held his hand under the cold water tap. The sudden icy douche made him jump and he saw that raw skin was peeled back and hanging loose. While she applied ointment and then a bandage he looked round the kitchen. At least the Mandels had avoided severe burning: Mandel himself had a few blisters on his right arm and he had lost half his eyebrows, but apart from a singed hair-line Etienne was untouched, probably because he had fought the fire from the seat of the power-grab. When he tried to thank them Mandel wouldn't listen, repeating that it was part of their war effort and that in any case the British were fighting for France as well as for themselves. Because there seemed to be no more to say Barnes went back outside to struggle with the engine.

The hull was still very hot but he found that he could cope and he spent half an hour checking for the fault, feeling an enormous sense of relief that the tank had survived and enjoying himself once more with mechanical work, work which gradually drained away the tensions from his body. When he climbed down inside the driver's compartment the engine started first time. They were on their way.

175

7. Saturday May 25

WEST AND THEN NORTH—that would be the route they would follow. The tank climbed up to the summit of the hill crest at top speed in the mid-morning sunshine. The rim of the turret was hot to the touch but this heat came from the steady blaze of the sun rather than from the incandescence of fire. Looking back for the last time Barnes saw the tiny figures of the Mandel family standing outside their farm, then they vanished as Bert moved down the other side of the hill. The road ahead to Cambrai was deserted and the only sign of movement came from people working in the fields several kilometres from the roadside.

In spite of his throbbing shoulder, his aching knee, his hand which burned as though a fire smouldered under Marianne's bandage, Barnes experienced a sense of quiet exhilaration: they were on the move again once more and now he knew exactly where he was heading for. His fateful decision to change direction—to head west and then north for Calais instead of north-west to Arras*—was based on a process of thought which had been going on inside Barnes's head for nearly two days, and he was compelled to rely on only two sources of information—the sketchy news bulletins and the evidence of his own eyes. It was what he had seen which more than anything else had convinced him that this was a revolutionary development in warfare based on the fantastic mobility of the tank.

* The Allied forces had withdrawn from Arras at 10 p.m. on Thursday, May 23. During their brief counter-attack, 1 Army Tank Brigade halted the 7th Panzer Division commanded by Major-General Erwin Rommel and caused a panic in the German High Command.

The Germans had disrupted all previous ideas of a static front line by driving their Panzer divisions non-stop across France, driving forward without any attempt to consolidate what they had conquered, relying almost entirely on the elements of surprise and terror to disorganize their enemy. The conclusion to be drawn seemed clear enough—providing one threw out of the window nearly all one's previous ideas of tank warfare. If the Panzers could move across such huge distances without waiting for the infantry to occupy them, then it should be possible for a lone British tank to come up behind them providing that it escaped detection. And then there was the question of the dumps. Barnes thought back over the conversation he had had with Jacques as he wrestled with the engine.

'If you can drive all the way here from Abbeville, Jacques, you must have plenty of petrol.'

'The Germans have plenty of petrol.'

'What does that mean?'

'You won't tell my uncle—he worries about these things?'

'I asked you because we're out here on our own.' Barnes stopped working for a moment. 'Look, Jacques, I've got to get an idea of the position as accurately as I can. You've been haring all over the countryside and you're the only one who can tell me.'

'I took it from a German petrol dump near Abbeville. All I had to do was to creep under a wire fence well away from the guards and take what I wanted. They've threatened to shoot anyone found on what they call German property—but that's to scare people off because they can't guard the petrol.'

'Something was said about ammunition dumps, too.'

'The same with them. I got inside one place with a friend and there were shells and boxes of ammunition all over the place.'

'I find that hard to believe, Jacques.'

He flushed and then grinned. 'That is because you do not know what is happening. The German tanks and guns have broken through with their supply columns but the infantry have not yet reached them—so they can't guard their dumps properly.'

'I'm beginning to get the idea,' Barnes encouraged him.

'It is like the curfew in Cambrai. They say they will shoot anyone found on the streets at night but that is to scare people. I have heard that you can walk all through the town after dark without seeing one German soldier except near the Town Hall. I think,' he said shrewdly, 'that the main reason for the curfew is so that people will not know how few Germans there are in Cambrai at the moment.'

'And you say the road to Abbeville is clear all the way?'

'Except for Cambrai and the three road-blocks outside Abbeville. I could mark their position on this,' he offered, pointing to the map spread out over the hull.

'Do that, would you?'

He went on checking the engine while Jacques marked the road-blocks and then asked a fresh question.

'What about the roads south towards the Somme?'

'I don't know the position there—I have not been that way, you see.'

'And which route do you take when you bypass Cambrai?'

'This way, to the south. I will mark it for you.' When he had finished he looked up, his expression blank. 'If you turned north beyond Cambrai you might get through to Boulogne. I know a way which goes close to St. Pol and Fruges, but it is not the main road—it ends up at Lemont where I live, near Gravelines. I have often used the route when driving from Lemont to Abbeville. I will mark that, too, just in case.'

'Might as well.' Barnes was peering at the engine.

'I feel perhaps I should have driven there instead of here,' went on Jacques as he marked in the route.

'You'd have run into the Panzers.'

'Possibly. I wonder? I think they went up the coast road here and my route is much further inland. From what I have heard I believe there is a gap between the Panzers along the coast and the Allied lines near the frontier.'

'Really?' Barnes kept his face blank, wondering whether he was fooling the sharp-witted youth. It hadn't escaped him that Jacques had carefully refrained from asking him which route they would be taking.

'I'm going back to Abbeville later this morning. I want to tell my sister that Uncle is all right. Then I may drive on to Lemont. Plenty of petrol!'

The trouble with this lad, Barnes was thinking, is that he's so excited by the war that he can't keep still, so he pinches Jerry petrol and then goes flying about all over the countryside to see what's going on. If he's not careful he's going to run into something.

But it was from this conversation that Barnes had gleaned the final scraps of information which led to his ultimate decision, and as the tank rumbled down the hill away from the Mandels he was pretty confident that the French lad had no idea which route he was taking—something he had been particularly careful about in case the lad were picked up by the Germans and made to talk. He scanned the sky and it was empty, further proof that they were still moving through a vast gap in the Allied lines, since had there been any Allied forces in the area the Luftwaffe would have been bombing them. An hour later they had turned off the main road to Cambrai and had almost bypassed the southern approaches to the town. He called a temporary halt to go down and see Penn.

'How's it going?' he asked him.

'Not too bad, although I do feel a bit woozy. I'm getting double vision every now and again.'

Penn was propped up with a wedge of blankets and he was trying to hold himself upright, but earlier when he had looked down into the fighting compartment Barnes had seen him sagging limply, his head flopped forward as though he couldn't hold it up any more. What the devil are we going to do with him, Barnes thought, but he spoke cheerfully.

'Can you stand a bit more of this? I know the movement of the tank must be giving you hell.'

'It's not so much that as the lack of fresh air down here. It's like sitting inside a furnace.'

The description was apt enough. Even standing on the turntable for only a few minutes was enough to bring Barnes out in a prickly sweat and he was surprised that Penn was still conscious.

179

'I'll be all right,' said Penn.

'Do you want to try and stick your head out of the turret for a while?'

'I doubt if I could get up there.'

Barnes kept his face blank but a chill of fear gripped him. He had to keep moving, had to keep the tank heading west and then north, but he had to find a doctor for Penn, too. It seemed as though fate had deliberately kept Penn in a state where he was wounded but not desperately ill until they had left the Mandel farm, and now Penn was becoming desperately ill, Barnes had little doubt of that. His skin was a strangely pallid colour and his eyes appeared to have sunk.

'The next place we come to we'll see if we can find a doctor,' he said.

'Not necessary. I'm not doing anything except sitting and I'll probably feel better by evening. It's just this heat.' He tried to speak lightly. 'Calais next stop?'

'We've a long way to go before we get there, Penn.'

'How far is it?'

'About a hundred miles.'

'Seven hours' drive if Bert goes flat out.'

'You're assuming there'll be nothing in the way, Penn. We can count on there being plenty in the way.'

It seemed an odd way for Barnes to be talking to a seriously wounded man but already he was foreseeing the moment when they would have to leave Penn behind if they could find a sanctuary for him. The realization of what they were driving into might make that moment when they left him a little less hard to bear. He hoped so. He also hoped that they found that sanctuary soon. Considering his physical state, Penn's mind was remarkably alert.

'A hundred miles, you said. Have we got the diesel for that?'

'Yes, with what we took off Lebrun, that is, providing we keep to the road all the way, which we probably won't. You know what happens when we move across country—fuel consumption is doubled.'

'You know what,' Penn began brightly, 'I think we're going to make it. I've had a bit of time to think down here and it strikes me there may not be all that much in our way if we keep a sharp look-out,' He paused and Barnes realized that Penn was wondering whether anyone was observing.

'It's all right, Penn. I told Reynolds to get out and stand on the hull while I was down here. Now, what were you thinking?'

'Well, Jerry is pushing on fast with his tanks and his popguns but the old foot-sloggers haven't put in much of an appearance down here yet. I reckon that with a lot of luck we could sneak up behind those Panzers before we run into much. Then it's up to us.'

'We might do just that, Penn.'

'And by that time I'll have pulled myself together. You'll see me hugging the old two-pounder again before we reach Calais. You can bet on it.'

'I never bet on certainties, Penn.'

With a heavy heart Barnes climbed back into the turret, told Reynolds in a loud voice that Penn was coming along nicely, and then gave the order to advance. Half an hour later he looked back along the road, frowned and grabbed his binoculars. The twin circles of glass brought forward a four-seater Renault with a single occupant, the driver. Jacques was racing towards them on his way to Abbeville.

The twin circles of glass focused and brought forward a toy line of white cliffs glistening in the sunlight. The white cliffs of Dover. General Storch lowered his binoculars and frowned.

'There we are, Meyer, the citadel of the enemy—the main enemy. Let us hope the 14th Panzer Division will be the first to be put ashore on the British beaches.'

'We have to beat them over here first,' Meyer pointed out.

'That will be dealt with in the next forty-eight hours. Here we stand on the coast west of Calais with our forward troops on the Gravelines waterline and Calais is under siege. Now we only have to take Dunkirk and the whole British army is surrounded.'

Meyer screwed his monocle into his eye and found that he was looking through a film of perspiration. In the hour of victory he felt exhausted, overwhelmed by the dazzling series of triumphs Storch had produced since that day so long ago when they crossed the Meuse at Sedan. So long ago? It was the afternoon of Saturday May 25 and they had made their way over the pontoons at Sedan on May 14. Meyer felt stunned. Perhaps, after all, this was a war for the younger men, for the Storches. The general stood gazing out to sea, talking rapidly.

'I want an immediate investigation made of this French Fascist's story—that informant from Lemont. He says there is a second road direct to Dunkirk—a road the enemy may not know about now that the sluice gates have been opened.'

'The French were very quick about that—the floods will make it very difficult for the Panzers to move on Dunkirk . . .'

Storch broke in impatiently. 'This is why this second road may be decisive. I want you to interrogate this man personally.'

'I can't find such a road on any map . . .'

'But that is the whole point, Meyer. Our Fascist friend has explained that for some reason it is not included on most French maps. So if the British are holding the sector at the other end they may not know it exists now it is under water. Even if there are French units in that sector they will probably come from another part of France. That road could be the key to final victory—the road along which the Panzers will advance to Dunkirk.'

'I don't think we should count on it.'

They paused as they heard the humming sound of a host of engines above them. Craning their necks they stared into the sky where an armada of small grey dots was approaching from the east, the humming growing steadily louder as the planes came forward like a swarm of angry bees. Storch nodded his head in satisfaction.

'General Goering is on time again and I see he has the sky to himself. When Mr. Churchill opened the cupboard this morning he must have found his shelves bare.'

'We mustn't count on air immunity any longer,' said Meyer sharply. 'After all, we can actually see England from here.'

Storch tightened his lips at this sign of caution. 'I want a very detailed report about your conversation with this Fascist.

He says this road will be covered by only a few inches of water—sufficient to conceal its existence but not enough to prevent the passage of the Panzers. Since he is a local he may well know what he is talking about.'

'I'd better go now.'

But Meyer did not go immediately because his sharp ears had heard a fresh sound in the sky, an engine sound different from that of Goering's huge aerial fleet. Whipping up his glasses he focused them towards the west while beside him Storch also stood with his binoculars aimed upwards. High above the Channel, at an altitude much greater than the Luftwaffe bombers, several squadrons of R.A.F. fighters flew steadily on course, heading for an invisible point which would take them over the heart of the oncoming bombers, although from the ground it seemed that the two air fleets were advancing on a collision course. Less than a minute later the R.A.F. formations dived to the attack, roaring down like avenging hornets on the massed planes below, weaving in and out of the pattern of bombers which was now becoming disorganized as the pilots forgot their objectives and desperately began to take evading action. In less than two minutes the huge German air armada was flying in all directions, its attack formation completely shattered. One bomber spiralled to the ground and crashed into the fields a mile away, to be followed by a second, but this one was heading for the coast close to where Storch and Meyer stood. As one man they dropped flat behind the hull of a nearby tank only seconds before the bomber hit the earth three hundred yards away, its bomb load exploding a few seconds after the moment of impact. The vibrations of the shock wave rattled the tank behind which they sheltered and a shower of soil rained down on Storch's neck and shoulders. Meyer spoke quietly.

'Mr Churchill must have found something at the bottom of his cupboard.'

'Driver, halt! There's a parachute coming down,' Barnes warned.

The air battle had raged over their heads, out of sight for

several minutes—out of sight even though the sky was cloudless because the planes were high and against the glare of the early afternoon sun. From the noise it sounded as though several machines were wheeling and diving as they fought each other to death in the sunlight. The engine sounds had come closer and faintly he had heard the stutter of machine guns, but they went on manoeuvring in front of the sun so that he had found it impossible to locate them until he had heard the ominous sound of a plane plunging into a tremendous power-dive. Then he had located a small dark shape spinning earthwards a long way to the west, much too far off to identify its nationality quite apart from the fantastic speed at which it approached the ground. It vanished and he heard a distant cough. Petrol tank gone. A thread of black smoke crept up from the horizon. Overhead the sky was full of warm silence. He gave the order to advance, reversing that order almost at once as he saw the tiny inverted cone of the single parachute floating down. He waited.

While he waited he thought about Penn. Since noon they had passed through three abandoned villages, and when he had halted the tank and walked through their deserted streets he had in each place found a house with the tantalizing word *Médecin* on a door-plate, but there had been no one behind the doors. Inside the third village they had stopped briefly for a quick meal from the Mandels' food parcel but Penn hadn't shared the meal because he appeared to have fallen into a state of unconsciousness. Alarmed, Barnes had checked his pulse but the beat was steady. When he felt his forehead it was hot and damp, and now everything in Barnes's mind was dominated by his new priority—finding a doctor. They were within four miles of the next village before the air battle going on overhead had attracted his attention as he halted the tank to attend to a call of nature. Reynolds twisted his head above the hatch to follow the course of the cone as it grew larger and larger drifting straight for them across the deserted fields. He called up to Barnes.

'Ours or theirs?'

'No idea.'

It was a good question, a vital question, in fact. The last thing they could cope with at the present was a Luftwaffe pilot as a prisoner. But if he had seen them and they let him go free it might be less than an hour before German headquarters in Cambrai knew of the presence of a British tank prowling behind their lines. As he watched the parachutist drift lower Barnes swore to himself. He had already shot one German for mercy reasons beside the wrecked infantry truck, but the idea of shooting one down in cold blood for their own protection was rather a different business. Maybe he'll open fire on me, Barnes told himself. If he does I'll let him have half the magazine. There was, of course, just the chance that the pilot wouldn't see them. The parachute was drifting lower and lower—and closer—the tiny figure underneath pulling at cords to guide himself, bobbing about so erratically that Barnes found it impossible to focus the glasses on him. Reynolds called up from the hatch.

'What if it is a Jerry?'

'Then we'll have a problem on our hands.'

'I'd shoot the bastard. He's probably just back from machine-gunning one of those refugee columns.'

Barnes was surprised. It was the first time that Reynolds had ever expressed an opinion without being asked for one. His burnt arms must be playing him up badly. Reaching down, he picked up the machine-pistol and tucked it under his arm. There was no hope now that the parachutist might not see them—as he drifted close to the earth he was floating nearer and nearer to the tank. From that height and distance he couldn't possibly miss seeing them. Climbing down from the turret he stood on the hull so that he could see the exact landing point. The parachutist was now tugging frantically at the cords so that the cone which had been almost overhead was floating away from them along the country road. He jumped down off the hull.

'I can follow him in the tank,' offered Reynolds.

'No, I'll investigate this blighter myself—get another machine-pistol out of the turret and wait here.'

'Watch yourself, sergeant. Don't forget Seft.'

That was the trouble at the moment, Barnes thought. We're in a general state of jitters. Apart from the Mandel farm, which had been a brief oasis of peace in a nightmare world, ever since they had arrived at Fontaine they had met either the enemy in the form of Panzers or treachery in the form of Lebrun; in the case of Seft the enemy and treachery had combined into one menace. So what was he going to encounter now? Let him give me just one reason, just one small reason, and I'll press the trigger.

He was running along the dusty road when the pilot landed in the field close to the verge, the parachute billowing as it dragged its owner across the grass. The cloth cone collapsed slowly. Barnes ran faster. He wanted to get there before the pilot disentangled himself from the cords, but as he came closer the man released himself from the parachute and climbed to his knees, facing Barnes who ran up with the machine-pistol thrust forward. Were pilots armed? He didn't think so but he wasn't taking any chances. The kneeling figure saw the gun and stayed on his knees, throwing his arms wide to show that he was unarmed. The next second will tell, Barnes thought grimly, and then the man spoke.

'And what is a Limey doing in this part of France, I'd like to know? Don't shoot the pilot—he's done his best!'

'You're an R.A.F. pilot?'

Barnes asked the question sharply, his pistol still aimed at the pilot's chest as his eyes roamed over every inch of the man's flying suit. From underneath goggles pushed up over the leather helmet a rugged face stared upwards at Barnes, the face of a man who might be any age between twenty-five and thirty-five. His skin was tanned brown, the texture almost as leathery as the suit he wore; his huge nose, strongly boned, overhung a broad, firm-lipped mouth, and his jaw-line suggested great strength of character. This, thought Barnes, is a tough egg, a very tough egg. But the overall impression of toughness was tempered by the humorous expression in his blue eyes, a humour which came to the surface with his reply.

'If I'm not R.A.F. the Luftwaffe is employing some pretty dubious characters.'

His accent was heavily American and this alone was disconcerting, plus the fact that the pilot himself appeared more amused than disconcerted, an unusual reaction when a man found himself at the wrong end of a gun. But Barnes couldn't forget that Penn had thought Seft a genuine Belgian, and it was just possible that the Luftwaffe employed a few renegade Americans.

'Get on your feet,' Barnes said tightly.

'Coming down I think I broke both me legs, sergeant.'

God, another lame duck to take aboard Bert. As if it wasn't enough having to cope with Penn he was now going to have another patient on his hands. The tank was rapidly turning into a casualty clearing station: the only trouble was that there was nowhere to clear them to. He went back several paces as the pilot clambered carefully to his feet. The stranger grinned.

'Correction, sergeant. I just *feel* as though I've broken both me legs. Ever landed in one of those things? The ground looks to be coming up so peacefully and then at the last minute it flies up and hits you like a steam-hammer.'

'I didn't know the R.A.F. were recruiting Americans,' Barnes said grimly.

'Canadians, please!' He lifted one gloved hand in mock horror. 'Although your error of geography is understandable, sergeant. My mother is Canadian and my father was American, but I was born in Canada. Ever heard of Wainwright, Alberta? No, I didn't think you would have. It's about the size of a pinhead but the C.N.R. expresses do stop there to unload drums of ice cream for the locals.' He gestured behind Barnes. 'Is that your tin can back there?'

'The tin can is a Matilda tank. Have you any way of proving your identity?'

'Sure. If I unbutton my jacket and slip my hand inside real slow you'll promise not to pull the trigger?'

Barnes didn't reply and he watched the pilot's hand carefully as it ferreted inside the jacket, but when the fingers came out again they only held an R.A.F. identity card. The pilot held it between his fingers for a moment.

'Now if I try and hand it to you there's a danger you'll think I'm going to try and jump you. On the other hand, if I drop it on the ground for you to pick it up I could just possibly land a boot in your eye. So which is it to be?'

'Drop it on the ground—then take six paces back.'

The pilot was still pacing backwards when Barnes stooped quickly to grab the identity card. Using only his left hand he fingered open the card, wondering whether he was carrying on with his check through caution or sheer cussedness at Colburn's attitude. Because that was the name in the card. Flying Officer James Q. Colburn.

'The Q is for Quinn,' Colburn explained helpfully, 'which comes from my mother's side of the family. The Quinns are an old British Columbia family—old, that is, by Canadian standard—although . . .'

'All right, Colburn,' Barnes skimmed the card through the air and the pilot caught it with his left hand. 'What happened up there near the sun?'

'You're satisfied with my identity, then, sergeant?'

'I think so.'

'Well how about letting me see your paybook—or am I supposed to take you at face value alone?'

Barnes looked at the six-foot pilot. He had a seriously ill loader-operator on his hands, he was in a great hurry to push on to the next village in search of medical help, and he had expected to find a Luftwaffe pilot struggling to free himself from the cords. He was certainly in no mood for wisecracks with free-lance Canadians.

'I'm Sergeant Barnes and if you think I'm going to show you my paybook you're out of your tiny mind. What do you think that thing standing behind me is—a Jerry tank? And even you must have seen a British army uniform.'

'All right! All right!' Colburn waved a placatory hand. 'And don't think I don't appreciate you've probably had a hell of a fortnight, whereas I'm just over here for the afternoon. At least I thought I was,' he added. 'But may I point out that

I'm wearing R.A.F. flying kit and that what you saw come down in flames wasn't a vacuum cleaner. It was, at the time of take-off from Manston, a perfectly good Hurricane.'

'It came down so quickly I hardly saw it till the crash. A Messerschmitt got you, I suppose?'

'Three of them—although that's no excuse. They chased me down here from the coast, which was a bad reaction on my part since I hadn't the petrol to make home base even if I could have clobbered the lot. Let's face it—they out-manoeuvred me. And sergeant, do I have to sing "Auld Lang Syne" before you'll put away the carbine?'

Barnes lowered the machine-pistol and nodded. 'Sorry, but we had a little trouble with a German fifth columnist who said he was Belgian so I'm taking nothing for granted. You could have been one yourself, Colburn.'

'Out of the sky?' queried the Canadian ironically, then his expression changed. 'I'm sorry—you're right to check everything. Those characters really exist, then? We've heard plenty of rumours—so many you'd think France was swarming with them.'

'The only thing this part of France swarms with is Panzers.' Barnes stared hard at Colburn before he went on. Was Colburn really as tough as he looked? 'You've come down in the middle of a gigantic no-man's land which could be at least twenty miles wide, but the only troops we've seen are parts of armoured divisions. We're completely on our own—just one Matilda tank.'

Barnes had relaxed a little now and he was prepared to wait a few more precious minutes while he made up his mind. He was studying Colburn quite dispassionately, without the least trace of sentiment, weighing him up ruthlessly. And Barnes had some experience of weighing up men. In this instance he was applying only one criterion—would Colburn be an asset or a liability? If he was going to be the latter then he wasn't coming with them. Colburn stared at him steadily.

'You mean the rest of your outfit got wiped out?'

'I mean we got separated from them at the very beginning

189

and it's been that way ever since. If you come with us you'd better understand we have one two-pounder gun, one light machine gun, several machine-pistols and three revolvers. That's the extent of our armament and so far we've escaped detection by three separate Panzer columns by the skin of our teeth.'

'Sounds a little one-sided. I'd have thought you could do with a little reinforcement.'

'We could, but tanks don't fly and you're a pilot.'

'You may have a point there. What's the alternative?'

'The alternative, Colburn, is to make your own way home.' He paused. 'Unless you'd sooner take the easier way out and walk down that road into Cambrai where the Germans are. Then you could spend the rest of your war in a nice quiet P.O.W. camp.'

He waited for the Canadian's reaction, but still nothing had changed in the steady expression. Even the voice was mild when he retaliated.

'I suppose if I were to hit you in the mouth for that, sergeant, your pal in the tank would gun me down?'

'I'm sure he would. Don't let me get under your skin, Colburn. It's just that I have to be sure.'

'Sure of what? I thought you'd have realized by now that I was taking off from Manston half an hour ago.'

'I have to be sure you won't get in the way. You're a Canadian, you say, yet you're in the R.A.F.'

'I volunteered. It was very hot weather at the time and the heat can make you do silly things . . .'

'What were you in civvy street, Colburn?'

'I took my medical degree and then . . .'

'You're a doctor?' Barnes didn't attempt to keep the eagerness out of his voice.

'No, I'm not. I never practised. I found I didn't like it so I became a chemist.'

'A chemist?' Barnes found it difficult to visualize Colburn behind a counter handing out aspirin.

'An industrial chemist. I developed an interest in high-explosives and had my own outfit after a few years. We supplied stuff for quarry-blasting operations all over Canada. So now you'll know how crazy I was to volunteer.'

'You had your own business and you gave it up?' Barnes stared even more closely at Colburn's sun-tanned features, wondering what made a man throw up everything to travel three thousand miles to fight someone else's war. His decision was crystallizing rapidly now.

'No, it wasn't as bad as that. I handed over to my brother and he's running things till I get back.' Colburn smiled faintly. 'Ed doesn't see any reason why the British shouldn't be left to fight their own wars. He could be right at that. Sergeant, what made you jump half a mile when I said I'd taken my medical degree?'

'My corporal's seriously wounded and I've been praying to run into a doctor for hours. Would you take a look at him for me?'

'Be glad to—but remember, I'm the most qualified non-practising doctor in the western hemisphere. Where is he?'

Barnes stayed behind to gather up the collapsed parachute while Colburn walked back to where Reynolds waited on the hull of the tank. It took him several minutes to bundle up the cloth and cords into a package which resembled an overblown eiderdown and then he hid it inside a drainage ditch. There was no point in alerting any German patrol which might arrive later to the fact that there was a British airman in the district. When he returned to the tank Reynolds was out of sight inside the hull but Colburn's head emerged from the turret. He looked down at Barnes, his voice quiet.

'The guy down there is a close friend of yours?'

'He's my corporal,' replied Barnes flatly.

'Sorry, that was badly put. The news isn't good, I'm afraid.'

'He may not make it?'

'He didn't make it—he's dead.'

It took them well over an hour to dig the grave out of the sun-baked French soil. They worked with the same shovels which had been used to dig them out of the tunnel at Etreux, and they took it in turns when Colburn insisted on helping.

During his rest period Barnes watched Colburn closely: on the basis of sheer physical strength there was very little to choose between the Canadian and Reynolds, but the main thing he liked about Colburn was his quick acceptance of an entirely new situation. By now the poor devil might well have expected to be landing at Manston prior to a trip to the nearest local: instead of which he was marooned in the middle of the battle zone helping to bury the body of a man he had never known alive. As he watched them dig out the final shovelfuls his mind was stunned. Penn had spent three years with him and in that time they had established a working relationship which functioned so smoothly they might have known each other all their lives. Penn, who had never really believed in anything, who found his sergeant's intense preoccupation with his profession rather amusing, Penn was a man who could always be relied upon. And, by God, they'd relied on him during that endless night when he'd stood sentry-go on the bridge while the Panzers rolled past. Penn had found his sanctuary now, although not the sanctuary Barnes had planned for him.

What had seemed to be the simplest part of their mournful task proved to be the hardest—the lowering of the body. The grave was ready and Colburn stood aside, leaving it to Barnes and Reynolds to lift the body which they had swathed in a blanket and then further protected by folding a groundsheet round it. To enable them to lower their burden slowly they had looped two ropes round the groundsheet—one over the chest and the other over the legs. All went well until the body was half way down inside the grave, then it stuck, wedged in at the shoulders at a point where the hole narrowed. They raised it and then lowered it a second time, but again it stuck. Barnes looked at Colburn.

'Would you take over this rope for me?'

He waited until the Canadian was in position and then he knelt down, placing the flat of his hand on the groundsheet. As he pressed he could feel the thickness of the bandage over Penn's left arm. Colburn had said that it was probably the shock of severe burning on top of his shoulder wound which had finally dictated that he couldn't survive. The heavily-wrapped body still wouldn't go down. He pressed harder, feeling that Penn didn't want to be buried here and was resisting him. What was it he had said? 'You'll see me hugging the old two-pounder again before we reach Calais.' Well, they were a long way from Calais and now Penn would never know whether they made it or not. He pressed harder still, knowing that they hadn't time to embark on fresh digging because out here they were horribly exposed to view. The body gave up the struggle suddenly, sinking down so unexpectedly that Barnes almost over-balanced. When he stood up his face and hands were running with sweat and all he wanted to do was to get away from this place.

'Shouldn't we say something over him?' mumbled Reynolds.

'No,' said Barnes abruptly, 'nothing. Didn't you know—he was an agnostic.'

When they had filled in the grave they erected a crude marker, and they used a shovel because it was the only instrument they could find for their purpose. The shovel was dug deep into the ground and on the handle Barnes had inscribed simple wording which he cut into the wood with his knife. '18972451 Corporal M. Penn. Killed in Action. May 25 1940.'

Before they moved off he asked Colburn to check his shoulder wound. While he had been leaning over into the grave, at the moment when the body had suddenly slipped down into its resting place, he had jerked his shoulder, feeling something give: he had ripped open the wound again. He sat on the warm hull while the Canadian removed the bandage and Colburn's voice spoke volumes of disapproval.

'I can see this dressing hasn't been changed recently.'

'You mean it's turned septic?' Barnes inquired quietly.

'No, you were lucky there. I'm talking about the state of the outside of the dressing. You've re-opened it again, all right, but it looks clean and that's the main thing. Now, keep still. This may hurt.

Cleaning the freshly-opened wound thoroughly, he applied a new dressing and then helped Barnes on with his shirt and jacket. The shoulder was starting to throb steadily, a nagging ache which absorbed far too much energy. When he was dressed he took out a pencil from the pocket containing Penn's paybook and diary, spread out his map over the hull and roughly marked the spot where the corporal was buried. One day Penn's parents might wish to make a pilgrimage to this spot, but by then anything could have happened to the shovel. Really, he told himself, it's a waste of time. All he could hope for was that the whole ruddy war wasn't a waste of time. He began discussing the battlefield situation with Colburn but soon found out that the Canadian could tell him little more than he already knew.

'As far as I can make out,' Barnes went on, 'the B.E.F. is roughly north of this line with the Belgian army on its left. We're standing in the middle of a huge no-man's land . . .'

'The gap,' said Colburn.

'You mean they're actually calling it that?'

'Yes, it's referred to as that on our briefing maps. As you say, you're slap in the middle of it but there's a lot of argument as to how wide it is. My squadron came over to mix it with Hun fighters but as a sideline we were told to shoot up any Panzers we found. They think reinforcements may come through here soon.'

'They were right—they came through early this morning.'

'Late again.' He smiled faintly. 'Going back to those Panzers, I raised a query about the risk of shooting up our own guys and you're not going to like the answer they gave. They said that if we found a whole lot of heavy tanks strung out along a road they were bound to be German—the British only have a handful and the French have cleverly scattered theirs in penny packets over the whole front.'

'You don't seem to know a great deal more than I do, Colburn.'

'Sergeant, you're over here in the thick of it, and it's my opinion that you're far too close in to be able to take in the general picture.'

'That, Colburn,' said Barnes irritably, 'is what I'm trying to extract from you. You get detailed briefings before you take to the air, you fly over the battlefield—if anyone has a general picture it should be you.'

'Oh, I've got it, all right, but from your questions I get the idea you're looking for some sort of clear pattern I should draw you, some nice neat little map which will show the Germans here, your lot there, and the French some other place. Well, I can't do that, and again it's only my opinion, but I'm pretty sure that when this war is only a memory and the historians get busy with their tidy little analyses they still won't be able to say exactly which unit was where and on what day. This, for what it's worth, is the biggest muddle of a battle that ever was.'

'What are you trying to say?'

'That there isn't any information worth a damn—these boys, the generals, are just making it up as they go along. Just like Wellington in the Peninsular War when he said it was like knotting a rope—you tie one knot, then you tie another and hope for the best. But don't try and kid me that any of them are working to a tidy little plan in a war room any more.'

'Not even the Germans?' Barnes asked quietly.

'Not even those bastards—not any more. Ask me how I know and I'll tell you it's the well-known Colburn intuition—that and the fact that I'm a minor student of the history of warfare. But there's one thing, Barnes, I'd bet money on—I'd bet that at this moment the German generals are so intoxicated with their success that they don't know what to do with it. Generals are always divided into pushers and pullers—one lot will be saying press on, push 'em into the sea, and the other lot will be yelling blue murder that they've overreached themselves and had better dig in quick before they get their heads chopped off.'

'It doesn't help me much,' remarked Barnes.

'Well, maybe this will help you. When I flew in today I came down south-east over Calais and I'm pretty sure there's another gap between the coast road and the main battle area to the east. That could just be the way for us to go.'

'It is the way we're going.'

'So I get a free ride to Calais, but on one condition—that you don't ever ask me again for the general picture. There isn't one. This is such a bloody mixed-up mess they'll never be able to describe it—not in a hundred years' time. Not unless they call on the aid of Shakespeare who did have a word for a complete one hundred per cent shambles. The general picture, Sergeant Barnes, is hugger-mugger.'

'Which simply means we could run into Jerry at any time now.'

8. Saturday May 25

THE STUKA BOMBER, one hundred feet up, smoke pouring from its tail, was heading straight for them as though aimed at the mouth of the quarry. Barnes stood perfectly still, his gaze fixed on the approaching projectile as he prayed that it would maintain its height for at least a few hundred yards more. It screamed in closer, its nose dipping like a suicide bomber guided to penetrate the quarry mouth and explode against the rear wall where Bert was parked. Beside him Colburn froze as he automatically assessed the Stuka's line of flight. Then it roared over them, still losing height, and ten seconds later they heard it hit France a mile away as its bomb load blew up.

'This place reminds me of high-explosives,' said Colburn.

The tank was parked inside a chalk quarry cut out of the hillside and the giant alcove was filled with shadow. It was half past six in the evening and they had been standing at the narrow entrance while Reynolds mounted guard on the rim of the quarry high above them. The driver shouted down to tell them that the plane had crashed a long distance off and then resumed his all-round observation.

'I'm none too fond of high-explosive myself at the moment,' Barnes replied drily as he swirled tea in his mug.

'That's because you've been on the receiving end—I'm talking about quarry-blasting operations. There's something very satisfying about laying the charges just right, going back to the plunger, pressing it, and seeing exactly the right area of rock slice away.'

'I thought you just supplied the stuff.'

'Oh, they were always asking me for advice and I ended up

by doing the job for them. I have a talent for destruction, Barnes. What's more to the point, I enjoyed my work.'

They walked away from the tank and through the narrow defile which formed the entrance to the quarry. Stopping in the entrance, they looked out across the fields of France. They had done very well, Barnes was thinking, and he estimated they were now less than thirty miles from Calais. All through the late afternoon and early evening Bert had moved at top speed along the road and only twice had they stopped and prayed. Once when a flight of German planes had flown across the eastern sky, and once when a cloud of dust had warned them of the approach of a German supply column. For over half an hour they had waited concealed inside a nearby wood, only emerging when the last escorting tank had driven out of sight in the opposite direction. And then Bert had ground forward non-stop heading north, always north towards Calais.

They had finished their meal and once again bully beef hadn't been featured on the menu. When they re-opened the parcel which Mandel had provided they had found several sticks of French bread, an earthenware pot of butter, a whole cold chicken, and four bottles of wine. They had dined well but Barnes had not enjoyed it because at the beginning of the meal he had remembered Penn who had never tasted any of the food. As a crew they were probably in better condition than at any time since they had left Fontaine, except that now the fighting crew comprised only two men—unless Colburn could absorb enough of a rudimentary training to make him useful. Beyond the quarry, several miles across the sunlit plain, Barnes saw a long thin trail of dust moving at an oblique angle to where they stood. It looked as though the column were heading for the coast. He focused his glasses.

'Panzers?' inquired Colburn.

'Probably. Too far away to see properly and that dust is fogging the view. They're not coming this way, which is something to be thankful for. Now, Colburn, let's see how much you can learn about a tank in no time at all.'

At the most, Barnes had hoped he might show Colburn how to use the Besa, but the Canadian was no sooner down on the

198

turntable when he wanted to know how to traverse the turret. Within five minutes he was showing that he possessed real mechanical aptitude and an ability to grasp the traverse system which surprised Barnes, a surprise which grew as he experienced the Canadian's endless persistence. Once he found he was able to traverse he asked Barnes to go up to the turret and give him instructions over the intercom. Settling down to indoctrinate his quick-witted pupil Barnes showed him no mercy, correcting his faults with the ruthlessness of a drill sergeant.

'Right, Colburn! I said traverse right! You now have the distinction of presenting our bloody rear to the enemy. That's better. Left! Traverse left!'

It quickly dawned on Barnes that he had a tiger by the tail. Colburn wouldn't give up until he could operate the traverse on instruction without mistake. He simply went on and on and on, tirelessly as though his life might depend on getting this right. And, Barnes thought, it could just work out that way. In all his experience he had never trained a pupil who learned so quickly, even though it was only the rudiments he was grasping. When he went back into the fighting compartment Colburn demanded to know something about the two-pounder, but here Barnes felt that any attempt to show him how the weapon worked would be a waste of time. He suggested, instead, that Colburn should tackle the Besa.

'Five minutes will do that,' said Colburn briskly.

Barnes stared. So the Canadian was a braggart, which meant he would be totally unreliable in an emergency. Colburn read something of the thought in his expression and grinned.

'You may have forgotten, Barnes, that we do carry a certain armament in the Hurricane. Like the Besa it's called a machine-gun.'

'Sorry.' Barnes closed his mouth tightly. The throb-throb of the shoulder wound had started up again and was pounding his mind to a jelly. 'I'd overlooked that. As you say, five minutes should do the Besa.'

Two hours later Barnes called a halt to the training exercise. It would be dark in half an hour and he wanted to move farther north to a more open position which still provided some cover: being trapped inside the quarry for the night didn't appeal to him when he remembered their experience under the bridge. By now Colburn had grasped some of the basic lore of how to fight a tank, including the use of the periscope for observation by the gunner. It was quite impossible to cram months of basic training into two hours even for Colburn, but Barnes was amazed at how much the Canadian had picked up. Calling Reynolds down from the top of the quarry he prepared to depart.

'That was fun,' said Colburn with enthusiasm. 'I'm not quite the spare wheel I was two hours back.'

'You'll do—in an emergency.' Barnes smiled drily.

'At least I can cope with the traverse and the Besa, so try and find me some running Germans within range, but if you're counting on the two-pounder,' he grinned, 'you'll be lucky.'

It struck Barnes that perhaps he shouldn't be too surprised at the Canadian's achievements; after all, it needed plenty of mechanical ability to handle a plane and the one quality no fighter pilot could do without was quick-wittedness. He was more surprised still when Reynolds spoke, pausing as he climbed down into the hatch.

'It just goes to show, sergeant, that training course is far too long like I've always said—strictly for village idiots. A right old load of bullshit.' He disappeared inside his own compartment.

For the first time it flashed through Barnes's mind that maybe Reynolds had always been so silent because Penn had always been so talkative. The relationships inside the unit were changing rapidly, and he was pleased to see that Reynolds obviously liked Colburn.

Three minutes later the tank left the quarry, moved on to the road and headed north. Up in the turret Barnes's expression was grim: he was conscious that they were approaching a crisis and that within the next twenty-four hours at the outside they might well all be dead or taken prisoner. There was, of course, the third alternative—that they might get the chance of striking a great blow against the Germans. If only they could locate a really vital objective. Over seventy two-pounder shells under me, he thought. They could make a mess of something.

He was still turning over an idea which he had not yet mentioned to the others—the idea of keeping going through the night, headlights ablaze like the Panzers. The Germans won't be expecting anything coming up behind them. He felt sure that their eyes would be glued to the battlefield ahead, and a vehicle moving through the night with its headlights full on looked very innocent from a distance, until they had the enemy within two-pounder range, anyway.

They were moving into a more populated area and now he saw people working in the fields some distance from the road. To the north several orange-coloured tractors moved slowly across the landscape which was so flat that it reminded him of Holland, although there was a small ridge over to the right. They were in the heart of the Pas de Calais now, roughly mid-way between Béthune and Etaples. It was incredible, thought Barnes, to have come all this way from Etreux in a vast semi-circle round the southern flank of the battle zone—but no more incredible than the lightning dash of the Panzer spearhead from the German border to the gates of Boulogne. I'll go on through the night, he decided, by God, I will. The people in the fields had stopped work to watch the tank, standing as motionless as scarecrows on a windless day. Then he caught sight of movement to his left, lifted his glasses, and his heart jumped.

Another of those sinister dust clouds, only just visible in the fading light, but under the cloud he could see small square shapes moving towards him across country. Panzers!

He issued orders instantly and the tank turned off the road to the right, moving over the field towards the low ridge, the only defence feature in sight. When they reached it he manoeuvred Bert until he faced the oncoming enemy in a hull-down position, the greater part of the tank concealed behind the ridge so that only the turret projected in the open. A quarter of a mile away a farmer on his orange tractor changed direction, heading across the field to take a closer look at the intruder. Flip off, Barnes told him mentally, or you'll cop a Jerry shell.

'Two-pounder. Traverse right. Right! Steady!'

The turret swung him round and steadied. Perfect. Davis could have done no better, and Davis had been good.

'Range six hundred. Six hundred.'

Barnes had the glasses pressed into his eyes as he watched the dust cloud's progress. It appeared to be moving *across* their line of fire now. Was it possible that in the uncertain light of dusk that they hadn't been spotted after all? In less than five minutes he knew that the Panzers had another objective altogether, somewhere far to the north. He didn't know whether to feel relieved or disappointed. It was almost dark as he gave them the news over the intercom, following it up with the order to advance.

To save time and to avoid the farmer on the tractor who was close behind him now, Barnes guided the tank towards the road along a different course from the one which had brought them to the ridge, moving at an oblique angle which would take them back on to the road some distance north of the point where they had left it. The tank completed its quarter turn and rumbled forward over the grass, leaving a faint trail of chalk as the substance disengaged itself from the tracks. It may have been the treacherous light of dusk, or it may have been the throbbing of his wound which grew worse towards night: it may have been a combination of these two factors which momentarily robbed him of his normal lynx-eyed observation, but whatever the cause Barnes failed to see the change in the texture of the land they were crossing, failed to see that whereas a moment ago they were passing over green grass and baked earth, now the grass was sparser, growing in isolated tufts, and even where it grew its colour was a strange, almost sinister acid green colour.

His first warning of the danger was the moment when the tank stopped moving forward, although its huge tracks continued to churn round, moving uselessly as the whole tank slowly began to tilt. The tilting motion was in a backward direction, so slight that at first Barnes wondered whether he was suffering from an attack of dizziness, but as the motion continued and he looked quickly over the side the awful truth dawned.

They were sinking, sinking more rapidly as the quagmire sucked at the tracks, dragging over twenty-six tons of tank downward into its drowning grip.

9. Saturday May 25

HIS INSTINCT was to give the order to reverse, to take the tank
backwards on to the firm ground they had left. Opening his
mouth, he closed it again without speaking. Work this out,
Barnes, and quickly. The front seems stable, so it may be on
solid ground; only the back is going down. It you reverse you
may never reach firm ground. Switching on his pocket torch,
he swept the beam behind the tank. They appeared to have
broken up a very thick crust of earth baked hard by weeks of
sunshine, exposing a horrible sticky ooze lower down which
gleamed in the torchlight. Go forward then? Climbing out of
the turret he walked forward over the left-hand track, sat down
and gingerly lowered one leg. Firm enough. But in the beams
of the headlights he had told Reynolds to switch on he could
see the same type of pallid baked earth, the surface cracked
with tiny fissures. Was that firm ground or were they perched
on an island of solidity with more quagmire ahead? At least
the tank had stopped tilting backwards now, as though it had
found a precarious equilibrium. Colburn came out of the
turret and climbed down on to the hull.

'What are you playing at, sergeant?'

'We've run into a bog. It's as soft as butter behind us now
and I'm not too sure of this lot. Get ready to grab me—I'm
going to test it for firmness.'

He lowered his full weight on his right leg and the ground
held, but it was rather like treading on a sponge. He slipped
the other leg down and stood up, felt a crumbling sensation
under his left leg and the ground caved in. He started to go
down, suddenly up to his knees in filthy ooze. Hands grabbed

him from behind, hauled him bodily backwards and lifted, sitting him back on the track, legs astraddle it. Carefully, he turned round and scrambled back on to the hull.

'Thanks, Colburn. You just about saved my bacon there. No way ahead and no way back. Get me a rope from that box near the compass. I've got to find out how far away we are from the shore.'

He waited until Colburn had emerged from the turret again and then tied a loop under his shoulders, handing the free end to the Canadian. The tractor had arrived now and it stood on the bank of the quagmire with its headlights beamed direct on to the tank, blinding Barnes as he made his way along the rear track while Colburn stayed on the hull. The farmer was shouting non-stop across the quagmire in French and with his limited knowledge of the language Barnes couldn't understand a word. If only they'd speak slower. He shouted back slowly in English that he was crossing to the bank and received an outburst in reply. Looking back to make sure that Colburn was in position, he pulled a face.

'Pity you don't speak French as well as handling machine-guns.'

'I know German. Do you think he might savvy that?'

'Don't try it, for God's sake. He's probably only friendly because we're British.'

'How can he know that?'

'Because of the uniform—he must have seen enough of them before we decided to trot off into Belgium. Here goes. Don't haul me back unless I'm in real trouble. I've got to find out how far it is to the bank.'

'You can see that by the tractor.'

'He'll be yards farther back than he need be. It must be this quagmire.'

Reaching out sideways well beyond the track his right foot touched firmness. But for how long? He put his full weight on it and the ground held. He put his other leg down and there was no feeling of sponginess. He was away from the tank now. Get on with it. A bold step forward with the right leg: it landed on more firmness, a tuft of grass. Were they really as close as

205

this to safety? He lifted the other foot and when it reached the earth it went on going down at an alarming rate, straight through the crust into liquid mud which sent up a dank nauseating smell. Jerking his foot off the tuft he thrust it forward as far as he could and it hit solid earth, his legs splayed wide apart in front and behind him. He tried to heave the rear foot loose but found he was in serious trouble: it had sunk in up to the knee and the quagmire was wrapped round his leg like some monstrous sea creature determined to suck him down into its lair. Fighting down a rising sense of panic, he heaved again with all his strength, feeling the leg coming up reluctantly, mud oozing and sucking as he pulled. Then it came free with a jerk and he fell flat on his face, aware that the ground under his body was hard and still. Strong hands locked under his shoulders and helped him to his feet. By the light of the tractor's beams he looked into the farmer's face, the long lean face of a man in his forties, still babbling away in French.

'Thanks,' said Barnes. 'Can you speak more slowly?'

Unlooping the rope from his shoulders, he looked behind the Frenchman to where the tractor stood and then walked up to it. Tied to the side were half-a-dozen iron stakes with ring heads: the stakes were at least six feet long and the farmer had obviously been erecting a fence. With sign language he indicated that he needed the stakes and the farmer nodded his head vigorously in agreement. Cutting the rope with his knife he carried three of the stakes to the bank and called out.

'Get Reynolds up on to the hull. He's to get the two steel tow-lines and attach them to the rear of Bert. I need a hammer over here, too. This chap's got some iron stakes—if we can fix the tow-lines to them it may stop Bert sinking any deeper while we think up something.'

'O.K.'

While he was waiting the farmer began to make a great effort to tell him something in a few words of English, spacing out the words one by one in his anxiety to convey the message.

'Stop . . . stop . . . there!' He pointed at the tank. 'I bring big big wood.' He was gesturing madly, scooping his hand as he pointed at the tank again. 'Big wood. Back soon. You wait.'

What the hell else can we do, Barnes wondered. Colburn had reacted quickly and he threw the hammer into the pool of light from the tractor just before the machine was driven off. To start with, Barnes had to hammer the stakes down in the dark, but once he had them firmly embedded he held the torch in his left hand and hammered with his right. Reynolds had attached the two lines to the rear of the hull long before Barnes had driven in the stakes so deep that he thought they should hold up Bert for at least a while, at least until the farmer came back, if he came back.

The quagmire was an eery place at night and even though it was now completely dark he could see the tank's silhouette outlined against its own lights. The shadows of Reynolds and Colburn waited on the hull and somewhere far above them a squadron of planes flew through the night at a great height. It was still very warm and muggy and the mosquitoes were active now, biting the back of his neck. He was only satisfied when the stakes were several feet into the ground and then he flashed his torch to show the edge of the quagmire.

'Before you throw me the tow-lines, is Bert still sinking?'

'I don't think so.' Colburn's voice. 'I think the tank's balanced on the island for the moment but it's still badly tilted at the back.'

'As far as I could make out that farmer is coming back with a load of heavy wood. That's all I could get but I imagine he's got some idea of bridging this gap. Now, I'll stand well back, Reynolds, so throw me the first line.'

The loop landed within inches of the stakes where Barnes had left his lighted torch on the ground. He wrapped the line tightly round the stakes close to the ground and then passed the end through an iron ring. When the second tow-line arrived he repeated the process. Now all they could do was to wait, hoping that the farmer would come back and that he would bring something they could use. Occasionally he called out to the men on the tank, but carrying on a conversation across the quagmire seemed pretty unsatisfactory so soon they said nothing and the minutes dragged by with agonizing slowness. Leaving the headlights on bothered Barnes because this drew

207

attention to them from the road, but he decided that they must risk keeping them on to make sure that the farmer could find them. They waited a whole hour before lights appeared across the field behind them, and then the tractor chugged across the grass and pulled up close to the bank. Barnes ran forward to see what the farmer had brought, and for a moment he couldn't see anything until the man pointed to behind the vehicle. He had dragged across the field two immense beams of wood which were attached to the back of the tractor by chains. While the farmer undid the chains Barnes measured their length by pacing. About ten feet long. He would have put the distance between the shore and the front of the tank at twelve feet, but that was only a rough guess. They'd just have to try it, anyway—as a fighting vehicle Bert might just as well be at the bottom of the swamp as immobilized on that island when daylight came. He stood on the bank and explained the plan carefully to Colburn and Reynolds, but that was the easy part. He now had to explain it to the farmer, and this was only achieved by careful gesturing. It became clearer when Reynolds had thrown two coils of rope on to the bank, and then they started.

The first stage involved careful co-operation between Barnes and the farmer because the wooden beams were enormously heavy and extremely unwieldy. They tied one rope tightly round the end of the longest beam and then began to invert it so that the roped end was lifted over their heads. As the huge beam rose higher and higher Barnes kept a firm grip on the loose end of the rope. The beam was slowly moving up to the vertical but the really tricky part was coming when they tried to control its falling movement as it passed beyond the vertical, lowering it under control so that the far end could be dropped just below the right-hand track and form a bridge to dry land—if the beam would reach that far. The beam reached its apex and began to topple. They just managed to prevent it crashing down as they both held on to the rope, and the farmer was sensible enough to let Barnes guide its controlled fall. It dropped lower and lower, scraped the front end of the right-hand track and settled. Would it begin sinking or had they managed to prop it on the tip of the island? The lights of the tractor were again beamed directly on the tank and as far as he could tell the beam was stable.

'Nice work,' shouted Colburn. 'Looks O.K. to me.'

'Right. Now for the next one.'

The second beam was successfully manoeuvred in direct line with the left-hand track, but it fell short. Not more than a foot, Colburn informed him, but it had fallen short of the island and was sinking slowly. Slowly? Barnes wondered—did that mean it had settled on a patch of fairly firm ground? The quagmire must be unusually solid at this particular point if a beam of such enormous weight was sinking slowly—whereas Barnes had felt his leg knifing through the mud. They'd just have to risk it, and at least they had the two beams placed so that they formed a bridge from the present position of the tank to the shore. He reached up and felt his shoulder gingerly. He'd ripped that wound open again. When he was lowering the second beam he had been aware of a slow tearing sensation and now he could feel stickiness round the edge of the dressing. He set about enlisting the farmer's aid for the final, possibly fatal, stage, and this time he was able to explain quickly what he wanted by sign language. They undid the tow-lines from the iron stakes after the farmer had reversed his tractor, then re-attached them to the rear of the tractor. Barnes tried to explain that he must synchronize his movements with those of the tank—that they must both move at the same moment, and he hoped to God that the farmer understood that the signal would be when Barnes shouted 'Maintenant'. Now. Since the farmer went on repeating the word about two dozen times Barnes felt that he had probably grasped it. Now to get back to the tank.

He was careful to choose the right-hand timber and when he walked along it he lit his way with his torch beam which splayed over the edge, showing a gleam of insidious ooze waiting for him where the crust had broken. Reaching the tank, he checked the position of the timber. The right-hand one was fine, perfect, in fact, but the left-hand one wasn't at all good. The breadth of the gap between timber and island looked more like eighteen inches. He explained it carefully to Reynolds.

'You'll have to reverse back along exactly the course we came over—then the tracks will move along the beams. This isn't going to be a picnic and you might as well know what could go wrong. The beams could crack under Bert's weight, and they probably will at some stage. One of them could slip off this island after we've started. Or your tracks could slip off the beams—take your choice.'

'Not much of a choice, is it, sergeant? But we can't stay here.'

'That's the whole point—we've got to risk it. You'll have to follow my orders very precisely. I've fixed up with that farmer chap to shout "Maintenant" when we're coming, and I'll do that as soon as you start moving. He'll drive his tractor like hell to help pull us out—every extra bit of power might just turn the trick. That's why he's revving up now.'

'You'll give me the usual order when you want me to go?'

'No, in this case I'll say "now." I want you to rev up first so that when we do go we'll go back at a hell of a lick. If we can shoot back fast enough before those beams give way there's a chance the rear tracks will reach the bank. If they do we might just make it—with the added pull the tractor will give us. And I can't guarantee it will work.'

'You're telling me you can't,' said Colburn. 'Once this weight moves on to the beams my bet is they'll sink like a stone.'

'You're probably right—but by then our impetus may take us on to the bank. There's no other way, Colburn. We're damned lucky that farmer turned up.'

'You're right there—I wonder if he has any idea what he's risking if a German patrol turns up? Don't tell me he can push off in the dark because he can't—not with all those tons of tank tied to his tail.'

'He must know that,' replied Barnes quietly. 'If the generals had fought this war the way some of these people fight when they get the chance we'd be over the Rhine by now.' He paused. 'I want you to stay on the rear of the hull, Colburn.

Then if anything goes wrong you jump. We're bound to move back at least a bit and with your legs you should be able to hit the bank.'

'What about you?'

'I'll be jumping off myself as soon as Reynolds is clear of the hatch.'

'Let's just see what happens, shall we?' Colburn suggested. 'And for your information you can stop treating me as a privileged person. There won't be any passengers on this trip.'

Reynolds moved on to the front of the turret to lower himself inside the driving compartment but Barnes stopped him.

'There's one point, Reynolds, and I'm sure you'll agree it's a good one—and no reflection on your driving abilities.' He grinned drily. 'When we do start to move be sure that you are in *reverse* gear!'

'I'll do my best, sergeant,' Reynolds replied stolidly. He climbed down through the hatch and began revving up.

At the last moment Barnes scrambled down inside the hull, collected a second torch, and handed this to Colburn when he emerged from the turret, telling him to shine it along the right-hand beam. He used his own torch to illuminate the other beam: at least they could now see where they were going and it was vital that he had as much warning as possible if they were on the edge of disaster. Any moment now. He waited a little longer to give Reynolds more time to warm up—the ultimate disaster would be an engine failure when they were half way back along those beams. And as he contemplated the weird scene behind the tank he felt that their attempt was doomed to failure. The torchlight showed up clearly the improvised bridge they hoped to move over and above it the tow-lines were taut and strained, vanishing in the darkness where they continued across to the rear of the tractor. In the brief intervals between the deep-throated revving up of the tank's engines he could hear the snarl and spit of the tractor's motor. Would there be enough horsepower to get them clear in time before the beams sank so deep that mud engulfed and choked the tracks—because of one thing Barnes was perfectly sure: those beams were going to sink rapidly under the tank's weight and they would probably split in half long before Bert reached the bank. Standing on the engine covers at the rear of the tank, Colburn should make it so long as he jumped quickly, but if their first rush didn't carry them to the bank Barnes didn't think that he would make it—he would have to stay behind to help Reynolds, and the driver had to climb upwards out of his hatch before he was even standing on the front hull. There was every chance that the twenty-six ton weight of the tank would sink like a stone long before Reynolds had come out, in which case they would both die without the aid of enemy action just as poor Penn had died. In fact, just as Davis had died. Barnes had an awful vision of what would happen as the tank went down, the mud and ooze rising hungrily up over the tracks, enveloping the hull, welling up over his chest and neck, his head going down as the quagmire swept over him and shut out the world for ever. His hand gripped the mike and he spoke.

'Now!'

Then he immediately bawled out 'Maintenant!' three times at the top of his voice and the tank was moving backwards. The tow-lines drooped, went slack. The farmer hadn't heard him! He opened his mouth again and saw the lines whip up, tighten, twanging as the tractor lurched forward. The tracks were on the beams now and instantly he was aware of a sinking sensation. Both beams had slipped off the island and Reynolds' end was going down. He was revving up non-stop and the tracks were churning through mud, sending up great gouts of ooze which sprayed through the torchlight rays as their bridge sank deeper and deeper. They weren't going to make it. The front end of the bridge was still firmly anchored to the bank so the rear end submerged more and more and now the tank was climbing at a steep angle. He looked back and saw liquid brown ooze lap over the end of the rear tracks, bubbling and slithering over the top. Soon the hull would be under. It was going to be too late, too late ever to reach firm ground and the tank was dropping like a slow-moving lift. Colburn still stood on the hull, leaning back now against the turret but still aiming his torch along the right-hand beam. Hand over the mike Barnes shouted to him to jump, removed the hand and sucked in his breath to order Reynolds up. Looking back he saw that the quagmire had reached the top of the hull—Reynolds must be frightened out of his life.

Inside the nose of the tank Reynolds was more terrified than he had ever been while under German bombardment, and he had been terrified from the moment he lowered himself through the hatch. His seat was jacked up so that when he sat down his head was well clear of the hatch rim and he could see exactly what was happening. It was the change of angle which finally confirmed that he was going to die horribly. Before Barnes had given the order to move the tank was tilted so that the nose was higher than the tail, and this had been of some comfort to Reynolds while they waited for him to rev up. If the tank did start to go down at the rear he might have time to get out and jump back on to the island. It was at least a chance. In the earphones he heard Barnes's order. *Now!* The tank began to move backwards, dropping to an even keel as the nose left the island and proceeded over the beams. Seconds later the angle began to change, so that now the nose was sinking, leaving the rear higher, and Reynolds knew that he was finished. The floor seemed to go down at an alarming pace and he could see mud flying past the headlights as the tracks churned deeper and his compartment went on sinking. The downward angle let him see the mud rising up over the tracks and he knew that in the next few seconds it would come over the line of the hull and creep towards his chin. Then, suddenly, it would be pouring into the hatchway, flooding his compartment as the quagmire swamped him. But Barnes hadn't yet given the order to bale out, so he stayed.

Colburn still hadn't jumped and Barnes had taken in breath to order Reynolds up when a tuft of grass flew past his torch ray. A second late the rear of the tank dropped and there was a slight bump as the tracks hit something solid. Colburn was shouting sentences Barnes couldn't hear but he understood what had happened. Climbing up over the steeply-angled beams the tracks had moved on upwards into the air until the centre of gravity had passed the end of the beams and they dropped. *They had reached firm ground.* The tracks went on up the shallow slope of the bank as he spoke quickly into the mike.

'Keep it up! We've done it!'

At that moment the engine coughed, sputtered, stalled, but they were ashore. The tow-lines were still taut as the tractor heaved at its immense load so Barnes jumped to the ground and ran forward to tell the farmer to stop. When the engine was switched off he thumped the Frenchman on the back and kept on thanking him regardless of the fact that the man couldn't understand half he was saying. He stopped suddenly as he heard Colburn calling out urgently and when he turned round to face the quagmire his body went completely rigid and he froze.

The giant vehicle must have driven along the road while they were preoccupied with saving the tank. They wouldn't have heard its motor because of their own engines and that of the tractor, and Reynolds, the only one facing the road, must have been too concerned with what was happening to notice the road. Worse still, the new arrivals could easily locate their position because Bert's headlights were still on, to say nothing of the tractor's lamp. The moon had now risen and this enabled Barnes to make instant recognition of the huge vehicle and the silhouette of its load—a tank transporter with a tank aboard. As if to complete the process of recognition a soldier walked past the headlights of the transporter, a soldier carrying something which could only be a machine-pistol and wearing a pudding-shaped helmet. The Germans had arrived.

It took a very short time for Barnes to recover from his stunned state, and this was replaced by an upsurge of cold, murderous fury. They had come all this way; they had lost Davis and Penn; they had almost lost their tank and their own lives a few minutes ago, and now this lot was poking its nose in to snatch it all away from them. Running back to the tank, he leapt on to the hull, grabbed a machine-pistol off the ledge inside the turret, and jumped down behind the tank. He spoke briefly to Reynolds and Colburn.

'Wait here—behind Bert. Don't switch the lights off—that will alert them.'

Then he was running back into the field, following as closely as he could the course the tank had taken when it first turned off the road. To avoid any risk of going into the quagmire he ran a little farther round than he thought was necessary, circling back so that he would come out on the road a good hundred yards behind where the transporter was parked. And as he ran his mind worked with icy detachment. How many Germans would there be? One transporter carrying one heavy tank to the repair shop: four men at the most, he guessed. Possibly only three—the Germans were short of ground troops. He dropped flat suddenly. The first soldier he had seen was standing in the field just beyond the grass verge, and now a second one had walked in front of the headlights and he was looking in Barnes's direction. He didn't think he had been spotted. He had kept his body crouched low and the moonlight wasn't very strong yet, its illumination blurred by a faint white mist rising off the field. The second soldier joined his companion and they both stood staring across the field. They couldn't be too worried yet because otherwise they wouldn't have walked in front of those headlights, and they could have no reason to suspect the presence of hostile troops in this area. Had they done that in the first place they would never have stopped the transporter. A third soldier appeared and stood right in front of the headlights, his machine-pistol clearly visible. He walked forward to join the others.

Barnes was very close to the road now and when he stood up the road was only a dozen yards away. A curtain of mist floated between himself and the Germans and he ran forward, crossing the road and continuing several yards into the field beyond. When he turned, the bulk of the transporter shielded him from where the soldiers waited. Why didn't they either investigate or go away? He found the answer when he looked back across the road and saw that the scene on the edge of the quagmire from that distance looked like anything but what it was. The lights of the tank were tilted downwards and he remembered the shallow slope at the edge of the quagmire. The odd angle of Bert's headlights gave the strange impression that there had just been a car crash. The turret of the tank was invisible and the light of the tractor was too far away to show up the tank's silhouette. The Germans might well be imagining that there was another road just across the fields, and from the passive way they were standing by the roadside he felt certain that Bert's engine had stalled just in time, otherwise they must have recognized the grind of the tracks. It was a tableau made to order, if only he could take advantage of it in time. He moved across the field towards the transporter, his boots making no sound on the grass.

He was close to the rear of the vehicle when he heard some-one call out in German. Peering round the end he saw two soldiers still standing on the verge just beyond the front of the transporter while a third one made his way across the field, flashing a torch in front of him. The mist was blurring Bert's lights now and hung over the quagmire like a noxious gas rising from the swamp. Was there a fourth man in the cab? The two Germans by the roadside presented a tempting target but Barnes waited. He had to try and get them all at once to avoid them scattering.

The soldier walking across the field had stopped, the machine-pistol tucked under one arm while he waved the torch with the other hand. The curtain of mist had drifted lower now and soon he would have to walk into it. He shouted across the field in German, waited, and then shouted again, several sentences. It was deathly quiet when he stopped shout-ing. The transporter's engine had been switched off and the mist seemed to cover the field like a leather glove which smothered even the slightest sound. Barnes waited. The Germans waited. He was fairly sure that the soldier in the field was going to give up his search and return to the others, which meant that for a brief moment all three men might be close together. He hoped so because as he stood by the elevated ramp at the rear of the transporter an entirely new idea was developing at the back of his mind, an idea which made it imperative that he should wipe out the whole German escort. Then he heard one of the men who stood by the roadside call out; the soldier with the torch answered and began to move deeper into the field, sweeping his torch towards the mist wall which was now less than a dozen yards ahead of him.

It happened without warning. The German walked up to the remnants of a wire fence, paused at a point where two posts tilted at a drunken angle, the wire between them sagging, and stepped over the wires, walking forward again. Then he fell forward, losing his torch which skidded sideways over baked mud, and shouted. His shout rose to a shriek of alarm. Jesus, thought Barnes, he's in the quagmire. One of the soldiers by the roadside ran forward, flashing on a torch beam, while the other stayed to guard the transporter. It was at this moment that Barnes climbed silently up on to the side of the huge vehicle, creeping forward and taking up a fresh position behind the German tank. The soldier was running across the field now, waving his torch in front of him as his comrade in the swamp screamed his head off, a scream of pure terror. As the running soldier stopped abruptly his torch beam focused on a horrifying sight: the first German was already up to his waist as the quagmire sucked him steadily downwards; his arms were waving frantically as he kept padding them down on the mud to arrest his sinking movement and he was still shrieking frenziedly. The third German by the roadside ran up to the transporter, feeling under the tank only feet away from where Barnes was crouched, pulled out a coil of rope and started running across the field. The soldier in the quagmire had sunk in up to the chest now, waving his arms high above his head, and only a few feet from where he struggled the lighted torch he had dropped lay on the top of unbroken crust. The man with the rope was close now and while he ran he held the rope coil ready to throw. As he reached the spot where the German holding the torch stood the struggling man sank lower, only his head and upstretched arms visible now, his voice an agonized moan. The rope was thrown, falling several feet short. The head in the swamp sank out of sight, the voice dying in a strangled gurgle, the vertical arms sliding under the surface, vanishing. Barnes wiped sweat off his forehead, slipped his finger back inside the trigger guard, stood up behind the tank and waited.

The two Germans came back slowly, machine-pistols hoisted over their shoulders, talking in low tones. They were less than a dozen yards away when Barnes lifted the machine-pistol. He fired one continuous burst, shifting the muzzle slightly from side to side to cover them both. They were still collapsing to the ground when he ceased fire, half a magazine still unused. At that moment the engine of the transporter kicked into life. There had been a fourth man—the driver, with instructions never to leave his cab. Barnes leapt down on to the grass verge and the door on his side was still open as he ran forward, pulling up short just before he reached the opening. Keeping back out of sight he shoved the muzzle of his pistol round the corner, aiming it upwards, firing one short burst. As he ran back to the rear of the vehicle, round the end and along the other side, the engine was still ticking over but the transporter hadn't started moving. He was still cautious when he reached the closed cab door. Grabbing the handle, he hauled the door open and jumped back, his pistol levelled, but the precaution wasn't necessary. As the door opened the driver's body toppled sideways, landing in the road with a soft thud. The German was dead, his right side riddled with bullets. Switching off the motor, Barnes went across to have a look at the other two soldiers. They were also dead. Sergeant Barnes was in sole possession of one German tank transporter.

10. Saturday May 25

THEY WERE ROARING through the night like a thunderbolt, twin headlights ablaze, the long beams stretching far into the darkness, the giant transporter swaying gently from side to side as Reynolds stepped up the speed. Fifty-five, sixty, sixty-five miles an hour. On the other side of the cab Barnes gazed along the beams which still showed only endless open road, while between them Colburn turned round to peer through the tiny window at the back of the cab.

'Don't worry,' Barnes assured him. 'Bert's still there—his weight alone will keep him on board even moving at this pace.'

His mind travelled back to what had taken place at the edge of the quagmire before they started their headlong dash to the north, and he smiled grimly as he thought that whatever happened now they had been responsible for eliminating at least one German heavy tank, even if the method used had been, to put it mildly, unorthodox. When he had examined the vehicle he found that it was in perfect working order except for the machine gun and the wireless set. To Barnes's mind it should have been possible to repair the firing mechanism in a few hours but instead the Germans had loaded the tank on to a transporter. This action alone pointed up the Germans' prodigal use of equipment. He had just finished his examination when he heard a heart-warming sound—the sound of Bert's engines tuning up faultlessly. By the time that Reynolds and Colburn arrived inside the tank he had decided exactly what he was going to do.

He was going to head all-out for Calais, the last port before

Dunkirk, possibly the twin keys to the whole campaign. If they could come up behind the Germans, causing the maximum possible damage to their rear, then they might be able to strike a heavy blow at a decisive moment. Above all else he prayed that they would find a really major objective. Bert, going all-out, had a maximum speed of fifteen miles an hour, whereas the German transporter, if driven to its utmost limits, could multiply that rate by four. But as a preliminary they had to get rid of one Wehrmacht heavy tank. This operation took less than thirty minutes.

First, they made a cautious reconnaissance to find out where the quagmire began. The wire fence proved to be the boundary and a short way from the gap through which the German soldier had walked to his death they found a faded notice board which carried a warning. The next stage was an even more cautious reversal of the transporter to a position close to the edge of the swamp. Barnes drove the vehicle while Colburn guided him with a torch. The third stage was the lowering of the ramp at the rear of the vehicle, followed by the infinitely satisfying moment when Barnes climbed into the driving compartment of the tank, fiddled with the controls, drove it backwards and forwards a few feet along the deck, and then reversed it for its final journey. He climbed out of the hatch and jumped clear as the machine was clattering down the ramp.

Wobbling erratically in the moonlight it proceeded across the field. It travelled backwards a dozen yards on an even keel like a robot moving through the night, then suddenly it lost its stability, the front tilting downwards as the tracks churned up a rain of wet mud. It continued at that angle for a short distance, advancing without pause, hurling back great goutfuls of ooze which made them jump sideways. A few seconds later the engine sound changed, coughing and spluttering as the huge tracks sank so deep that only the hull and turret were visible. The hull went under. The engine sound cut out altogether while the turret submerged and Barnes saw with amazement the turret disappear in a matter of seconds, leaving behind only a disturbed whirlpool of mud and water. They had been lucky—they had driven Bert into the harder end of the swamp.

'What happened to that farmer?' he asked Colburn.

'As soon as he heard the rattle of your machine-pistol he cleared off across the fields. I don't think he liked the idea of being mixed up with dead Germans.'

'And yet he had the guts to fetch those beams.'

'I guess he thought he'd done his bit—you can't blame him, he probably has a wife and family.'

'I don't blame him but I'd like to have thanked him with a bottle of Mandel's wine.'

It took them another ten minutes to put Bert aboard the transporter and to cover his silhouette with the tarpaulin they always carried. Under Barnes's instructions, Reynolds had reversed Bert back up the ramp and along the deck until his rear rested behind the cab wall so that in an emergency he could be driven off in the minimum possible time. Then they had carried the dead Germans well away from the roadside into the field opposite the quagmire, collected all the spare machine-pistol magazines they could lay their hands on, and climbed aboard.

It was surprising, Barnes thought as he sat in the cab of the transporter which was now thundering north like an express train, it was surprising what you could do in thirty minutes. The question now was what they could do behind the German lines near Calais. He looked at his watch, Penn's watch. Thirty minutes to midnight. At this rate they would reach the Calais area soon after midnight, that was assuming they drove all the way without interception, which of course wouldn't happen. It was the surprise element which they had on their side, surprise plus audacity. He had a vivid picture of that Panzer column which had driven through the night with its lights full on. Well, they had their lights full on and this was a German vehicle they were driving. Finally, there would be an element of near-chaos close to the battle zone.

'I still say these might come in very useful,' remarked Colburn. He produced three German helmets piled on top of each other from under the seat.

'Under what circumstances?' demanded Barnes. 'Put one of those on and you can get shot as a spy.'

'Just a thought.' He put them away again and produced a machine-pistol. 'This baby is very good. While you were killing Germans back at the quagmire I found out from Reynolds how to use it—just in case. Look.'

Extracting the magazine, he hunched the weapon under his shoulder and gave a demonstration. Then he replaced the magazine and slipped the pistol under the seat. The energy of the Canadians, thought Barnes. This laddie never stops going. A distinct asset.

'I still can't understand why you like handling explosives as a peacetime occupation,' he told Colburn.

'The satisfaction of doing a good job.' He paused. 'Hell, let's face it—I'm a bastard who likes a good blow-up.'

'You've come to the right place.' He pointed to the right.

Beyond Barnes's side window the night was lit up with distant flashes, flashes which succeeded each other almost instantaneously like an electric storm. They were racing north through Colburn's 'gap' with the southern flank of the main battle area on their right, although as yet they couldn't hear the sound of the guns. For the third time in a minute Reynolds glanced in his rear view mirror.

'I thought so, sergeant. We've got company. There's a truck coming up behind us and I think it's like the one Penn put a shell through.'

'How far back?'

'Coming up on our tail. I think he'll be passing us in a minute. He's coming at a helluva lick.'

'Keep your present speed.'

Barnes tightened his grip on the machine-pistol which lay across his lap and Colburn produced the German helmets again with a flourish.

'Sergeant Barnes, how many men do you think there could be aboard this truck?'

'At least twenty,' said Barnes shortly.

'And we would like to get to Calais rather than fight Custer's Last Stand here?'

'That is the general idea.'

'Then may I offer these—going very cheap? I've noticed that in wartime you don't look at a soldier's face—you look at his uniform, and the most distinctive part of a German soldier's uniform is this elegant helmet.'

They said no more, they put the helmets on, and it struck Barnes that he had never seen anyone look more like a German soldier than Reynolds in his helmet, which was perhaps just as well since he would be closest to the truck. They could hear the horn blaring behind them now, warning the transporter they were about to be overtaken, and now a chill silence descended on the cab as the tension rose rapidly. Barnes remembered the open-backed trucks which Penn had described and how the sea of faces had stared at him as they went past.

If this lot suspects anything, Barnes thought grimly, all they have to do is to play innocent, pass us, and the next thing we'll know is when a spray of bullets comes through this windscreen. One burst should do for all three of us. He crouched lower in his seat, peering from under the rim of the helmet which was too large for him, changing his grip on the pistol so he could raise and fire in one movement. The only comforting thing was that Reynolds would keep on driving without his nerve cracking as long as he was physically capable of the action. Ah, here they come.

He could see the headlights of the truck now. It seemed to drive part way along the side of the transporter and then hold its speed. Had the tarpaulin come undone? Could they see that it wasn't a German tank under the sheet? He peered back through the little window and the bulk of the tank blocked his view, but he could see that the tarpaulin was still firmly in place over the rear. The trouble was it was the side which counted. The headlights were moving forward now and out of the corner of his eye he saw the cab of the other vehicle draw level and then move ahead. Any minute now. The cloth-covered side of the truck slid past and the truck was ahead of them. A huddle of helmeted German soldiers stared back into the fierce glare of the headlights, their faces white under the pudding-shaped helmets. Barnes stared back, knowing that they couldn't see him because of the headlights. They looked dazed, bored, tired. As the truck sped away from them he wondered how many of those soldiers would be alive when the war was over. They took off their helmets and handed them to Colburn.

'Well, that worked,' he said, 'but I can't say I fancied the experience all that much. Have you had a lot of this sort of thing since you left Etreux?'

'Not more than six times a day,' Barnes replied humorously.

'Oh, well, that's fine. I thought maybe it happened frequently.'

You could sense the drop in temperature inside the cab, the relief at still being alive, the sheer enjoyment of still being in one piece. Colburn found he had an almost uncontrollable impulse to chatter and it was with difficulty that he restrained himself from overdoing it. These boys really had something to put up with; this long-drawn-out business wasn't his forte. Give him the air every time. It was short but sharp up there, over with quickly. Ten minutes later the tension crept back into the cab when Reynolds informed them that there were headlights behind again.

'Another truck?' queried Barnes.

'No, I think this is a car. He's in a hurry, too. I thought I was driving this bus over the speed limits but some of these drivers need certifying. The car behind came up from nowhere like a dirt-track rider.'

'Let him pass.'

'Helmets on?' queried Colburn.

'Not this time. Whoever it is won't be able to see clearly into the cab from a car.'

'He'll see Reynolds if he looks,' Colburn objected.

'I don't like wearing Jerry helmets,' said Reynolds flatly.

Headlights had appeared beyond Reynolds's window and the car began to move up fast. Reynolds glanced down, looked ahead quickly, and then glanced down again. The car moved forward and then stayed alongside the transporter's bonnet, the driver's arm projecting and waving madly as he flagged them down. Barnes's eyes narrowed and he lifted the pistol, a movement which caught Reynolds' eye.

'Don't, sergeant.'

'What's the matter?'

'It looked like Jacques. I think he wants us to stop.'

'Jacques! It can't be. He passed us this morning on his way to Abbeville.'

'It's a green Renault and I'm sure it's Jacques. In fact,' Reynolds concluded heavily as though not enjoying contradicting Barnes, 'I saw him twice. It's definitely Jacques.'

'All right. Slow down and then pull in, but keep your engine running. Was he alone?'

'As far as I could see, yes.'

The darkest suspicion flooded into Barnes's mind and he put one hand on the door handle ready to jump out as soon as the vehicle stopped. If this really was Jacques no possible stretch of the imagination could explain his presence up here in the Pas de Calais, yet what was he doing so far from the Mandel farm and Abbeville? Still not at all sure that Reynolds hadn't made some ghastly mistake, he jumped down as soon as the transporter pulled up. When he reached the ground the Renault was stopping a dozen yards ahead. The engine was switched off and a man got out. He ran back towards them, shielding his eyes against the powerful beams. It was Jacques.

'I've been driving up and down this road for three hours hoping to see you, Sergeant Barnes. But I didn't really expect I ever would—I thought you'd follow that route I marked on your map, though.'

'I didn't expect to see you either,' Barnes replied grimly.

'You amazed me when I saw Reynolds in that cab—it is a German transporter, isn't it?'

His face looked chalk-white, although it might have been the light of the beams, and his voice was harsh and strained.

'Yes, it's a transporter. What are you doing here, Jacques? You said you were on your way to Abbeville.'

'A terrible thing has happened. The Germans have shot my sister.'

Had his voice trembled? Barnes thought so, but the fleeting

expression of pain was succeeded by an expression of bitterness and hate.

'How did it happen?' Barnes asked quietly.

'The Germans are trying to say it was an accident—their interpreter told me that—but they killed her. She was standing in a square in Abbeville and some German tanks arrived. Someone leaned out from a window and shot one of their men in the tower of a tank. They fired their machine guns all round the square and my sister was killed. Boches!' He spat out the word.

'I'm very sorry to hear that, Jacques.' Barnes spoke gently. 'But what are you doing in this part of the world?'

'After what happened I decided I must come home to tell my father. I live in Lemont—that is near Gravelines. I told you that,' he ended accusingly. 'Then I shall kill some Germans.'

'I'd think about that, if I were you. Killing Germans takes training and skill.'

'Not with a knife in the back in a dark street.'

He spoke without hysteria, his mouth tight. He means just what he says, Barnes thought, and he'll do it coldly and clinically. This was the lad who led a gang to put wire across a road, wire which killed a German cyclist.

'On the other hand,' Jacques said suddenly, 'I could come with you.'

'Thanks, but nothing doing.'

Jacques was peering up at Colburn who leant out of the cab window to listen to the conversation. He frowned and turned to Barnes.

'Who is that?'

'A soldier—someone we picked up on the way.'

'And where is Mr Penn?'

'He died.'

'I am so sorry. I liked Mr Penn. He was so jolly, is that the word?'

'Jolly would do.'

'And you will not let me come with you?'

'Sorry. No. You get home to your people at Lemont.'

'This is the road to Calais as well as to Gravelines. You are going to one of those places—to Calais, perhaps?'

'Perhaps.'

'I could drive ahead at least some of the way and warn you of danger.'

'It's not good, Jacques. That would put you in a crossfire between us and the Germans.'

'I don't mind. No, that won't make you change your mind.' He paused. 'You are travelling on the main road at the moment, the most dangerous road. If you are going to Calais I know another road which turns off this one and it would be much safer, I'm sure. The Germans are less likely to expect someone coming that way. If I take you along it I can leave you before you reach Calais and drive back to Lemont. In fact,' he added slyly, 'if I insist on driving ahead of you, you can't really stop me, can you?'

In the end, reluctantly, Barnes agreed. Before the night was out the lad was going to do something silly, anyway, and he was within a few months of being called up when he would have no choice. If they were very lucky they might get him behind the Allied lines where he would be safer while he got over his sister's death. The only alternative, in view of his obstinacy, was to throw away the ignition key and leave him stranded, and he wasn't prepared to do that. He gave Jacques careful instructions—he was always to drive at least one hundred yards ahead of them and if they ran into trouble he was to leave his car at once and run. Climbing back up into the cab, Barnes watched him walk back to the Renault.

'I still don't like it,' he told Colburn, 'but if he keeps that distance ahead of us it won't look as though he's leading the way.'

'There's a war on and he looked pretty mature to me. If you'd made him leave us he'd have been up to his back-stabbing tricks and sooner or later they'd get him.'

'Let's go, Reynolds,' said Barnes.

As the transporter moved on through the night the air of tension returned to the cab and it never went away again. There was no longer much conversation and Barnes found himself holding the machine-pistol in a vice-like grip as his eyes followed Jacques' tail-light. He had already made up his mind that as soon as Jacques put them on the side road the lad would have to leave them and go home to Lemont. Telling Colburn to keep a close eye on the tail-light, he took out his map folded to the Pas de Calais area and found Lemont, a dot little more than a large village close to Gravelines, the town east-north-east of Calais. Both places were on the waterline, a system of canals with sluice gates to control the flow. Closing the map, he lowered his window and looked to the east where the flashes now rivalled the moonlight as they illuminated the sky, but it was no longer the flashes alone which told him they were moving very close to the battle area, for now he could hear in the distance the thump of big guns. He wiped more sweat off his forehead and dried his hands on his trousers. The rising sense of tension had almost become a physical presence inside the cab, something they could all *feel*. Was it simply the growing sound of the guns or was it also the realization that with every second which passed, with every yard they moved forward, they drew closer to the inevitable encounter with the Germans? Five more minutes passed, five minutes of loaded silence, and then the crisis broke with alarming suddenness.

They had followed Jacques round a sharp corner and immediately Reynolds was jamming on the brakes, the huge vehicle still trying to move forward against the restraining pressure. The Renault was stationary perhaps seventy yards ahead, and no farther than fifty yards beyond the stopped car lights were strung across the road. One of the lights, a red lamp, moved from side to side.

'Road-block,' said Barnes tersely.

Colburn stirred beside him. 'Hadn't we better move up closer to Jacques?'

'No, we stay here. Reynolds, switch off the headlights but leave the side ones on—we may have a visitor in a minute. And turn off the motor—I want to hear what's going on—but get ready to start it again as soon as I tell you.'

Leaning out of the window, he turned his head and listened. The big guns had obligingly paused with their cannonade and he heard a voice, a staccato voice probably speaking in German. Then Jacques began to turn the car round in the road. He had only commenced the operation when a burst of machine-pistol fire shattered the night. The car stopped in mid-turn and ran back into the ditch, its front wheels still on the road. Barnes had his head poked out of the window when he heard another burst. As it broke off he detected a faint noise and looked up the road but it was difficult to see anything between the transporter and the Renault, whose light were now beamed across the road. Colburn grasped Barnes by the arm.

'For God's sake . . .'

'Quiet! I think he's almost here.'

The running footsteps were very close and as Barnes jumped down into the road Jacques appeared, his breathing laboured, his expression bleak. He spoke rapidly.

'I'm all right. They opened fire when I wouldn't drive up to them. As far as I could see there's only three or four of them but they've got a pole across the road . . .'

'Any sign of a field gun? A gun with a shield and a big barrel?'

'No, but there was one man crouched by the roadside behind a sort of rifle on legs.'

'Anti-tank rifle. Which side is he on?'

'The left as you approach them. I saw a motor-cycle and sidecar behind the rifle . . .'

'Any one in it?'

'No, but there are three more men behind the barrier—it was one of them that fired at me. I managed to get out of the car on this side.'

'Get up here quick.' Barnes was unfastening one corner of the tarpaulin and he held it while Jacques scrambled up on to the transporter deck. 'Get on to the tank behind the cab and lie flat on the engine covers—the turret should shield you from any bullets that may be flying about.'

'We're going through it?' asked Jacques.

'Yes, so keep your head down.'

Re-fastening the tarpaulin, he climbed back into the cab

229

and gave the order to move. He held the muzzle of his machine-pistol well below windscreen level and Colburn extracted his own pistol from under the seat. The transporter began to move forward, headlights blazing again, while inside the cab three men gazed fixedly ahead.

'No shooting unless we can't avoid it,' Barnes warned. 'We stopped and they'll think there's something funny about that but they'll recognize their own vehicle. We're not stopping whatever happens and they may lift the pole. Reynolds, get up some speed and keep going—I'd like at least forty miles an hour when we reach that barrier, more if you can manage it.'

The transporter began picking up speed fast as Reynolds put his foot down. He had reached a speed well in excess of forty as they flew past the abandoned Renault and ahead the lights of the road-block rushed towards them. Barnes was leaning well forward now, straining his eyes to see as much as possible before they reached the obstacle, which was clearly visible in their headlights—a narrow pole mounted several feet above the road. And something else, too. On the left a soldier lay behind the anti-tank rifle, while beyond rose the silhouette of the motor-cycle and sidecar, a soldier already astride the cycle. The pole remained obstinately down. Barnes shouted.

'Reynolds, if you can, drive over that rifle and the cycle—as long as you can get us back off the verge to the road. Leave it to you . . .'

Reynolds made no reply, his broad shoulders hunched forward over the wheel, his head quite still as he stared through the windscreen. They hadn't opened fire yet. The fact that it was a German vehicle was confusing them. Barnes braced himself for the impact, grabbing the edge of the window and spreading his left arm across Colburn's chest to hold him back. Cleverly, Reynolds left his manoeuvre until the last possible moment, driving straight down the centre of the road, heading for the middle of the barrier, increasing speed. Twenty yards. Fifteen. Ten. He turned the wheel. The anti-tank rifle, the soldier, the man on the cycle, rushed towards them and then the huge transporter loaded with twenty-six tons of tank smashed past the impediments. The wheels ground over something, the cycle and sidecar were hurled sideways, the soldier catapulted through the air, and then they were through the barrier as Reynolds swung the transporter back on to the centre of the road. Not a shot had been fired. In his concentration on the anti-tank rifle Barnes had never even seen the pole go: when he leaned out to look back all the light had disappeared and the beams from the Renault were fading into the distance. He gave one simple order.

'Accelerate.'

GENERAL STORCH stormed into the Lemont farmhouse which was his temporary headquarters, his voice preceding him down the narrow passage.

'Meyer! Where are you?' He reached the entrance to the room serving as his office, closed the door quickly and took off his cap. 'Ah, there you are! What has gone wrong?' He was talking rapidly as he strode to a table clothed with a large-scale map of the area. 'I have just heard that you have sent an instruction countermanding my order.'

'Only provisionally, sir.' Colonel Meyer stood up behind the table and screwed the monocle into his eye, his expression worried. This was going to be another bad night.

'But it was only an hour ago that we went over the order together—the order to attack at dawn, at o.400 hours. That road to Dunkirk is only three inches under the waterline in spite of the fact that the French opened the sluice gates at Gravelines—so what has happened since?'

Meyer picked up the message form from the table and held it out for the general to read, but Storch ignored it, stripping off his gloves, his voice urgent.

'You've read it, so tell me.'

'It is a message from G.H.Q. which came in after you'd left, sir. It was because of this that I issued my order—to be confirmed later subject to your approval.'

'What are the arm-chair lot up to now?'

'The message is not complete—it was garbled in transmission. We're still having trouble with the wireless but I'm sure the meaning is clear.'

'We haven't much time,' the general reminded him, examining the map as he spoke.

'It orders us to halt on the waterline, to stay where we are now. General von Bock will attack the B.E.F. from Belgium. I gather that General von Rundstedt is worried about the condition of the tanks, and that's why he's halting us.'

'May I see it?' Storch took the message and read it through several times, then looked up cynically. 'It doesn't really say all that—and it's certainly garbled.'

Meyer took a deep breath. 'When I was talking to Rundstedt on the field telephone several days ago in your absence he explained his views—he wishes to preserve the armoured forces for the coming battle against the French south of the Somme.'

'Yes, I remember.' Storch hardly seemed to be listening. 'I have just heard from Keller that this submerged road is not covered by the enemy—our patrol advanced half way along it before dark without meeting any opposition. I've had the patrol pulled back to Lemont for the night.'

'On the surface it does look promising,' Meyer reluctantly agreed.

'Actually, the road is under the surface.' Storch flashed a confident smile and it made Meyer feel even more exhausted to see the general looking as though he had just risen from an excellent night's sleep. 'So the road to Dunkirk really is open, Meyer. Even allowing for a cautious passage by our tanks the advance forces will be inside Dunkirk two hours after dawn. And once we have Dunkirk the whole B.E.F. is in our hands —over a quarter of a million men.'

'But the message from G.H.Q. . . . .' Meyer began.

'I think we can deal with this. It's badly garbled and the most recent order we received was quite clear—advance up the coast and seize the ports. That is what we shall do—we shall seize the last port. Dunkirk.'

'I have asked the wireless operator to try and get through to obtain clarification.'

'Then we shall have another confused reply which will make matters worse. Cancel the request for clarification.'

He waited while Meyer picked up the phone and gave the order, replacing the receiver reluctantly.

'What is really worrying you, Meyer?'

'I'm bothered about the huge concentration of ammunition at the dump. In this confined area inside the waterline . . .'

'You have sufficient for the operation?'

'Too much really . . .''

'We can never have too much.' He pulled his cap on firmly. 'So we record the receipt of this latest message as being so garbled that it is meaningless. And now you can send off the confirmatory copy of my order to attack to Advanced Head-quarters. We should be able to spare one staff car from our entry into Dunkirk. Send off the car within the hour.'

The colonel swallowed. Storch had now covered himself completely. By the time the staff car reached Advanced Headquarters the Panzers would be on the move along the partially submerged road.

'Our rear, sir,' Meyer persisted. 'It is hardly protected at all, everything is facing north and east.'

'Precisely! The British are in front of us, Meyer, not behind us. We advance at dawn as planned.'

The clock on Meyer's desk registered 12.10 a.m.

Racing through the night, the transporter weaved steadily from one side of the road to the other and then back again as Reynolds struggled desperately to prevent the German truck from passing them. Again, the crisis had arisen with hardly any warning. Barnes checked his watch. 12.15 a.m.

Reynolds had warned them that headlights were coming up behind them very fast and that he thought it was another truck-load of German soldiers. A sixth sense had told Barnes that it was highly unlikely that they would be able to repeat their previous deception and then he heard the horn blowing. The horn had gone on blowing ever since, and for a while the truck had been content to stay on their tail.

'Sounds as though he'd like a word with us,' said Colburn.

'I'm sure he would,' replied Barnes grimly.

'I don't see how they could have cottoned on to us.'

234

'That road-block we smashed up. Someone must have sounded the alarm and sent this lot after us.'

Reynolds glanced in the rear view mirror. 'He's going to try and pass us.'

'Don't let him.'

So Reynolds had started weaving the giant vehicle backwards and forwards across the road, blocking the truck's path each time it attempted to move up. Colburn had been surprised that they hadn't opened fire, but Barnes had pointed out that behind the cab stood a tank with a 70-mm. armour plating and that the Germans must realize there was a tank aboard from the shape of the tarpaulin. They must also have realized that machine-pistol fire would scarcely scratch the plating, let alone penetrate the full length of the tank to reach the cab. And that, Barnes supposed, was why they were so anxious to pass—so that they could send a blast of bullets into the cab from the front. It couldn't go on like this much longer, he was quite sure. They had to do something about that truck. He explained his plan briefly to them and then he opened the door and threw it back flat against the side of the transporter. The horn behind them was still blowing like a banshee. He went out backwards, holding on to the upper door frame while his right foot stepped inside the metal climbing rung. Looped over his shoulder, the machine-pistol didn't help his balance and at the speed they were travelling the wind velocity buffeted his body like a minor hurricane and tried to tear him away from his precarious grip. He stayed there for a second and wondered whether he was in full view of the truck, but the tarpaulin-shrouded tank was acting as a screen. Very carefully he sent his left foot out into space, feeling for the deck behind the cab. The foot felt nothing as the transporter lurched sideways and he nearly came off. There were too many things to cope with at once—keeping his grip, anticipating the violent swerves of the transporter, feeling around for the deck —and all the time the wind rush tore savagely at his body. This was worse, far worse, than he had expected. It was taking him all his time to hang on. Then his shoulder wound began to throb viciously and suddenly he felt dizzy and his head started to swim. That decided him. All or nothing. Gritting his teeth he made a supreme effort, lifting his left leg high, bringing it down where the deck should be. His foot hammered down on hard flat wood. He let go with his left hand and grabbed for the tarpaulin rope, praying that it was firmly attached to the rear of the cab. He pulled at the rope and when it held firm he let go with his right hand, his whole weight suspended from the rope now. At that moment the transporter swerved again and the violence of the momentum hurled him outwards.

His body described a complete arc of a hundred and eighty degrees, his left foot pivoting under him, his hand sliding down the rope, then his body slammed back against the tank with fearful impact and he ended up facing outwards, still clutching the rope with only his left hand as his right foot scrabbled for a hold on the deck. For several seconds he hung there help-lessly, dazed with pain because when the swing of the arc had brought him round to crash backwards against the covered hull the first point of impact which took the shock was his wounded shoulder. Waves of dizziness trembled through his brain, a feeling of sickness welled up, and beyond it all the guns boomed, the horn shrieked, and the transporter swayed crazily from side to side. He was done for, he couldn't summon up enough will-power to do anything but hang on. He fought down the sickness, tasted salty blood in his mouth where he had bitten through his lip, and then felt Jacques grasp him, one hand round each upper arm. The grip steadied him while he grasped the rope with both hands, hauling himself in between the cab and the rear of the tank. Then he flopped forward on the canvas over the engine covers and lay quite still, gulping in great breaths of air, desperately fighting for self-control as his wound screamed at him. He was vaguely aware that Jacques was lying beside him next to the turret. And all the time the vehicle swayed insidiously from side to side under him as he tried to push away the feeling that he was blacking-out.

It was a terrible struggle to recover quickly, to get his choking breath back to normal, to push under the blinding waves of pain, but two things stimulated his recovery—the rush of fresh air and the insistent shrieking of the horn which continually alerted him of the imminent danger. Telling Jacques to keep flat he forced himself up on his knees, scooping up a ridge of tarpaulin to conceal his position. Then he extracted two spare magazines from his pockets, rested them behind the ridge and lowered himself flat, the machine-pistol next to his shoulder. Clubbing his fist he gave the agreed signal, banging three times on the rear of the cab.

The transporter stopped weaving and pulled over to the right side of the road, still moving at high speed, allowing free access for the truck to pass. I've got to get this just right, Barnes told himself. Head down until the exact moment when the covered part of the truck is alongside us—the part which sheltered the troops inside. No need to fire at the driver at once—I want to get the lot—and they won't shoot at Reynolds from their own cab for fear he swerves into them. He kept his head down and heard the truck coming up as Reynolds drove well into his own lane. The truck was coming up with a roar. He felt the transporter lift slightly as they started going uphill. Now! He flattened the canvas ridge with the gun muzzle and his heart sank—the truck was much further past than he had expected, the cab already beyond Reynolds, the covered side spread out in front of him. Pressing the trigger he swivelled the gun methodically low down along the canvas wall, just above the wooden side, sweeping the muzzle in slow arcs. Empty! He was ramming a fresh magazine when Jacques called out: a German soldier peered round the end of the truck, machine-pistol aimed. Barnes fired, the man fell into the road as Barnes swivelled the muzzle back again, his finger pressing steadily on the trigger, a stream of bullets ripping and tearing through the canvas along one continuous strip. At that moment Reynolds took a hand.

The road was climbing an embankment up to a bridge and the driver gave the pre-arranged signal, two long blasts on his own horn. Barnes shouted to Jacques to hold on tight and braced himself for the impact as the transporter began to speed up and edge across the road, moving ahead of the truck as it shifted its course to hit the truck broadside on. They were close to the summit when the German driver lost his nerve, swerving away when the colossus was only inches from him. Lifting his head Barnes saw the truck spin over sideways, falling from view. As they went over the bridge he heard a muffled thump, a boom, and then flames flared in the night behind them. The petrol tank had gone. The next thing he heard was a terrifying shriek of brakes, the transporter's brakes.

The view from the cab was frightening. Reynolds had heard the stutter of Barnes's gun, had concentrated half his attention on that final manoeuvre which had destroyed the truck, then he was sweeping over the bridge at high speed. The road was going down now and he saw what faced him in a flash. Headlights blazed on a stone wall dead ahead, a right-hand turn at the bottom. Then the headlights were swinging wildly as he desperately tried to negotiate the unexpected hazard, braking, turning, going straight through the wall with a tremendous smash, the immense weight of the vehicle piercing the wall like butter. The whole transporter shuddered, knocking aside a small tree, skidded across the garden, then it stopped.

Barnes lay still for a moment, collecting himself, still clutching the machine-pistol. He had been warned by the shriek of brakes and he had been saved by the pillow of spare canvas between himself and the rear of the cab, and his own body had saved Jacques when the lad was thrown against him. They got up cautiously, like men expecting a limb to fall off, and Colburn was waiting for them at the foot of the open cab door, his pistol under his arm, blood oozing from a cut on his forehead and a gash on the back of his left hand. He said they were little more than scratches.

'Is Reynolds all right?' asked Barnes.

'Reynolds is all right,' said Reynolds from the cab. 'I don't know why, but he's all right. Probably only because he was inside this brute—we went through that wall like going through paper. I'm sorry, sergeant,' he added, 'but I was concentrating on the truck and when we got over the bridge the wall was on top of me. And by the way, this job,' he banged the wheel, 'is a write-off. So it's back to Bert now.'

'You did damned well. No one could have survived in that truck—I riddled it before you bounced it over the edge and then the petrol went up—but I'll go back and make sure in a minute. It's a good job you braked when you did—we wouldn't have gone through that like paper.'

He pointed to the house. Barely six feet beyond where the transporter had pulled up stood an ancient three-storey mansion. All the windows were broken, a wall creeper almost covered the front door, and the garden in which the transporter rested was knee-deep in weeds. No one had lived there for a long time, which was probably just as well: opening the front door to find a tank transporter in the garden could be a disconcerting experience. Reynolds tried the engine several times but it refused to function, and while Barnes went back over the bridge Colburn and Jacques helped the driver to pull the tarpaulin off Bert.

Barnes approached the bridge with caution. Reaching the top he crouched behind the wall and peered over the edge to where the wrecked truck was still on fire. There was no sign of life but there was every sign of death. The vehicle had landed with its wheels in the air and by the light of the flames he saw huddled shapes lying in the grass, but the only thing which moved was the flames. Few of the men in the back could have survived the murderous fire of his machine-pistol, and any who did would have perished when the truck tumbled down the steep embankment. He doubted whether anyone was alive when the petrol tank blew. When he turned round to walk back he froze, his taut nerves trying to cope with the fact that a new crisis was at hand.

Headlights were coming down the road from the opposite direction. They were still some distance away but he gained the impression that they were approaching at speed. Running down the slope he heard the welcome sound of Bert's engines starting up, but they still had to lower the ramp and bring Bert down it, and he knew there wouldn't be time to do that before the oncoming vehicle arrived. Colburn must have seen something in his face because he asked the question immediately.

'More trouble?'

'I'm not sure. There's something coming down the road from the north—on it's own.'

'We'd better set up an ambush. I'll take the other side of the road . . .'

'No, stick with me—otherwise we may end up shooting each other. Jacques, tell Reynolds to switch off his engine and sit tight. You get behind the end wall of the house and stay there. Come on, Colburn . . .'

The vehicle was quite close now and it sounded like a car, but it was still hidden by the bend in the road, and it was still travelling at high speed. They ran a short distance into the garden, stopping at a point where an undamaged section of the wall was shoulder-high. Peering over the wall-top beyond the bend Barnes saw that the headlights were quite close. He ducked out of sight and heard the car begin to lose speed as the headlights reached the bend. Well, they wouldn't get far once they turned the corner and found half the wall strewn in their path. He looked back and wasn't too happy to see that the glow of fire beyond the bridge clearly silhouetted the transporter with a British tank nestling on its deck.

'I think it's stopping,' Colburn whispered.

'It's bloody well going to have to.'

'It may be a civilian.'

'Only people like Jacques are mad enough to drive about in battle zones.'

He timed it carefully, keeping low as the car crawled round the bend and then pulled up, its engine still ticking over. As he lifted his head he heard a clash of gears and the car began to reverse back round the bend. He had a quick impression—a black Mercedes staff car, the hood back, a German soldier driving and beside him an officer in a peaked cap clutching something to his chest. It was almost beyond the bend now, reversing rapidly. He lifted the machine-pistol, cradled it into his shoulder, and rested the barrel on the wall-top. Aiming about two feet above the headlights he fired. One long burst. He heard a brief shatter of breaking glass and the car went crazy, still reversing but snaking from side to side. He fired again, arcing the gun. The car swung wildly sideways, crashed its rear into the wall and halted, its headlights shining on the opposite wall. The engine had stopped.

The driver was hunched over the wheel, head and shoulders drenched in blood. The passenger seat door was open and the officer lay in the roadway on his back, capless, arms outstretched, staring up at the stars. A few feet from his right hand lay a half-open brief-case, the case he had clutched so firmly to his chest when the emergency had arisen. Barnes checked the officer, whose chest was torn with bullets where the arc had moved across him, and lifted one shoulder. He was a major, a dead major. Picking up the brief-case, Barnes took out a paper while Colburn examined the rear seat; holding the paper in front of the headlights he grunted.

'This is your pigeon. You said you could speak German, Colburn, can you read it as well? This looks as though it could be interesting.'

'Let me have a look.'

He scanned the lines briefly and then looked up, his face very serious. 'This *is* interesting. It's a battle order and this copy is for some Advanced Headquarters. Let me check it again to make sure I've got it right.'

'This staff car can tell us something,' said Barnes thoughtfully. 'They can't possibly be expecting anyone coming up from this direction or else it wouldn't be travelling without escort. We may surprise the bastards yet.'

'This document* is going to surprise you, Barnes. The German 14th Panzer Division is going to attack Dunkirk at dawn. They've found some secret road to the port just under the water—the whole area must be flooded along that part of the front as far as I can gather. Apparently this road is built up from the surrounding countryside so it's only a few inches under the floods.'

---

* Not only sergeants are lucky with documents. Twenty-four hours earlier, Lt.-Gen. Sir Alan Brooke, commander 11 Corps B.E.F., was handed a battle order captured from a German staff car which warned of an imminent offensive by Gen. von Bock's Army Group B—just in time for him to move more troops into the threatened area.

'Does it give the start-line for the attack?'

'Yes, the funny thing is it's Jacques' home town—the attack is being launched from Lemont at 04.00 hours.'

Barnes knew that at the eleventh hour he had found his worthwhile objective. He checked his watch. 12.25 a.m.

'We'll forget about Calais,' he said. 'Jacques is going to take us home.'

'It gives the name of the general who's leading the attack.'

'Really?' Barnes wasn't too interested as they hurried back to the transporter.

'Yes. A General Heinrich Storch.'

12. Sunday May 26

STORCH JUMPED OUT of the staff car, checked his watch, briefly acknowledge the salute of the waiting officer, walked down the hedge-lined lane on the outskirts of Lemont. 12.45 a.m. Less than four hours to dawn. The lights of an armoured car at the end of the lane showed him the way while beyond the hedge on his left, to the north, the light of the moon shone down over the flooded areas, a vast lake which might have been the sea. When he reached the car he stopped and turned to the officer who had followed him.

'So here it is, Keller—the start-line of the final advance. It doesn't look much from here, does it?'

The lights of the armoured car beamed north across a flooded field below the level of the lane. Water stretched as far as the eye could see towards Dunkirk, but standing up above the surface of the lake ran a double line of six-foot poles like slim telegraph poles immersed by the inundation.

'Keller, how far do the marker posts stretch?'

'Ten kilometres, sir. We felt it inadvisable to mark the passage any further at the moment.'

'Quite right, Keller, quite right.'

Storch paused, slapping his gloves slowly against the side of his leg. He was in an excellent humour and when this mood took him he liked to show his subordinates that their general was capable of a certain light-hearted touch.

'So, Keller, you are telling me that between those posts lies the road to Dunkirk—that we do not have to possess super-natural powers like Christ to walk upon the waters?'

Keller, a religious man, as Storch knew well, blinked and

stirred uneasily. What could be in Storch's mind now? He kept his face expressionless and answered with admirable brevity.

'Yes, sir.'

Keller waited anxiously. He was never quite sure how to deal with the situation when Storch talked like this for it was closely akin to another mood which could be the precursor to an almighty row. He said nothing further and waited while the general walked to the front of the armoured car, standing to gaze for a moment through the gap in the hedge. Then, without warning, Storch marched forward between the posts, his boots splashing up water but never sinking more than six inches below the waterline. He walked on and on, almost out of sight, and then came back again, deliberately kicking up great spurts of water like a small child on its first day by the sea. Reaching the armoured car, he paused and lifted his night glasses to look the other way, focusing his gaze to the south where a line of heavy tanks was drawn up along the extension of the road on higher ground. Beyond the tanks he could see the small airfield which was serving as the main tank laager and beyond the groups of small dark shapes loomed the hangar, the main ammunition dump. Meyer had once again complained that everything was crammed into too confined an area but the floods had dictated that. At that moment Keller had the misfortune to say the wrong thing.

'I hear, sir, that the main dump is very close to the laager.'

'You'd like to move it, Keller?' Storch inquired.

'No, sir. I just thought . . . that is . . . Coloney Meyer . . .'

'Meyer has been here recently?'

'Only for a few minutes—to check the water level . . .'

'Really, Keller, it is most fortunate for you that I have only wet my boots. Had the water risen to my thighs we might well have had to look for your replacement. Till 04.00 hours, Keller!'

Barnes rubbed his eyes and checked his watch. 12.45 a.m. The tank rumbled along the side road, its lights full on, the tracks churning round at top speed. In the turret beside him Jacques warned that they were approaching the southern outskirts of Lemont. The French lad knew exactly where he was and now he felt strangely excited as the road he had known since boyhood rolled past under them. He had chosen a roundabout route to enter the village and Barnes had asked him to find a place where they could park Bert safely for a short time. He thought he knew just the place.

Inside the tank Colburn sat behind the two-pounder in Davis's old seat. A loaded machine-pistol lay across his lap and already he was becoming accustomed to the small metal room, the gentle sway of the hull, the endless grumble of the tracks. He missed the fresh air of five thousand feet up but at least here he had solid ground under his body. Oddly enough, now that they were so close to the battle zone the thunder of the guns had died, as though preserving their energies—and their ammunition—for one final effort when day came. And daylight was close now. But he was on edge because he had nothing definite to do, and in this respect he envied Reynolds. The driver in the nose of the tank had his head projecting above the hatch and gazed stolidly forward. His hands held the steering levers stiffly because his arms felt as though they were on fire and even the slightest movement increased the pain. They were almost there, Barnes had said, and Reynolds was anxious to get it over with. Now that they were so close to the Allied lines and that Dover was just across the water he found himself thinking of England and home. With a bit of luck they'd soon be there. He'd be able to get some leave and go back to Peckham. A pint of bitter at The Grey Horse. It made him feel thirsty and then he forgot about it as Barnes's voice came down the intercom with a fresh instruction.

'You turn left,' Jacques had just told Barnes, 'just beyond that white building.'

Barnes gave the order. 'And that farm you mentioned, Jacques, those isolated outhouses . . .'

He broke off as the tank turned down a narrow track. At the edge of the headlights he could see a strangely familiar shape, and when the track curved the beams played full on the bulky silhouette. Barnes stiffened and as Jacques pointed to the farm

245

buildings beyond an open gateway he gave the order to halt. The stationary vehicle which had startled him was tilted over at an acute angle, lying just inside the field with one track caught in a deep ditch. It was Bert's twin brother—a Matilda tank. Jumping to the ground he walked towards it, hearing Colburn's footsteps behind him. When he played his torch over the tank he saw that it was derelict, half the turret blown away, its right-hand track torn loose, the rear of the hull burnt black.

'Looks like one of yours,' Colburn suggested quietly.

'It's one of ours all right. There's been a helluva a scrap here. Look.'

In the field behind the tank uniformed bodies lay scattered across the grass, on their stomachs, on their backs, on their sides, and sometimes the uniforms were German but many were British and all dead. Barnes picked up several rifles and found them empty. There was only one tank, the single Matilda, and in its solitude it seemed to emphasize the terrible shortage of armoured forces with the B.E.F.

'The Panzers came through,' he remarked to Colburn, who made no reply.

They walked further down the track and by the gateway they found more empty rifles, British .303's, their dead owners lying close by. Barnes followed his torch beam cautiously into a yard surrounded by out-buildings and when they searched them they found that the place was deserted— deserted of human life but there were several British flfteen-hundredweight trucks parked round the edges of the yard which had obviously been some minor transport depot. Inside the buildings were more trucks and further evidence that a unit had been in residence recently—a pile of unwashed billy-cans, a dixie full of scummy water, several respirators and a Lewis gun without a magazine.

'I'd like to have another look at that truck in there,' said Colburn, flashing his torch on a truck with an R.E. flash at the rear.

'I'll be back in a minute. I want to get Bert parked.'

Barnes left the Canadian and explored the area immediately round the buildings, finding only empty fields which were strangely still and silent in the pale warm moonlight, the air heavy and muggy as the earth released the heat of yesterday, the buzz of unseen insects in his ears. Across the fields he could see a roof-line which looked as though it had been cut from cardboard—the roofs of Lemont—and behind them a solitary searchlight wearily probed the sky. When he returned to where he had left the Canadian he found him inside the truck which carried the R.E. flash. He was shining his torch over layers of wooden boxes.

'I want to do a recce into Lemont on foot from here,' Barnes told him. 'Jacques has agreed to take me in so I'm leaving you and Reynolds with the tank. This is a better place than I thought we'd get to park Bert—the Germans are hardly likely to come poking around a place where there's already been a dust-up and this stuff's no use to them. It's only a handful of bits and pieces, anyway.'

'There's more than a handful of these, Barnes. You know what they are, of course—detonators. There's enough stuff here to blow up half Ottawa—including gun-cotton, a plunger, and God knows what else. This truck belonged to a demolition unit.'

'For God's sake mind what you're doing, then . . . Sorry, I'd forgotten. Detonators are your business.'

Barnes sat down on an old wooden crate pushed against the wall and tried to think straight. His shoulder wound had been playing him up foully ever since he had crashed back into the tank transporter when he was trying to reach the deck from the cab. It was pounding like an iron hammer now and he wondered whether he had the energy to walk one step further. Well, he'd have to walk quite a few steps further if they were going to try and find out what the position was inside Lemont, and Jacques had blithely told him the best thing would be to try and reach his father. The fact that his father lived in a house in the main part of the village on top of a small hill overlooking some private airfield, and that this meant a long walk from where they were now, hadn't seemed to worry Jacques, but it worried Barnes when he thought of them making their way through enemy-held streets. He made the effort and was walking out to give instructions to Reynolds when he stopped in the doorway in surprise. Colburn was whistling under his breath, a tuneless melody. Colburn was in his element as he explored more boxes.

'Barnes, there's wire here—there's even some phosphorus. This god-damned truck is one huge potential bomb . . .'

'Well, we shan't be needing any bombs,' Barnes replied, his voice edged with irritation.

'Can't understand the bastards leaving this lot unguarded.'

'They haven't got enough men to guard their own stuff according to Jacques.'

'This I could really do something with, Barnes. I haven't had my hands on such a hoard since I joined the R.A.F. If I'd bumped into this outfit instead of your own mob I could really have earned my daily bread. And say, look you here . . .'

Barnes wasn't too interested in Colburn's enthusiasms and the Canadian's burst of energy seemed to underline his own state of desperate fatigue to an extent which made him feel more irritable than ever. He spoke quickly.

'I'm off with Jacques now. Reynolds is staying with Bert next door so you'll have someone to chat to.'

'I'm quite happy here. You're going to Jacques' father's place?'

'I doubt if we'll get that far.'

'The old boy might know what's what. And watch yourself —we don't want any nasty accidents now we're at the end of the line.'

'That's right. So for Pete's sake, Colburn, don't drop one of those detonators.'

Barnes checked his watch, Penn's watch. 2.25 a.m. Ninety minutes to dawn. The recce was completed and they were almost home, if you could call 'home' three out-buildings they had never known before, one of them stuffed with high-explosive. He looked back along the silent street and saw Jacques a long way behind him—Jacques who was still a problem because the village of Lemont was abandoned, all the inhabitants either evacuated or driven away by the

Germans when the tide of war had rolled this way. The lad waved a hand and pointed ahead, an unnecessary precaution because Barnes was already trying to locate the German sentry they had skirted on their way in. He had been standing on guard outside a small single-storey house where light had shown round the edges of drawn blinds. On the outskirts of Lemont all the houses were single-storey and this was the only house which had shown any sign of life in the deserted tree-lined street. Who was hidden behind those drawn blinds? And where was that damned sentry now? The empty motor-cycle and sidecar was still parked in front of the house.

He took several cautious steps forward again and halted. He could still see the light round the blinds but the sentry had vanished. It worried Barnes and he glanced back again to make sure that the lad was still behind him. Jacques opened his hands to express puzzlement and Barnes knew that he also had spotted the sentry's absence. The only thing to do was to go round the back way as they had before, but cautiously. He held up a warning hand to indicate to Jacques that he should stay well back and then he crept forward, turning down a path which led between the houses.

His nerves were keyed up tautly, his mind oscillating between two impulses—the need for caution on the last lap and the need to move quickly because they were running out of time just when he had found his supreme objective. The path was bordered with shoulder-high stone walls and he knew that when the path turned at the bottom the walls continued along the backs of the houses. Keeping his head down, his revolver in his hand, he crept past a closed gate let into the wall. He was concentrating on placing his feet carefully because he remembered that there was a deep ditch on the left. Perhaps he heard something at the last moment. He might even have started to turn his head, but he could never remember the details afterwards. A rifle butt struck his head with such vicious force that he lost consciousness immediately . . .

When he woke up he knew that he was going to be sick, but he forced it down into the churning pit of his stomach. His wound ached abominably but now the pounding hammer was

249

at work inside his head, and because it felt hollow he seemed to receive each blow twice as the blows echoed. Get a grip on yourself, man. With an immense effort he forced open eyelids which felt to be made of lead. A blinding light hit him, so he closed them quickly. A voice spoke gutturally. In English.

'So pleased you are recovering, Sergeant Barnes.'

Barnes jerked his eyes open a fraction and peered through slitted lids. From behind the lamp a uniformed arm appeared and lowered the light cone so that it shone on to the desk. The arm belonged to a thin faced man of about thirty who wore the uniform of a German officer. Glancing round the darkened room Barnes could see no sign of Jacques; the French lad must have escaped into the village during the ambush.

'Tell me when you are ready to speak,' the German suggested.

Barnes swore inwardly. He was seated in a high-backed wooden chair and his wrists were bound with wire to the arms. When he tried to shift his body surreptitiously he felt a broad band strapped round his waist; only his legs were still free. They had sewed him up nicely. Another uniformed officer appeared from behind his chair and like his colleague behind the desk he was wearing his peaked cap. He spread pine needles along the desk under the cone of light, arranging them carefully in varying lengths, apparently taking no notice of Barnes while he completed his little display. Barnes gritted his teeth, wondering whether the prelude to torture was a bluff to sap his nerves. The officer behind the desk spoke.

'I am Major Berg. You, of course, are Sergeant Barnes.' He lifted a British army paybook off the desk and waved it. 'And if you are wondering why I speak such good English it is since I was military attaché in London before the war.' His voice changed and he spoke rapidly, his manner bleak. 'Barnes, where is your unit and from where will the British be attacking us in the rear?'

Barnes said it. Name, rank, serial number. Then he shut his mouth. He opened it a moment later when the officer who had been bending over the desk swung the stiffened side of his hand savagely across Barnes' lips. He felt something give inside his mouth, felt around with his tongue, tasted blood and spat out a broken tooth. Through half-closed eyes he saw Berg shake his head as though cautioning his fellow-officer.

'I should have introduced you,' Berg went on. 'This is Captain Dahlheim. Normally our method is to ask questions politely first and then exert pressure later, but we are short of hours. I should warn you that Captain Dahlheim becomes annoyed when people do not answer my questions properly.'

Barnes said it again. Name, rank, serial number, adding that under the Geneva Convention this was all the information he was obliged to give. Dahlheim was fiddling with the pine needles now and while his body temporarily masked him from Berg, Barnes lifted his wrists hard against the wire. It was quite impossible to get his hands loose.

'But you are a spy,' went on the unseen Berg. 'Show him the clothes he was wearing when we found him.'

Dahlheim picked up a bundle from a chair and showed the clothes. For a horrible moment Barnes wondered whether they belonged to Jacques but he saw that they were a jacket and a pair of trousers of blue denim, common apparel for French workers in the fields. Jacques had worn a lounge suit. He must have escaped.

'I've never worn those in my life and you know it.'

'Captain Dahlheim can confirm that we took those clothes off you while you were still unconscious. We can say you wore them to hide your uniform. And you had no means of identification. No paybook.' He dropped the paybook into a drawer and closed it. 'So you are a spy and can be treated in any way we like.'

Was Berg bluffing? Barnes could see his white face now and as he became accustomed to the single desk light he thought the German was older than he had thought at first. He felt sick with fury. He had been on the last lap, had completed the most difficult reconnaissance he had ever undertaken, had been within a five-minute walk of Bert's refuge, and because of a momentary lack of alertness he had been captured. And as the realization dawned on him, the realization of how unlikely it was that he would ever escape, he found one thought torturing his mind. He had come to Lemont because the battle plan they had taken from the German staff car showed beyond doubt that here was the point of maximum peril for the B.E.F. And now he believed that he had found a way of striking a crippling blow against the 14th Panzer Division, the spearhead of the attack on Dunkirk, only to find himself a prisoner. What was it Berg was saying?

'We have not a great deal of time, Sergeant Barnes.'

'None of us have that here.'

'For various reasons it is a matter of urgency that you answer my questions quickly. Where is your unit? What is the British plan?' He paused. 'Dahlheim! Barnes is not going to reply again.'

Dahlheim straightened up and turned round. The needles were arranged in a neat row, their sharp points turned towards Barnes under the cone of light. Beneath the peaked cap Dahlheim's face was round, his eyes seeming half-asleep, and for the first time Barnes saw that he wore a black and silver collar-patch bearing a curious runic sign. Captain Dahlheim was a member of the S.S.

By now Barnes found that his eyes were growing accustomed to the semi-darkness beyond the cone of light and behind the seated Berg he could see a window. The curtain was drawn across it but at one side there was a gap, and because of the deep shadow beyond the desk light he could see a wedge of moonlit night. Dahlheim was reaching his hand to his side and Barnes expected him to draw the pistol from his leather hip holster, but instead he took a length of cord from his pocket and wrapped it round both hands. He took his time over this little exercise, watching Barnes carefully, then without speaking he went past the chair and disappeared behind it. Guessing what was coming, Barnes tensed himself.

Reynolds could see the sentry standing outside the small house and he also saw the stationary motor-cycle and sidecar close by. It was the first sign of life he had seen since entering the village. He took several quiet paces away from the road down a pathway between stone walls. Now he was well under cover, two houses away from where the sentry mounted guard. For a minute he stood there, undecided what to do. It was probably the first time in his army career that he had performed these two actions and both of them worried him—he had disobeyed an order and he had taken an initiative without reference to any superior. He kept wondering whether he ought not to go back.

Barnes had specifically told him to stay with the tank and now Bert was a good five minutes' walk away. Only an overwhelming feeling that something had happened to Barnes had prompted his action and he had firmly refused Colburn's offer to come instead. A pilot's place was in the air—they weren't much good on the ground, Reynolds had reasoned to himself. Now his great dread was that he had missed Barnes and Jacques coming back and that already his sergeant was asking Colburn where the devil Reynolds was. He'd better go back, he decided, but not along the road—that was far too dangerous. There must be another way back along the rear of these houses. Yes, he'd go back immediately. Barnes was able to look after himself.

He reached the end of the wall and lifted his head cautiously. Light from a window two houses away spilled out into the night. It must be some sort of German H.Q., a good place to keep away from. He started retreating along the footpath which ran behind the back garden wall and then looked over his shoulder. The light puzzled him. Perhaps he'd better check: Barnes might want to know who was there. In for a penny, in for a pound, as his father was fond of saying. Keeping his head well down, he crept along the back wall, counting gates. This must be the right one. The gate wasn't quite closed and when he pushed it gently it swung back inwards without making a sound. The vague outline of the lighted window was broken up by the branches of fruit trees which stood in the garden. He listened carefully and peered round the end wall to look along another pathway which led back to the road. If the sentry decided to walk up there while he was inside the garden he would be nicely trapped. In for a penny . . .

Creeping down a garden path he reached the back of the house close to the window and saw that there was a gap in the curtain. Ten-to-one the people inside would be staring straight at the window when he looked in, but he felt he must see what was going on, so he pressed one hand against the wall, eased himself forward, caught a quick glimpse and stepped back. He had glanced inside at the moment when Dahlheim had walked behind Barnes's chair. He had seen his sergeant helpless, the only time he had ever seen Barnes in this state, and for a few seconds he was stunned, but his mood swiftly changed to one of fury.

He went back up the garden, out of the gateway, down the pathway between the houses, his hand extracting the knife from its sheath, a knife which he had carefully honed to a razor's edge, the point like a needle, the condition in which an ex-fishmonger was prone to keep his knives. At the end of the path he waited behind the wall and listened to the sentry's footsteps. The German must have become bored with standing and now he paced a steady sentry-go—ten paces away, ten paces back again. While he listened Reynolds remembered a certain guard duty he had mounted late one night at a remote camp outside Hull. Alone in the dark, he had particularly disliked the moment when he had stopped to turn, still keeping step as he revolved through one hundred and eighty degrees, and this was the moment he was waiting for now.

The sentry was coming his way again. Eight, nine, ten . . . Leaving the safety of the wall Reynolds moved with a terrible determination, seeing the back of the German only six feet away. His hand rose above shoulder level and with the same movement he crept forward three quiet paces, driving the knife savagely down into the uniformed back. He felt it sheering through cloth, driving down deeper, jerking briefly as it grazed the bone and then sank deeper still. The back fell away from him and the sentry let out one howling shriek. Reynolds was sure half the street had heard the sound as he bent over to grab the rifle and fixed bayonet, tearing the strap loose from the limp arm.

His reactions now were an echo of his early basic training—

254

taking up the rifle, one hand gripping the stock, the other stretched well along the barrel as he grasped it close to the bayonet. He was running full pelt for the front door when it opened in his face, revealing a uniformed figure. Dahlheim held a Luger pistol in his hand but before he could press the trigger Reynolds was on him, his headlong rush carrying the bayonet deep into Dahlheim's stomach. He groaned and went over backwards, carried to the floor by the still-moving impetus of Reynolds's violent charge. Automatically, the driver stood a foot on the sprawled body and used it as leverage to withdraw the bayonet with one quick hard pull, his eyes searching the room beyond.

When they heard the sentry's awful cry Dahlheim had just gripped Barnes round the neck. At Berg's instant command he had taken out his Luger and rushed to the front door, opening it as Berg came round the side of the desk, his own gun already in his hand. Barnes heard Dahlheim's horrible groan while Berg was passing him. Shooting out his left leg, he caught the German between his own legs and tripped him. Berg was on the floor when Barnes flung his whole weight sideways, carrying himself and the chair over on top of Berg, the fall smashing the left chair arm so that his wrist was immediately released, still encircled with wire. He was half on top of Berg, still tied inside the chair as he raised his left fist and clubbed him viciously in the face. Then the chair slipped and took him over further sideways so that now he was lying on the floor trapped by the chair behind him. He saw Berg blink, spit blood from his mouth where the fist had broken teeth, and then he raised the revolver which he still held and aimed it point-blank in Barnes's face. Anchored to the floor by the heavy chair, just too far away to get at Berg, even in that moment of terror Barnes was aware of movement above him and then the rifle butt in Reynolds's grip smashed down on Berg's head with a terrible impact. The hand fell back with a thud to the floor and the Luger slipped from the hand as it went slack.

'Good work, Reynolds.' Barnes gasped out the trite phrase automatically and just as automatically thought of Dahlheim. 'Make sure of that other bastard.'

255

'He's finished. Keep still while I get your hand free.'

'Smash the support off under the chair arm with your rifle butt and then I can slip my wrist off. Go on, man, we're hellishly short of time.'

They could hear Dahlheim groaning continually behind them as Reynolds aimed the rifle butt carefully, destroying the wooden support under the chair arm so that Barnes could slip his wrist off the end. Then he pressed the wire bracelets down over his hands while Reynolds unfastened the leather belt which bound him to the chair. Barnes had his back to Dahlheim but he could still hear the agonized moans of the S.S. officer, the clumping of his shoes on the floor. The moment he was released he swung round and instantly shouted a warning. Dahlheim was turned over on one side, clutching his left hand to his stomach, a hand covered with blood, his face twisted almost out of recognition with the pain, but his right hand had found the pistol. At the moment when Barnes shouted the gun went off.

Dahlheim had fired at random, Barnes felt sure of it because the barrel had been wobbling all over the place. Two more shots entered the ceiling and then the gun fell harmlessly on the floor. Jerking his head round as the pistol skidded against the wall, Barnes looked up and saw Reynolds topple, an expression of amazed disbelief on his large face as he fell and hit the floor with a tremendous crash. Groggily, Barnes climbed to his feet and his legs nearly gave way under him as he picked up the rifle, wobbled forward, and took up a position behind Dahlheim who was now rolling on the floor. He managed to lift the weapon several feet and bring it down again. Even in his weakened state the force of the blow was so great that the rifle jumped out of his hands and fell beside the now motionless German.

Kicking the rifle away against the wall he picked up the pistol which still held five cartridges and pushed it down inside his own empty holster, wondering what the devil they had done with his own gun.

'Reynolds!'

He had a terrible job turning the driver over and then

256

Reynolds began stirring and cursing foully. There was plenty of blood on his left thigh but on making a quick examination Barnes found that the bullet had passed through without lodging in the flesh. He applied a field dressing he always carried and managed to seat the driver in Berg's chair, an operation which took away nearly all his remaining strength. Inwardly he was swearing. Of all the bloody bad luck. Davis killed by the accident of falling rock. Penn shot down by an envenomed looter. And now Reynolds wounded by a wobbling hand that had hardly been able to hold the gun, let alone aim the bloody thing. Then his eyes fell on his watch. When the chair had gone over sideways the face had been smashed in the fall and the hands had stopped at 2.40 a.m.

He stood by the desk for a moment, looking down at Reynolds's haggard face, his thoughts torn and muddled between his wounded driver and the knowledge that within eighty minutes the Panzers he had seen with Jacques from the ridge above the airfield would be on the move, creeping along the underwater road which the French lad had pointed towards. He pulled himself together, refusing to give way to the fatigue clogging his limbs. Think, Barnes, there are things to do.

He opened Berg's drawer to collect his paybook, found his own revolver inside, still loaded, and substituted it for the German's gun.

Reynolds suddenly became talkative and told his sergeant to leave him there since he couldn't possibly walk or drive. But Barnes just nodded, went to the front door and looked carefully along the silent street. He wasted several precious minutes dragging the dead sentry's body inside the house, but if a patrol came along he didn't want the alarm raising if it could be avoided. Dropping the body next to Dahlheim's, he took a deep breath and began the intricate manoeuvre of hoisting the driver on to his back. Bent double under the great weight, hearing Reynolds's feet trailing on the floor, he staggered out of the house and wrestled him inside the sidecar while his burden protested that the noise of the engine would give them away. Without replying, Barnes went back into the house, switched off the desk light and came out again, closing the door behind him.

The starting of the motor-cycle seemed a louder noise than any he had ever heard, but he had made up his mind—he must find a safer place to park Reynolds. The street was still deserted as he drove away from Lemont and reached the outbuildings, cutting the engine quickly and calling out to warn Colburn who emerged from behind a wall with a machine-pistol at the ready. They made Reynolds as comfortable as possible by sitting him on some straw inside one of the buildings—Barnes was determined that this time he would take no wounded crew member on what might be Bert's final journey. And, he thought grimly, for this journey his crew was now reduced to two—himself and Colburn.

At 3.20 a.m. they were ready to move, but only because they had worked like Trojans. Barnes looked up at Colburn who now occupied his own position inside the turret—the tank commander himself was going to have to drive Bert on his last trip.

'You really think it will work, Colburn?'

'It's more likely to than your idea of firing shells into the dump. That way there's no guarantee at all that you'll get a major explosion, but you can bet your sweet life that when this lot goes it'll lift the whole dump sky-high—just supposing we ever get close enough and just supposing we don't go up before we get there. If we do, they won't have any burial problems with us. Just look down there—this tank is one ruddy great bomb.'

The floor of the turntable at the base of the turret had been tightly packed with gun-cotton slabs and to this lethal foundation Colburn had added a quantity of instantaneous detonating fuses, several cans of petrol, a quantity of phosphorus and some grenades he had found in a satchel. The remaining grenades were still in the satchel hanging from the top of the turret where he could reach them easily. Even closer to hand was the plunger mechanism and a large spool of wire. Colburn pointed to the plunger.

'And just supposing, Barnes, that we do get a chance to get clear of the tank before this lot goes up . . .'

'Don't bet on that, Colburn.'

'Hell, I'm not betting on a damned thing. But just supposing you're on your own then, don't forget to take the coil of wire as well as the plunger with you. The wire's paid out through the gun slit so you can ram the lid shut—ramming the lid shut is important because it locks everything inside and increases the power of the explosion quite a bit . . .'

'We've got to get moving, Colburn.'

'For Christ's sake, I know I'm telling you twice but it may save your life. Before you press the plunger you must turn this switch. This device is as harmless as a kitten until you do turn the switch. Come to think of it, Barnes, I reckon we've got rather too many "supposings" in this equation.'

'We've also got seventy two-pounder shells and the boxes of Besa ammunition to pep up the explosion.'

'I know. I just hope I'm around when that lot goes up—it will be the crowning blow-up of my career to date. When I say "around" I do mean at the very end of that paid-out wire,' he added.

'We'd better get moving, Colburn. I've a nasty idea we're too late already with fiddling around with your little toy. You'll have to handle all the observation and talk to me over the intercom. Think you can manage?'

'A damn' sight better than I'd manage driving Bert. O.K. As the bomber crew guys say, this is the final run-in.'

'Which is pretty appropriate since it's a mobile bomb we've got for delivery to General Storch.'

Three minutes later the tank was moving through the village at full speed, its headlights ablaze, rumbling down the deserted street like an avenging phantom. It was their only chance, Barnes felt sure of that—to press forward as though they owned the place in the same way that Mandel had described the advance of the Panzers across France. And it was their one advantage—the element of total surprise, an element which must be rammed home ruthlessly right up to the moment when they reached the airfield, if they ever did reach it. The appearance of a tank in the early hours with its lights full on must cause a reaction of doubt, of indecision, for at least a few vital seconds, and in that time Bert should pass any patrol they might encounter. It was all a question of how soon they ran up against the big stuff.

They were moving past the house where Reynolds had saved him, he felt sure of it, although his vision was limited and he was relying heavily on Colburn's guidance over the inter-com. The driver's seat was closed to its lowest level and the hood over his head was shut, sealing him off from the outside world so that his only view was through the slit window in front. Four inches of bullet-proof glass protected that slit while 70-mm. of armour-plate shielded him from shell-fire—the thickest plate covered the front hull—so theoretically he was fairly safe. Unless the tank caught fire and when he rolled back the hood he found the two-pounder barrel pointed straight ahead and depressed to its lowest elevation, in which case the barrel would form a steel bar preventing him from climbing out at all while the tank burned. Cynical drivers said that was why the driver was issued with a revolver—to give him an easier way out than frying alive. Why the hell am I thinking like this, Barnes wondered? Perhaps only now he was really appreciating what poor Reynolds had gone through.

He hoped that if it really came to it, Colburn did know how to use a Mills hand grenade. The Canadian had told him that a British staff sergeant had demonstrated their use on a bomb-ing range and Barnes could imagine Colburn taking a great interest in how the mechanism worked. Still . . .

'Barnes,' Colburn's voice came clearly over the one-way intercom. 'We're approaching a square and from that sketch-map you drew me we go straight over, but there may be a problem—I can see lights. Keep moving, I'll keep you in touch.'

Up in the turret Colburn stared anxiously ahead. The lights shone through some trees in an open square surrounded with two-storey houses and the beams were stationary. He couldn't see any sign of troops, any hint of danger, just those lights coming through the trees. Barnes had told him that as far as he had been able to make out when he reconnoitred the village with Jacques the place had been evacuated of civilians, which would be logical since the Germans were using it as a forward base.

They had penetrated as far as the house of Jacques's father and he had not been at home. So any sign of life was likely to be hostile life. The square, apparently deserted, came closer and Colburn moved from side to side as he tried to see behind the trees. There was something there, then he saw them.

'Barnes. A couple of motor-cycles and sidecars at the edge of this square. They've got lights on but there doesn't seem to be anyone about . . .'

Barnes coaxed a little more speed from the engines, staring along his headlight beams which now stretched across the small square to the street beyond. He sat wedged in between the boxes of detonators which were stacked on either side and the proximity of so much explosive wasn't a comfortable feeling, but he had insisted on loading these spare boxes to increase the power of the bomb. Now he wondered whether he had overdone it. Highly unstable, British detonators, Colburn had said. The Germans used Trotyl, which was far less temperamental. And Colburn was a man who should know. They were half way across the square now and subconsciously he was listening for the first sound of Colburn's voice, because if he spoke now that would mean trouble. The avenue of darkness ahead moved towards him and then they left the square and the beams stabbed along a straight street. Colburn's voice was tense.

'They came out just as we left the square—a couple of Germans. They stopped and stared for a few seconds and then ran for one of the bikes.'

Barnes gazed ahead. It was starting already. There was a turning down to the left he had to negotiate soon and that would mean reducing speed a lot, and this was the last moment they should be slowing down if one of those motor-cycles was after them. He wished to God that the intercom was two-way, that he could warn Colburn to watch the man in the sidecar, the one who would be carrying a machine-pistol. Colburn's voice again.

'The cycle is following us down this street. I know there's a left turn soon but keep up your speed. Don't worry, I'll handle it.'

Colburn was really worried. He looked back to where the lights of the oncoming cycle were closing the gap rapidly. He realized the danger to himself perched up in the turret—if the cycle was allowed to come close enough the man in the side-car would blast his head off with the machine-pistol he had seen him running with. He took one grenade out of the satchel and then he took another, laying the second one behind the plunger box where it couldn't roll; it wasn't an action that many would have taken but to Colburn the box was dead until the switch was turned. He also glanced down inside the turret towards the bed of gun-cotton. Don't drop this little feller down there, he told himself. He had his finger inside the ring-head of the pin now. Get it right, Colburn; allow for the tank's speed and the onrush of the cycle. And get it good. You're pitching the ball at Toronto. Removing bomb from pin, he counted. One, two, three, four. He threw. Without waiting his hand whipped over the second grenade, inserting his finger. Withdraw. Count. He had his head down as the first grenade blew only feet in front of the Germans. A hard lethal crack split the street. The flash lit the walls and the cycle climbed, taking the side-car with it, wheels spinning futilely, the sidecar ripping away from the cycle. He threw the second one from inside the turret, just to get rid of it now that it was no longer needed, and by the flash of the second bomb he saw a shadowed wreck in the street behind it. Even the lights had gone. He let out his breath and the sound travelled down the intercom to Barnes.

'Got them.'

Colburn leant back against the turret and wiped sweat off his hands on his flying suit. He had shot men out of the air but this was different. He had caught a brief glimpse of the man in the sidecar pitching out head first towards the ground and he was amazed it was all over so quickly. He had been very frightened for those few minutes, so frightened that he had made a bad mistake in not wiping his hand earlier—that second grenade had nearly slipped, had nearly gone down inside the turret. The very thought of it made him sweat again but now that it was all over he felt enormously relieved, relieved that he was still alive. And this was a mere bagatelle, a single motor-cycle and sidecar. What faced them somewhere just ahead would be on a far bigger scale. The headlights played on a distant wall with wording painted on the plaster. Restaurant de la Gare. He spoke quickly into the mike.

'That building's coming up—the restaurant place. Prepare to turn left. I'll guide you.'

Barnes was already reducing speed and he began turning very slowly, his hands an extension of Colburn's instructions as they eased Bert round. The turning was sharp and almost at once they moved on to a downward slope of cobbles. He had to crawl round, edging his way as Colburn leaned out of the turret to check wall clearance, talking down the intercom all the time. They nearly scraped the right-hand wall, then they were round the corner, the tank straightening up and proceeding down the cobbled street, its metal tracks grinding and clattering over the stones. That was close, Colburn was thinking, but we managed it nicely between us. He peered along the beams, still savouring the sensation of relief, wondering how Barnes was feeling.

Inside the nose of the tank Barnes was experiencing a rather different sensation—Barnes was in serious trouble and he wondered whether they had a dog's chance of making it as a chill of fear seeped through him. *One of the detonator boxes had broken loose.* It had happened on that last bend while he was struggling grimly to negotiate the corner and allow for the drop in street level. They were almost round the turning when he felt a heavy blow strike his right shoulder. Still in the process of taking Bert round the corner he only had time for a quick glance sideways and this showed him the heavy box projecting well beyond the one it rested on, kept stable now only by the obstacle of his own body. As he moved down the hill, the tank wobbling slightly as it rumbled over the cobbles, he tried to ease the box back into position with his shoulder.

The action nearly made him jump out of his seat as pain from the maltreated wound screamed through his body, stabbing at his brain. For one terrible second he thought he was going to faint. He bit down on his lips to drive away the dizziness and reopened the cut in his mouth, tasting his own blood for the second time that night. The heavy box was pressing against his shoulder all the time and there wasn't a thing he could do about it, except to pray that at the next right-hand turn the box would regain its balance. Was he still driving straight? He forced himself to concentrate on the view through the slit window.

'Barnes, I can see the canal embankment beyond the bottom of this street, so we're on the right road. And we turn right in a minute.'

Barnes had been waiting for that right-hand turn but he knew that with both hands occupied with the steering levers his shoulder was still going to have to bear the brunt of shoving that box back against the wall. Would he be able to stand the pain; Colburn's voice again, a voice edged with tension, the sure sign of further trouble.

'Something coming up . . . a soldier in a doorway, a sentry, I think. Keep moving at this speed—we'll have to turn in less than a hundred yards . . .'

Colburn ducked his head inside the turret and waited, waited for the challenge, the pause, then the first burst of fire from the machine-pistol the sentry held across his chest. His own machine-pistol was gripped in his hands and he looked upward beyond the open rim of the turret. The tank clattered down over the cobbles, the dark silhouette of irregular rooftops slid past beyond the turret rim, cold specks of starlight glittered distantly in the late night sky. The moon was low now and an early morning chill prickled the back of his neck. Still no sound from the sentry. He couldn't stand it any longer: he peered over the rim. Nothing moved but he thought that he could still see the shadowed figure by the doorway, a motionless figure.

It was incredible. Some of his astonishment travelled down the intercom.

'Barnes, he never moved—he never moved. And we're in a British tank.'

It worked, Barnes thought, the element of surprise worked there. Perhaps the sentry hadn't done his homework on tank silhouettes. He might have been posted there from other duties and he was tired out, so when a vehicle came down the streets of German-occupied Lemont with its headlights blazing he assumed that it must be all right. He could even have been asleep on his feet. But the main thing was it had worked once and it could work again. Colburn's voice spoke urgently.

'I can see the embankment clearly now—we're close to the turn. You'll have to watch this one, it's narrow. I'll guide you round . . .'

Barnes reduced his speed close to zero. He remembered this bend and it was the worst one they would have to negotiate. The route they were following had been so simple that he had known exactly where they were ever since leaving the farm building. Once they had entered the village the way had led straight forward down the first street, across the square, continuing along the street beyond up to the first left-hand turn down the hill. At the bottom of the hill they turned right and then it was straight on again by the side road at the foot of the canal embankment. If they could only manage this corner . . . They were almost round the sharp turn when it happened. They were moving slowly forward and then there was a terrific jolt and the tank stopped, its engines still ticking over. Barnes had jammed on the brake, warned by the impact and the scraping sound he had heard just before the jarring crash which rammed the detonator box savagely against his shoulder. He struggled against an overwhelming desire to be sick, too shaken to try and thrust the box back while his hands were free. Then he heard Colburn.

'Track's jammed against the left wall. Sorry—my fault. We'll have to get out of here quickly—that sentry has started to walk down the hill. Reverse slowly. We can't go forward.'

Inside the hull Barnes heard the harsh grind of metal plate along immovable wall as he reversed carefully. Then the tank stuck. He grimaced and thought for a few seconds. If they

265

weren't very lucky he could immobilize them. He remembered once seeing a track split and come apart, so that the tank hull moved for a few yards while it splayed out track like unrolling a metal carpet. If that happened they were done for, and there was that little matter of the sentry coming down the hill to investigate. They couldn't go forward so they'd have to go back. Gritting his teeth, he reversed, hearing, feeling, the agonized grind of metal over stone. Then they were free again. And still intact. Colburn guided him round without haste and then they were moving along the next street, the headlights probing its emptiness and desolation. Barnes glanced at his watch, the one he had borrowed from Colburn. 3.30 a.m.

Up in the turret Colburn put the revolver back on the ledge next to the plunger box and wiped both his hands dry. The revolver had seemed a more appropriate weapon for one sentry. Taking a last look back at the dangerous corner he concentrated on observing the view ahead, issuing occasional instructions to keep Barnes in the dead centre of the street, his mind chilled. On his right a row of two-storey houses ran down the side of the street as a continuous wall, the upper floor windows just above the level of his turret. To his left ran the high embankment of the unseen canal, a steep-sloped embankment at least twenty feet high which closed off the view across open fields. Ahead lay the street, a canyon of shadow, apparently deserted, the forward movement of the beams exposing only empty road. It seemed quite uncanny and as the tank ground forward Colburn found his nerves screwing up to an almost unbearable pitch of tension. Within the next few minutes they were bound to run into something very big.

Barnes was experiencing the same emotion, as far as he could experience anything beyond the mounting pain which gripped his whole body. The tenderness of the shoulder wound was almost unendurable now as the side of the detonator box sagged against him, a relentless pain which should have obscured all others, but he could still feel the aching bruise on top of his head where the German sentry had knocked him out and the back of his burnt left hand felt strangely disembodied, as though it might float off the end of his arm. And over it all flooded a tidal wave of fatigue which threatened to drown his mind, a wave held back more by pain than by any effort of will.

Another part of his mind mechanically operated the steering levers and the two control panels—the gear box clutch pedal on the left and the accelerator on the right. There was a hill in front of them, a hill which rose almost level with the embankment, then a steady drop with a side turning off to the right, then another hill beyond that . . .

Colburn's voice was taut. 'We're running alongside the canal embankment now—there's a line of houses on the right. Still no sign of trouble.'

Which was exactly how Barnes was visualizing it. Had they got away with it? Already they were driving along this road at the very edge of Lemont—the village ended abruptly at the embankment and beyond there was open country. Jacques had told him that it was very much of a side road, which was why they had reconnoitred along this route. And now they had left behind what Barnes had anticipated might well be the grimmest part of their journey—the dash through the village. What lay ahead didn't bear thinking about but it almost looked as though they might reach the airfield. In his mind's eye he saw the lie of the land ahead. They had come in one way, along this road to the empty house of Jacques' father, and then for safety's sake they had come back across the fields on the far side of the embankment . . . He heard the shot, one single report. Then another.

Colburn had been striving to watch all ways at once—the road ahead, the road behind, the line of two-storey houses to his right and the silhouette of the high embankment which showed more clearly now against a faint glow. Dawn was on the way. He looked for his watch and remembered that he had loaned it to Barnes. The line of the embankment was dropping now as they began to move uphill. He knew that soon he would be able to see across it and he kept reminding himself to keep a sharp eye on those houses. There was no reason to suspect any danger from their darkened windows but they worried him because they were so close and the upper windows looked down on the tank. He picked up the revolver and the weapon gave him a sense of security.

The emergency happened so unexpectedly that it almost took his breath away. A window on an upper floor was flung open and the curtain must have been attached to it: a pool of light flooded out and illuminated the tank below. Colburn looked up and saw a German soldier, his pudding-shaped helmet clearly visible, staring down. He heard him shout, saw him reach back into the room and then lift a machine-pistol. Colburn reacted instantly. Raising his revolver, he fired twice. As the tank moved on the German toppled into the garden below.

'Barnes, a Jerry opened a window and spotted us. He was going to shoot but I got in first.' Colburn wished that the damned intercom wasn't simply one-way. It was like talking to a ghost. 'If they've got a phone in the house they'll be all over us soon now. Unless he was alone with a girl. He had his helmet on,' he added with unconscious humour.

Barnes thought of the joke and smiled grimly. He hoped that the German had been with a girl: if that were the case she'd probably try and get a neighbour to dump the body into the convenient canal. Not that it was likely if the village had been evacuated, so they'd better assume a warning was going out. They must be close to the top of this hill now, and close to where he had crossed the canal with Jacques over that huge barge. Was there something wrong? He could have sworn he had heard Colburn suck in his breath. Colburn had sucked in his breath and now he was no longer looking at the houses or at the embankment. He was gazing straight ahead and as they moved over the hill-top his mouth was dry with fear such as he had not known since they started their fateful journey through Lemont.

From his vantage point at the hill crest he could see over the summit of the hill beyond where a chain of headlights moved towards him, an endless chain which threw up a great glow of light behind the next hill summit. He had no doubt at all that he was looking at a column of armoured vehicles advancing down the road they were moving along, probably a

268

column sent for the express purpose of intercepting them. My God, he thought, and I was kidding myself up that we might have got away with it. We're finished now, finished.

'Barnes! There's a whole stream of traffic on the road ahead. It's still some distance off but it's coming towards us and we'll meet it in the next few minutes. They're on to us—it must be Panzers, a helluva lot of them..

Barnes's reaction staggered him. He felt the tank pick up speed as it moved down the hill, the tracks grinding round faster and faster as they rumbled forward at ever-increasing pace as though Barnes couldn't wait to meet the oncoming column in head-on collision. For a moment he thought he had gone mad and then they reached the bottom of the hill and stopped. The headlights went out and Barnes rolled back the hood. He paused for a second while he heaved the detonator box back into position, using both hands to push the case firmly against the side of the hull. Then he jacked up the seat so that when he sat down his head would be above the hatch. He called up to the anxious Colburn.

'How far away are those vehicles?'

'Half a mile, I'd guess. I can't be certain.'

'Maybe only a quarter?'

'No, at least half a mile. Barnes, our lights have gone.'

'I put them out. I don't want to risk them seeing us go up the embankment.'

'Up there?'

Colburn stared in horror up the steep slope which rose twenty feet above them. Had Barnes lost his judgement? He must have decided to make a last stand from the top of the embankment, if they ever got up there. He couldn't have realized the strength of the column which was moving against them. He called down from the turret.

'There must be at least twenty or thirty vehicles heading towards us.'

'Listen, Colburn.' Barnes's voice was urgent. 'We're not going to fight them—we're trying to dodge them. I came back over this canal with Jacques dead opposite this road behind us which leads back into Lemont. We came over a huge barge

269

with a deck like an aircraft carrier—it almost fills the canal. We're going to reverse into this side street until Bert's nose is pointed up that embankment—then up there is where we go.'

'Will the tank make it?'

'I don't know till we try it but it's our only chance. It's close to dawn, so if we don't make it now we never will. When we reach the top there'll be a split second for you to see whether we're driving on to the centre of the barge. I'll be ready to brake, but I can't do that till we're off the slope. You'll have to react damned quickly. Got it?'

'If it's O.K. to go on, I'll say O.K. If it isn't I'll say stop.'

The side road which led off at right-angles to the embankment was wide enough to give ample room for Barnes to reverse into quickly. Then he paused briefly to flex his fingers. Without thinking about the chances against success he went forward, guessing that Colburn thought it was a maniac's last throw, and up in the turret confidence was the last of the emotions which inspired Colburn. He would have liked to look two ways at once—up to the hill crest behind which the armoured column was advancing and straight ahead where the slope loomed like the side of a mountain. Beneath him the tracks began to claw and grind up the gradient as though finding it difficult to hold on to the lower slope and Colburn found himself tilted backwards against the rear of the turret. Barnes seemed to be going up at a fantastic pace. Supposing the barge wasn't in the right position to act as a bridge?' Supposing the enemy column poured over the hill crest when they were half way up the embankment? Grimly he recalled his remark to Barnes just before they had started out. Were there, after all, too many 'supposings' in this equation? I don't think we'll make this one, Colburn told himself.

Barnes had decided, and now he never asked himself whether or not they could make it. His pain-battered mind was concentrated on one idea only—get Bert over the top. Because the tilt of the tank was longitudinal rather than sideways the detonator boxes were holding their position well, but could they stand up to this sort of treatment? The tank rocked badly as the forward tracks moved into a depression and then climbed out of it, the engines revving madly as Barnes fought to take the tank higher. Very unstable, Colburn had called British detonators, the Germans use Trotyl. The left-hand track sank alarmingly into another depression and the box slipped again, slamming hard against his shoulder, grating its weight into the sensitive wound. He stiffened abruptly, swearing that he would throw out that box if they ever reached the other side, and, knowing that he was approaching the summit, he accelerated.

Colburn was standing upright in the turret now, holding himself erect by grasping the front rim with both hands, because it was vital to see instantly whether they were correctly placed to move across that barge, a barge he couldn't even see yet. But he felt the acceleration and knew that Barnes was going to rush it. Anxiously he leaned further forward. They reached the top.

'O.K., Barnes! O.K.! O.K.!'

There it was—the barge. They were going to hit it dead centre. The tank paused, its forward tracks in the air briefly, then dropped level to the towpath. It moved forward again across a few inches of water and landed in the middle of the flat deck. The barge shuddered under the impact of its immense visitor and the tank moved on until it was half way across the deck. Then the engines stalled.

Colburn forced himself to say nothing. They were now trapped on top of the embankment in full view of the approaching column once it breasted the summit of the hill. He heard Barnes trying again and again to start the engine. Instinctively his eyes swept over the summit of the hill behind which the column was advancing. Nothing yet, but the front of the column must be very close now. He could imagine the scene so clearly—the first heavy tank cresting the hill, spotting them clearly silhouetted against the pale light, wirelessing back to the column, continuing down the hill as more vehicles followed, the barrage of shells aimed point-blank . . . He found he was holding his revolver tightly and forced himself to relax his grip. His eyes rested on the plunger below him and then he looked again at the glow of light behind the hill, a glow which seemed to grow stronger every second as Barnes repeated his efforts to start the engines without success. Colburn glanced back the way they had come and the street was still deserted. Who had summoned the armoured column? Probably the owners of the second motor-cycle and sidecar in the square they had crossed. Then the engines fired, the tank jerked forward, left the barge and plunged down the far slope at speed. At the bottom Barnes turned in a wide curve and halted the tank facing along the canal. He switched off the engines, rolled back the hood and climbed out quickly.

'I thought we'd stall at the top,' he remarked. 'No sign of that column? Good. Colburn, could you come down and give me a hand to dump this bloody box?'

He check his watch. 3.40 a.m. Twenty minutes to zero hour.

The field below the embankment was firm hard earth and there were no hidden quagmires to hold up their advance, although not so far off to the left was a vague glimmer of flooded areas. The tank rumbled forward as Barnes gazed through the slit window from his lowered seat, following the same course he had taken when he had returned from the reconnaissance with Jacques. The next twenty minutes would decide the whole issue, would decide whether the 14th Panzer Division would advance across the water-line to spring on an unsuspecting Dunkirk, or whether they could muddle things so drastically that the Panzers would be delayed, perhaps fatally. Colburn was talking now.

'I think I can see the archway under the embankment.'

That archway was the end of the line, a phrase Colburn had spoken just before Barnes had set off on the reconnaissance which had deprived them of Reynolds, but without that reconnaissance they would never have reached this point. Through the archway lay an open field with the aerodrome beyond—the site of a huge ammunition dump and the laager of the waiting Panzers. Tight-lipped, Barnes peered through the slit window as the tank rolled forward in the early morning light.

He found that he had increased speed without realizing it and he wondered about that archway. Would it be wide enough? He had paced out its width, immediately thinking of Bert when he had crept under it with Jacques, and he had estimated that in an emergency they should just be able to manage it. They *had* to manage it—the archway was the only means of approaching the target from this side of the canal. The growing light was apparent even through his narrow window and he prayed that the defences had not been reinforced since they had left the place, but there was always the chance that the Germans would confidently rely on the heavy column they had sent along the road to investigate the intruders. He wondered how Colburn was feeling, knowing that these might be his last few minutes of life.

In the turret Colburn kept looking to the east where the pale glow of dawn was spreading across the horizon. If they had been half an hour later they would never have passed through the village successfully—and even if they had got through the 14th Panzer Division would already have been on the move. Would they really manage it? He glanced down at the plunger again with a feeling of wonderment, suddenly conscious of the fact that he might be dead within the hour, or sooner. It was an odd sensation and involuntarily he shivered. There was a sharp chill in the air now and white mist was rising off the fields. He had seen the same mist rising off the early morning fields near Manston. Then he saw the archway clearly and Manston faded.

The archway looked far too narrow to allow the passage of the tank, its stone walls so close together that Colburn thought they could let through nothing larger than a farm wagon. A feeling of bitter disappointment swept through him—they were going to be stopped at the last moment because of a single archway. There was no question of driving the tank up the embankment a second time—the slope here was even more steeply angled, to say nothing of the fact that if they reached the top their advance would be stopped by the canal itself. A sense of overwhelming frustration was in his voice when he spoke.

'Barnes, this archway's too narrow to get through—I'm sure of it.'

The tank ground forward, moving away from the embankment in a wide semi-circle until Barnes had brought it into a position where it directly faced the arch, and now he could see that the field beyond was shrouded in mist, masking their approach from the Germans. Colburn gave up protesting and leaned far out as he guided Barnes forward every inch of the way, his gaze switching backwards and forwards between the incredibly narrow arch and the forward tracks. The ground was very uneven at this point and Barnes found it difficult to follow the Canadian's instructions precisely. He was close to the archway when Colburn called out urgently for him to halt: he was too far over to the right. He reversed some distance and changed his angle of direction a fraction, moving forward at a crawl, his eyes straining to see more clearly, forcing himself not to look at the wrist-watch which was ticking away vital minutes. They must get through this time. The dark archway crept towards him and now the light beyond was stronger, illuminating the semi-circle clearly. It was almost daylight now. The front hull moved inside. Suddenly there was a jarring sound, the screech of steel grating along stonework. The tank shuddered violently throughout the length of its hull and then stopped abruptly as Barnes braked. Perhaps it was useless. This could be one obstacle they might never overcome, not even in broad daylight. He rolled back the hood and from above him a torch beam flashed along the wall.

The vicious clash of steel against stone had frightened Colburn and now he tried to estimate the position by the light of his beam. They had driven into the left-hand wall, of course. In their anxiety not to repeat their earlier mistake they had erred too far in the opposite direction, but was the manoeuvre even possible? He flashed the torch on the other side and the light penetrated a gap between tank and wall, a gap no more than six inches wide, if that. So theoretically it was possible, but with such a narrow clearance they would be extraordinarily lucky to pass clear through the archway in this light. He called down direct to Barnes.

'Six inches' clearance on the other side. Six inches maximum, maybe less.'

'Then we can do it, provided nothing gives when I reverse.'

'It'll take a miracle.'

'Maybe we're entitled to one.'

For the second time Barnes went into reverse, handling the controls with a concentration he had probably never equalled before, hearing the metal scraping harshly against the wall every inch of the way. But they were moving. The tearing sound petered out following the painful withdrawal, his heart in his mouth until he saw that they were clear of the imprisoning arch once more. They had to manage it this time. Colburn guided Barnes back a short distance and then gave no further instructions. The change of direction required was so fine that unless Barnes could *feel* what was needed they would end up smashing into the other wall.

Gripping the rim he saw the arch coming towards him again, his torch shining on the right-hand side now to make sure that Barnes hadn't overdone it again. He ignored the other wall completely, knowing that if they could move through with the right-hand track barely scraping the wall they should be able to make it. So great was his concentration on the wall that Colburn nearly died at that moment. Just in time he remembered the solid stone arch coming towards his head: he dived down inside the turret and something brushed the crown of his head, and as he went down a fresh fear darted into his mind—would the turret go under the arch? He reached up a hand and felt his fingers graze stonework as the tank rumbled forward. They were almost through when their nerve ends were seared again as the familiar grinding noise started. The tank increased speed and they were out in the open, driving across the field in a weird early morning half-glow mingled with white mist.

Barnes halted the tank briefly, switched off the engines, and stood up to listen. The vaporous fog bank was dispersing and beyond it he detected a staccato mutter which sounded like the power-drills of a tank repair shop, and beyond that he was damned sure he could hear the mechanical grumble of Panzers on the move. With a bit of luck these two background noises might help to conceal Bert's approach until the very last moment. And now he looked at his watch. 3.48 a.m. Twelve minutes to the Panzer attack.

'The mist's clearing,' said Colburn quietly. 'I can just see the ammunition hangar. I'll stick it out up here until we get close and then I'll pop downstairs and observe through the periscope.'

'If you don't, you'll be dead mutton.'

'And I'll use the Besa when the time comes—machine guns are my forte. The mist's clearing rapidly. That hangar is dead ahead. Good luck, Barnes. Advance!'

'Thanks for coming, Colburn. Thanks a lot.' It sounded trite, horribly trite, but he felt he must say something at this moment. Sitting down again, he closed the hood.

The tank moved forward rapidly over the level ground, brushing mist trails aside, picking up more speed every second. Colburn felt chilled to the bone, scared stiff of what was coming, but he looked curiously at the high bank which rose immediately behind the rear of the hangar. The houses behind the ridge were a faint silhouette of rooftops in the early morning light. It was from this ridge that Barnes and Jacques had looked down on the airfield, from here they had seen the sinister huddles of tanks which comprised the armoured striking force of the Panzer division which General Storch was about to hurl against Dunkirk. Ahead he could see the outer defences of the tank laager, a screen of barbed wire hastily thrown up to cordon off the airfield, and as the pale glow of the coming day increased he saw beyond the hangar a score or more of low dark shapes. His heart thumped when he saw them. Heavy tanks of the 14th Panzer Division. The laager was in view.

Quickly he gave Barnes an instruction to veer on to a fresh course which would head him straight for the entrance to the hangar which they were approaching broadside on. As to going below and watching through the periscope, that would be useless: he'd have to stay in the turret to keep the perfect observation they needed. He lifted up his machine-pistol. As

276

they approached the line of barbed wire Colburn almost forgot the holocaust which must await them; there was so much to see, to note. An armoured car parked close to the hangar, the outline of another vehicle which seemed familiar, signs of movement over to the left behind the mist. He recognized the vehicle now—a giant transporter with a tank on its deck. It was then that he saw the first Germans—small figures on the deck working by the light of shaded lamps. His hands tightened on the machine-pistol as the tank rumbled closer and closer. Surely those men must have seen them, must have heard them coming? But as he watched he saw a violet glow and sparks flashed strangely in the mist. They were using welding equipment and the sound of their tools had smothered the sound of Bert's engines. Still there was no indication that they had been spotted and the line of wire was very close now, coils of mist like gun-smoke floating behind the tangled network.

It was pure luck that he turned his head in the right direction and saw movement low down on the ground just beyond the wire, fifty yards away to the right. In the deceptive light he made out a square shield, the profile of a long barrel, a barrel which was swivelling. The barrel of the field piece was traversing as though it had not yet locked on to its target. Scrambling down inside the fighting compartment he jammed himself into the gunner's seat, hugging the shoulder grip, his hand grasping the traverse lever. The compartment rotated too fast and too far, so he had to bring it round again, his eye glued to the telescopic sight. The range was point-blank, for field-piece as well as for two-pounder. He had to get his shot in first. The cross-wires locked on to the shield smudge as he depressed the barrel a few degrees. He squeezed the trigger and the tank bucked under the impact of the recoil. God! The explosives! He waited for the tank to disintegrate but it was still grinding forward. He traversed to find the target and saw a cloud of white smoke replacing the white mist swirls. Dead on target. Climbing back up into the turret he looked round quickly. The tank had reached the wire and then the scratching noises began as it threshed over the coils. The field-piece had vanished inside the smoke and from now on it all became a kaleidoscope for Colburn as he went on speaking to Barnes automatically, guiding him towards the hangar entrance.

Men had appeared from nowhere, running towards the stationary armoured car. Colburn realized the danger at once and he raised his machine-pistol and took careful aim. As his finger pulled firmly on the trigger he swivelled the gun. He swivelled from a point close to the armoured car outwards, so that his hail of bullets cut them down before they could reach the vehicle, bringing down three men while a fourth man ran straight into the fusillade, stopping suddenly in mid-stride as he flung up his arms and fell to the ground. As Colburn inserted a fresh magazine he gave a direction change. The tank was still moving forward, passing within inches of the steel-plated sides of the armoured car, its nose pointed towards a machine gun which had just been manned by a soldier who had darted out from the shadow of the hangar. Colburn ducked, hearing bullets spatter the sides of the turret, and the tank accelerated, its steel bulk thrusting forward and driving over man and gun, crushing flesh and metal under its pulverizing tracks.

Their course was now taking them close to the trank trans-porter and Colburn remembered the men who had worked on it. Pressing the trigger, he swept the deck with a semi-circle of fire, seeing men falling over the side. He heard a brief burst of answering fire before another German fell forward after his machine-pistol had dropped under the tank's tracks. Colburn knew that he had been hit in the left shoulder, which had suddenly gone numb. He also realized that he had emptied his magazine as a capless figure in overalls came out from behind the tank and jumped from the deck on to Bert's hull. Dropping his machine-pistol on to the ledge he grabbed his revolver as the overalled figure lifted something he held in his hand—a spanner?—Colburn never knew as he raised his revolver and shot the German once in the face, saw him topple backwards and fall under the tracks which ground forward over him. He spoke breathlessly into the mike.

'We're almost there. Keep straight on . . .'

It was the tanks which worried Barnes. His own kind. He

knew what they were capable of. They had to reach the hangar entrance before the Germans brought up heavy tanks. Without a loader-operator to re-load the two-pounder Colburn would never stand a chance against them, even supposing he could hit one of them if he tried. Down in the tank nose Barnes never knew about the smashed field-piece. He was concentrating on keeping going. The element of surprise. Ram it down their bloody throats till the end. He thought they *must* be pretty close now, close to General Heinrich Storch. Colburn was coping well. He could hear machine-gun bullets ricocheting off the hull now, angry metal bees glancing harmlessly off the armour-plate. Sweat streamed off his face and hands but the pain had receded as his nerves strung up to fever pitch took over for one last effort. They'd almost made it. If they were hit with a shell which penetrated, this lot round him would blow and it ought to take the dump up with it, but he'd like to be certain, absolutely certain. He wanted Bert in the mouth of that hangar. Through the slit window he saw men coming round the end of the building, but had Colburn seen them? Colburn had seen them. With great difficulty he had inserted a fresh magazine and now he was slumped forward over the turret, the machine-pistol crooked under his right armpit, his right hand curled round the trigger as he lifted the muzzle high. It was like lifting a cannon and the tank seemed to be rocking strangely like a ship in a choppy sea. His left shoulder was beginning to ache now, a thudding ache which affected his whole body as though it were being plucked like an immense violin string.

He managed it, he lifted the gun higher and squeezed hard, vibrating the muzzle madly from side to side as he sprayed it wildly over the running group of men. They collapsed in a heap, too closely bunched together to spread out in time, only one man firing a few random shots, so random that they missed even the tank which was bearing down on them non-stop. Colburn's finger relaxed on the trigger and he slumped forward over the turret rim, still holding on to the pistol, the weapon now held up between his chest and the rim.

Colburn was still hanging on desperately to consciousness

279

when Barnes reached the end of the hangar, braked his right-hand track, carrying the tank round on the left-hand track, advancing several yards again and then stopping in the mouth of the open hangar. Colburn was vaguely aware that they had arrived and he lifted his head, catching a brief glimpse of the shell dump, of great stacks of wooden boxes. Then his eyes switched to the next hangar corner which he instinctively felt to be the danger point. A group of helmeted figures ran recklessly round the corner and he operated the gun with one arm and one hand, swivelling the muzzle as he poured out a hail of bullets at point-blank range into the compact mass of running bodies. It became a muddle and a massacre, the front men falling, the ones behind tripping over their bodies and dying in the subsequent rain of fire. Then his magazine was empty and he knew that he could never re-load. Beyond the inert bodies he could see a squat dark shape moving from the laager towards him. He whispered down the mike.

'Tank coming . . . don't forget . . . close lid.'

Looking sideways, he stared dazedly beyond the open doors of the hangar into the vast stockpile of shells and ammunition, his last sight before a German soldier hidden behind a pile of crates aimed his rifle and fired once, killing Colburn instantly. The machine-pistol fell and narrowly missed Barnes who was beginning to emerge from the hatch, his revolver in his hand. He looked quickly towards the corner where the huddle of Germans lay and then switched his gaze to the inside of the hangar. His revolver jerked up and he fired twice. The German with the half-aimed rifle collapsed behind the crates. Jumping to the ground, Barnes ran round the back of the tank, climbed on to the hull, took a quick glance at Colburn and went down inside the turret. The Canadian who had just come over for the afternoon had been shot through the temple.

Settling himself into the gunner's seat, he remembered that the two-pounder wasn't loaded. Cursing, he stood up, flopping in a fresh round with sufficient force to make the breech-block close, settled himself again and traversed the turret. Using the shoulder-grip, he elevated the barrel several degrees. The German tank came up behind the cross-wires, crawling forward like a huge dark beetle, a silhouette he had seen so many times in the past battle-scarred fortnight.

He squeezed the trigger and Bert shuddered under the spasm. The shot reached the target, the German tank stopped, flames flaring over the superstructure. Bert had just killed his first German tank. Barnes climbed back into the turret and looked at the plunger. It was extraordinarily quiet all of a sudden. Without thinking about it he gripped the handle firmly, paused, then pressed down.

Nothing happened. He had forgotten the switch. He lifted his head above the rim and looked round the airfield. The burning tank was well ablaze now but he couldn't see any sign of Germans. Again without thinking about it he picked up the plunger-box and the spool of wire. Climbing down on to the hull, he closed the lid and dropped to the ground, paying out the wire which led back inside the gun slit. Peering round the corner of the hangar along the side they had come he saw no sign of life. He began to walk rapidly back under the hangar wall, paying out wire from the spool, going past the Germans Colburn had killed, past the tank transporter where an arc welding torch lay on the deck, still spitting out a spray of sparks. Feeding out the wire behind him close to the wall, he kept on walking like a robot, wondering whether the wire would last out.

To his exhausted, pain-racked mind the act of forgetting to turn the switch had seemed a sign, a sign that he might just survive if he refused to give up. He reached the end of the hangar and found that the area between the rear wall and the high bank was deserted. Still paying out wire, he crossed the concrete strip and began to climb the slope, the same slope from which he had looked down on the airfield with Jacques before they had made a detour round the airfield to the point where Barnes had seen inside the open hangar mouth with his field glasses. He had almost reached the top of the slope when he heard trucks arriving on the concrete strip below him. He flopped on the slope, still holding the box, and lay perfectly still, his head turned sideways. Soldiers were spilling out of the trucks and forming up into two sections, then one section made its way down one side of the hangar while the second section followed the officer along the other side. Barnes climbed over the top of the ridge and staggered down inside a huge bomb crater close to the houses. Sitting down on the floor he looked at his watch, Colburn's watch, stared up at the pale sky he might never see again, turned the switch and pressed the plunger. At 3.58 a.m. the world blew apart.

The initial explosion came in two shock waves which blew away from Lemont straight across the laager—the detonation of the tank bomb followed almost at once by the subsequent blowing of the immense dump, which was then succeeded by fire which created a chain reaction of exploding ammunition. The first two shock waves swept over the laager like a tidal wave of destruction, caving in the tank walls like paper. Beyond the laager the shock waves smashed in the walls of the farm which housed German headquarters, and when Meyer, blood streaming from his forehead, staggered into his general's office he found Storch lying across the floor, his skull crushed under a rafter which had fallen from the ceiling, one clawed hand stretched out towards the telephone which lay in a heap of plaster. Reaching down for the phone, Meyer sank to his knees, picked up the receiver and found that the field telephone had survived. He asked for Keller. He knew exactly what he must do—he must retrieve the situation from the disaster he had always feared since that day so long ago when they had crossed the Sedan pontoons. He had already heard the report that British tanks were moving up through Lemont to attack their rear and a column had been despatched to intercept them without success. What Meyer had dreaded had now happened—the enemy had counter-attacked. The tremendous explosion which had just killed Storch was the final confirmation: there were no enemy planes reported so the British must have heavy artillery which had blown up the dump. He heard a voice speaking and broke in.

'Keller, this is Meyer. General Storch is dead. The British are attacking from the south—yes, the south. Cancel the order for the advance on Dunkirk immediately. Do you understand? You have the waterline at your backs so now you must . . .'

Half way through the conversation the line went dead, but Meyer was satisfied that Keller had grasped his order. From the tank laager there was now a series of explosions of increasing violence and for the first time Meyer had the terrible thought that he might be wrong. He *could* hear planes now, planes flying low overhead, and the ack-ack guns had opened up. With a curse he left the wrecked office and ran out into the garden. He heard the whistle of the bomb coming down and turned to run, just in time to receive the relics of the farmhouse full in his face as the bomb scored a direct hit.

At exactly 3.55 a.m. Squadron Leader Paddy Browne was approaching the coast of France, leading his Blenheims on a dawn raid. His instructions gave him unusual latitude, but then the situation was, to say the least of it, unusual. Evacuation of the B.E.F. imminent, the German Panzers lording it over the battlefield, the position changing almost from minute to minute. 'Fluid,' as the war communiqués would say. His primary objective was the key rail junction at Arras, but if he saw enemy ground forces and could positively identify them, the choice of target was left to his discretion. 'But for Pete's sake, don't paste our own chaps,' the briefing officer had added.

Browne wasn't particularly concerned with the Gravelines-Lemont area, but as he led his squadron over the coast his attention was drawn to it by a huge mushroom of smoke rising into the early morning sky, a mushroom which rose higher every second as though the whole of that corner of France were detonating. We'd better have a quick look, thought Browne, so he signalled to the squadron and took his Blenheim down. Two factors quickly convinced him that this lot was the other lot—he met flak at once and his keen eye saw beetles scuttling about on the ground as though they had gone mad. He could hardly believe it for a moment but he believed it the next moment. Hun tanks—a whole laager of them. Browne exercised his discretion: he gave the order to bomb. An avalanche of high-explosive rained down and when the squadron turned away there was no sign of movement anywhere between the breaks in the smoke pall. Browne's only comment on the way back was typical.

'Good of them to send up a smoke signal.'

Lieutenant Jean Durand of the 14th French Chasseurs found it difficult to believe his eyes as he focused his glasses across the flooded zone. His unit was charged with the defence of this forward sector of the Dunkirk perimeter and so far it had been a quiet morning, but then this is what he had expected because how could Panzers advance across water? And, Durand asked himself, how can this idiot advance across water? Speaking into the field telephone, he asked the British liaison officer to come at once. This was a sight which must be shared.

The lone figure on the bicycle was crouched low over his machine as though he could hardly stay on it, but still he cycled steadily across the sheet of water, never once looking up, as though he knew the way by heart. Barnes had to ride in that fashion because it was the only way he could see the road surface under six inches of water. His pedalling motion had long since become mechanical, a movement which had no relation to thought. In fact, he had now reached the stage where he hadn't looked up for some time and he had no idea he was so close to the Allied lines.

The British liaison officer, Lieutenant Miller, had now joined his colleague and his eyes narrowed behind the field glasses as he recognized the uniform. Apart from the fact that the cyclist could cross water, this sudden arrival of another apparition was not a complete surprise to Miller because in the present state of the battlefield men kept stumbling into the perimeter with increasing frequency. A dog's breakfast, that's what it is, Miller told himself. All over the bloody shop.

The cyclist was within a hundred yards of where they stood when there was almost a disaster. Unknown to either Durand or Miller, because they had been unaware of the road's existence, and unknown to Barnes because he hadn't been this way before, the road suddenly dipped and before he knew what was happening he was cycling up to his chest in water, and then he fell off. They dragged him out spluttering and choking, holding him up between them until they reached dry land where they laid him out on the grass. Barnes was desperately trying to say something and in spite of Miller's attempt to restrain him he burst out with it.

'Road goes all the way . . . all the way to Lemont . . . Jerry Panzers.'

'Got it,' said Miller. 'Not to worry. Hospital for you, my lad.'

Barnes spent two days at the Dunkirk field station for the seriously wounded although he kept trying to tell them that he was only seriously exhausted. In spite of his efforts to leave, they refused to listen to him, so he waited his opportunity until the ward was empty of staff and then he crept out behind the hospital still in his pyjamas, his bundle of clothes under his arm. It took him half an hour to dress himself behind the hanging wall of a bombed house, and when he reached the beaches he made a tremendous effort to walk upright as though there were nothing wrong with him. He was still only vaguely aware that a total evacuation was taking place and he was frightened that they might not take him if he didn't look fit.

Afterwards he could only recall the journey as a blur, like a film run too quickly through the projector. The endless wait on the beaches, the sand coughing up as bombs fell, the crowded boat which threatened to sink under the great weight of men who sat shoulder to shoulder, the incredible calm of the Channel as they crossed to England under bombardment and in a blaze of sunshine. Then Dover. Dover was the same thing all over again. A tremendous muddle, hundreds of men moving off in trains with hardly any supervision so far as he could see.

He waited alone for long hours, searching the sea of faces so intently that eventually he feared he was incapable of seeing what he was looking for. Twice he had persuaded a military policeman to let him wait a little longer and he was on the point of giving up when his heart jumped. Three soldiers were helping a fourth along the platform to a waiting train and he recognized the stoop of the broad shoulders, the tilt of the head of the limping man who was being helped. Reynolds! He could hardly believe it as he ran forward and when the three men saw his stripes they left the driver in his care and wearily climbed aboard the train. Reynolds managed a faint grin, leaning on his stick.

'Those three Jocks found me outside Lemont—we helped ourselves to one of the fifteen-hundredweight trucks. I woke up as they drove inside the Dunkirk perimeter.'

They were boarding the densely packed train when the military policeman questioned Barnes for the third time, enquiring his destination.

'Colchester,' Barnes replied.

Colchester was his base depot. Barnes now had one fixed idea in mind. He had to get a new tank.